**Netta Muskett** was born in Sevenoak College, Folkstone. She had a varie teaching mathematics before workin of the 'News of the World', as well as serving as a volunteer during both world wars – firstly driving an ambulance and then teaching handicrafts in British and American hospitals.

It is, however, for the exciting and imaginative nature of her writing that she is most remembered. She wrote of the times she experienced, along with the changing attitudes towards sex, women and romance, and sold millions of copies worldwide. Her last novel 'Cloudbreak' was first published posthumously after her death in 1963.

Many of her works were regarded by some librarians at the time of publication as risqué, but nonetheless proved to be hugely popular with the public, especially followers of the romance genre.

Netta co-founded the Romantic Novelists' Association and served as Vice-President. The 'Netta Muskett' award, now renamed the 'RNA New Writers Scheme', was created in her honour to recognise outstanding new writers.

# HOUSE OF MANY WINDOWS

*Netta Muskett*

This edition published in 2014 by House of Stratus, an imprint of
Stratus Books Ltd, Lisandra House, Fore St., Looe,
Cornwall, PL13 1AD, UK.

www.houseofstratus.com

Typeset by House of Stratus.

A catalogue record for this book is available from the British Library and the Library of Congress.

ISBN 0755142861
EAN 978 0755142866

# Chapter One

# 1943

He was watching her as he had watched her, every day almost, for the past three weeks.

He watched the lithe, very young grace of her, the way she ran over the rocks at low tide, sure of herself on bare feet even when the rocks were slippery with seaweed or rough with sea-lichen or studded with limpets. Occasionally she slipped, and saved herself with out-flung arms, or slithered down asprawl, when her laughter would come to him, clear and fresh and joyous.

Only the very young could laugh like that nowadays; in his homeland not even they would be laughing now. At the thought, his lips pursed and his brows contracted in pain. It didn't do to think of his homeland in the summer of 1943, with the world still, waiting for the liberation which seemed so intolerably slow in coming.

It was bitter-sweet to watch her. He had never actually seen her face, not as a close-up. As soon as she came from her daily bathe, a forbidding-looking female appeared from some hidden viewpoint and shrouded her in a beach-wrap and towels and hurried her off out of sight. Paul wondered even if he would know her if he saw her in the little town, and dressed. He was not sure he wanted to see her like that. It would not be in human nature to come up in features to the promise of that slender, immature body with its breasts mere buds, its movements and unawareness the prerogatives of early youth. In the life that seemed to have belonged to another world and another personality he had been an artist. It was that artist which was content to watch her from afar, not to know her as an individual but as no more than a fantasy, a dream of beauty unsubstantial and intangible.

Unaware that she was observed, except perhaps by the hidden dragon, she posed on the extreme point of the rocks where they dropped steeply into the sea, her arms spread wide, her head flung back so that the wind blew into a rippling pennant her corn-gold hair.

Her carefree happiness communicated itself to Paul Esterre so that by just watching her some of the restlessness and torment of frustration were eased.

She left her sea-girt rock and wandered off, picking her way amongst the seaweed, dropping down into the little hollows, climbing up again, until the arm of the tiny bay hid her from view. She had gone on into the next bay. Since he could no longer see her, he let himself become drowsy and slept in his sun-warmed niche until something roused him. It was the sea lapping at his feet, splashing them when the waves broke.

He rose and stretched himself and then became aware of the fact that he was cut off by the tide. Between him and the foot of the cliff there was now a stretch of what he knew would be deep water.

Oh well, it didn't matter. He had already had his swim, but it was not too difficult to undress and get into his wet trunks again and tie on his head the small bundle of his clothes, no more than sleeveless singlet and blue jean trousers and canvas shoes.

He would have to go to the point of the rocks before he could swim back if he wanted to avoid swimming over jagged rocks with which he had made acquaintance on such another occasion.

He picked his way out to the point, turned for a moment before dropping down into the water, and in that moment he saw a flash of blue which made him look again.

He was not mistaken. It was the girl he had called, to himself, *'ma nymphe'* – my nymph. She was lying on a patch of dry sand, one arm across her face as if to protect her eyes from the strong sun, her body in its blue swim-suit motionless.

At first he thought she was hurt and unconscious. Then, climbing over the rocks, he slipped, fell with an instinctive exclamation, and she woke, sat up and rubbed the sleep from her eyes.

He clambered on towards her, and she sat and watched him, interested speculation on her face and no suggestion either that she was afraid or he unwelcome.

When he was close enough to see her face clearly he stopped and found himself tongue-tied. No, she was not actually beautiful, but his artist's mind at once recognized something far to be preferred to mere beauty of feature. Her brow was wide and thoughtful, her high cheekbones gave the face its heart-shape to small pointed chin, her mouth was large and generous and full of humour, its redness that of natural, perfect health and contrasting with the sunburnt skin and the eyes, as he drew close enough to see them, of deep, dark blue. These eyes were her best feature, if one could pick out and separate everything that made up the attractive whole, but Paul Esterre had no wish to analyse any part of her. She had so much less actual beauty than he had pictured, so infinitely more in reality.

He smiled at her, and instantly, and unafraid, she gave him back his smile, a wide and lovely grin.

'Hullo,' she said, propped on her two hands.

''Allo,' said Paul, drawing the rest of his long body out of the water and laying the clothing bundle on a dry rock.

'Have you had to swim to get round here?' she asked.

'No, but it is necessary that you do for get back,' he said, picking out his English carefully.

'Oh, are you a Free French?' she asked. 'A sailor? I've always wanted to talk to one.'

'I am sailor, yes. Esterre. Paul Esterre. I wait here for a sheep,' with a sigh, a smile, a shrug, all very French.

'What do you want a sheep for?' asked Diana.

'A sheep, a *sheep*,' he reiterated. 'For go across the sea to my country.'

'Oh, a ship! Have you been over here a long time?'

'Only since three months so my English she is bad, yes? It is long time for to go from France into Spain and there again they keep me but I escape again and in a small sheep—ship, you say?—I come at last to England and then to 'ere but 'ere we are all matelots but no sheeps. You can understand my so bad speaking?'

3

She smiled encouragingly. 'You speak very good English considering that you've been over here only three months,' she told him.

'Ah, but always I like the English and so I learn to speak so that some day if I meet a beautiful lady, I speak to her as I speak now.'

'Heavens, I'm not a beautiful lady! I'm only a schoolgirl,' she said. 'Now that you've told me your name, I suppose I'd better tell you mine. It's Merrimayne—Diana Merrimayne.'

'That is long and difficult to remember, Merri—Merri ... But Diana. That is better. But in English it is a beautiful name with a sound that is what you call—*fort*? Strong? No, hard. It has a hard sound. In my country we say it *doucement*—Diane. It is better, is it not so, than your Diana?'

'Diane. Yes, it is, isn't it? They call me Di at school, but I hate that, and nobody ever calls me that at home.'

'And where is it, this at home? You live here?'

'In Wales? No, I live in England, in London, but they've sent me here because of the bombing. I'd rather have stayed with Gramp. I hate leaving him alone, but he's promised to come down here before the end of the holidays.'

'And who is it, Gramp?'

'Oh, grandfather really, though I call him Gramp. He's a great person. I love him better than anybody in the world, I think.'

'You have no father? No *Maman*?'

'Oh yes, but I've never been with them very much. You see, Daddy's a sailor—oh, like you! Only he's in submarines now, and Mummy's in the Wrens. Daddy wasn't a sailor before the war. He just looked after the estate, but Gramp says there won't be any estates when this war's over because taxation will not allow anybody to have enough money. Do you think that?'

'Me? I could not speak. I do not know how it will be in your country. In mine—all is so sad, so terrible. For me there is perhaps nothing any more.'

'Where did you live? In Paris?'

'No, in a little village called Sept Saules, with a small river and the old inn. And now—no country, no home. But we wait. We wait,' and he looked beyond the horizon, across the sea.

Diana, still sitting on the warm sand, her hands embracing her knees, looked at him with interested curiosity.

Since she had been in the cottage outside the town, she had watched the Free French sailormen stationed in the small coastal town in North Wales. Though the majority looked jaunty in their round caps with the red bobble and seemed to have made many friends, there was a look, Diana thought, which all of them shared – the watchful, uncertain, rather lost look which was in Paul Esterre's face.

It was a good-looking face, lean and bronzed, his dark hair with one or two deep waves in it, his eyes very blue and thickly fringed with dark lashes. He was tall, his body lithe and active. How old would he be? she wondered. At sixteen it is difficult to assess the ages of older people, but she guessed about twenty-five.

Actually he was twenty-three, but his adventures and the need of looking after himself, of getting out of tight spots, of avoiding capture, of making up his mind very quickly whether or not he must kill to remain alive – all these things had set their seal on his face.

He brought his eyes back to hers and saw their speculative wonder and smiled.

'I will not make you sad,' he said. 'Me, I am not sad. The day will come. The day of liberation! When my beautiful France will arise and we shall throw the Hun out and kill him—kill him in his thousands and his millions, kill him for ever! Now we do not talk of me. We talk of you, Diana. You live in a great house in London?'

'It's quite a big house. In Collett Square near Park Lane. I like Mayne Downe best because it's in the country, in the middle of Kent, but they've made an aerodrome in the park now and the R.A.F. have taken the house over, so we've only got Collett Square.'

'But you're living here in Abernendy now?'

'Just for the holidays. I'm here with Frizzle. She used to be my governess, but when I went away to school she stayed on with Mummy and helps with the house, does all the sewing and odd jobs, but she's so scared of the bombs that they all thought it would be a good thing if she came down here to look after me—all of them except me, of course!' with a laughing grimace.

'Is she the so serious lady who wraps you with your coat?' asked Paul, watching the changeful face, its delicate moulding, its clean lines. His fingers moved mechanically as if they held a pencil. He wanted to catch some of those moods.

Diana nodded.

'Her real name's Miss Frith, but somehow I turned it into Frizz and then Frizzle.'

'And now your father and your mother are both sailors, and there is only you and—how you say?—Gramp—and Frizzle. Where is she now, the excellent Frizzle—Ah, *sacré nom d'un chien!*' as he suddenly remembered why he had come to find her.

She followed the direction of his suddenly startled gaze and jumped to her feet.

'Golly! We're cut off!' she said, for the sea, coming in quickly over the rocks, was only a few feet now from where they sat.

'That is why for I came, to tell you and to help you, but now—how can we?' asked Paul.

They looked at each other solemnly and then she began to laugh.

'We've done it now,' she said. 'We'll just have to stay till the tide turns again. There's a cave back there, and at this time of the year the sea doesn't come right in. Poor old Frizzle! She'll be frantic. She's got a cold so I persuaded her to stay in, but when I don't come in for lunch she'll leap out of bed and almost wade into the sea. Come on. We'd better make a dash for it,' and she left him to speed ahead, into the mouth of one of the many cavernous openings made in the sheer face of the cliff by the thundering winter seas.

He picked up his clothes and followed her, and when they had reached the opening of the cave, examined it with some interest.

'I think you are perhaps wrong,' he said. 'See, here is seaweed, and the rocks not quite dry. Can you, do you think, climb a little if the sea comes?'

Diana nodded joyously.

'Of course. It'll be easy,' she said, looking at the sloping sides of the rocky cave, with ledges for footholds and a wide shelf jutting out some ten feet above. 'Up there we shall be quite safe. Isn't this fun? Life's been such a bore since we came here, nothing to do, nobody to make friends with, and Frizzle such a fusspot all the time. It's always been the same. She's so afraid I shall make what she calls "undesirable acquaintances".'

He threw back his head and laughed. It echoed round and round the cave and they both laughed again.

'Will she not think that a French sailor is that—how did you say— "undesired acquaintance"?' he asked.

'Probably. What else are you, Paul, except a sailor? I mean, were you always a sailor?'

'No. I am only sailor for war. Before I was student for art, for the painting. Now?' and his shrug told her what he thought about that as a future. 'Well, if we go up soon,' with a glance at the shelf of rock above their heads, 'it will perhaps be well, yes? I go first,' and he tossed his bundle up first and then, as agile as a cat, chose the best footings and came down to give her a hand.

She did not need his help, being as agile as he, but it was a novel sensation to her, up to now an unconsidered schoolgirl, to be treated as a grown-up by this good-looking Frenchman.

Seated in complete safety on the ledge of rock, his white singlet round her shoulders now that they were out of reach of the sun, they watched the sea cover the flat sand with incredible speed and encroach on the floor of the cave. They talked and laughed, and Paul showed off to her by climbing, cat-like again, to higher and higher ledges of rock.

'Be careful,' said Diana, suddenly anxious for him, and he climbed down again and sat beside her and looked at her with eyes which gave her an odd, new feeling that was not exactly fear but which dallied on the very edge of it.

'Why do you look at me like that?' she asked.

'Because you're beautiful,' he said.

'Now I know you're romancing,' she said. 'Nobody could call me that! Mother says I'm a little horror and wonders why I couldn't have been like her or Daddy. I'm not like either of them, except that I've got her coloured hair.'

He put out a hand to touch the shining gold cap. It was like silk, and at the passing of his hand over it, it crackled with the urgent vitality of her.

'It's such beautiful hair,' he said, 'but I do not think she says what is right. You are beautiful, Diane. I have so great wish to make a picture of you. Some day perhaps? But no. After today I do not see you, no? I am the undesired acquaintance for the Frizzle!'

Their conversation roamed easily over all sorts of subjects. She told him of as many of her sixteen years as she could remember, the young happiness of life at Mayne Downe with only occasional visits to Collett Square which they had not enjoyed but where Mother had spent many months in the year.

'She's so lovely and everybody loves her and she used to give big parties and all sorts of important people came. I used to look over the banisters and watch them arrive, evening dresses and jewels and uniforms and orders, though Gramp and I liked it best at dear Mayne Downe. Gramp didn't often come to town with us, though when he did, he was very grand indeed, with ribbons and orders that we knew all about, though I think some of the tales he told us were just for fun and not true at all.'

Paul scarcely listened. It was joy enough to watch her, but he gathered that the Merrimaynes were quite important people, not just rich, and Diana, when she had ceased to be a schoolgirl, would also be an important person.

In return he told her of life in a small French village, his father a farmer, his mother a bustling, capable housewife with her three sons, her marketing, her friends in Sept Saules and neighbouring hamlets, the feasts and junketings which used to take place, at the old inn, famous for many miles around for its food and its wines so that parties came from far and near to hold their wedding receptions, their christenings, their coming-of-age celebrations there.

'Where are your family now?' asked Diana.

The expressive gesture of his hands told her.

'My eldest brother was killed on the first day of the fighting, and when the Germans came they took my father and Jean, my second brother, away and we did not hear again of them. My mother? Who knows? She say she stay to keep the farm if she can, but I have to get away or the Germans take me too. So—I am here. When the liberation comes, then we see. Do you speak French, Diane?'

She laughed, glad of the chance to relieve the tension she felt at the incredible tragedy of this, only one amongst thousands, millions of such tragedies.

'School French,' she said. 'You know—*la plume de ma tante est dans le jardin avec la table de mon oncle.*'

'Ah, but you have a good accent! Me, I teach you French, not *la plume de ma tante*, but real French, yes?'

'Yes, Paul, but how?'

'Ah, *mais oui.* How, as you say?' he echoed. 'After today, I shall not see you again, *ma petite* Diane. That is sad, not so?'

'We can come here,' said Diana. 'I don't mean climb up here every time, but round the point where Frizzle can't come.'

'You would do that, Diane?'

'Why not? Where is the harm? It would be good, actually, because I'd be learning French!' with a little chuckle.

How sweet she was, he thought. So young, so innocent still. If she had to make an 'undesired acquaintance', better that it be he, Paul Esterre, than some he knew!

All too soon it became clear that they must go. It still meant a little swim, but Diana had known for quite a time now that there would be pandemonium in the cottage. It seemed that every day she and Frizzle came down to the beach with Mr. Evans, who brought two churns of milk down into Abernendy, and he called for them again on his way back, giving them about three hours on the beach. Today he would have looked for her in vain and gone back to the cottage to tell the tale to poor distracted Frizzle.

'Where are your clothes?' asked Paul, as after clambering out to the point over the wet rocks they slid into the sea and began the short swim to the shore of the next bay.

'There's a little hut there where I put them,' she said. 'Oh, look! There are people! Do you suppose they're looking for me?'

'I think yes,' said Paul. 'They will see us both together and it will not be happy for you. I think they have not seen us yet. You go on and I stay here and hide somewhere in the rocks until it is good for you. You will be all right?'

'Yes, but—Paul, I shall see you again?' wistfully.

'Tomorrow perhaps? By the cave?'

She nodded and swam on and into full view of the little collection of people who ran towards her with cries or relief, questions, admonitions; these last from the local policeman, Tom Tones.

'Now where can you have been, Miss Diana?' he asked. 'We have all been that worried, we have.'

'I'm quite all right, but I got cut off by the tide and had to wait in a cave until it turned again,' she said, and ran past them all into the tumbledown hut where she had left her clothes.

It was maddening to have to turn into a little girl again, she thought, with people fussing over her and having the right to ask where she had been, what she had been doing. Paul had not thought of her as a little girl. They had seemed the same age, both grown-up people.

Tomorrow she would see him again. She was determined on that. How wise he had been not to swim right ashore with her!

When she was dressed, she found 'Evans, the milk' waiting for her with his old horse and little cart.

'Oh, Mr. Evans, have you come down specially for me?' She had imagined she would have to walk the three miles to their cottage.

'I had to, Miss Diana. There's rare goings-on up at the cottage because your mum and dad have come.'

'Oh no, Mr. Evans, have they?' she asked. 'How sudden of them. Are they in a state about me?'

'Miss Frith is, but your mum and dad seem to think you'd be all right. We'd best be going on up now,' and Diana hopped up into the little cart, wondering what effect this unexpected visit might have on her new friendship with Paul.

They were all of them outside the cottage when the old horse ambled along the lane – her mother in the smart uniform of a Wren officer, her father unfamiliar and quite a shock with a huge, bushy brown beard!

Miss Frith gave a little cry as the trap appeared.

'Oh, Diana, there you are! I've been nearly out of my mind,' she said. 'Wherever have you been? And the only morning I let you go alone— and you promised me solemnly—'

'Don't be a fusspot, Frizzle. I'm all right,' she said. 'I only got cut off by the tide and had to wait till it turned again. Hullo, Mummy and Daddy.'

Had Paul Esterre been able to watch her at this moment he would have believed her a different person from the one who had laughed so happily with him. Her smile had a nervous, conciliatory look about it, her approach to her parents almost timid.

Clementine Merrimayne looked her over. She was classically lovely, and the uniform seemed to accentuate the feminine allure of her. Everything about her was as perfect as nature and art could make it. Beside her, her daughter looked *gauche*, untidy, ill at ease.

'What a sight you are now you have come, Diana,' she said, but her tone was careless rather than admonitory. 'Your skin's like a gipsy's. How are you ever going to get that sunburn off?'

'I suppose I shall go through the usual yellow Chinee stage.'

Commander Merrimayne gave a chuckle. It always amused him to see the two of them together, Clementine so exquisite, so sure of herself, and this changeling child of theirs so plain, if not downright ugly by comparison.

Diana turned to him and took a half step towards him, her eyes doubtful, and he laughed again.

'Not sure whether you'd like to be kissed by a beard?' he asked, and bent down and rubbed his thick bush against her cheek.

She had always been afraid of her father. It was not that he had ever given her real cause. In fact, as a parent, he was particularly indulgent and easy-going, but Diana had felt that he had never really had time for her. Diana was cared for, educated, and well dressed but she felt that as a person she did not exist for her parents.

'Got cut off by the tide, did you?' he asked, with his rather bluff laughter. 'Never make a sailor's daughter if you won't watch winds and tides, you know. Expect you're hungry, aren't you? Better cut along in with Frizzle and get some lunch.'

'And do something to your hair,' added her mother in her easy, careless fashion. 'How about a walk over the hills, Piers? Or shall I change first?'

Their eyes met, laughing, excited, mutually understanding eyes, and then he linked his arm with hers and turned her about and went back with her into the cottage and up to their own room, the large front bedroom from which they could catch a glimpse of the sea.

Piers closed the door and looked round the room with a smile. He had not been in it before. It was a typical cottage bedroom, a double bed dominating it, pieces of well-polished mahogany furniture, rag rugs on the shiny linoleum, spotless frilled muslin blowing gently in and out at the wide-open casement windows.

'An odd setting for you, my sweet,' he said.

She laughed and threw off her three-cornered felt hat and tossed her uniform jacket over a chair and stretched her arms in their crisp white blouse above her head.

'At least it's out of bombs and things,' she said. 'Off the earth. Like it that way?' with a provocative smile at him.

He came to her and put his arm about her and drew her face to his and muffled it in the wiry whiskers.

'How're you going to like 'em?' he asked her.

'I don't know. A new experience, anyway. I think perhaps I'm going to, but if I don't like 'em—off with them or off with me. Oh, Piers, isn't it heaven to be together again?' melting in his arms, clinging to him, her slender, taut body strained close against his.

He pushed his fingers through the thick, close-set waves of her hair, the same bright corn-gold as Diana's, shaking her head from side to side, making her hopelessly untidy before he kissed her again, deeply, satisfyingly, as if slaking an intolerable thirst at her lips.

Seventeen years married, still in their thirties, these two had never ceased to be lovers, all in all to each other, their child a mere incident outside their real life. On that, nothing ever did more than impinge. Theirs was that rare and priceless thing, a marriage of twin souls and twin bodies and these brief, snatched hours together the only life they now had.

'A walk over the hills!' he mocked her between their kisses. 'Away from me for three months solid and the first thing you can think of for us to do is to walk over the hills!'

She laughed. It was the low, happy laughter of a supremely happy woman in love and in her lover's arms.

'It wasn't the first thing,' she told him.

'Then what was the first?'

'Don't you know?' Her eyes of dark and lustrous blue teasing him between their narrowed lids, her whole body relaxed into complete surrender to him.

Downstairs Diana was eating with healthy schoolgirl appetite whilst Frizzle questioned and upbraided and complained.

Diana let the flow of words go over her unheard. She was thinking of Paul Esterre, of his laughing dark eyes, of the tones of his voice, of the way he had helped her to climb the rocks, of the feel of his arms about her for a single instant when he hard held them for her to jump into as she got down. Of course, to him she was only a little girl, she thought with that exasperating consciousness of the slowness with which one was allowed to grow up.

Above her, someone had laughed. Her mother. It was not the sort of laugh with which Clementine greeted a joke. It had an excited quality in it, and the next moment she heard the deeper sound of her father's laughter.

The colour flooded her face. Why had they not gone for that walk in the hills? They were always, at Mayne Downe, talking about the benefits of fresh air, of not staying indoors when the sun was shining and yet they were up there instead of out of doors.

Vaguely she knew why. The half-knowledge made her ashamed and embarrassed for them. People should keep 'that sort of thing' for the darkness, for the proper time for being in bed. At sixteen, she was far less knowledgeable than most girls of her age, partly owing to the fact that she had none of the curiosity about sex with which some of her contemporaries seemed so preoccupied.

But she felt that there was something not quite decent about her parents shutting themselves up in here on this sunshiny day for that express purpose; besides, they were quite old. Piers was thirty-six and Clementine only a year younger, and to Diana at sixteen such ages were completely alienated from the years of youth.

At dinner she could scarcely bring herself to look in their direction. Her mother was no longer in uniform but in a lovely dress of black taffeta. Piers was still in uniform. He had only thirty-six hours' leave and had brought no luggage. Clementine had come from London to meet him because in that way they could get another hour or two together.

Diana had thought, with secret rapture, that they had come to Abernendy to be with her, but just before dinner she had overheard something which undeceived her.

'You look marvellous, my sweet,' said Piers from the foot of the stairs, watching Clementine come sweeping down them, 'and much too beautiful for this little hole. I ought to have met you in Town instead of bringing you down here.'

'Darling, if you'd come to me in Town, we'd have lost hours together,' said Clementine, her voice like a purr, not a bit the sort of voice she used to anyone else.

After dinner Piers rang up for a car and took her into Llandudno to find somewhere to dance, and they were not back until the early hours, though Diana knew her father had to be in Cardiff by ten the next morning.

She was having her own breakfast with Frizzle when Clementine came down, trim and uniformed again.

'I suppose I'd better have a snack of something,' she said. 'Goodness knows when I shall get anything else. And eggs, Frizzle?'

Miss Frith bustled out to the kitchen. Mrs. Evans came in every day to do the work of the cottage, but Frizzle liked to do some of the cooking, especially when she could make a fuss of Mrs. Merrimayne.

'Mummy, do you have to go today?' asked Diana pleadingly. 'Didn't you say you hadn't to be back till Friday?'

'Yes, dear, but I've got a thousand things to do in Town, and I shall sleep at Collett Square a night or two. I want to have a real bath and get my hair washed,' said her mother indifferently.

She was watching the stairs, listening for Piers, never at peace or content unless they were together. Already, Diana knew, the desolation of the coming separation was on her again.

'Couldn't I come with you, Mummy? I wouldn't be any trouble really, and—it wouldn't be so lonely for you after Daddy's gone.'

Her mother's face softened. She was not entirely without maternal feelings towards Diana, and she was punctilious in personally seeing that she was well cared for, and yet her daughter knew that no one would ever reach the core of her life, which was for Piers alone.

'Sweet of you, Diana, but I shall be all right. Gramp will be there. Besides, London's no place for you just now.'

'I'm not afraid, and I'd rather be with you and Gramp. You might get killed, Mummy!' her voice rising with an anxious inflection. It was her daily and hourly fear when any of them were in London, though she had had to school herself to acceptance of the fact that her beloved Gramp would not be torn away from London. Gramp, at sixty-eight, felt himself to be far too young to be pushed away out of sight, and though persistent attempts to get into one of the fighting services had failed, he had found unending jobs to do once the bombing of London had started. He was a warden in one of the most heavily bombed areas, and his cheerful face, red as an apple above the thick white moustache, his blue eyes merry with laughter, had brought courage and calm to thousands of petrified women and children as he went steadily on his rounds.

Diana had begged and wept because she wanted to stay with Gramp, but they had been adamant and Gramp himself had put her on the train with Frizzle, who was unashamedly glad to get away.

'I'll soon have this war over for you, my pet,' said Gramp, 'and then you can come back and we'll get up to high jinks again.'

'But there'll be nobody to take care of you, Gramp, and I *know* you won't take care of yourself,' she wailed.

'I'll pop under the table every time I see a bomb anywhere near,' said Gramp cheerfully, his blue eyes still twinkling but with a rather misty look in them. Diana was the light of his life.

The train had carried her remorselessly away, and though human nature makes its merciful adjustments in time, every letter, every visit of her parents, brought back vividly and terrifyingly the knowledge of the danger in which they all stood, these three people about whom her life was entwined, whether they wanted it or not.

# Chapter Two

Diana and Paul were meeting nearly every day, Miss Frith remaining sublimely unconscious, since they had taken care not to repeat the occurrence of that first day, when they had been cut off by the tide.

On the days that Diana could not bathe she was in a fever of embarrassment to explain the position to Paul until she found, to her even greater embarrassment, that she had no need to explain.

'*Chérie*, I am not just stupid, or so very young,' he told her. 'But she blushes! That is very sweet and beautiful that she blushes! Now we go over the rocks to our cave, and I make some drawings of you, yes? It will be for my so great painting that some day I shall make,' and he laughed and caught her hand and swung it, and she made an effort to overcome her embarrassment and went with him.

He made other sketches, too, finding her a delightful and ready model, though he complained constantly that he could not work as he had once been able to do.

'The hands, they are rough and stiff and I need more to learn and to learn. I cannot make you as you are. But how could anyone make you as you are, my Diane?'

If he were making love to her, it was such delicate, tender love that she did not know it for what it was. He was just her friend, a little different because he was French. He never touched her, except to swing her hand in his as they picked their way over the rocks, or to give her his when they were climbing up to their ledge in the cave, or to move the position of her head, to tilt up her chin, for one of the innumerable sketches he made of her. It was an odd friendship, stranger for the man than for the unawakened girl.

Only on their last day together did there flower the exquisite, fragile bloom of romance.

They knew it was to be their last day, unless chance should play one of its puckish tricks and bring them together again, for Diana was going back to school and both felt it unlikely that Paul would still be in Wales, waiting for the Great Day, in three months' time.

As if the sun were reluctant to see their parting, it was a wet day, with gusts of wind whirling the sand into eddies which got into one's eyes and throat and ears and made life on the beach untenable. Frizzle had advised a quiet day indoors, or at most a walk in the hills with rubber boots and mackintosh, but Diana had almost tearfully insisted on their going to the beach.

'You needn't come with me,' she said. 'I'll be quite all right on my own. What harm can I possibly come to?' but Frizzle had stoutly refused to allow her to go alone and had hauled herself to the wind-swept deserted shore.

'You're surely not going to bathe?' asked Frizzle in amazement.

'Why not? You can sit in the hut,' said the girl and ran ahead with the uncalculating cruelty of youth.

She was late already, for Frizzle had made such a fuss about their coming, and the thought that Paul might not have waited was like physical pain.

But he was there, sitting on the rocks. It was still half an hour before the water would be low enough for them to get to their cave.

She laughed as she joined him, sitting on his coat.

'I couldn't see you at first,' she said. 'I thought you hadn't waited!'

'But of course I wait, Diane. Here I do not think the Frizzle will see us, no?'

'She's so short-sighted and I expect we look like a hump of rock, done up like this in your raincoat. Of course it would be a wet day!'

'The sky weep for us,' he said with his comical, half-serious, half-laughing expression. 'It know how soon you now exchange yourself into little school mademoiselle again and poor Paul just a *matelot*. But let us not talk of sad things. Look, Diane, the sea how she run now quick so we attend our cave.'

'Oh, Paul, how I'm going to miss your funny English! I've found myself starting to copy it. I told Frizzle last night that I thought I should mount, when I meant go upstairs. She thought I had gone batty.'

'And my so funny English, is it all you will miss of Paul?'

'Oh, but I shall miss everything, everything. I've never had a real friend before, not the way we've been. I wish you could write to me, but they'd never let me. All our letters are censored, and they'd soon write to Mummy if I suddenly acquired an uncle, and a French one at that! Oh, Paul, what if I never see you again?' mournfully.

His dark eyes were very tender. How sweet she was, and how touchingly unaware of the power she held, the power of beguiling and bewitching a man. If she were older, he would have made love to her, and it a little surprised him that, for all her youth, he had not done so. He mocked himself for a prude, and yet was glad that he was letting her go untouched and unawakened. Some other man, on some future and happier day, would teach her the meaning of life.

He rose and pulled her to her feet, cautiously in case Miss Frith chanced to be looking and should see the astonishing sight of a hump of rock rising and producing feet.

'*Allons.* We go I think now further?' and in a few minutes they were climbing up to what he called *la planche* – the shelf of rock on which they had spent so many hours of their strange companionship.

Diana's school had been moved away from the Kent coast into the comparative safety of Wiltshire.

'I'd rather be in London,' she told Paul fiercely. 'I don't want to be safe. I'd rather be in the bombing with Gramp.'

'It is better that you be safe, *petite*. So Papa and *Maman* and the Gramp do not worry about you.'

'But I worry about them, Daddy down below the sea in his horrible submarine and Gramp always out in the raids and Mummy—I never know where Mummy is, but I suppose it is something secret. They're all I've got, Paul, and what shall I do if anything happens to them?'

It was her constant anxiety. The ground which had seemed so solid beneath her feet had been cut away by the disintegration of her family through the war. She was not of the kind that wants to stand alone. It terrified her to have nothing to which to cling.

And now Paul, who had been for a time that needed support, was also to be torn from her.

He comforted her with an arm about her, a brotherly arm which, at the feel of her young, immature body, tensed with a feeling far from brotherly.

'You are cold, *ma petite*,' he said tenderly and he held her more closely and she let her head lie back against his shoulder. The scent of it was in his nostrils, a silky frond touched his lips.

'Ever after,' he was thinking, 'I shall remember this to my credit, that I left her as I found her, that I did not spoil one part of her fragrance and bloom.'

Too soon it was time to part. There was last-minute packing to do, and Frizzle had been adamant about not leaving her whilst she herself went back to the cottage to do it.

'I shall have to go,' said Diana unsteadily, her eyes filled with tears which she tried to blink away.

'Yes, Diane.'

'Paul, I'd like to—kiss you goodbye. May I?' and she lifted her lips towards his cheek and touched it softly with them.

Instinctively he turned his head and she felt his mouth on her own, at first the gentle touch with which one kisses a child, but then, at her swift, unexpected response, the kiss of a man for a woman.

For a second she felt herself recoil, but it was no more than the primitive instinct of virgin woman, for a moment later she was clinging to him, her lips hard on his, her whole young body surging with a wild, uncomprehended tide on which every inhibition, every precept, drifted out to nothingness.

'Paul—oh, Paul, darling Paul,' she whispered against his lips but scarcely knew she had spoken.

Shaken himself, he released her and stood up. She was only a child in years still, though now he knew she was ready to become a woman even though she herself had no consciousness of it. It was so unlikely, he felt, that they would meet again. A world at war had them both caught in its hideous, ruthless wheels.

'You must go, *chérie*,' he said. 'This, it is not for us. It is *un conte de fée*, how you say—for the fairies? Do not cry, *petite*. The Frizzle, what does she think? That you swim and come back with eyes that have cried, why for in the sea?'

She rubbed at her eyes with the back of her hand.

'I won't any more,' she said, 'only—my life seems to be nothing but saying goodbye to people I—love. I do love you, Paul, very much,' with sweet simplicity.

'As I love you, *ma Diane*,' he said lightly, determined that there must be no more surrender to that unexpected, disturbing passion.

There was nothing more to say about meeting, nothing they dared to say about parting, but when they reached the point so that in another moment Diana would see Frizzle searching the shore with hand-shaded eyes, he released her fingers gently.

'*En avant, petite*,' he said. 'Do not look behind. It is better so, *n'est ce pas?*' and she found that he had left her and was picking his way steadily, head bent, over the rocks away from her.

She was very quiet and subdued for the rest of the day, a day which held yet another parting, for they had to change at Bristol and her grandfather had contrived to get there to meet her. They were going to spend the afternoon together and he would see her off for school before there was any danger of raids starting.

Francis Merrimayne was the sort of figure at whom most people looked, and often looked twice. Tall, broad-shouldered, with thick white hair and fierce white moustache, his upright carriage and movements proclaiming his long years of soldiering, he looked many years less than his sixty-eight.

He and Diana adored each other. During her life, her parents had done much coming and going between Mayne Downe and Collett Square, leaving their daughter in whichever place she happened to be, usually at Mayne Downe, but Gramp had been there nearly all the time. It was he who taught her to ride, had taken her fishing, though she could never bear to see the fish on the hook. She would not go shooting with her father, hating to see things killed. She had gone with Gramp, however, when he went shooting alone, this being an unsolved mystery to her parents. The truth, known only to Gramp and the old gamekeeper, was that when he was with her, though Gramp aimed at things, he never shot them.

'Ha! Missed that time,' he would say, shooting wide, or 'Got away, the blighter,' lowering his gun after taking careful aim.

Diana would slip her hand into his. She knew.

Today he eyed her critically.

'What have they been doing to you in old Welsh Wales?' he asked. 'You look peaky, even though you are brown. Your mother said you looked like a gipsy.'

'I know. She's sent me some stuff to take it off, but I don't suppose I shall use it. I don't mind looking like a heathen Chinee at school. Oh, Gramp, do I *have* to go back?'

The day was still wet, so they were sitting in a café drinking endless cups of tea and consuming platefuls of cream buns.

'Why, what's all this?' he asked in surprise. 'Of course you must go, poppet. Look what a row I should get in with the parents if I let you do anything else.'

'But, Gramp, I'm sixteen, nearly seventeen, and it's silly to stay on at school. I could be doing something useful, not all the senseless stuff I do now.'

He stroked his white moustache contemplatively, his blue eyes twinkling.

'Heaven knows, my dear,' he agreed. Tell me what you've been doing in this place. Abernendy. Clementine tells me it's the last place on earth and that she'd have died there after more than one night.'

'Yes, it was dull,' agreed Diana.

'Your mother says it's full of those Free French chaps, *matelots*, I suppose. Poor chaps. One wonders what's in store for them. I suppose one of these days we shall give them a few old ships and they'll go over the Channel and probably be blown to bits.'

Diana swallowed hard. She had wondered whether she would be able to tell him about Paul, but now she knew she could not. Even Gramp might not understand. She did not understand it herself.

'Gramp, I don't want you to go back,' she said.

'Hey, hey, what's all this?' he asked. 'Don't make me sorry I came. You know I've got to go back, and you've got to go back. It won't be all that long either. I'm not supposed to tell you this, but Clementine says if she can wangle leave, we'll all spend Christmas together somewhere.'

'But it's three months to Christmas and you may get killed. Gramp, promise to take care,' in such obvious anguish that he felt worried about her.

'I'll promise to take care,' he said with exaggerated solemnity. 'As soon as the sirens go, I'll flash to the nearest shelter and stay there. Gramp first, and then women and children.'

He took back to London with him that memory of her, her face white under the sunburn, her mouth trembling, her eyes drowning in tears. She would have been better left with him, bombs or no bombs. Somehow he would have looked after her. No fear in life could be greater for her than this fear of losing those she loved.

Still, it was not his affair to settle. Clementine and Piers were doing what they thought best, though he knew their desperate anxiety for each other precluded any intense interest in anyone else, even their own child. Neither of them was cut out for parenthood. Almost children themselves when they had rushed into marriage, Piers nineteen, Clementine a year younger, they had provided one of society's gayest spectacles and disaster had been freely fore-told for them. How could they know what they wanted at that age?

But they had known. It was impossible not to be with them without knowing how right they had been.

Diana had been a solitary child, brought up by Frizzle, whose idea of the status of the Merrimaynes was so exalted that scarcely anyone was considered by her to be suitable as a boon companion, and until Diana went away to school her circle of friends consisted of dogs and cats, the oldest and least aristocratic of the horses, a collection of animals from the home farm, especially the weaklings, a lame duck or a battered hen or a motherless lamb.

She had not been unhappy or conscious of loneliness. In fact, when she went to school she often felt oppressed by the constant nearness of so many other girls, of never being alone, not even at night, for though something to cling to was an essential to her, the intrusions of others were irritating and unnecessary. She made none of the furiously intimate friendships which other girls made. The only deep affection she felt for anyone at Bourndene was for Miss Alliott, the science mistress, but Joan Alliott was a sensible, modern type of school-teacher who did not encourage such unhealthy affections as girls often develop for their elders.

In the holidays, until Mayne Downe had been taken over by the R.A.F. and she had been doomed to Abernendy, she had started to live again after three months of suspended animation. After her beloved home had been closed to her, however, she had felt like an outcast and had tried the harder to cling to her parents, and then, when only Gramp remained, to him.

He was thinking of all this, knowing part of it and guessing the rest, one night a week or two later, a night which promised for once to be raidless. Had he had any means of knowing that beforehand, he might have slipped down to see Diana.

The door of 5 Collett Square stood open, as always. Francis Merimayne, now known once again, affectionately, as 'the Colonel', though he had not been able to get back into uniform, passed through the hall and went up to the first floor where now the private living quarters had been arranged. He was surprised and pleased to find his daughter-in-law there.

'Why, hullo, m'dear. Nice to see you,' he said.

He thought she was looking thin and fine-drawn, her cheekbones too prominent, her eyes deep-set, her voice staccato-bright.

'Just for the night. I want a bath,' she said in that tone.

'Don't they have baths on your ship?' he asked with a smile.

'They have what they call baths, but that's not what I call 'em. The last one I had there, I had to scrape off barnacles and anoint my seat with lanoline afterwards. I only hope the merry tribe downstairs haven't taken all the hot water.'

'I've had them put an electric affair in your bathroom,' he told her. 'That makes you independent of downstairs.'

'Oh, Francis, that's sweet of you, bless you. I'll fly up at once. It seems quiet this evening. Aren't we going to have a raid?'

'They don't think so. I called in at the post on the way. What are you doing tonight? Other than the bath?'

'Nothing. I didn't think I should have such luck as to find you free. How about taking me out?'

'I should be charmed,' he said at once, with real delight.

When she rejoined him she was lovely in a gown of gossamer seagreen. She talked a lot, wittily, gaily, completely at her ease, loving him only less than Piers, who some day might so much resemble him. He was proud to be with her as she with him.

'Well, what do we do now? Want to have an early night?' he asked when they had dined at one of the fashionable and so far unbombed restaurants in strange, dark London.

'Heavens, no!' she said. 'Could we dance somewhere?'

'If you can put up with a rheumaticky old man,' said the Colonel, knowing quite well that he was still as good a dancer as any young man there, and better than most.

'You're wonderful to be with,' she told him. 'You've solved the riddle of life, haven't you? You've eaten your cake and yet you still have it. I suppose there's nothing now that you really want in life?'

'Indeed there is. I want the end of this war,' he said.

'Oh, so do I, so do I!' she cried, all her gaiety gone in an instant so that he saw what he had already divined, that it had been no more than a mask dragged forcibly over her face.

'Let's go home,' she said at last.

Upstairs in their sitting-room he poured out a drink for her, and one for himself, but as she was taking it from him, her hand shook so much that she set it hastily back on the table.

'Clem, my dear,' he said in concern, and the next instant she let the last tattered remnant of her pride go and came to him and put her head down on his breast and leaned her slender weight against him.

'Oh, Francis—Francis!' was all she could say and, stroking her head, he wondered just how bad her news was and whether she was remembering that Piers was also his son.

She lifted her head at last to look at him.

'Is it—the worst, Clem?' he asked, his own voice not quite steady.

'No! No! How selfish I'm being! I ought not to tell you. I ought not really to know, but things come through, and at the time nobody even remembered how much it matters to me. It's overdue. It was four hours when I came up to Town. I've kept telephoning. You must have wondered what was the matter with me and been too much of a gentleman to ask. There's no news. I'll ring up again from here,' crossing to the telephone.

Afterwards they sat by the fire which he had had lit, though it was only September.

'There's plenty of sense in hoping,' he told her. 'After all, many things might have happened to cause the delay, and Piers wouldn't risk trying to make contact with H.Q. too soon.'

'I know. I keep saying those things to myself too. It doesn't make any real difference, does it?'

'No,' he agreed sadly, and then, in an attempt to distract her thoughts, spoke of Diana and of seeing her off at Bristol.

'The child seemed quite upset, crying almost. Wanted to come back with me. Said it was much worse being away from us all than being in the raids.'

'Of course she can't come back,' said Clementine, her ears still strained to catch the first sound of the telephone bell.

'No, I suppose not,' he said thoughtfully, 'but one wonders whether one's proportions are right. The whole world is upside down, and reason is no longer what it was. Keeping her safe may not be the only and most important thing. She's—sort of lost, Clementine. She feels we are all pushing her hands away as she tries to cling on to us. She's not like you, you know. Not like Piers or me, either. She's like her grandmother, my Stella. She would have stood up to a thousand deaths rather than be parted from the people she loved. I believe it was sheer hell for her in the '14–'18 war.'

'It's sheer hell for me now,' said Clementine in a low voice.

'That isn't only because he's in danger. It's much more because you're not with him. You'd be quite happy sharing it with him, wouldn't you?'

'Yes.'

'That's how Di feels.'

'She's only a child. She can't possibly feel the way we do,' she said almost impatiently, not really interested.

He persisted as much to distract her mind a little as for Diana's sake.

'You were only two years older than Diana when you married Piers,' he reminded her.

'I know, but I was different. I was so much more mature. She's only a child. I'm sorry, Francis, but just at the moment I can't get het up about Diana. My mind's too full of Piers. Piers,' repeating his name as if it were some charm that might keep him safe.

There was no thought for either of them of going to bed. They sat all night by the telephone, waiting for it to ring, making repeated fruitless calls. By the morning they realized that, unless some quite unprecedented thing had happened, another submarine had gone down with its human freight, never to rise again.

Clementine dragged herself to her bedroom, that room so poignant with memories that she could scarcely bring herself to enter it, and dressed again in her uniform. She looked suddenly a middle-aged woman. There were deep lines in her face, her mouth drooped, even her hair seemed to have lost its gold. Her voice was toneless, her feet carried her like automatons where once they had danced.

Neither of them had spoken again of Diana, but at the last moment Clementine remembered her.

'I suppose I had better write to Di,' she said.

'Isn't it a bit precipitate? I mean, we can still hope,' said Francis.

He too, had aged visibly. Piers was his only son. His daughter, married and prosperous, did not trouble herself much about him. He and his son had been very close. Not even his love for Clementine had been able to diminish his love for his father.

'You know there's no hope,' said Clementine harshly.

'Leave it for a few days anyway. Then, if you like, I'll go down and tell her myself. When we really know, that is.'

'Thank you. Thank you a lot, Francis. We do really know now, don't we? I shall never see him again. Never hear his voice or be in his arms again—oh God! God!'

He laid a hand on her shoulder and held it tightly and gradually she was calm again.

'Isn't there one of the Ten Commandments about making idols?' she asked in her grim, toneless voice. 'I called on God, but that isn't much use, is it? If there were one, I've flouted Him anyway. I made an idol of Piers. He was my God, my everything. But there isn't a God, is there? You've only to stand and look up at the stars as I often do, to realize one's utter insignificance. There may be some power, something that puts out a careless hand or puts down an uncaring foot, and—pff! a few million human beings are gone like ants under a gardener's boot.'

'I think there is some power, something better than that,' said the Colonel earnestly.

'I prefer to think there isn't,' said Clementine bitterly. 'Better that there should be nothing there, than that something could be so fiendishly cruel and callous. What harm have Piers and I ever done anybody? Or any of these other millions of suffering, wretched tortured people?'

When she had gone the Colonel returned heavy-hearted to his many jobs, thankful for them, aware of an overwhelming sense of impotence and of failure, aware too of that aching emptiness in his own life.

He wondered how much it would mean to Diana. Piers as a father had been happy-go-lucky, generous, carelessly affectionate, but like Clementine, the core of him had held only the one love.

# Chapter Three

# 1947

The war was over before Diana Merrimayne could be expected to take any active part in it, a fact for which she was profoundly glad.

Since her husband's death Clementine had been a greatly changed woman. She was as witty, as brilliant, as beautiful, but with a difference. The wit was pointed, the brilliance had a brittle quality, her beauty that of a perfect mask which revealed nothing of the woman who dwelt within it. She attended all the fashionable functions; her dress was described in detail by the fashion correspondents at Ascot, at Henley, at the smartest night dubs.

Diana, now twenty, was not in the least inclined to go with her to these functions, nor was she encouraged by her mother to do so.

'I'm thirty-nine but I have no intention of keeping that in my own or anybody else's mind all the time by displaying a grown-up daughter,' she said frankly. 'Still, if you want to have a social life, I'll launch you.'

'Thanks. I don't,' she said. 'I'm perfectly happy with what's left of Mayne Downe and with Gramp.'

'What's left of Gramp,' said the old man with a wry grimace. 'The Colonel' had aged a lot between sixty-eight and seventy-two. When the house in Collett Square had received a direct hit in one of the last raids on London he had taken the disaster to heart.

He was never the same after it, and as soon as the need for air raid wardens was over he went back to Mayne Downe, where Diana only too gratefully joined him, first in her school holidays, and permanently when she had left school.

Mayne Downe was in a sorry state. The grounds had been churned up by countless lorries and other vehicles, its three-hundred-year-old lawns now a sea of mud or a desert of dust according to the weather.

From the house itself all valuables had been removed before it was taken over by the Royal Air Force, but such things as age-old panels on the walls and carved baluster rails bore traces of the senseless vindictiveness of ignorant vandals.

When Francis Merrimayne had his first sight of his home when it was declared ready to be handed back to him there was no longer any merriment in his blue eyes, but rather the mist of tears.

'They might have left that,' he whispered, his hand on a mutilated carving. 'What good did it do anyone to hack at it?'

Clementine refused point blank to live at Mayne Down. So, with little more than the pension paid to her as Piers' widow, she took a tiny flat in Kensington, and lived the sort of life she had chosen.

Diana and her grandfather made a modest home for themselves, like an oasis in the desert, by living in one small suite of rooms. A small modern kitchen and an extra bathroom were devised out of one enormous bedroom, and the pair of them lived in tolerable comfort with two old servants, Ben Good and his wife Ethel, to look after them.

Diana was perfectly happy, happier than ever in her life before. Once she had got over her horror and grief of what had happened to her home, she found many compensations. For one thing, what she had most dreaded had never come about; there were no longer the balls, the enormous parties, the garden- and tennis-parties of the old days; no more hunting and shooting with their nauseating visions of dead and bleeding little animals.

She would have helped Mrs. Good in the house, but Ethel was old-fashioned and had been 'with the family' since before Diana was born, and it was unthinkable to her that one of her young ladies should soil her hands with broom or duster, though now and then she let her experiment with cakes and puddings in the new kitchen.

So she spent nearly all her time with her grandfather, walking or riding with him, passing only by courtesy of the new owners over most of what had once been the Merrimayne lands.

Very occasionally Clementine swooped down, bringing with her a medley of people of all kinds and ages, the only qualifying necessity, according to Gramp, being that not one of them was capable of a single intelligent thought. They arrived by train or taxi, or in small, noisy sports cars or in opulent super-monsters that purred soundlessly up what had once been the drive.

The unused bedrooms were opened, aired and warmed. A special one was always kept ready for Clementine. There was a bathroom attached, and whether Clementine came alone or with her retinue of friends, extra help was brought in from the village so that she should miss none of the comfort she had always associated with Mayne Downe. Gramp laid himself out to please her, was the perfect host to her friends, appalling though he found many of them, and when they had gone he and Diana exchanged sighs of relief though neither was disloyal enough to make much comment.

After her careless 'You'll have to do something' to her daughter, she had left Diana alone. She sometimes commented disparagingly on the girl's hair, or complexion, or dress, but did nothing about them.

'I suppose if you like looking like that, and Gramp doesn't mind, it isn't up to me to bother,' she said on one occasion, 'but if you've got a decent dress, put it on for dinner this evening.'

'I've got my blue,' said Diana doubtfully.

'That old thing? Don't tell me that's still in existence!' said Clementine. 'Oh well, I suppose it doesn't matter. With your hair like a bird's nest and your skin like sandpaper, you'd look much worse in a Molyneux. And your hands, Di! For heaven's sake do something to them before this evening.

Her grandfather was also there, sauntering down the length of the picture gallery and the two exchanged guilty grins.

'I've got to put on my blue for dinner tonight,' said Diana.

'Have you, by Jove? That means I've got to dress too. Wonder if I've got a clean shirt? I suppose we ought to be glad that we're kept civilized,' he said, and they sauntered down the gallery, whose walls were now bare, his eyes going unconsciously to the patches on the walls where for generations the portraits of his ancestors had hung.

'Where are they all, Gramp?' asked Diana.

'Oh—put away somewhere. Some of 'em sold,' he said.

He was not very comfortable about those pictures, nor about the other treasures which had once graced this lovely old house. He did not want to admit it to Diana, but he had sold nearly all of them to satisfy the never-ending demands of Clementine for money. She lived extravagantly, far beyond the limits of her small pension, but she had been Piers' wife, and utterly beloved by him, and had not Piers given his life in the service of his country, all this would some day have been hers. It was unthinkable to him that she should know the pinch of poverty. Yet he felt slightly guilty about selling so much. They were his to sell. Only the house itself was entailed. He had not even been obliged to obtain the consent of the next heir, a middle-aged son of his deceased younger brother, to sell the village and the farms in order to pay the taxes.

Blaize Merrimayne had been only once to Mayne Downe since Piers' death had left him heir to it. With his nose, and that of his wife Hester, in the air, he had walked through the rooms, condemned by his supercilious glance everything he saw, and remarked on leaving that probably the only thing to be done with the place would be to get rid of it by leaving it to the National Trust. Since the death duties would not be payable until his own death, the Colonel did not feel inclined to pursue the matter.

Still, there was not only Blaize to consider. There was Diana. As time went on he began to worry about her and to wish she would find some nice young fellow who would take a fancy to her and she to him.

That night, at dinner in her old blue dress, her hair brushed into smooth, heavy waves and dressed with becoming simplicity, Diana seemed more than ever to stand apart, isolated by her youth and simplicity, by her shyness and self-consciousness.

Clementine had surrounded herself as usual with a crowd of young, or would-be young, sycophants. In particular there was a man whom they both found especially revolting, a tubby man in the late fifties, whose Savile Row clothes, diamond studs and huge diamond ring set him apart from the crowd of mere scroungers and hangers-on to Clementine's hospitality. He had a red face and a loud laugh, and his accent and uncultured manners grated on the sensibilities, not because the man lacked education and was obviously self-made, but because of his complete lack of natural refinement. There was no snobbery in the Merrimaynes but to both Diana and her grandfather the presence of Joseph Bloggett, *Sir* Joseph Bloggett, at their table was an abomination.

He sat at Clementine's right hand and she was dazzlingly gracious to him, laughing at his cheap witticisms, deferring to his opinion, listening with flattering attention to his loudly expressed opinions.

After dinner, Clementine took a number of the guests, including Sir Joseph, through the house. Diana followed as if by compulsion, though her mother made no attempt to include her.

In the great library, which had been kept for the use of students amongst the R.A.F. officers and men who had been quartered at Mayne Downe things were much as they had always been; the thick Turkey carpet still on the floor, the ceiling-high shelves with their glazed fronts packed with books on every conceivable subject, most of them sombre leather-bound classics of all nations and in all languages, with biographies, travel books, philosophies, dissertations on every known religion and some almost unknown.

'How dull!' said somebody, with a little shudder. 'Clem darling, how frightfully cultivated your ancestors were!'

'Not mine,' said Clementine. 'I'm only a Merrimayne by adoption, a sort of weed that's been allowed to take root temporarily on the old stem, if that's botanically speaking possible!'

Sir Joseph, near her as always, must have said something not for everybody's ears, for she gave a little gurgle of laughter, almost a snigger, and Diana found her lip curling. For Mummy to be like that! For her even to tolerate such a creature!

She moved apart from the chattering, irreverent group of sightseers and stood looking at one particular bookshelf. Here there were books belonging to her childhood, books as beautiful and solidly bound as their betters because neither Gramp nor Piers nor, she had believed, Clementine, could bear to possess things that were cheap and meretricious.

Her eyes filled with sudden tears.

She became aware that the pandemonium of voices and laughter had died down, but that she was still not quite alone.

Standing looking at her out of his small piggy eyes was Sir Joseph Bloggett, and there was something in his look which brought the quick blood to her cheeks

'No need to be scared of me, y'know,' he said in his rough, uncultured voice.

'I'm not, thank you,' she said politely.

'Y'know, you're quite a surprise to me. I'd no idea yer mother had a grown-up daughter, nor such a pretty one,' leering at her and coming so close that she could smell his whisky-laden breath.

'We'd better join the others,' was all she could think of to say, and would have passed him on her way to the door when, to her horror and disgust, he laid a hand on her arm to detain her.

'Not so fast!' he said. 'I've had my eye on you ever since I saw you. "Now there's a pretty little filly," I said to myself, "and out of a good stable, or I'm a Dutchman," but you could have knocked me down with a feather when yer ma told me who you were. Not like her, are you? Except for the hair, and of course she has to touch hers up now. Like yer dad, perhaps, eh?' still eying her up and down.

'Not very much,' said Diana rather wildly, wishing someone would come in and yet terrified that they might do so.

He chuckled.

'Frightened, aren't you? Well, I like women that're a bit standoffish at first. Now you and me could be good friends, little girl. Do you know that? I'll bet you do, inside that pretty noddle of yours. I could do a lot for you. I expect you like pretty clothes, and a bit of a do in Town now and then, and perhaps a sparkler or two, eh?' – making the diamond in his ring flash under the electric light.

Diana did not know what to do. She was trapped by him and by one of the great library tables, and the wheeled trolley which was used when the books lying about the room had to be collected and restored to their shelves at night. She had wild thoughts of giving that a push and making him lose his balance so that in the commotion she could escape, but knew it would be silly and undignified.

His hand still held her arm, fingering it and pinching it and giving her a frantic desire to scream hysterically.

'Please let me go,' she said as steadily as she could, trying to make her voice sound like Clementine's when she was displeased. It still sounded like the squeak of a frightened schoolgirl, and he laughed again, softly and ingratiatingly,

'She's still frightened,' he said. 'Well, it's a nice change. Most of 'em are all over you at the first hint of a new dress of a bit of jewellery. I bet you like pretty things, though, don't you?'

'I don't like jewellery and I've all the clothes I want, and in any case I wouldn't let a man buy them for me,' said Diana, and had managed to control the shaking of her voice and achieve the semblance of dignity. 'Please let me go. My mother will be wondering where I am.'

'Your mother! Your *mother*!' he repeated, tickled. 'Yes, I bet she will—or where *I* am. All right,' taking his hand from her arm. 'We'll have another little talk presently, eh?' But she had run from him and scarcely heard the threat of the last words.

She ran across the room, and instead of going out by the door into the hall, where she might have met any of them, she raced up the little iron staircase in the corner which led to a gallery round the room and thence by another door into another part of the house. She knew he was unlikely to follow her up those winding stairs.

Once safe, she stood with her back to the wall, her breast heaving, her heart beating painfully, her eyes shut tightly against the threatened tears of fear and release from fear.

He could not have hurt her, she kept telling herself. There was nothing to be afraid of. She was safe. Soon they would all be gone, and she and Gramp alone again.

Yet she knew she had been petrified with fear, and disgust. How could her mother bear to have people like that near her? Yet undoubtedly he had come at her invitation. Clementine, who had always been so fastidious, so proud!

In the ballroom, its fine floor scored and ruined, its satin-panelled walls torn and dirty, its great chandeliers giving a ghostly light through their protective coverings, Clementine Merrimayne tapped a foot impatiently and tried to disguise the little glances she was giving towards the door. When Sir Joseph came sauntering in the glance quickened into one of suspicion. Where had he been? Who, in this derelict, deserted house, had been responsible for that expression on his face? It could only have been one of those little minxes Mrs. Good had got from the village to help with the work whilst the visitors were there.

Her lip curled and she turned away as he strolled up to the group.

'Have I missed anything?' he asked jauntily.

'Missed anything?' she repeated, looking puzzled.

'I got ... er ... detained, but managed to find you all here.'

'Oh! I thought you were with us,' said Clementine indifferently, and his eyes narrowed.

Had she thought that? If she had (and one could never tell with her), things were not quite as he had imagined, and for the rest of the evening he was assiduous in his attentions to her.

Diana did not appear again and nobody asked for her or appeared to miss her.

She carried a tray with her breakfast and Gramp's into his room the next morning.

'Well, this is nice,' he said.

'*They'll* be coming down at all hours,' she said, 'so I thought we'd get ours over quietly. It's eggs. I've poached them,' taking off the silver covers and settling the tray comfortably for him.

'Quite the little housewife,' he said with a smile. 'Any sign from any of them yet?'

'Not a whisper. Gramp ...'

'What is it, poppet?'

'Gramp, would it be too awful if I went out for the day?' she asked with a kind of desperation.

'Much too awful. Out where?'

'I don't know. Anywhere. I could make up something I had to do.'

'You can't do that, Di. You're the hostess,' he said.

'*I* am? Oh no, Gramp. Mummy's the hostess. They're her guests.'

'Nominally. Actually they're mine. Ours, poppet. This is still my house, you know, and as your mother doesn't make it her home, you're my hostess. I'd have liked you to sit opposite me at dinner last night, but your mother had arranged the table and I didn't want to start any trouble. You're grown up, you know, duckie, and if things had been as they ought to be, you'd have been presented and come out with a splash by now, all sorts of orgies.'

'I'd have hated that,' she said fervently. 'I couldn't, *couldn't* have gone through it. I should have passed out straight away.'

'Well then, you certainly wouldn't have had to go through it after that, would you? Seriously, dear, I often feel I've done badly for you in letting you bury yourself down here with me. It isn't the right life for you.'

'It's exactly the right life for me, Gramp. I'm utterly happy here, just with you and what remains of poor Mayne.'

'No. You ought to be meeting people; people of your own age; men.'

'I hate men,' she said, and he was further convinced that some man last night had frightened her, curse him.

He wondered which of them it could have been, casting his memory over the bunch of them without alighting on one of them who had appeared to take any interest in her. In her shabby blue dress she looked like a field flower which had got by mistake into a bowl of hothouse blooms. For himself, he preferred field flowers, but surely none of Clementine's new crowd would even notice them?

'You haven't met the right sort,' he told her, frowning over the problem of how to contact the right sort for her.

Her mind flashed back over the years.

When she had first parted from Paul Esterre, she had thought of him constantly, hugged to herself a memory she would not share with anyone, least of all the other girls at school, who always came back after the holidays bragging and boasting and whispering in corners about their, 'boy friends'. He had been to her something so private and to be cherished that it seemed almost sacred, and she had kept him so.

He had never written, though she had given him her address and told him that in any case she would be at the cottage again the next holidays. When that time came, the Free French navy men had gone from Abernendy and no one seemed to know where, nor what, had happened to them.

For months she had been anguished for him, time and separation turning the friendship into the semblance of a romance so that she half believed she had been in love with him and he with her, though deep in her heart she knew that this was absurd and that nothing between them, except that one kiss, had been in the least love-like. Gradually, as these things do, the hurt grew less and memory dim, and now it was years since she had even thought of him.

He came back to her now, merry-eyed, tender, careful of her, as men in her limited experience seemed no longer to be careful of their women. Would he have been what Gramp called the right sort? At that time he probably would not have been, she the daughter of the Merrimaynes, he the son of a struggling French farmer, an art student, but actually with no home, no country even.

But values were now all different.

Still, why think of him at all? They would never meet again. He might not (and this sent an odd little shiver through her), he might not even be alive any more. He would have been in the fighting. He had wanted to be in it, had been waiting there in ever-growing irritation because he was not in it.

To think that the same world could hold a Paul Esterre and a Joseph Bloggett!

'I'm perfectly happy with you, Gramp dear,' she said lovingly.

'I believe you are, poppet, and I'm glad you are, though my better nature knows you ought not to be! You're grown-up now, rising twenty-one. We'll have to have some sort of a celebration, I suppose.'

'Oh no!' she cried in horror. 'Promise me we shan't have that.'

He laughed, but rather shamefacedly, passing a hand over the white stubble on his unshaven chin.

'I daren't promise you,' he said. 'That'll be for your mother to decide. If she says junketing, then junketing it will have to be.'

'Well then, that's all right. Mummy won't be anxious to tell the world that she has a daughter of twenty-one! Though you'd never think it, would you? Isn't she lovely? Different, but lovely.'

'Different, as you say.'

'You couldn't expect her to stay the same, could you? Without Daddy, I mean. They were very much in love, weren't they?'

'Yes, very much. Very much,' he agreed sadly.

When they had finished breakfast she stood for a moment looking down somewhat dejectedly at her grandfather.

'You really think I've got to stay with them today, Gramp?'

'I really do, my duck. It's only for today, you know. They'll be rushing off in their noisy cars, all shouting and screaming at one another, by about tea-time, perhaps earlier.'

'All right,' she said with a sigh, and carried away the tray.

As it happened, any fears she might have had about Sir Joseph appeared to have been unfounded, for he took no notice of her until the longed-for moment came when they were all ready to depart.

She stood with Gramp on the front steps to play the good host and hostess, finding it much easier to be pleasant to them all now that they were going.

Clementine bent her head and brushed her daughter's cheek with her lips, lightly, so as not to disturb their careful painting.

'Bye-bye, my dear,' she said, 'and for heaven's sake get yourself some new clothes. Ask Gramp for some money.'

'Mummy, couldn't you give me some?' asked Diana in a whisper. 'I don't like asking him for everything.'

'I haven't got any,' said Clementine crossly. 'It's all I can do, and more than I can do, to pay my own bills. Tell him I'll pay him back, though goodness knows when.'

Diana could not decide whether Sir Joseph, who was standing near, had heard the whispered exchange, but the next moment he had her hand in his and Clementine had gone out to the car, his car, one of the most gleaming and vulgar of them all.

'Don't you forget what I said,' he whispered to her. 'Anything you want—within reason, of course!' with a wheezy chuckle. 'You can trust me, y'know. Honest Joe Bloggett,' with a squeeze of her hand and a wink.

Diana said nothing. Her mouth was dry and her throat hurt and her whole body was revolted by his nearness.

He let her hand drop and joined Clementine in the car, and the uniformed chauffeur climbed into the driving-seat and they shot off down the drive in the wake of the other cars.

Diana went in quickly and washed her hands.

# Chapter Four

Diana's chief and, in fact, only close friend at this time was that same Joan Alliott who had been science mistress at Bourndene and to whom as a schoolgirl she had been innocently devoted. Joan was now married and living with her doctor husband, Ian Hurst, in Maidstone, and when Diana made her weekly expedition for shopping, driving the dilapidated old car, she had formed the pleasant habit of spending the afternoon with her.

Joan Hurst was a good friend for her, steady, practical, unsentimental, with a fund of good humour and common sense which was exactly what the girl needed to save her from turning her thoughts in on herself too much and becoming a neurotic. With Joan and her small son, Christopher, a most engaging toddler, Diana was her best and most natural self.

Joan, watching the two together and seeing what a different person Diana became after the first half hour in the little house, felt that the best thing for the girl would be an early marriage. Though she adored her grandfather and Mayne Downe and seemed perfectly contented, making them the centre of her life, Joan felt that Diana was too young and had too much reserve of affection and emotion to be so circumscribed. The old man was seventy-two, and though he still seemed hale and hearty, in the normal course of things Diana would have the greater part of her life without him.

So she took trouble to bring to her home on Fridays a collection of young men, her husband's friends and patients, students at the hospital, the brothers of her own friends, and persisted even though Diana shut up like a clam at the very first contact with them. She had an attractiveness all her own, a quality not dependent on conventional attributes of beauty but something elusive and fadeless.

With only one of the *habitués* of Joan's house was she at all at her ease, and that was because he was older, rather of her mother's generation than her own.

Andrew Shawn was thirty-six, the head of a reputable stock-broking firm and a man of considerable means, though he made no show of his wealth, had simple tastes and was devoted to Joan and the baby for their own sakes as well as for the fact that he owed his life to Ian Hurst. He lived at Sevenoaks and went to Town every day, but at weekends he had made a habit of driving to Maidstone in his elderly Daimler and spending the time with the Hursts. It was on some of her Friday visits that Diana had met him.

He was a Scot by birth, though southern by adoption, and his voice still held the undefeatable trace of his Scottish speech, the lightened vowels, the delightful role of the 'r'.

One Friday, when the Merrimaynes' ancient Morris had for once let her down, Andrew Shawn offered to run her back to Mayne Downe.

'I couldn't let you do that,' she said.

'It would be a pleasure to take you. As a matter of fact, though you don't seem to have been aware of it, I've been angling for some weeks for an invitation to see your wonderful old home.'

Diana flushed, quick as ever to feel embarrassed.

'I'm afraid you won't think it so very wonderful now, though,' she said. 'The grounds were completely ruined during the war.'

'I don't think even a war can altogether destroy anything like Mayne Downe, since mercifully the house was not bombed,' he said.

'Oh, do you know it then?' she asked, surprised.

'No, I've never been there, but I've read about it. One quite often comes upon references to it and its treasures in books on antiques. They're by way of being my hobby, in a humble and somewhat ignorant fashion. So you see you'll be doing me a favour by letting me drive you home,' with another of those smiles which transformed his plain, square face.

He had no claims to good looks, but his firm mouth and chin, a largish nose, small, twinkling eyes of a sailor's blue and thinning hair of sandy brown all contributed to the make-up of a man whom one felt instinctively could be trusted, a wise counsellor, a man of kindly sympathies but unromantic, not at all the sort of man to make an appeal to a young girl. Joan, thoughtful, intelligent and now in her middle thirties, appreciated his friendship, but the girls of Diana's age whom she invited as part of the young social circle with which she tried to surround her thought him stodgy and dull. This did not prevent them from taking advantage of anything they could get out of him, occasional lifts to Town, theatre tickets given him by clients which he did not want to use, sometimes an introduction to someone who might give them a good job.

He stowed away Diana's parcels in the ample saloon, and Joan looked after them thoughtfully when he had driven off.

Her husband, putting off for a few minutes the daily routine of 'surgery hours,' linked an arm in hers as she stood at the window of their pleasant sitting-room.

'Not at it again, surely?' he asked with a smile.

It was a standing joke between them that she could never resist match-making.

'Don't you think it might be a good idea? Diana ought to be married, to have a life of her own apart from that mouldering old ruin and the companionship of an old man.'

Meanwhile Diana, seated in the front beside Andrew, was showing him the short cuts, taking him to the house through the old drive which, not having been of any use for the airport, had remained almost untouched.

'How far does your grandfather's land go?' asked Andrew.

'Oh, very little of this is ours now,' she said. 'We weren't able to get full compensation, and in any case, with the terrific taxation, it is impossible to maintain it as it always has been maintained. Gramp has had to sell most of this, and the village too. Our land starts where that big barn affair is. If you go round to the left, we can get to the house without going through what used to be the farm.'

He could hear in her voice her bitter resentment at what had been done to her home, her grief over her memories, and he felt sincere sympathy with her. He himself came of good middle-class Scottish stock, with no knowledge of more than one generation of his forbears and no history or tradition to cherish. His interest in antiques, however, made him able to appreciate what it must mean to a family like the Merrimaynes to know that its history was finished, its traditions broken, its pride laid low.

He glanced at her. There was about her that indefinable look of race, of breeding. She seemed to him pathetic, the product of so much that would never be again. He wished that this girl might have been left, the dreaming princess in her guarded tower, rather than thrust out into a life of which she seemed no part.

He drove on, and gave a little sigh of pure delight when the great house came in view, grey-faced, many-windowed, one of its flanking towers long gone into ruin.

Diana heard the sigh and turned to him, her face alight with pleasure.

'You think it's lovely?' she asked, and he knew that here was the core of her heart.

'Beyond words,' he said. 'You're very fortunate to have this for your heritage, in spite of what's happened to it now.'

'Yes, I know. Only it isn't actually a heritage, if you're thinking of the future. You see, my father was killed in the war, so after Gramp it goes to a cousin, a man I don't know very well.'

'Nor like very much, your tone says,' said Andrew.

'No, nor like very much,' she agreed. 'It's hard to believe he was my father's cousin, though I suppose cousins need not be much alike. And Gramp and I loathe his wife. We hate to think of her living here with her horrid children!'

She spoke with underlying laughter, but he knew that there was pain in the thought, not pain for herself but for the beloved house, her home, which she felt would be given into unworthy hands.

Colonel Merrimayne had heard the sound of the car, a more aristocratic sound than the wheezes and coughs that were time's legacy to the old Morris, and came out on the terrace. He looked so exactly right, thought Andrew Shawn. His tall, spare frame, the proudly held head with its crown of thick white hair, the acquiline nose and fierce white moustache – all of them helped to make up this last survival of a proud line of Merrimaynes.

Diana sprang out and hurried to him.

'Darling,' she said, 'poor old Jane let me down. She's got something quite vulgar the matter with her—trouble in her big end! So Mr. Shawn very kindly offered to bring me and a thousand parcels home. Mr. Shawn,' as Andrew came up the broad, shallow steps of the terrace towards them, 'my grandfather, Colonel Merrimayne.'

'My dear sir, how very kind of you,' said Gramp in his courtly fashion. 'I do hope it hasn't inconvenienced you too much? Do come in. The servants will see to the packages,' leading the way into the great house, with its echoing emptiness, his manner and tone suggesting that he might be completely unaware of the passing of its former glory.

Diana slipped away to get Ben Good to unload the car, whilst she consulted Ethel about the possibility of having a guest to dinner.

'There's a chicken, Miss Diana, only really enough for you and the Colonel,' said Mrs. Good, 'but if I carve it and grill some of that bacon, there'd be enough. I've done plenty of vegetables, and there's a plum pie, and I can do devilled eggs as a savoury.'

'Oh, thank you, Ethel. You're a gem,' said Diana and ran upstairs with the intention of conveying to Gramp privately that there would be enough if he liked to invite Andrew Shawn to stay.

It was as well Ethel had made it enough, for Andrew had already been invited. Gramp was above such petty difficulties as that of stretching the meal from two portions to three.

Andrew Shawn was greatly attracted to the old man, and the attraction was mutual, for when he left, much later, it was with the Colonel's warmly expressed invitation to return again soon.

In the friendship which sprang up between the two men Colonel Merrimayne seemed to take a new lease of life, and it was largely her joy in this which took from Diana the last vestige of her shyness with Andrew and cemented the three of them into a harmonious whole. Andrew was not a man of country tastes and pursuits, but at Mayne Downe, even in its deteriorated state, he was learning some of its joys. Among the few luxuries which Diana and her grandfather allowed themselves were their horses, the Colonel's bay gelding and her little chestnut mare, both middle-aged if not actually elderly. Andrew admitted that he had not ridden for years, but Diana persuaded him one evening to accept Gramp's offer of a mount.

'I shall probably fall off,' he warned her with his dry smile.

She laughed. It seemed to the two men that she laughed more easily and often nowadays. It was a delightful sound, young and happy and wholesome.

'You couldn't fall off Robert,' she said.

'Take me somewhere away from this world in case I do manage it,' he warned her, and presently, in some old riding breeches and boots dug out by Good, he set off beside Diana on her gentle old Frolic, whose manners entirely belied her name.

'You're all right,' she said approvingly when the horses were picking their way carefully across the fields, apparently familiar with the rabbit holes and other dangers. 'You've got a good seat. I don't know why you made such a fuss about it!'

'I thought I might have lost the knack, but, as you say, Robert has the most accommodating ridges. Which way do we go now, or do the horses know?' as they passed out of the field through one of the many ungated gaps in the once trim hedge.

'They do know, as Gramp and I always go the same way, but they like to pretend it's we who're choosing,' she said. 'Left here, and through the village, and we can get up on the downs where they do a decorous canter.'

'Then I *shall* fall off,' said Andrew.

'There'll be no one there to see, if you can manage to cling on until we're through the village,' she laughed, thinking that he really looked rather well on a horse.

After that day they rode together several times, and on other occasions they went in Andrew's car, sitting in it in comfortable warmth when he had drawn it up facing the wild winter sea on the promenade at Hythe or on the heights above Dover. Occasionally the Colonel went with them, though as a rule he said he preferred the fireside, or just ambling about in the old walled garden.

Diana, watching the sea on one of these occasions, was remembering how she had sat with Paul Esterre on their *planche* and watched the waves breaking in foam over the Welsh rocks. Between that time and this, she had so very rarely even seen the sea, her life circumscribed by Mayne Downe.

Andrew had been watching her, the soft mouth, the half-smile on it and in her dreaming eyes.

'Thoughts?' he asked, and she gave herself a little shake and turned to him.

'Only browsing amongst things I've almost forgotten,' she said. 'I was thinking of a Frenchman I used to know, when I was only a schoolgirl. We used to sit and watch the sea like this, though it was summer then, and in Wales. I wonder what happened to him.'

'What is this? A romance?' asked Andrew, aware of a most unexpected little stab of regret.

'Oh, no. Nothing so exciting. He was a lot older than I was. I was only sixteen and, now I look back at myself, most astonishingly innocent. He must have been a very nice person even to bother about a schoolgirl. We spent many stolen hours together and nobody ever knew. I've never told even Gramp. He'd probably have disapproved, and my mother would have been horrified and thought the worst at once!'

'Tell me about your mother, Diana.'

'Oh—there isn't really much to tell. She's, I think, the most beautiful person I've ever seen, and she always looks lovely, too. I'm not in the least like her,' with rueful self-deprecation.

'Does she ever come to Mayne Downe?'

'Very occasionally she descends on us, and brings the most ghastly people with her, but it's so wonderful when they've gone back that Gramp and I always feel it's been worth it for the sake of the contrast.'

'I wonder why she married your father, if she's so different from you two? If your father had lived, wouldn't she have been expected to live at Mayne and be the grand lady?'

Diana's expressive face changed, as it did so often, so en-chantingly.

'Ah, but then everything would have been different. She was quite, quite different when he was alive. You see, they were most terribly in love with each other. He was her whole life and I don't think it would have mattered to her where or how she lived if they could have been together. When he died, she was left not wanting anything, not even wanting life at all. People think she got over his death quickly and enjoys her freedom, but I don't think it's that. I think all the time she's trying to forget, trying to make some sort of life for herself even though she knows that inside she's dead.'

'She may marry again,' he suggested.

'Mummy? Oh no! No, she'd never do that.'

'She's too faithful to a memory?'

'Yes. I don't think anybody could possibly care again, not after the way she loved him. It was something—well, I don't think it often happens for two people to feel as they did.'

'You don't think you ever will, Diana?'

He scarcely knew why he had asked the question.

She turned to him her sweet, warm smile which he knew held nothing personal to him.

'I don't know. I should like to think so, but people like my father don't come every day.'

'What about the French friend?' he asked with a teasing little smile.

'I told you there was no romance in that,' she said. 'I was so young, and it's so long ago that I doubt if I should even know him if I saw him again. Mr. Shawn, it's wonderful sitting here and I hate to suggest going, but haven't you forgotten that you wanted to get back early to see somebody or other?'

'I'd like to forget, but perhaps we'd better go,' he said, and backed and turned the car for the homeward journey.

He did not want to give his thoughts full rein just then. He was not at all sure he wanted to let them go in that direction at all.

By one of those odd coincidences which seem almost uncanny, when they reached Mayne Downe again they found Clementine there, and for once alone.

It was obvious that her father-in-law was worried, and Diana felt the stab of an unaccustomed resentment against her mother for having the power to disturb him. She had thought he had not been so well lately.

Clementine looked with interest at Andrew Shawn, and sent a quick, half-amused look in her daughter's direction. What was this?

Diana watched the two during the brief half-hour or so for which they were together. What if Andrew fell in love with her beautiful alluring mother? And what if Clementine decided that she could bear to marry again and that she could marry Andrew? How would she herself feel about that?

She thought that she would be glad. She was sometimes worrier in an almost maternal way about Clementine's restless gaiety and the kind of life she led. With a man like Andrew Shawn she would have something stable and worthwhile in her life again, a proper background, someone who would really care for her happiness not merely try to get something out of her tremendous vitality.

Yes, Diana decided that it would be a good thing if they could fall in love. Their ages were right, too, though Clementine hated people to know how near she was to forty.

After Andrew had gone, Diana spoke artlessly.

'Don't you think he's nice?' she asked.

'Shawn? Oh yes. Quite nice,' she said carelessly. 'Who is he? A beau?'

'Of course not! Why, he's old enough to be my father. He's almost as old as—'

She stopped in dismay of what she had been about to say, but her mother finished the sentence.

'As I am? That makes him a Methuselah, doesn't it? Who is he? What is he?'

'He's something in London. A stockbroker, I think Joan said. It's his own firm.'

Clementine's lovely eyes widened.

'Shawn Greenfold? Is he *that* Shawn? My, but you fly high,' with a look of surprised approbation at her daughter.

Is he an important person, then?'

'If he's that Shawn, he is. It's a very prosperous firm indeed, and apart from that, his name's on quite a lot of boards of directors. Well, well, well,' with another of those looks of amused surprise.

'Pity I've got a car here,' she said, laughing a little. 'He might have driven me up to town in his elderly Daimler.'

'You're not going back tonight, are you, Mummy?' asked Diana.

'I must. And right now,' she said, looking at her watch, an extravagant trifle in diamond-set platinum.

'What a lovely little watch!' Diana said. 'I didn't know you had that.'

Clementine pulled her driving glove over it. She had dined there but had not taken off hat or coat.

'I don't often wear it,' she said. 'It's too showy. See me off, dear? I'll just run up to Gramp to say goodbye.'

'I'll turn the car round,' said Diana, and as she was doing it noticed a silver disc attached to the ignition key. She looked at it in careless curiosity. The initials on it were J. B.

Joseph Bloggett?

The initials need not have been his, of course, but Diana had a nasty feeling that they were. She hated the thought of her mother, exquisite and fastidious as she had always been, even borrowing a car from that horrible old man. Her flesh began to creep as she remembered those few moments in the library, his hand on her arm, his nasty insinuating voice paying her silly compliments and offering to give her clothes and jewels.

She hoped the car was not his, but she dare not ask her mother. Clementine had never invited curiosity about her personal affairs and would certainly resent it now.

She kissed Diana coolly but with an unusually interested smile.

'Clever girl,' she said as she got into the car and drove off.

Clever? That was a new one, especially from Clementine, but why? How was she being clever? Surely, surely her mother didn't think that she, Diana, had designs on Andrew Shawn? The idea was too fantastic. She laughed aloud at it as she went in and upstairs.

Her thoughts fled at once away from herself and to her grandfather when she saw him, stretched back in his chair, his hands, old now and gnarled with what he refused to admit was rheumatism, working unconsciously at the chintz covering on the chair arms.

She kissed the top of his head.

'Tired, old man?' she asked.

He put out a hand and drew her to him.

'A little. Perhaps it's your mother's bounding energy. It shows up my lack of it and makes me feel about a hundred and eight. You're a dear child,' he said. 'What should I ever have done without you all these years?'

'What should *I* have done without *you*, you mean,' she said.

'That's one of the things that worry me. You'll have to some day, perhaps some day soon. Who knows?'

'Now we're surely not going into that again!' she said, for she could usually tease him into joining in her laughter when he started to talk about dying. 'Want me to ring up Mather?'

Mather was the local undertaker.

But tonight she could not jolly him out of his mood of black depression, so she tried another diversion.

'Clementine was quite impressed by the fact that we know Andrew. It seems he's quite a big noise. She thinks I'm out to snatch him. Andrew! I nearly slipped up and reminded her that he's almost the same age as she is. I thought he seemed to like her rather, but then she's so terribly attractive, isn't she?'

'I don't think she's quite his style,' said Gramp grimly.

'Not just now, but then he hasn't seen her as she *really* is, as she used to be before—you know.'

'It's four years ago now. Perhaps this is how she really is and the other was just a phase.'

'Oh no, Gramp! That was what she's like in herself. I've been thinking it might be a good thing if—well, if she and Andrew got fond of each other. They might, you know. She's so attractive and he's very nice, and if it's true that he's got a good deal of money, that would make it better for her, wouldn't it?'

'I'd say anybody with money could make it better for your mother, poppet,' he said in that grim voice which he seemed to keep now for references to Clementine. 'No, I don't somehow think Shawn will fall for her. You exaggerate her attractions a bit, you know. She isn't everybody's cup of tea, and she's damned extravagant.'

Diana could not think what to say, for she had not been able to escape the knowledge that her mother was constantly asking for money from Gramp, in spite of his very reduced circumstances.

The next topic she chose was not altogether a change of subject.

'Darling, I don't really want a big do for my twenty-first,' she said. 'Let's just have Joan and Ian and Andrew in for the evening and get Ethel to do us a chicken with mushrooms the way we like it, and one of her wonderful *soufflés*, and a cake if she wants to. It'll be much more fun than a big party. Besides, who'd come?'

He passed a hand over her hair.

'I'm going to have my own way for once,' he said. 'I'm going to give a party for my only grandchild, and nobody's going to bully me out of it. As for who's coming, you'll see soon enough! I was talking about it to Clementine only this evening, and she's going to get out the list.'

'*Her* friends? Oh, Gramp, it'll be awful!' in real distress.

'Not just her friends, though I expect she'll want some of them. You've lived a hole and corner existence long enough.'

'Oh, Gramp, I shall be miserable. And it is going to be *my* birthday, you know.'

He laughed and she saw that at least the conversation had had the effect of cheering him up, and though her whole soul recoiled from the idea, she brought paper and pencil and helped him compile a list of their reasonably near neighbours, especially those known to have young people in the family.

# Chapter Five

To Diana's infinite relief, though she deplored the reason, the proposed twenty-first birthday never came off.

With the invitations printed and all ready to go out and plans made for the opening and redecoration of the ballroom and for catering by a big London firm, with Diana's dress designed and in the hands of Clementine's dressmaker, Colonel Merrimayne was taken suddenly ill.

Ethel, going into his room with his early tea one morning, found him lying half in and half out of bed, unconscious. She had thought at first that he was dead.

Diana telephoned frantically to Dr. Jenning and they managed to get the heavy old man back into his bed by the time the doctor came.

'I'm afraid he's had a stroke, Miss Merrimayne,' said the young doctor, and told her what to do, which she felt was little enough, and left her with the two servants in a state of great distress.

Later in the day she rang up Joan Hurst, and in the evening, to her surprise but great comfort, Andrew Shawn's car drew up outside.

'How good you are to come,' said Diana shakily, going down to the door whilst she left Mrs. Good in the sick-room. 'I'm afraid he's very ill. I can't bear to think he might—might not get better.'

But the Colonel was made of tough fibre, and it was very soon established that he was going to recover, but too slowly to admit of the possibility of holding the twenty-first celebrations.

Clementine, who had not come down whilst the old man lay unconscious and possibly dying, came later, but seemed worried and distracted on her own account rather than his.

'Will you at least see that everything possible is cancelled for the fourteenth?' Diana begged her, worn to a shadow herself with anxiety, and with nights of watching when she would let no one relieve her.

'Very well. I expect the dress has gone too far, but perhaps he'll find someone to take it off our hands without too much expense. Heaven knows I don't want to have to pay *your* bills.'

Diana coloured.

'Gramp will pay for the dress when he gets better,' she said with an unusual touch of acerbity.

'I didn't mean I won't pay for it. Of course I will if it has to be paid for,' said Clementine, realizing that she had been more than a little ungenerous. 'The only thing is that I'm so desperately hard up just now and more bills would completely sink me.'

Diana could not forbear a glance at her mother's turn-out, exquisite as ever; perfectly tailored suit, its matching accessories beyond reproach, a coat of dark mink over her arm.

Clementine could not fail to interpret that glance and she shrugged her shoulders.

'I know. I know,' she said. 'Nothing's paid for, though. The mink was a present and I daren't sell that to pay for the rest. How long do you think it will be before one can talk to Gramp?'

'If it's to ask him for more money, then never,' said Diana with a new firmness. 'He's frightfully hard up. I'd no idea how hard up until I've had to see to his affairs for him whilst he's been ill, and he can't give you anything else. He really can't afford the allowance he's making you, and there's no reason at all why he should be making it, but I expect he'll go on doing it. As soon as he's well enough, I'm going to try and get a job.'

'A job?' echoed Clementine with unflattering amusement. 'What on earth can you do that people will pay you for?'

'I don't know, but there must be something. I can ride, and drive a car and do accounts after a fashion, and I dare say I could learn to use a typewriter. Anyway, I'm not going on being a parasite on Gramp once he's better.'

'Meaning that I am a parasite?' asked her mother angrily.

'No, but I think you ought to manage to live on your pension and what Gramp gives you without always asking him for more.'

Clementine turned away and Diana looked after her with astonishment at her own temerity. To dare to criticize her and tell her what and what not to do!

Driving furiously away in the little car which she seemed able to 'borrow' at any time, complete with as much petrol as she wanted, Clementine became aware that in the distance, heading leisurely towards her, was Andrew Shawn's Daimler. With its high, old-fashioned body, it was unmistakable even at a distance, and quick as thought she pulled up at the side of the road, sprang out, opened the bonnet and disconnected a wire lead in the engine. This had given trouble on the way down, but a temporary repair had been effected at a garage so that she could make the journey.

When Shawn drew level with her she straightened up and let him see who she was.

He stopped at once, pulling his car into the side of the road.

'Mrs. Merrimayne? In trouble?' he asked.

She gave him a devastating smile.

'Isn't it maddening? It was a nuisance on the way down and I got them to fix it at a garage and innocently thought they'd done so, but look at me now! I suppose I ought to have turned back then, but I was anxious about Gramp and I haven't seen him for a week and thought I could just make it. It's infuriating, as I simply must get back to Town tonight,' giving him one of the helpless, appealing glances which were always effective with a member of the opposite sex.

This occasion was no exception.

He gave a would-be wise look at the engine, about which he knew even less than she, and then closed the bonnet.

'Perhaps I could push it into this field,' he said, 'so that it could wait to be collected. Then, if you'll allow me, I'll run you back to London. I think I can just make it on my petrol, but at any rate I can get you within reach of a good train service. Oh, here's someone coming,' walking into the road to attract the attention of a cyclist, who obligingly helped him to push the coupe through the gateway and safely off the high road.

Clementine settled herself contentedly beside the driving-seat. Surely, since they had now met several times and he seemed distinctly interested, she could turn this heaven-sent opportunity to really good account? Andrew Shawn was not at all her idea of a man, but then she would never find that again, and he was at least presentable and had good manners and if not out of exactly the same drawer as the Merrimaynes, he subscribed to the same code and would never disgrace her. She wondered just how rich he was.

When they reached Sevenoaks he decided that there would not be sufficient petrol to take them up to London, but he told her he had a private store in his garage.

'By the way, just how desperate is your hurry to get to Town? And by what time must you be there?'

She felt a stab of sheer relief. So far the conversation had been so impersonal that anybody might have joined in. She was, in fact, finding him heavy going, and was the more surprised at the fact that Diana, usually so tongue-tied and awkward, seemed to have found no difficulty in holding a conversation with him.

She gave him an encouraging little smile.

'Well, it's fairly desperate,' she said, 'but actually it depends.'

'On what?'

'On what alternatives offer,' she said flirtatiously.

Andrew Shawn's experience was much limited by the fact that, since the death of a girl he had worshipped and had wanted to marry many years before, women had held little attraction for him. He was known amongst his intimates as a complete and confirmed bachelor, and he had made his life so comfortable that until very recently he had felt no lack in it.

He had, however, welcomed the unexpected opportunity of this meeting with Clementine Merrimayne away from Mayne Downe and free from interruptions. He had a particular reason for welcoming it.

'I won't test that too far,' he said with a smile. 'I was only going to suggest that you take tea with me.'

'I shall be enchanted,' said Clementine, and when he drew up before a substantial, old-fashioned double-fronted house of red brick, she looked at it with interest.

It was well kept, as was the small, formal front garden, and she caught a glimpse of more garden at the side and the back.

There were white steps to the double front doors, and gleaming, well-polished brass. Inside there was an air of solid comfort.

The housekeeper came forward, looking a little surprised but not displeased to see the visitor.

'Tea, Mrs. Castle, please, and some of your special efforts in cakes if you've got any.'

'I made some only this morning, sir,' said the woman, 'and I'm glad somebody's going to eat them this time,' bustling away again.

'My drawing-room is upstairs,' said Andrew, leading the way up the thickly carpeted stairs. 'I expect you'd like to wash your hands after having had to fiddle about with your car. There is the drawing-room,' indicating one of the several closed doors, 'and there is a bathroom here,' opening another door for her.

'A bit of an old fusspot,' thought Clementine, 'but all this is nice,' looking round the bathroom which was not modern but almost palatial in its size and comfort.

He brought her fresh towels, some highly perfumed soap, and left her to enjoy them. She noticed with secret amusement that he had sent surreptitious glances along the passage towards a door which undoubtedly sheltered a convenience he could not bring himself to name to her, but when presently she went along the corridor, knowing he would not have permitted himself to be anywhere near, she opened another door and peeped in.

It was, she could see, his own bedroom; another superbly male place with heavy dark furniture, dark red carpet and curtains, no knicks-knacks or ornaments of any kind.

She closed the door again, softly. Well, it seemed pretty obvious that there was no feminine influence here; everything was too austere.

The question was, could she bear it? Could she endure to live with a man like Andrew Shawn, so difficult of conversation, so out of touch with her kind of world, so difficult from her kind of associates? Those associates, at least, which had been hers since Piers died?

Piers.

She stood still for a moment, her body tense, and there swept over her that feeling of desolation which she could not conquer, even after four years of reckless crowding of her life with what was called pleasure, making herself so tired that she had to sleep from sheer exhaustion, filling every hour of every day and most of the night with noise, movement, the ceaseless chatter of parrots and magpies.

Andrew Shawn was not Piers, might be endurable for the very reason that he was so different that he would never remind her of Piers.

She went to his drawing-room, her decision made. She would marry Andrew Shawn. It never occurred to her even as a remote possibility that she would not be able to accomplish this. All her life she had been courted and flattered and desired, and she knew the effect she could produce in all sorts of men by her extraordinary beauty, her wit and her charm.

He was aware of them all as she sat before the tea-table with its shining silver and delicate china. He was aware, too, that she was not now wearing the platinum and diamond watch he had seen on her wrist in the car.

He mentioned it.

'Have you by any chance left your watch in the bathroom? I see it isn't on your wrist,' he said, 'and I shouldn't like to be left responsible for anything so valuable!' with a smile.

For an instant she was faintly flustered. It was unprecedented.

'Oh no, I—it's in my bag,' she said, and recovered herself at once. 'It isn't too comfortable to wear. It's a bit tight.'

He wondered, and thought he knew, why she had taken it off and was not flaunting it before his eyes. He guessed that Joseph Bloggett had given it to her. Diana was so transparent that it had been impossible not to see what was in her mind when she had made references to him, connecting him with her mother in a way she had no idea he could so easily recognize. She was far too loyal to say anything against Clementine and would have been horrified if she had known that she had told the whole story to him.

He thought it was a pity. She was so lovely. Even his eyes could see that. Surely she need not prostitute her beauty and all her other graces for the enjoyment of men like the one Diana had so artlessly described to him?

And beyond doubt Clementine was charming. He watched her and listened to her with a mind that appreciated without being in the least dazzled. He liked simple things, natural things, whereas Diana's mother was perfected art.

He glanced at the clock. If he were going to say what he had gladly seized this chance of saying, he must say it now.

He brought the subject round to Diana.

'One wonders how she will accept the inevitable transfer some day from her present home,' he said, when they had glided over the girl's love of the country and skill with the horses, the dogs and her amateur efforts at farmyard farming. 'It seems so exactly the right setting for her.'

'Yes. She ought to have been a boy,' said Clementine casually. 'When my father-in-law dies we shall have to leave Mayne Downe and heaven knows where we shall go then.'

'It will mean a lot to Diana, I'm afraid. I didn't realize it meant so much to you, though.'

'Because I'm not often there? Well—there are reasons. For one thing, we're terribly poor, with taxes, and the changes in everything, and Gramp lost a lot because of the war, foreign investments and so on, and my Piers was never a good business man. Whilst Gramp's alive, of course, we've a home there, but neither Di nor I would ever contemplate living with the Maize Merrimaynes!'

Was this the approach he wanted? He cleared his throat and wished he did not find it so difficult to say it.

'Mrs. Merrimayne, I've been thinking about that quite a lot, about what—you and Diana will do when the old man has gone, and I have a solution—something I'd like to suggest to you—I feel a little diffident about it. It seems—almost presumptive on my part. I've never married. I was engaged once, but she died, and until now I've never found it possible to care for anyone enough to feel I could make her happy. I can't even now be sure that I could, but I'd devote my whole life ... Mrs. Merrimayne, tell me frankly, what are my chances?'

She moved, pushing the wheeled table a little so that it was no longer between them. She was smiling. Her eyes were alight and soft. Her lips were parted in indulgent amusement.

'Andrew,' she said, using his name for the first time, 'are you by any chance proposing to me?'

He caught a swift, astonished breath. Heavens, what frightful *gaffe* had he made? Was it possible that he had made her think that?

'I'm trying to ask you to let me marry Diana,' he blurted out.

Clementine sat motionless for one appalled moment. Then the training and habit of years came to her rescue, and she smiled.

'Do you know, I believe I had you foxed?' she said with a little light-laugh. 'Confess now. In that first wild moment you thought I was serious, didn't you? Poor Andrew, what a trick to play on you! As if I didn't know you wanted to marry Diana! It's written all over you. I dare say the only person who doesn't know is Diana herself. Or does she?'

'No, I don't think she has any idea. I've never said anything to her. I wanted to speak to you about it first. The Colonel knows, and approves, but I felt I could not say anything to her until I'd spoken to you. I suppose I am almost Victorian. I am many years older than Diana. I'm thirty-six against her twenty-one, but I'm hoping she will think I have other things to recommend me. She likes me. I'm sure of that. We're very good friends. I understand her ways. In fact, I'm prepared to alter as many of mine as I can to suit her. This house, for instance. It suits me very well, but it won't do for her. For one thing, it's too formal and too far in the town. Sevenoaks is growing and is no longer the little country town it used to be. It's almost suburban. Diana would be happier further out. I've had the agents' lists already, and there are one or two nice properties for sale in the surrounding villages, Otford, perhaps, or Seal, or Romney Street. I could still get to Town several days a week, though there is now no actual need for me to be there unless I want to. I'm not a wealthy man, but I could make my wife comfortable, give her everything she could want within reason. And Diana, bless her, has no very extravagant tastes!' with a little reminiscent and very tender smile which assured Clementine, if she had needed assurance, that she would be wasting her time trying to attract him away from her daughter.

She was furious, humiliated, wretched, frightened, but she showed him none of these things. Her brow was unruffled, her eyes calm, her smile sugary, as she listened with only half her attention to the flow of his now voluble speech, making plans for Diana, offering Diana happiness, security, freedom from all these carking anxieties which weighed her own life down.

It was maddening, but what could she do?

'Of course you *are* a great many years older than Diana.' she said when she had to say something. 'However, if that's what you want and what she wants, it's nothing to do with me. Go in and get her and let me dance at your wedding!'

'You really mean I should be acceptable as—it sounds rather silly, but as your son-in-law?'

'So long as you don't call me Mother,' she said, and thought he must be an idiot not to see that she was fuming in impotent anger. 'I think we'd better go now, hadn't we?'

'You're sure you won't have another cup of tea? No? Then I'll put the petrol in the car and be ready in about five minutes.'

On the run to Town she sat without speaking, and Andrew, who liked to concentrate on his driving, made no attempt to divert her, having no idea that she needed to be diverted. He was glad that he would have no opposition from either Diana's mother or grandfather. It now remained to be seen whether he would have any from Diana herself. He was under no delusions. He did not see himself as any knight of romance. In fact, he underrated his possible advantages as the husband of a young girl. If it had been the mother with whom he contemplated marriage (she was right when she thought that for one wild moment he had not realized she was joking about that!) he would have looked at things differently, assessing as the most important factor his quite considerable means. With Diana, that would not count. It would always be the man himself that would matter to her, and what had he to offer in that category? Good health, good temper, stability, tolerance.

He paused. Was he tolerant? He thought of the many things he disliked intensely, things like vulgarity of thought and speech, deceitfulness, unfaithfulness to a promise, slanderous gossip, light behaviour in a husband or wife – but there was not one of those intolerances to which Diana herself would not subscribe.

He left Clementine at the entrance to the expensive block of flats in which she had a service suite. Looking at the sort of place in which she chose to live, when she was free to live anywhere, he was glad that her daughter had so little of Clementine in her. Diana would have hated to live in one of those tiny, costly boxes.

The uniformed liftman spoke to her as he whirled her up to the fourth floor, but she did not reply. She needed to be alone, to relax, not even to have to think, though how was she ever going to get away from her thoughts?

'I'm tired and disagreeable and thoroughly bad-tempered,' she said to the maid when she came to take her coat and hat.

'I'll run a bath,' said Flora, who was deeply attached to her.

Relaxed in a hot bath, she felt better able to cope with the problems which had become too insistent to be pushed aside any longer. She wondered if she might not have made more of her early opportunities with Andrew Shawn, and then told herself that if what he really fancied was someone like Diana, then it would have been a waste of time for her to try to get him.

'Get me Sir Joseph on the 'phone, Flora,' she said when she was resting after the bath.

'That you, Joseph?' she asked in a tone of languor. 'I've changed my mind. What shall we do this evening? ... No, not there. I'm bored with it ... All right. We can have dinner there in any case. Afterwards? ...' She gave a low, murmuring laugh. 'No promises, but we'll see.'

'Find me something glamorous to wear,' she told the maid with a sigh. 'Sir Joseph's calling for me at eight, so I needn't start to dress for another half-hour. I think the gold. It's ornate and it'll be overdoing a restaurant dinner, but he'll like it. No jewels. Oh, the diamond earrings, I suppose.'

She never had to pretend with Flora. The girl knew almost as much as there was to be known. She dreaded the prospect of her mistress marrying Sir Joseph Bloggett, but since there was nothing she could do about it she wisely accepted the possibility.

Sir Joseph was kept waiting fully twenty minutes in the too warm, too softly stuffed sitting-room, but when Clementine appeared in the doorway his irritation vanished.

'By gum, but you're a smasher tonight,' he said admiringly, and she smiled as if the result had been achieved without effort.

'And mine,' he thought gloatingly. 'I'm going to have her, by all the powers. Somehow, I'm going to have her. I'll jolly well see no other feller does.'

She knew just how to treat him, with a lofty disdain that was almost rudeness, as if he were beneath contempt and she did not care whether he stayed or went. He always had to offer her the very best. Anything less she would have spurned, not with indignation but merely with that cold contempt which blew him into a white-hot flame of desire for her. And he had scarcely even been allowed to kiss her, and then only her cheek! What was he, he thought, giving his order for the most expensive champagne on the list and preparing his usual heavy bribe to the head waiter – what was he, man or mouse, that he let her treat him like that?

After the dinner he wanted to dance. She always felt slightly absurd dancing with him, for she was almost half a head taller, and in his close embrace she was bent in the middle to fit over his tubby contours. Still, she could not hope to get everything for nothing, and she graciously agreed. She had intentionally drunk more champagne than she usually drank, so that she might not feel too much affronted by his vulgarity and proximity.

'Come into my place for one for the road?' he asked her when they were in his car ready at last to call it the end of the day.

She shook her head with an understanding smile.

'No. I know that one,' she said. 'If you want a drink, I'll give you one though, if you promise to be very quiet.'

'Like a mouse,' he said, and as if facetiously carrying on the simile, scrabbled and pinched at her bare arm under the mink coat which she was wearing cloakwise.

He remembered that it was another of the things he had given her and for which, in the clever fashion he could never really fathom, she had again failed to give payment.

She drew her arm away and wrapped the coat round it.

'A cigarette, please,' she said serenely.

When he took a woman out in the evenings he preferred not to drive the car himself. Helping her out when they had reached her home, he told the chauffeur curtly to wait.

Flora was waiting up, but at a meaning glance from her mistress she faded away. She had a bedroom in the flat which Clementine had furnished for her as carefully and daintily as her own.

Flora went to her room but not to bed. She knew that Clementine was often exhausted and depressed after an evening with Sir Joseph, and she wanted to be at hand if there were anything she could do for her. She sat in her comfortable armchair and thought rather sadly about the man who seemed to have become inseparable from their life. If only she could have got enough money some other way! But so few people they knew were rich nowadays. Most of them were in the same state as the Merrimaynes, and it was as unthinkable to Flora that Clementine should be without money as it was to Clementine herself. They just had to get it somehow.

Clementine was pouring out cocktails.

'No bubbly?' asked Sir Joseph.

'All gone,' she said.

'I must get you some more.'

She shook her head. Her heart was beating fast. What if she messed this up as she still felt she must have messed up things with Andrew Shawn?

'No. Nothing,' she said.

'What do you mean, nothing?' he asked in the slightly bullying tone he used to all women, even to Clementine.

'I mean exactly what I say,' she said, her eyes averted, her voice very calm and aloof. 'I don't want to take anything else from you. Sir Joseph. I've been wrong in accepting your generosity, your very great generosity. It can't go on.'

'Oh? And why not?' he demanded, blustering a little.

She handed him the cocktail she had mixed for him, but set her own down on a little table and stood with her hands just touching the edge of the wood.

'Because it's not being fair to you,' she said, and now she looked at him calmly. 'I haven't been brought up to do all the taking and I find that it does not come easily to me now, so though I'm very grateful, it must end.'

'Well, well. That takes some thinking about, y'know. Not that I'm not with you about doing all the taking, and I'm not saying it isn't what you've done, y'know. Not been what you might call exactly generous yourself, now have you, Clem, my dear? Not that I only give so's to get back. Don't think that, but a man likes to know that what he gives is— well, appreciated, y'know.'

She wondered if she would ever get used to his saying 'y'know' or if she could get him out of that habit, as she would have to get him out of others if she were to be able to live with him at all.

'It's exactly what I have been saying,' she told him calmly. 'That is why I feel I cannot go on taking from you, Sir Joseph.'

'Not so much of the *Sir* Joseph,' he complained. 'You say you can't go on taking—not without giving, I suppose you mean? Well, what's wrong with that? What's wrong with doing a little bit of giving, eh? Eh, Clem, my dear?' putting down his glass and coming round to the other side of the little table and attempting to put an arm about her.

She moved away.

'You see, that's what I mean—Joseph. I'm not prepared to do that sort of giving, and there isn't any other kind, is there? Not from me to you.'

'I'd be good to you, Clem. You know that. I'd look after you, and if you wanted it, I'd settle something on you. I'm not the sort to leave you flat, either. I don't chop and change, and you're what I want. You're what I've always wanted.'

She shook her head, but there was a sort of wistful regret in her eyes. At that moment they looked like Diana's though the thoughts that lay in her mind could never be Diana's.

'I'm sorry, but—I'm not really what you want, Joseph,' she said, and her voice was soft with that same regret she had contrived to get into her eyes. 'What you want is—someone who could be to you what I could never be to any man.'

'Get along with you. You're a woman, aren't you? And not a bit of ice, either, or I don't know women. You be old Joe Bloggett's little friend, girlie, and he'll show you what he can do in that line as well,' with a fat, unctuous laugh which made her feel faint and sick. Could she possibly go on with it?

Then she remembered the pile of bills, the threatening tone which had now replaced the polite reminders. There had even been a writ, which had horrified her and brought her to this, since Gramp had not been able to do any more for her. The man who had served the writ on her had indicated that the next step would be the bailiff!

She shook her head again.

'I'm sorry. Joseph. I like you so much. What woman would not? You've been so good to me, so kind and thoughtful and generous. Don't think I haven't appreciated it because I have, more than I can say, and—it isn't going to be easy to say goodbye to you.'

'Hey, hey, what *is* all this? About goodbye and so on? Who says we're saying goodbye? I've told you, Clem, that when Joe Bloggett makes up his mind, it stays put, and I'm staying put with you.'

'No, my dear. I've got to be fair to myself as well as to you, and it's not being fair to myself to—feel all the time that I'm under a debt that I can't discharge. It isn't in my nature. And—I can't discharge it. That isn't in my nature either,' dropping her voice very low.

'Bless my soul, nobody would know. How could they? You could keep on this flat if you wanted to. Go on living here, have your friends, your bridge and so on. But we'd have another little nest, you and I. I've got my eyes on it. Just the thing. Not in the West End, of course, because that's how people see you. It's out Harrow Road way, not much to look at outside, but inside I'd spend a mint o'money on making it all right for you, new bathroom, everything new, and you could go to Harrods' or wherever you liked and buy all the furniture you wanted ...'

She shook her head, this time with more determination.

'No, Joseph, my dear. I keep saying no, and I really mean it. I'd never be on those terms with any man, never. So—you see, it's got to be goodbye, hasn't it?' lifting her eyes to his with just the right expression in them – sadness, regret, even affection.

She lifted her arms and deftly removed the diamond earrings and laid them down on the table, giving him at the same time another of those swift sad smiles.

'What are you doing?' he asked uncomfortably.

'Giving them back to you, and thank you for letting me wear them. I'll send the other things to your bank. And now—goodbye,' and she held out her hand to him.

He did not take it.

'You can't mean it, Clem,' he muttered. 'You can't mean you're pushing me off.'

She did not reply, but stood there looking at him with that unmanning look in her eyes. Dammit, where would he ever find another woman like her? He didn't even want any other woman. Never had, not seriously, ever since he'd first set eyes on her.

'I—I—Clem, I'm not a marrying man,' he said at last, thickly, and not looking at her. His short, stumpy fingers were moving the diamond ear-studs about on the table. He was thinking of his freedom, his lovely, cherished, vaunted freedom, the thing he loved more than almost anything else in the world. One of the two exceptions was his money. The other – was it Clementine herself?

'I've been married, y'know. My wife died a matter of ten years or so ago, but I never minded that much. It wasn't much good as a marriage. We didn't get on, and she never had any children, and I suppose it was things like that that put me to making money. It was the only thing left for me to do. But I made up my mind that Joe Bloggett would never marry again. No more of that, I said to myself. You stay free, Joe. I told myself, and that's how I've stayed, ever since. Free. But—it's no good blinking at facts, and the fact is—I want you, Clem. You mean a lot to me, too much for me to give you up, and if you say there's no other way—well, what would you say to that? Would you marry me, Clem, if I asked you to?'

She smiled, putting a little more warmth into the smile.

'*Have* you asked me, Joseph?'

'Have I? I dunno. Well, perhaps I have. I'm burning my boats. I'm asking you now. Will you marry me, Clem?' taking out his handkerchief and passing it across his forehead as if the effort had been a prodigious one, as indeed it had.

She hesitated. She had made up her mind long ago, even before the evening had started, but she had to hold him, she had to be top dog. She must not appear too eager.

'I—don't quite know,' she said slowly. 'It's rather a shock to me. You see, I hadn't really thought about it. I'm not a marrying woman, either. You see—my first marriage *was* a happy one, a great success. I loved my husband very dearly. I could never feel like that towards anyone again.'

'Well, I wouldn't expect that, but I'd expect a *loving* wife, Clem, even if she didn't really love me. You know what I mean?'

She gave a little shiver which she hoped he did not see. Yes, she did know. It was an inescapable part of the price she would have to pay.

'Yes, I understand,' she said, 'and of course I wouldn't expect—or want—marriage on any other terms.'

He had a vision of her as his wife, surrendered to him, her white body in his bed, for the taking. He would string her nakedness with jewels, see them glitter on her pale flesh. Furs, too. He would cover her in them and then uncover her again ...

His brain seemed suffused with hot, racing blood, the blood of a young man again. Veins stood out purple on his forehead. His eyes were hot and rimmed with red.

He stretched out his hands and touched her, pulled her into his arms, crushed her against him and bruised her lips with his own. She struggled and fought, mad with fear and with hatred of him. Then she remembered and went limp and let him have his way with her lips, her throat, her white shoulders, but pushed him away when his greedy fingers would have explored further.

'Can't you wait?' she forced her outraged lips to say with a forced smile.

'Not too long,' he panted. 'Don't make me wait too long. There's nothing to wait for, is there? Is there, Clem, my darling?'

'No, there's nothing to wait for,' she said slowly.

'Tomorrow we'll go and buy the ring. I'll buy you a beauty, my love. Good night, my lovely. All right. Fight me now if you like, but some day it'll be my turn, and then you won't be able to fight me. Though I like a bit of fight in a woman. I never have thought much of the sort that are off with their clothes and into yer bed before you can say knife,' and with another bear-like hug and a triumphant laugh, he left her.

Flora heard him go and came to see what she could do for her mistress, but Clementine without a word pushed her aside and went into her bedroom and the maid heard the key turn.

Out of a drawer where she had put it long ago, Clementine took a leather case, opened it and looked at the face of her dead husband. Her own face was white, her eyes tragic.

'Oh, Piers, Piers?' she whispered, and pressed the cold glass against her breast. 'Forgive me. My darling, forgive me!'

# Chapter Six

Andrew Shawn, once he had made up his mind, lost no time in his approach to Diana.

On the day following his interview with Clementine, instead of going to his office, he went to Mayne Downe. It was not much after twelve, and Diana looked up with surprise. She was on her hands and knees, weeding her herb bed. They had given up all thought of restoring order to the ornamental and pleasure gardens, but she and Good, with the occasional help of Mrs. Good and much well-meant but disregarded advice from Gramp, had managed to restore some semblance of order to most of the walled kitchen garden.

She was dressed in an old pair of jodhpurs and a yellow jersey, and she had tied a bright scarf over her head.

'Hullo, gipsy,' he said, startling her.

"Oh, Andrew! You quite scared me,' she said, laughing and jumping to her feet. 'What on earth are you doing here at this time of the morning? Aren't there any stocks to broke today?'

'I've left them to the other brokers and given myself a holiday,' he said, smiling. 'I thought I might prevail on you to give me some lunch.'

She pulled a grimace and wiped her grimy hands on the seat of her pants. One of the things he loved about her was her complete naturalness.

'Heavens, what on earth shall we be able to give you?' she asked. 'The everlasting egg?'

Ethel said she would make an omelet, but would Miss Diana see if there were any mushrooms?

Diana went back to the garden and picked up Andrew on his return journey from the ever-burning rubbish heap, and together they went to the shed where he had been helping, with advice at any rate, to make and establish a mushroom bed. So far, though they had carefully followed the instructions in every detail, no mushrooms had materialized. This morning was no different from any other morning in that respect.

'We'd better go back and tell Ethel,' said Diana resignedly.

'She'll never have expected us to bring any in, so why worry?' said Andrew, setting down the empty basket. 'Let's sit in the sunshine and talk—if it's not too cold for you?'

'I never feel the cold here. Isn't it wonderful for December? And soon it will be Christmas, and then the spring again!'

'Wonderful to be young enough to long for every new spring,' he said, half in jest, half in regret. 'Since my blood's not as young as yours, shall we take advantage of the south wall?'

They sat there where many generations of Merrimaynes must have sat, the sun-warmed wall behind them, in front of them the neat rows of vegetables, the cordons and espaliers getting into shape again, some sort of order restored to the wire-caged soft fruit bushes.

'I saw your mother yesterday,' said Andrew, telling her of the car breakdown. 'We talked about you.'

'About me? But whatever is there to say about me?'

He laid a hand very gently on one of hers.

'Dear,' he said, using his first endearment to her, 'would it surprise you very much to know that I've grown very fond of you?'

She gave him one of her quick, shy glances.

'Well, I'm fond of you, Andrew,' she said, much too frankly and innocently for his liking.

'I'm glad you are because I'm going to ask you if you think you could get rather more than just fond of me. You see, I happen to have done something that surprises me very much, and pleases me very much. I've fallen in love with you, Diana.'

Now the glance was much more startled.

'Andrew! You don't mean ...?'

He nodded, smiling as sheepishly as a schoolboy with his first girl-friend.

'Yes. I do mean. I'm more than *in* love with you. I love you. With all my heart and soul. How do you feel about my telling you that?'

'I don't know. It's so—unexpected. I never dreamed of anything like that,' frowning a little and looking thoughtfully on the ground.

Her first reaction was a feeling of loss. She was going to lose the first real friend she had ever made, the first man friend that is, since she could hardly count the dim memory of Paul Esterre.

'Why do you look so troubled about it, Diana? Am I such an old buffer that you can't think of me in terms of love and marriage?'

'You mean you want to marry me, Andrew?'

'I do, very much. That's why I talked to your mother yesterday, and to your grandfather last week. They both seem to think it quite a good scheme, but what do you think about it?'

She was silent for some moments. It was such a new idea to her, one which had never entered her head. Her thoughts were spilt all over her mind. She could not even begin to gather them up. To marry? Andrew? *Andrew?*

'Well, my dear?' he asked.

She looked at him with troubled eyes.

'Have I got to say yes or no right away?' she asked.

'No. but I rather hoped you might want to say yes at once. If you need time to think about it, it rather suggests that you don't love me. I wonder if you do, or think you could, Diana?'

'It isn't that I don't love you. I think perhaps I do. Anyway, I'm not a bit in love with anybody else,' she said honestly .

'Well, that's something, anyway. I start with a clear field in spite of handicaps. Do I seem old to you, Diana?'

'Oh no, Andrew, not a bit! At first I did think you'd be more likely to be Mummy's friend, but I soon saw that you were going to be mine, and now I never think about you being a lot older than I am. You see, I'm not quite like most girls, am I? I mean, I don't care all that much, for dressing up and going out and having what they call a good time. I love being at Mayne, and I'm happy doing all the things I do here, and the time never drags.'

'It's because I know that that I dare to ask you to marry me. There must come a time, perhaps not too far ahead, when—you'll be obliged to make a change in your life. You know that, don't you?'

'Yes, I know. The doctor told me that if dear Gramp has another attack, which he may do at any time, he won't get over it, and then of course Mayne Downe will belong to Blaize.'

'You wouldn't want to live here then?'

'Oh no, I couldn't, even if they wanted me, which they won't. They've got the most ghastly ideas of what they'll do to the house when they get it. They're going to run it as a sort of country club, hotel business. Isn't it dreadful? Mayne Downe!'

'It's as well that you know and have begun to face it, my dear, and it makes it easier for me to say what I want to say. I can't give you Mayne Downe. Nobody can do that. But I'd give you the best substitute we could find. I saw just the place the other day. It's at a tiny place called Ivy Hatch, no more than a few houses and cottages, but there's one fairly big house there, not too big but comfortably sized. The joy of it is that there are about seven acres of land with it, some of it laid out as a garden, some of it woodland, part of it fields where, if we liked, we could have a cow or two, or whatever you wanted. I couldn't get inside the house without an agent's note, so I looked through the windows and it looks comfortable and roomy, and you could arrange things as you wanted them. The place would have to be done up inside and out ...'

He was full of a young eagerness and energy such as she had never seen him display, and behind it was the light of his tenderness towards her, and a devotion which she knew to be something very well worth having. But she was still a little dazed and unable to think clearly, the idea too new.

He saw how she was feeling and checked the eager rush of words.

'Diana dear,' he said, taking her hand again, for she had unconsciously withdrawn it in her startled shyness, 'I can see I've surprised you and that you hadn't any idea I felt like this towards you. Would you like a little time to think it over and get used to the idea?'

She caught at that eagerly.

'Oh yes. Yes, I would, Andrew. You see—I never thought—'

Gently he saved her the need to finish her stammering sentence.

'All right, dear. I won't ask for an answer now, but you won't make me wait for it too long? I'm not a young man, as you think of youth, though at thirty-six one isn't really in one's dotage, you know,' with a smile.

'It isn't that, Andrew. Really it isn't that,' she said quickly. 'It's only that I'd like to think about it—please, Andrew.'

He got up and pulled her to her feet by her two hands and stood holding her like that for a moment, looking down into her eyes with such love and kindness in his own that she felt a warm flood of affection for him.

'Dear Andrew,' she said softly, and for once she did not run away from a thing which caused her deep feeling.

'I believe you're fond of me, aren't you?' he asked gently.

She nodded, her eyes misty.

'Then let's leave it at that for the moment. At least you haven't turned me down,' he said, and dropped her hands and linked an arm in hers and went back to the house with her.

Neither of them even thought again about the mushrooms, but Mrs. Good, watching them from her kitchen window, gave a little sigh of satisfaction. That was what she wanted to happen. It would be the best thing. As for the mushrooms – well, she hadn't expected there would be any, in any case.

Though it seemed outwardly as if nothing had happened, both Diana and Andrew were acutely aware that much had taken place. Watching her obvious indecision, her quick, shy glances away from him, her little worried frown, her closer clinging to her grandfather, he knew he was seldom out of her thoughts. There was a sadness in his own thoughts as he realized that she could not be completely in love with him to be so undecided, but as the days went by he could see that she was getting used to the idea, that she welcomed him now as her own visitor and missed him when he did not come.

One day her grandfather spoke to her about him.

The old man had never entirely recovered from his seizure, though he was up most of the day even if he sat before the fire, the inevitable dog at his feet, the inevitable cat on his lap.

Diana came in from a walk, her cheeks pink, her eyes bright, her hair wind-blown, the embodiment of youth and health.

'Look!' she said. 'The first primrose!' and she laid it in his hand. 'Isn't it lovely to think it's spring again?'

'Yes. Yes,' he said with a little sigh. 'Not everything gets renewed each year, though. Old men, for instance.'

She put an arm about his shoulders.

'Got the grumps?' she asked him tenderly.

'Not especially, but I wish one didn't have to rub out so infernally slowly.'

'Now, Gramp! You're getting on fine. Why, look at you, up every day now and talking of going out as soon as the wind has dropped.'

'Yes, my dear. Yes,' he said, and she did not know what an increasing and great effort it was for him to get up every day.

'Di dear, come and talk to me,' he said.

'Not about dying,' she told him decidedly.

'More about living. About you, not me. Di, what have you said to Andrew Shawn?'

She flushed brightly and stooped to caress the old spaniel who, like his master, was taking a long and weary time to die, though both were comfortable with their fireside.

'I haven't said anything, really. I don't know what to say.'

'How do you feel about him?'

'I like him. I like him very much, but—Gramp, there must be something else. There is, isn't there? Look at my parents. They had it, hadn't they?'

'Yes, they had it, but it's very rare, poppet. Not many people find it.'

'Did you, Gramp?'

'Not entirely, though your grandmother and I were very happy and made a good life together. It was actually what you'd call a marriage of convenience. It was a long time ago now, and life was very different. We'd grown up together with the idea of marrying. She had the money and I had the property, and a strip of what she would inherit ran between our land and the village, and altogether it was a most convenient arrangement, and we were very happy.'

'I don't think that would satisfy me, Gramp. I want to find what Mummy and Daddy had. I think I'd rather not marry at all than without that.'

'It's too rare a thing, my darling, and you ought to marry and have a home of your own, and children. There are so many things in marriage apart from the story-book romance of love. I think what you feel for Andrew is much what Stella and I felt for each other when we married, but it developed into something very beautiful and valuable.'

'You want me to marry Andrew, don't you, Gramp?'

'Not unless you feel you could be happy with him, poppet, but I feel sure you could. He is a good man. You would have some one you could rely on absolutely, and I'm sure you would get to love him dearly. That's part of your nature, to love the people who are good to you, and you must have someone to love. It's for when I've gone, my darling—'

She laid her fingers against his lips.

'No, Gramp,' she said in swift pain.

He kissed her fingers and took them away.

'It's got to be faced even if we don't talk about it, but it worries me night and day, wondering what you'll do then. You see, there won't be anything for you, Di, and it's been my fault, most of it. I've—well, never mind what I've done—'

'I know, Gramp,' she said steadily. 'You've been giving money to Mummy, but I know why you felt you had to. Don't worry about it on my account. I shall manage.'

'I've been wrong. I know I've been very wrong. I ought to have kept it for you, but—she was Piers' wife, and I couldn't let her be without money. She's always had it, and it's a part of her.'

'You mustn't blame yourself, dear,' said Diana comfortingly. 'You've done what you felt was right, and I don't see what else you could have done, but don't worry about me. I shall be quite all right, and at any rate, it's going to be years and years yet. Whilst we live at Mayne Downe, and don't increase our expenses, we can keep going as we are now. Don't you worry.'

After lunch he settled down for his nap whilst Diana decided to take advantage of the lingering early spring sunshine to work in the garden. She was always happy doing that. She could even forget the constant worry about Andrew and the still unsolved question of what eventually she was going to say to him. She was quite sure that she was not in love with him, but not quite sure how much that mattered. It was only when she let herself remember the passionate love of her father and her mother, which never let them be happy apart, that she realized what glory there could be in the world, and that if she married Andrew she would miss it.

Strangely, she remembered now with increasing frequency that far-off, tender little friendship between the child Diana and Paul Esterre. Looking back at it with eyes of a woman, even an inexperienced and unawakened woman, she knew that that had held the seed of a true romance. She remembered their one kiss, which had lain like a flower in her mind for so long afterwards, to be looked at in secret, touched with tender fingers, its fragile perfume delicately savoured. When the other girls had whispered and giggled and compared experiences and talked of their 'boys', she had kept as aloof as ever. Not for anything in the world would she have let them know anything about Paul. Their giggling curiosity and comments would have been intolerable and profane.

Why should she think of him now? She supposed it was because, if she decided to marry Andrew, she must put away from her thoughts for ever any such romantic, other-worldly dreams.

As she knelt on the path, busily weeding a rock garden which she had discovered under overgrown bushes and rank grass, she heard the sound of a car and looked up to see the smart coupe which her mother drove. Her brow furrowed into a frown. She supposed Clementine was coming for money again, and Gramp would be worried, and the only thing any of them could do for him was to try to keep that from happening.

Still, she could hardly ask her to go away without seeing him, so she wiped her hands and went forward as the car drew up.

'Hullo, Mummy,' she said, conjuring up a smile. 'Don't tell me I look a sight. I know I do. I've been doing wonders with the old rockery, as you can see.'

As they went into the house, Clementine asked in her casual fashion after Gramp.

'Oh, he's fairly well,' said Diana. 'Worried a bit. Things aren't too easy. They aren't for anybody, are they?'

'You mean money? Well, for once I haven't come down to ask for that,' said Clementine with a little laugh which held a bitter note. Diana wondered why.

Colonel Merrimayne got up stiffly from his chair in spite of her quick 'Don't get up, Gramp,' as she hurried across the room to him.

'When I can't get out of a chair when a pretty woman enters the room, I hope it'll be because I'm dead,' he said with his special smile for his dead son's wife. 'How are you, my dear? You look delightful—delightful.'

'Thank you, Gramp,' she said gently, an arm slipped through his to take him back to the fireside.

She was always at her best with her father-in-law. The hard surface which she had cultivated ever since Piers had died seemed to soften in his kindly presence. She sometimes thought that he was the one person in the world whom she truly loved, and yet her love had not been enough to keep her from worrying him and getting from him money which she really could not spare.

'Are you staying tonight, dear?' he asked her. 'Your room is always kept ready, you know.'

'No, not tonight. I've got to get back. I came down for a special reason, to tell you something—rather important. The fact is, I'm going to marry again.'

Diana felt a little chill run through her, though her common sense told her that this was bound to happen. After all, it was more than four years since her father's death, and Clementine was not the sort to remain a widow for the rest of her life.

'Well, that certainly is important news,' said Gramp cheerfully. 'Very interesting news. Do we know the lucky man?'

'Oh yes, you know him. It's Sir Joseph Bloggett,' said Clementine very clearly, her head high, her eyes holding the same defiance as her voice.

There was a moment's shocked silence, broken only by Diana's gasp of incredulous dismay. Then Colonel Merrimayne spoke slowly.

'I'm sure you must have given the matter a great deal of thought, Clementine dear,' he said, not looking at her.

'Yes. Yes, I have, of course,' she said. 'I agreed some weeks ago to marry him but it's only just being announced. We are to be married on the fifth of April. That just escapes the first!' with a faint curl of her lip.

'Mummy, you can't—oh, you can't!' breathed Diana almost under her breath.

Clementine turned to her.

'My dear child, why not? It is a most suitable marriage,' she said. 'I came to get one or two things I left here. There's a small pigskin dressing-case somewhere. Do you know where?'

'All your things are in your own room or else in the one we use as a box-room,' said Gramp heavily. 'Diana will get it for you.'

'Thanks. I may as well throw out one or two things that I shan't want again,' she said, and went out of the room and along the passage to the room which was always called hers and kept for her though she seldom slept in it.

Diana paused, looking beseechingly at her grandfather, but he nodded his head at her.

'Better go along and see if you can find what your mother wants,' he said, and she went miserably away, her heart filled with resentment and pain and disgust.

She found the case and took it to her mother's room.

Clementine was turning out the contents of the drawers on the dust-sheeted bed.

'I don't want any of these things,' she said. 'These silk things— they're quite good and will last you some time. There are some stockings too—here,' tossing them down, 'and I've forgotten what's in the wardrobes, but I dare say you can have the lot—'

'I don't want them,' said Diana stormily, letting the proffered stockings and lingerie fall on the floor. 'I don't want any of your things, ever.'

Clementine looked at her in surprise. It was the first time she had ever seen her like this.

'Good heavens, Di, why this tragedy queen stuff?' she asked. 'If it's about my marrying again, I fail to see how it can affect you, since we don't live together and are not likely to.'

'It isn't that. You know it isn't that. I don't mind you marrying again. I always thought you would some day. But to marry—*him!* Mother, you can't do it. You can't marry him!'

'Don't be silly. I've told you I'm going to. Look!' with an expression that was bitter derision, holding up her left hand for her daughter to see the huge, ostentatious ring, an enormous diamond solitaire, on the third finger. It replaced the 'eternity' ring of small diamonds which Piers had given her to wear above her wedding ring.

'But how can you, how *can* you, after Daddy?' she cried, beside herself with disgust. 'He's a horrible old man.'

Clementine turned on her, her face white and tense.

'Stop talking like that,' she said. 'Do you understand? Stop talking like that. Stop talking about your father for always. He's dead. He's been dead for four years. Four years! My God—four—years!' and suddenly she crumpled up and put her hands on the corner of the tall swing mirror and bent her forehead down against them.

'Four years,' she whispered again.

Her anger fleeing as swiftly as it had come, Diana ran to her and put an arm about her and held her closely in almost the first spontaneous embrace she had ever given her.

'Mummy, don't. Don't, darling,' she said. 'I'm sorry if I was beastly. I know you've always loved Daddy and always will, that you'll never be able to forget him. Don't cry, darling. Please don't cry.'

She had never seen her mother in tears before, not even after Piers had died. She had been stony-faced and dry-eyed all through that terrible time.

Diana held her and softly stroked her shining hair and murmured to her and presently Clementine lifted her head and found a scrap of lace handkerchief on which to dry her eyes.

'How idiotic of me,' she said. 'I suppose I'm a bit overwrought, what with making up my mind about marrying, and then the way Gramp looked, and now you. Give me a dry handkerchief, will you? There are some on the bed,' picking up her bag and taking out her compact and lipstick.

Diana dare not start again. The storm she had evoked had frightened her, showing her places in her mother's mind which she must not again penetrate. Instead she began mechanically to pick things up from the floor and lay them on the bed, whilst Clementine repaired the damage to her face and said nothing.

'You—you really have quite decided, then?' asked Diana nervously.

'Yes. I can't expect you to understand. You like being poor, pottering about here, living on grass and eggs and wearing those disgraceful garments. I couldn't do it. I'm not made that way. If I don't have good clothes, nice things to eat, places to go to, things to look forward to, I wouldn't want to live. I know that to anyone like you, young and— unspoilt (you know, Di, you're quite sweet), it must seem unthinkable for anyone of our sort to marry someone of Joseph's sort, but he isn't so bad. He's very kind, very generous, and he'll be good to me. He spoke about you too. Said that if I wanted it, and you liked the idea, you could live with us. He'd give you an allowance, he said.'

'Oh no, Mummy, no!' cried Diana, shrinking away from the very thought. 'I couldn't possibly!'

Clementine gave a shrug.

'All right. I told him I didn't think you'd want to, but it was nice of him to offer.'

Diana could not even agree to that. She could not forget those few minutes in the library. She felt she would never forget them.

They went back to Gramp and the tea-table which Mrs. Good had just wheeled in.

After she had left the room and Clementine was pouring out the tea, she looked across at her father-in-law and her daughter.

'Is it any good hoping you two will come?' she asked.

'I'd rather not,' said Diana at once, and Gramp added something about it not being very easy for him to get about now.

'We'll just stay quietly here and wish you well, my dear,' he said. 'We do wish you well, Clementine. You know that, don't you?'

'Yes, I know you do. Thank you, Gramp,' she said in a low voice, and no more was said about her marriage.

After she had gone, and Diana stood at the window watching the car vanish in the dusk of the spring day, he came across the room and put an arm about her shoulders.

'I don't often quote the Bible to you, m'dear,' he said, 'and it surprises me that I can do it because I'm going to do it now. Two quotations. "Judge not that ye be not judged", and "The heart knoweth its own bitterness." I think they're the Bible, but they may be Shakespeare. Both very wise books.'

She leaned her head against him.

'But—*that* man,' she said.

He did not reply. He never told her, or anyone, what he thought about that marriage.

But that night, lying awake, Diana felt she could not marry Andrew Shawn.

'I don't love him,' she thought, 'and if I married him, it would be the same as Mummy marrying that horrible man—for money.'

# Chapter Seven

Diana had intended to tell Andrew of her decision the next time she saw him, but she could not bring herself to make the opening, and he did not offer her one.

He knew that she was upset by her mother's approaching marriage to Sir Joseph Bloggett, though he tried to get her to look at it from a worldly point of view and even managed to persuade her to go to the wedding. He went with her and stayed closely beside her at the small but very smart reception.

Sir Joseph had wanted a church wedding, but on this point Clementine had been firm and he had yielded. With no other man would she ever go through that ceremony which had united her to Piers, both of them heart-touchingly young and so much in love.

She was a brilliant figure at this, her second wedding. Her bridegroom certainly had nothing to complain of in his bride, for she was radiant with a happiness in which not even the most observant and critical could detect one false note.

Diana hated the innuendoes and the sniggers. Their authors, she felt, would have done the same thing themselves if they had had the chance, but it was hateful, *hateful*, that it should be her mother, the adored and cherished of Piers, who for money had become the wife of this elderly, vulgar man.

Yet, with Andrew's comforting presence at her side, his hand occasionally touching hers in understanding sympathy when some particularly ribald comment reached their ears, somehow she got through the day, and was with the little crowd of fashionably dressed people who saw the bridal pair leave in Sir Joseph's monster of a car.

'Well,' said one of the guests standing next to Diana, of whose identity quite a number of them had no idea, 'she puts up a good show. The happy bride off to Paradise in the arms of her gallant young hero! Wonder how much she really got for the sale?'

'I'd want a lot before I'd let Joe Bloggett crawl into my bed,' said another.

'My dear, look at her pearls to start with! And it wouldn't be so bad in the dark. By the way, hasn't our Clem got a grownup daughter tucked away somewhere? If she hasn't revealed her to old Joe, it'll be a bit awkward for her.'

'I've heard she's a bit of a clot. Anyway, let's trickle away, shall we? Another drink on Joe Bloggett first?'

'Might as well,' and they went back into the hotel whilst Diana, who had been hedged in by them so that she could not escape, turned mutely to Andrew.

He laughed. He felt it was the only thing to do.

'Come along, clot,' he said. 'Let's go. I've got tickets for the ballet tonight and it's Fonteyn, and if we walk it'll just get us there in time and also blow away the fumes of old Joe's champagne. You won't want a meal first?'

She shuddered.

'The thought of more food makes me feel quite sick,' she said.

She remembered that walk all her life, with gratitude to Andrew for his understanding kindness and his sturdy common sense. He did not make the mistake of talking exclusively of other things, since it would have been impossible entirely to distract her mind, but he brought the events of the day into focus, poking gentle, not too malicious fun at things and people and contriving to give the whole thing a more normal and healthy look than it had worn for her.

He took pains over the ballet, too. She realized that he must have booked the seats a long time ago, as soon, in fact, as they had known the date of the wedding. She knew, too, that he was not a lover of the ballet, and the evening must have been devised exclusively for her benefit, to interest and divert her.

She came nearer to loving Andrew Shawn that day than she had dreamed possible, and when at parting (she was staying with the

Goods in an hotel that night), she knew that he wanted to kiss her, she lifted her face to his in what seemed to him an enchanting mixture of the child and the woman.

Her lips were cool and soft and unresponsive, and though at their touch all his senses quickened, he held himself so rigidly in check that it was the kiss of no more than a friend, a brother even.

She was able to tell Gramp about the wedding, keeping away from bitterness, though in her heart she was still revolted by the thought of her dainty, fastidious mother in the arms of Joseph Bloggett.

Could she ever feel able to marry? To accept such a position, even with a man she loved?

Inevitably she was thinking of Andrew, but he did not revolt her and she could, though shrinkingly, begin to imagine herself his wife, He was so kind, so gentle. Surely it would be easy to love him, if she were his wife?

And then, almost without warning, Colonel Merrimayne died.

Diana herself found him one afternoon, lying back in his chair unconscious and breathing stertorously. Frantic, when she had sent for the doctor, she telephoned to Shawn's office, a thing she would never have done had she not been distracted.

'Andrew, it's Gramp,' she said when his voice came to her, comforting and strengthening even at that distance. 'He's—he's going to die, I think. He isn't conscious.'

'Would you like me to come?'

'Oh, Andrew, could you?'

'At once. I'll come by train, and get a taxi from Maidstone,' he said and rang off.

The comfort of his presence was unbelievable. She had known from the moment she had found Gramp that he was going to die, and she did not know how she would have got through the hours of that heavy day without Andrew's thoughtful care. He took into his capable hands the strings of the disordered household and got it working again as if he had always been there, and when early the next morning the old man died quietly and without regaining consciousness, it seemed natural to turn to him. Clementine was away on her honeymoon in

Italy and in any case would not have managed things as he did, without fuss or bother.

It was impossible to keep the funeral a quiet, family affair.

Francis Merrimayne was another snapped link between past and future, and his passing could not be ignored by either. From the uneasy, uncertain present there came to stand at his grave those who had shared the vanishing past with him, and those who would never know the stability and peace in which they had been reared.

Diana, flanked by Blaize, fussily important, with Hester Merrimayne, large of bosom and self-esteem, on her other side, was cut off from Andrew and realized her need of him. Her eyes constantly sought him, his reassuring smile telling her that he was watching her all the time, guarding her.

The press of the public stayed outside when the coffin was borne down into the great vault and only the family followed. Diana gave a frightened, appealing look in Andrew's direction, and he went to her at once and, ignoring the slightly affronted glances of Blaize and his wife, she slipped a hand into his, and they stood like that during the rest of the committal service.

Once her eyes went to the rows and columns of memorial tablets round the vault bearing the name of long-departed Merrimaynes. The newest of them was that for Piers, whose body lay fathoms deep in some unknown sea.

Andrew went back to the house with them, vouchsafing no explanation when he found Blaize's arrogantly enquiring eyes fastened on him. Hester touched her husband's elbow and whispered to him, and he nodded. His wife had suggested that the uninvited guest might be 'interested' in Diana, and it would suit them better if that were so.

The old man's will was read, but it was a hollow mockery, for it had been made years ago, and the bequests in it were no longer his to give away. The lawyer explained to Diana what she already knew, namely that when one or two debts had been settled, and the funeral expenses paid, and legacies to Mr. and Mrs. Good, who were the only ones left to receive benefit under the very old provisions for 'indoor and outdoor servants', there would be practically nothing left. The residue, bequeathed to 'my beloved grand-daughter Diana', might be a hundred pounds, possibly a hundred and fifty, but no more. Everything not entailed and therefore unrealizable had been sold, most of it to pay Clementine's debts and keep her in luxury.

Though Andrew Shawn had loved the old man, he found it hard to forgive him that. Still, if things went as he hoped they would, Diana would never be in want nor feel the wasting of that money which should have been hers.

She was staying on at Mayne Downe for the moment, as were the Goods. There were personal matters to be seen to; her own and Clementine's private belongings, things like the dogs and the hens, her own and Gramp's horses.

'I must go back to Northampton tonight,' said Blaize importantly, 'but Hester will stay with you and help you.'

'I can manage, with Ethel,' said Diana, who disliked Hester intensely.

'I shall remain,' said Hester, more than ever like a pouter pigeon in her tightly stuffed black. 'After all, Mayne Downe *is* ours,' and Diana drew back at once, flinching.

'Of course,' she said quietly. 'I am not forgetting that, and I won't intrude on you any longer than is necessary.'

'Oh, stay as long as you like, of course,' said Hester grandly.

'In fact, Blaize and I have been talking about it, and if you care to stay on here, being helpful of course, we shan't raise any objection. Blaize has written to Lady Bloggett about you.'

But for her deep unhappiness, Diana could have smiled. Blaize had married a little below the usual Merrimayne standards, and Hester was of the type to like rolling a title on her tongue.

'Thank you,' Diana said in her quiet, well-bred voice. 'That is very kind of you and Blaize, Hester, but I won't trouble you like that. I understand you have asked the Goods to stay on.'

'Yes. We have not made really complete plans, but of course nobody could *live* in the house, not actually *live*, I mean. It's too big, too sprawling. No, Blaize and I are seriously thinking of turning it into an hotel. I thought, Diana, as you will now, I suppose, have to get something to do, you might stay on here if we do turn it into an hotel. I don't mean as a guest, but in some helpful capacity, housekeeper or in the reception desk or something. We should pay you, of course, and you could have quite a nice little room for yourself, though I am afraid not the one you have now. We should take that suite for ourselves, and Brian would want your room. There's quite a nice little room on the floor above, though—'

'In the servants' quarters, you mean?' asked Diana calmly, though she felt the reverse of calm inside her. 'Thank you, Hester, but I shall not need to trouble you either for hospitality or for a job. I have—made other arrangements.'

Mrs. Merrimayne flushed with annoyance. She and Blaize had certainly talked it over down to the last detail, and even to the salary they would have to pay Diana ; not a large one, of course, as they were giving her a home. It was most annoying to have her refusing it. It upset all their plans, which they had been laying ever since the Colonel had his first seizure. Where else would they find anyone who would fit in with them so well as Diana? They had arranged that she would not only have some useful position in the house, but as she seemed to like gardening and outdoor work, she could also take over the care of the kitchen garden and look after the hens and ducks, and as she could drive a car, she would be so useful if any of the guests needed to be taken to or from the station, or for shopping. And now the silly girl, quite blind to the really wonderful chance she was being offered, had refused it!

Most annoying. Most. And other arrangements, indeed! What arrangements had she been likely to make, with no knowledge or experience or anything?

Andrew had come quietly into the room through the open french window as they were talking and had stood with his back to them until they had finished their conversation, apparently taking no interest in it, but when Diana, walking swiftly, her head held high, came past him and into the garden, he followed her, purposely not catching her up until they were out of the range of vision from the windows of the house.

He slipped a hand under her arm and walked with her.

'Good for you,' he said, quietly amused.

'You listened? You heard?'

'Did you mind? It seemed a bit my business as well as yours.'

'No, I didn't mind. I was glad you were there. Offering me a job and one of the servants' rooms! Why, Gramp and I didn't think those rooms were good enough for Ben and Ethel, so we put them on our floor. Blaize was going to see if he could arrange for me to have a bath occasionally, too! I should have thought they wouldn't consider it necessary for anyone who hasn't a home to have a bath!'

'You've got a home, Diana my darling, whenever you want it *And* a bathroom,' he said in his quietly humorous way, and suddenly the tension snapped and she turned to him and buried her face against his shoulder and wept her heart out. They were almost the first tears she had shed since Gramp's death. Pride had sustained her. Now there was no pride left.

He held her, stroking her hair, and when she lifted her face, wiped her eyes and very gently kissed their reddened lids.

'Will you come to me?' he asked.

'If you want me, Andrew.'

'You know I do, with all my heart and soul. Darling, I know you don't feel quite as I do. I don't think you're *in* love with me, but you do *love* me, and that's the most important thing. We're good friends and sincerely intend to make a happy life together. We do intend that, don't we, my darling?'

How could she not love him? He was not only her port in this storm and tempest in which she drifted, rudderless. He was everything she cared for most – kindness, sincerity, honour, unselfishness. How could she *not* love him?

'Oh, Andrew, yes! Yes!' she whispered. 'I want to make you happy. Do you think I can?'

'I know you can.'

He held her fully within his arms and she lay quietly against his breast, her eyes closed, her whole being filled with a peace which she had not known since first Gramp was taken ill. It was a feeling of home-coming. This was right for her, this was her destiny and her happiness.

She lifted her face and gave him her lips.

'I do love you, Andrew,' she said, and did not know that in the kiss she gave him there was anything lacking.

Though there was actually nothing for them to wait for, both of them felt that they would enjoy their happiness in marriage more if they let at least a few months elapse to cover the deep grief of Gramp's death. Diana did not remain at the house more than a few days, working feverishly with Mrs. Good to sort out, throw away, pack up, everything that was purely personal to herself and her mother.

The Goods had decided to stay on for the time being, though Diana could see that before long Hester would rub them up the wrong way. They were used to being treated as friends, and never with any suggestion that they were considered inferior to the people for whom they worked. Hester did not understand such an attitude, filled as she was with a sense of her newly acquired social status as mistress of Mayne Downe.

'I don't know that I shall be able to put up with her way of going on, Miss Diana,' said Ethel. 'The only thing is, Good and I want a job together, and they're not so easily come by now. I hope you don't mind, but I spoke to Mr. Shawn about us yesterday, and he said to see him again if later on we thought we'd make a change.'

'Oh, Ethel, I'd love to have you and Ben,' said Diana, 'but I didn't like to suggest it to Mr. Shawn. You see—he's doing so much, and I don't quite know where we're going to live. You've promised Mrs. Merrimayne to stay for a bit though, haven't you?'

'Yes, three months, but I'm quite sure we shan't want to stay longer than that,' said Mrs. Good happily. 'Well, if you can do the last of those drawers yourself. Miss Diana, I'd better go and start the lunch or she'll be up here again. As if I didn't know how long it takes to make a rabbit pie!'

In less than a week Diana had left her old home and gone to stay with Joan Hurst until she was married.

Andrew came to fetch her and would allow her no backward looks, and no lingering. She had gone round saying goodbye to all her favourite haunts the day before. The horses and two of the dogs were being taken care of by a neighbouring farmer friend until Diana and Andrew had settled in their home. Gramp's old spaniel, fretting badly and refusing to eat, had been mercifully put to sleep, Diana holding him in her lap, her eyes so blinded with tears that she did not see the last grateful, loving look the old dog gave her.

Andrew got her at once involved in the preparation of their home, knowing that it was the best remedy for her home-sickness for Mayne Downe. As soon as he had shown her Wayside at the little Kentish hamlet she had fallen in love with it.

'Oh, Andrew, we must have it whatever it's like inside,' she cried. 'Just look at the vegetable garden! And we could make that into a real rockery instead of a heap of stones. And there's a field for Robert and Frolic, and would you let me have a few hens in that corner? They wouldn't be seen from the house, and as soon as they were used to the place they wouldn't need to be kept in with wire netting. There's even a pond for the ducks. This, I take it, is a dog kennel, though can you imagine the disgust of Robin and Simon if they were asked to sleep there?'

They were puppies which Andrew had given her when it was decided that Gramp's old spaniel must go. Robin was a bull mastiff, a huge and lordly creature, Simon a golden cocker, merry and with no dignity whatsoever but with a wealth of frenzied affection in his ecstatically wagging body.

These two, with the two horses and Milly the hen, would be well housed at Wayside, so, as Andrew said in his dry fashion, he supposed it would be all right for him and Diana too.

'We'd better look inside at our own quarters,' he said, 'or do we take over the kennels for ourselves?'

She laughed and linked an arm with his.

'Poor Andrew. Do you know what you're taking on? If you want to change your mind, please change it before we've been inside the darling house.'

'I shan't change it, my sweet. Come along in.'

It was very small compared with Mayne Downe standards, but compact and convenient; three rooms and a kitchen on the ground floor, four bedrooms above. The hall, staircase and landings were large and light. The whole house was full of sunshine – or would be when some of the trees had been cut back and thinned out.

Standing at the window of the room which would be their bedroom, Andrew's arm about her, Diana imagined that in the distance she could see the sea, though she knew it was impossible.

'I didn't know you'd have liked to live at the sea, darling,' he said, 'or that you were so fond of it.'

'I'm fond of it, but I don't think I want actually to live beside it. I had a wonderful holiday once by the sea.'

He nodded his head.

'I know. Paul, the Frenchman.'

'Oh, Andrew!'

She had forgotten she had told him.

'Did you think I should forget my hated rival?' he asked lovingly.

She leaned her head against him.

'You haven't got a rival,' she said. 'You're alone in my heart, quite, quite alone.'

He kissed her and she clung to him for a moment. He had become very dear to her and the prospect of life with him a happy one with which to occupy her mind. It could even make acceptable, almost, her exile from her beloved home. She was determined that she would harbour in her mind and her heart nothing that could make their marriage anything but the perfect thing they both meant it to be.

If now and then she thought of the love which her father and mother had had for each other, she knew that she and Andrew lacked something of its quality, but she felt that was not altogether to be regretted, for she wanted children but would not let them be shut out of their parents' lives as she had been. She would have had a desperately lonely and almost an unloved childhood but for Gramp.

Andrew had bought the house, though he had asked her whether she did not think they ought to let the horses and the dogs, and Milly the hen, have a look at it first to see if it would suit them. His dry sense of fun, the tender way he teased her, were very endearing things about Andrew, and as they planned and furnished their home and made preparations for a September wedding, she felt they had drawn very close to each other with happiness surely within their grasp.

It was to be a very quiet wedding. Andrew would have liked a bride in conventional white, with a train of bridesmaids and the organ pealing and even the bells ringing, for he was proud of her and felt that her wedding day should be her great day.

But Diana had pleaded for a quiet wedding.

'I should be terrified of a lot of fuss, Andrew. I should fall over my train, or muff my words or something and probably never get properly married to you at all. I'd like it to be in a church,' remembering the cold, businesslike performance her mother's wedding had been, 'but only just the people we know best, the Hursts, and Ethel and Ben, and some of the village people.'

So it was arranged that way, and early in September Diana went up to London to get herself a dress and a hat. Joan was to have gone with her, but she was expecting her second baby and having a few bad days, so Diana went alone, having lunch with Andrew first.

He had been more than generous to her, insisting on opening a banking account at his own bank for her and persuading her to let him pay for much of her trousseau. It was to take some time yet to get her grandfather's estate settled up, for there had been complications arising out of his sale of things which Blaize maintained belonged rightly to the entailed property. Whilst the lawyers argued about it and would in the end acquire for themselves whatever money might have come to Diana, she was penniless and she had agreed to accept money from Andrew only on the understanding that she be allowed to repay it as soon as the estate had been settled.

Andrew, guessing that she would never be able to do so, had agreed. As by that time she would be his wife, there was no point in arguing about it.

Diana wandered about in the West End in pleasant contemplation of all sorts of outfits. There was no particular hurry and actually she would prefer to leave the actual buying until Joan could come with her. Her mother, writing from Cannes, where they had just rented a villa for the winter, had sent her a substantial cheque.

*This isn't a wedding present (she had written), but to make sure you don't appear on your wedding night in the awful garments that used to hang on the line at Mayne, I'm enclosing some addresses. Go there for your things, and say I sent you. Joseph says you can spend this and have some more if you want it. Whatever he is, he isn't mean.*

But Diana could not bring herself to use the money. The cheque still lay in her bag, uncashed. If it had been her mother's own money she would have taken it thankfully so that she need not be quite so much beholden to Andrew, but she could not forget that it was Joseph Bloggett's money. In her letter, Clementine had given her advice and warnings about her clothes.

*Don't get that hideous colour known as beige; it's death to people with our colour of hair.*

*Do lose that idiotic habit of asking if a thing will 'wash'. What does it matter? Andrew Shawn can afford to give his wife clothes.*

*Don't be frugal over your unders. You can often patch up a quarrel with a pair of lace panties. Buy plenty.*

*Mind your shoes, gloves and bag. The best, and matching, whatever you do.*

Some of the advice made Diana laugh. Fancy quarrelling with Andrew! One couldn't. He didn't quarrel.

But she knew he could be angry, terribly angry. She remembered an occasion when a man had come to him for help, a distant cousin who was down and out, largely through his own fault. She had persuaded Andrew to help the man, and he had sent for him, fitted him out with decent clothes, found him a job and paid for his first month's lodging.

Before the month was up the man had absconded, robbing both his landlady and his employer. It was then that she had seen Andrew angry. He had had him pursued relentlessly, caught and imprisoned.

Diana remembered how Andrew had looked, and the tones of his voice.

'It's the betrayal,' he said. 'It's the lying and deceit and the sheer insincerity of the man, with his fair promises, which I could have sworn were honest, though now it turns out that he was laying his plans to do this from the very first. It must have taken him it least a fortnight to make those duplicate keys, the police say, so he started the first week he was there. The man's rotten. Would you keep a dog that bit the hand that fed it?'

His eyes had been like pieces of polished steel, his mouth grim. No, he wouldn't quarrel, but he could certainly be angry and she could not imagine that even the laciest of panties either on or off could do anything about that!

She was smiling at the idea whilst she hunted in her purse for pennies for the ticket machine on the Underground.

A tall man in front of her was putting a shilling into the machine. His ticket was delivered to him but not his change.

'Zut!' she heard him say, and he gave the machine a vigorous shake without producing any effect.

'*Crois donc—*' he began, turning to the waiting girl for sympathy.

Then he stopped, the words dying on his lips as he stood staring it her.

Diana was gazing back at him, her eyes wide, her face suddenly pale until the blood came rushing back to it with a flood of gorgeous colour.

'Paul! Oh—*Paul!* It's you, isn't it? Don't you remember me? Diane?'

# Chapter Eight

After that first moment of incredulous half-recognition, memory came rushing back fully to Paul Esterre.

'Diane,' he said. '*Ma petite* after so long, so many years, and me same, just, just the same!'

She laughed ruefully.

'I can't be so much the same,' she said. 'You didn't really recognize me, did you? But I knew you at once.'

'Ah, but a man does not change in—how many years is it?'

'Nearly five,' said Diana.

'Five—but you, you have turned from a little girl into a so beautiful young lady. I was *ébloui*—dazzled, you say?'

She laughed again.

'Oh, Paul, you're just the same!'

'But my English, it is a lot better, yes?'

'Yes, a lot,' she agreed.

Their hands had met. They were still clinging whilst people jostled and pressed by them to use the machines.

'We must talk,' he said. 'But here, no. Where do you go now?'

'I was going home, but I need not. Let's go and have tea somewhere, shall we?'

'Ah, your English tea! Well, we go. Where?'

'Oh—anywhere,' said Diana vaguely.

'I think perhaps you do not know your London and I do, so come. I know where we will go.'

'You haven't got the change for your shilling out of the machine.' she reminded him thriftily.

He gave one of his characteristic French shrugs, so expressive, so impossible for an Englishman to imitate.

'Ah, what would you? For my change, I get you, my Diane! Come,' and with her hand in his, he took her out of the booking hall and into the street again.

He hailed a taxi, put her into it, gave the man an address and got in beside her.

'A taxi,' commented Diana. 'Are you in the money, Paul?'

It was exhilarating and joyous to feel all the old ease with him. Between her and the rest of the world, even between her and Andrew, there was always a veil, fine as mist where Andrew was concerned, but there, always to be felt. Between her and Paul there was nothing.

'A poor artist in the money, *chérie!* When is he ever?' he replied lightly, 'but I am having a little holiday, and when one has a holiday one is rich. And how should I not be rich, finding Diane again? And to take her on a bus, but no! A bus is for the common people. For my Diane, a carriage, isn't it?'

'Oh, Paul, isn't it wonderful being together again? And doesn't it seem to you now that we've always been together? Though we don't know anything about each other?'

'Yes. *petite*, wonderful. And you are beautiful, Diane.'

She shook her head in laughing protest.

'Oh no. I'm certainly not that.' she said.

'But you are. To me, you are. This lovely line,' tracing with his finger, very gently and lightly, the moulding of her cheek, 'and this—and this. To me you have always been beautiful, Diane. So many drawings I made of you. Do you remember?'

She nodded her head. Suddenly she was unable to speak. The touch of his finger had done something to her, something she could not understand, dare not try to understand.

In the dimness of the taxi she could see his dark eyes glowing with light. She did not know that her own were shining too, that all about her was a shining radiance as if a lamp had been lit inside her.

She did not ask where they were going. It did not matter. She was with Paul again.

He took her to a little unfashionable restaurant where they could sit in a corner and talk. She had tea and Paul an *aperitif*.

'Still I do not like your English tea,' he told her. 'It is a drink for a barbarian.'

It was a miracle that either of them ate or drank anything. They talked all the time, though he had so much more to tell than she. He told her of the day he had sailed for France, skated lightly over what must have been hell let loose, told her that he had been wounded.

'Oh, but a little, a little,' he assured her at her quick response. 'It was the arm all the time that I had fear, but this was the leg. A bagatelle. Sometimes if I am a little tired or the time is bad, I go the dot and carry,' laughing at the expression.

She laughed with him.

'Dot and carry one,' she amended. 'Oh, Paul, you got that from me! I used to say that. Remember? When I fell on the rocks one day and twisted my ankle a little, and I taught you that expression? Have you always used it?'

'No, I think I only just remember it. I think I remember now so many things, perhaps everything, my Diane,' leaning a little towards her, his eyes on hers. There was a deep tenderness in them.

Diana felt as if her whole being moved towards him, reaching for him, meeting somewhere in the space between them the very heart of him. She was remembering nothing, thinking of nothing, needing nothing in that enchanted hour but Paul.

How could she ever have thought she had forgotten him, what he looked like, the way he spoke and moved his hands, the way his eyebrows went up when he laughed, the little shrug of the shoulders, every smallest thing that made him – Paul?

He stretched a hand across the table, and she put hers into it. It was her left hand, and his fingers found her ring, held it for a moment and then he was looking at it, noticing it for the first time.

'What is it, Diane?' he asked softly. 'Does it mean ...?'

She nodded, suddenly stricken. It was the first time she had thought of Andrew.

'Yes, it does,' she said. 'I'm going to be married, Paul.'

'Married? But—you're a little girl, Diane.'

'Not any longer. I'm twenty-one, Paul. Nearly twenty-two.'

'Twenty-two! A very very old woman, I see. Now tell me, my dar-r-rling, how is it you still walk about, and without even a stick?'

She laughed. How easy it had always been to laugh with Paul!

'Sometimes that's what I feel, a very old woman,' she said.

'But not now? Not with me, Diane?'

The laughter died. She was sweetly serious and she did not know what lay in her eyes, but he knew.

'No, not with you. With you, I'm—sixteen again.'

He shook his head, his eyes holding hers.

'No, Diane, not sixteen, not a little girl still. You're a woman, Diane—a woman who did not wait.'

'Wait?'

She felt a stab of something like fear.

'For me.'

'But—how would I know we should ever meet again, Paul?'

'We had to meet, *ma mie.* How could we not see each other again? I think it was in the stars.'

'But what about you? You couldn't have been waiting, and being sure we should meet again, because you didn't even know me, not at first.' she said triumphantly.

'Why then do you think I turned to you? You of all the people who were down there on the *metro?* It was because it was you, *vois tu*! You of all the people drew me to speak to you.'

She disclaimed it laughingly.

'Not at all. You were so angry because you'd lost your change that you turned to anyone, just anyone, and it happened to be me.'

'Do you not like better to think it was because it was you?'

'Yes. Yes. Paul. I do like it better that way.'

'But this man you are to marry. Tell me, then. You love him?'

'Yes.'

It was true, she told herself fiercely. She did love Andrew. She did love him.

'It is a marriage you make for yourself? They, your family, do not make it for you?"

97

'No. We don't settle our marriages like that in England. I'm going to marry Andrew because I want to, because I love him and I am going to be happy with him.'

'There is something in your Shakespeare that says "the lady doth protest too much, me thinks",' said Paul with a smile that subtly mocked her and brought the swift colour to her cheeks.

That's not fair, and not right,' she said hotly.

'All right, all right.' He spread out his hands in laughing protest. 'Do not jump at the throat. You love him then, this André. Well, so my little friend she is a woman. *Helas*, Diane is a woman and she does not wait for Paul. She grows up, and at once—pff! she fly into the arms of some other man. Tell me of him, this André.'

'Andrew,' she corrected him.

'An ugly name,' he said.

'I don't think so. Anyway, I've drunk all the tea there is, I don't want another pot, and if I'm going to get back to Maidstone in time for dinner, I'd better be going. I shall be late as it is.'

She did not tell him that that would not matter, that Joan had told her not to feel she must watch the clock, that if she were enjoying her day in town she need not let her know she would be home late. She had begun to panic. Refusing to put it into words, even in her mind, she knew she must not stay longer with Paul.

'Late? What is late, when two old friends meet? The evening is still to come. Spend it with me, Diane. We will do what you like, some dinner—'

'I've only just had tea,' she pointed out.

'Oh, not now, but presently. A theatre? A movie? Or we will get a bus somewhere and sit on the top and just talk. That, I think, would be nice, but the buses are so full now, with such crowds. What can you think that we can do in this London? In Paris I would know, but in London?' with one of his expressive shrugs.

She hesitated. Would it matter so much, just an hour? One little hour? One hour out of all the years they would not be together?

'We could go into the park,' she said.

'What does one do in a park?'

'Oh—walk about.'

'Walk? You English with your walking!'

He bent down and touched her ankle. The touch sent a thrill through her and she drew away her foot, tucking it away under the table again.

Paul laughed, but tenderly.

'Yes, she is a woman, my little Diane,' he said. 'Well, if we must walk, we walk, and later the stretcher will take me back to my hotel without doubt.'

It was a lovely evening, fine and warm. They took a taxi to Hyde Park. ('I feel like a millionaire today,' he told her) and walked as far as the Serpentine and found two chairs where they could watch the people in the boats and talk.

How easy it was to talk to him! Their minds seemed to flow together along one channel so that there were times when words were almost superfluous.

At last she knew she must go or Joan might be getting anxious, in spite of what she had said. Also with every minute spent with Paul her sense of guilt and fear was increasing.

He went with her to Charing Cross and waited with her for the train. Nothing had been said about their meeting again, but at last he spoke the words she had longed and yet dreaded to hear.

'You will meet me one day, Diane? One day very soon?'

'No, Paul. It wouldn't be fair.'

'Fair to this André? Or fair to me?'

'To—all of us,' she said in a low voice. 'You're going back to Paris, to your work, and I'm going to be married and make a new life. I—I won't see you again, Paul.'

'You mean you will be afraid to see me, Diane?'

'Yes, I suppose that's what it is.'

'Why?'

'I don't know. Only—I feel it wouldn't be right,' she said in the same low, hesitating voice, not looking at him.

'Look, Diane. You want to marry your André and be a good little wife. *Eh bien.* Well. But to have just one day for yourself, and for me? One day out of all the many days you will have for André?'

'Paul, no. It isn't—wise.'

'You think you might love me a little too much?'

'Don't. Please don't.'

'Just one day, *chérie*. You come to London—when? Monday? I meet you here—ten o'clock? Eleven?'

'Oh, Paul, no!' she said, and then she caught sight of Andrew.

He was threading his way through a crowd of people towards the entrance to the platform, where they were standing. In another minute he would be there, face to face with them.

In a panic she gave Paul a little push from her.

'It's Andrew,' she said. 'He's coming along the platform. Go. Please go.'

'Then say you will come on Monday or I shall stay,' he said.

'All right, then. I'll come,' she said recklessly, and with a smile but no other word Paul turned on his heel and left her. A second or two more and it would have been too late.

Andrew caught sight of her and smiled in pleased surprise.

'Diana! What a bit of luck! I thought you'd gone hours ago. Have you got your ticket?'

She gave him the return half of her third-class ticket, and he smiled, had a little discussion with the ticket collector at the barrier and put her into a first-class compartment.

'You don't have to travel uncomfortably, you know,' he said, as she relaxed, obviously tired, against the softly padded seat-back.

'It isn't uncomfortable travelling third,' she said, 'but I admit this is much nicer.'

'Then travel first next time.'

'No. Not yet,' she said firmly.

'What an obstinate little person you can be when you like,' he said. 'Don't you know it's my greatest happiness to do things for you and make life easier?'

They were alone in the compartment, and she slid an arm under his and drew him close to her.

'Dear Andrew,' she said, 'I do love you,' and he could not know that it was her conscience speaking, and the memory of those hours with Paul when, if no word of love had been spoken, she knew they had been making love with every look, every word. Light, unmeaning love, but it had been love-making all the same.

'What have you bought?' asked Andrew, looking at her parcels which by some miracle she had still retained.

She told him.

'No wedding dress yet?' he asked.

'No. I want Joan to come with me when I get that.'

'Whatever it is, it will be right for me on that day,' he said lovingly. 'How about fixing on that date, by the way? It was to be later on this month, so I suggest the—let me see,' taking out his pocket diary, 'the twenty-fifth? And as the house won't be ready for us for quite another two months, if we do want a change from Ireland, we could take a trip to Cannes to see your mother, if you'd like that?'

'No,' said Diana definitely. 'I should hate it. That awful man!' with a little shiver.

He had guessed already that there had been some sort of episode with Joseph Bloggett which had disgusted and frightened her.

'All right. We can probably think of somewhere else to go if we get tired of being in Ireland. Can we settle on the twenty-fifth?'

'I—yes—yes, I think so,' said Diana uncertainly.

The thought of her marriage had suddenly become difficult and remote. Struggle as she might against it, Andrew had become another person, or perhaps the same person but a long way away. From being very near, he was tiny and distant as if she looked through the wrong end of a telescope at him. It was terrifying.

She put her hand into his and held it tightly.

'Yes,' she said again, covering the uncertainty. 'Please let it be the twenty-fifth, Andrew.'

He gave her a searching look.

'Diana, nothing's happened, has it? Nothing to upset you?'

'No, nothing. Of course nothing's happened,' she said with a sort of defiance. 'What makes you think that?'

'I don't quite know. Just an idea. I thought you seemed—upset a little. You do want us to be married this month, Di, don't you?'

'Yes, I do. It can't now be too soon for me,' she said, and though there was nothing in the words at which any man could cavil, he still had that feeling that she was not quite as usual.

Still, he was not the man to exaggerate and dramatize a woman's moods, and he proceeded with eagerness and delight to the arrangements for their marriage in three weeks' time. They had decided to go to Eire for their honeymoon rather than to one of the continental countries. They now decided to go first to Dublin by air, make it their centre, and then go to the western side of the island. He was glad she did not want to spend part of the time in Cannes with the Bloggetts, though Clementine had been most pressing in her invitation to them to do so.

The new Lady Bloggett was doing what from the first she had determined to do. She was making the best of it and of Joseph. He was kindness itself to her so long as he himself felt he was getting a fair deal. He was intelligent and shrewd. If he had not been, he would not have made a fortune out of his small beginnings, even considering the benefits of war. He knew that Clementine had married him for his money and that she was not in love with him. On the other hand, she yielded her charms to him fully and gracefully, beyond his rosiest dreams, and he was grateful and generous. He heaped on her everything she could desire which money could buy. Her jewels were a sensation amongst their friends in London. In Cannes she had not lost caste so much by becoming Lady Bloggett as she had done in her former social circle. Many of the Merrimaynes' friends, impoverished now and living secluded, austere lives, would gently drop her when she returned to England, since there were still people to whom money was not the one thing of importance. In Cannes, money was all-powerful, and though there were many occasions when Clementine Merrimayne stood aside to watch, with supercilious disdain, the smilings and posturings of Lady Bloggett amongst her new friends, she did not in the least regret her marriage.

Exquisitely dressed, and wearing (to please Joseph) a galaxy of jewels far too elaborate for the occasion, she dispensed lavish hospitality from their palatial villa, showing herself off because in that way she could best show her gratitude to the man who had made all this possible. The more she glittered with diamonds, the more blatantly scintillating her whole personality, the better he was pleased.

Just at first, in those humiliating and nauseating nights early in the marriage, she had to steel herself to bear his touch, force her jangled and screaming nerves to respond to him. In those hours of martyrdom, when she hated him, hated herself, despised herself, Piers seemed to be in the room with them. His eyes glowed in the darkness, steely with condemnation of her. At such moments it was all she could do not to scream aloud and push Joseph away, but gradually she became used to it, just as, she supposed, one could get used to anything if there were no alternative and one did not die.

Gradually his essential kindness, which was something deeper than and apart from his generosity with money, reconciled her to the payment she was making. She was determined to give such value as she could, and the humble appreciation of this naturally arrogant and self-important little man made it easier to endure it.

'Gee, but you look lovely,' he said to her one night when they were ready to receive their guests at an evening party. It was the most important function they had given so far. Ten guests had been bidden to dinner, but later about a hundred were expected to fill the long reception room with its windows overlooking the Gulf. The smaller rooms were for games, bridge for those so inclined, roulette and 'chemmy' for others when they were not dancing to the music of the smartest band on the Riviera.

Joseph had told his wife he wanted her to 'knock 'em all flat' and she had certainly done her best. Her strapless gown was of ivory brocade, cut perfectly plain to form a background for the most glittering and vulgar of all the glittering, vulgar jewels he had given her. There were diamonds round her neck and falling in a cascade of liquid fire to the soft hollow between her breasts, great flashing rubies in her ears and a coronet of square rubies and clusters of diamonds set in her dark-gold hair; one wrist was encircled with a three-inch-wide bracelet of diamonds, and several slender jewel-set bands lay one after another on the other arm; her fingers, their nails exactly matching her lips and the rubies, were stiff with a king's ransom.

What wonder, she thought rather acidly, that Joseph exclaimed at sight of her! Even Flora had gasped when the last bracelet had been fastened and the final ring put on.

Clementine had laughed then.

'Have you ever seen anything like me?' she asked.

'You look beautiful, my lady,' said Flora and meant it.

'I look incredibly vulgar,' said her mistress, picking up her platinum evening bag, needless to say also set with diamonds.

But in her husband's eyes she was perfect, and after all, since he had bought the things, and bought her to show them off, what reason had she to complain?

She stood with him at the head of the stairs to receive the long line of guests and many of them, meeting the enigmatical smile in her eyes, forbore to make their comments on her until they could be quite sure they were out of earshot. Most of them, the women at any rate, looked at her with grudging respect. She might have to put up with Joseph Bloggett and even sleep with him, but the majority of them would have thought it worth it, dazzled by the sparkle of her jewels.

One of them, a man, was obviously not amongst these.

He was Garry Prosper, the writer of several plays which owed their considerable success to his biting tongue and scurrilous attacks on the manners and habits of the very people who paid most to see them. He was spending a few months in Cannes getting fresh material, and Lady Bloggett's reception was a rich hunting-ground for him.

He was a man who might have been any age from twenty-five to fifty-five, and who was actually forty-five, dark, heavily built, divorced from his wife and apparently not inclined to replace her. He had met Clementine several times at the houses of mutual friends, but for some reason which she did not try to analyse, she had not sent him an invitation to her own party.

His inscrutable grey eyes mocked her, ran over her dazzling figure, and mocked her still more derisively.

'I see you go in for gate-crashing,' she said to him, avoiding his outstretched hand.

Joseph at the moment was busy with another guest.

'I knew the omission was accidental,' said Prosper.

'On the contrary. It was intentional,' said Clementine sweetly.

'Why?'

'Because I dislike you intensely, and because I don't intend my house and my guests to be used merely to provide you with your nasty material. However, now you're here, you may as well stay.'

'Thank you, lady,' he said, his eyes boldly impudent, and he sauntered off to what he thought would be the liveliest and most entertaining of the little groups that were forming.

Later he managed to get his hostess alone.

'Are you eating anything?' he asked. 'Or are you really made of ice as well as encrusted in it?'

She smiled. She liked his impertinence though there was something about him which gave her a sick feeling of recognition. He was as different from Piers in looks as anyone could well be, and yet he was reminiscent of him.

'Don't you think my jewels are wonderful?' she asked with a gibing note in her voice.

'Magnificent,' he said mockingly. 'I've seen you decked out before, but never in the full regalia. How satisfying it must be for the good Joe to see and actually be able to touch the reward of the rich.'

She found herself flushing. The inference was intentionally obvious; she herself was one of those things which he could see and touch.

'I could hate you so much,' she said.

'I know. I could loathe you. You're representative of everything I most despise. You've sold your exquisiteness for filthy lucre and haven't cared how filthy.'

The words were unforgivable, but his tone and his expression robbed them of some of their offence. He was claiming her as a kindred spirit, one of the very few to be found in all this noisy, glittering, sycophantic throng.

'I could say the same about your plays,' she parried.

'You could. A lot of people do,' he said with a chuckle.

'But they flock to see them.'

His eyes took in the scene around them.

'They flock here too,' he said.

She laughed, feeling with every moment that sense of belonging to his sort of people. She had missed that so much since she had been Lady Bloggett.

'Are we birds of a feather, Garry Prosper?' she asked him.

'If it were not too presumptuous to liken my execrable self in any way to the beautiful, the successful, the sought after and admired Lady Bloggett, I might say we are,' he told her, and signed to a passing waiter to ask him to bring something to eat and drink.

'Where shall we have it?' he asked, detaining the man whilst he turned to his hostess.

'Bring it to the Chinese room,' she told the waiter, who was one of their own staff, not one of the many specially imported for the evening.

The servant brought them food on a little wheeled table, and champagne in a silver ice-bucket.

'Will there be anything else you require, milady?' he asked.

'I don't think so, but will you find Sir Joseph, please, and tell him I am in here with one of the guests and ask him if he would care to join us? If he would, bring some more sandwiches and another bottle of champagne.'

When the man had gone, Garry Prosper made a wry grimace in protest.

'Now was that necessary? Or kind?' he asked.

'I think so,' said Clementine smoothly, taking one of the little sandwiches.

'Or was it merely—prudent?'

She refused to be drawn, though he had the satisfaction of seeing the little smile that hovered over her lips.

'The servant has probably told some of the other servants,' she said, 'and I do not choose that there shall be any cause for gossip.'

'But to send for your *husband*!' he complained.

She gave him a steady glance. She was by now aware that this man had something to give her and to ask from her which she did not intend should be given.

'You may as well understand, Mr. Prosper, that I am quite happy with my husband and he with me, and that that is how I intend things to remain. No side turnings have any attraction for me at all.'

He smiled.

'Well, that was straight from the shoulder, anyway. I can only bow gracefully to such a decision—though I should still like to be told why you deliberately refused me an invitation.'

'I've told you. I don't like you,' she said, but her eyes danced a little. She was realizing how absolutely without spot or blemish her life had been since her marriage, and that it was fun to be with someone like Garry Prosper again.

'How mutual of us,' he said. 'May I open the champagne or do we wait for an official opening by Monsieur le Mari?'

'As you like,' she said, and with his eyes on hers, gay and impudent and quite unsuppressed, he unwired the cork and let it fly out with a resounding pop.

Joseph pushed aside the door curtain as he was pouring out the wine. He looked from one to the other for a moment, clearly in some perplexity about why she had sent him the message which had brought him here.

Clementine came to him and linked an arm with his and drew him to the table again.

'Do you mind, Joseph?' she asked. 'I thought you might be as glad as I was to get away for a little while from all that noise and commotion, and, as Mr. Prosper realized, I shouldn't have got any supper in there, nor would you. Do you know Mr. Prosper? He's Garry Prosper, who writes those amusing and immoral plays which show us as others see us—or at any rate, as Mr. Prosper sees us.'

Joseph nodded to him curiously, wished he understood half what people were getting at but supposed that as Clementine had sent for him, it was all right.

Presently, after a sandwich or two and two glasses of champagne, Prosper excused himself and left husband and wife together.

'I suppose we ought to go back,' said Clementine regretfully.

'You sound as if you didn't want to. Aren't you enjoying your party, eh? Eh?'

'Of course, but ...'

How could she tell him that she was engulfed in a wave of nostalgia for the things that had been and could never be again? And she knew that it was Garry Prosper who had done this to her because he had that odd, indefinable likeness to Piers.

She shook her mind free of the bitter-sweetness of feeling that she had actually been with Piers.

'Funny idea you coming in here with that cove, wasn't it?' asked her husband, peering at her with his beady little eyes.

'I told you. I wanted something to eat and a little peace and quiet,' she said with a touch of the hauteur which always had the effect of reducing him to apologetic submission.

'Yes. Yes, you did, didn't you? And sending for the—yes, of course,' he said fussily.

She smiled and moved towards the door and stood waiting for him to open it. She was improving his manners towards her, though it was uphill work. He was of the type and standard of education which did not perform these little courtesies to women, particularly their own womenkind. Before their marriage, he had been known to say there were only two places and attitudes for women – on their knees and on their backs. He did not say this in Clementine's hearing, nor did he now say it at all.

His mouth twisted wryly as he obeyed her silent gesture and opened the door.

All the same, he felt an odd satisfaction in being made to do her behests in these little matters. She was a winner, a thoroughbred.

'You look a queen tonight, Clementine,' he said.

She had stopped him from calling her Clem because, to her horror, it was beginning to develop into Clemmie.

She smiled carelessly.

'Thanks to the regalia,' she said. 'A burglar would have a good haul if he had a go at me this evening, wouldn't he?'

'It's all well insured,' said Joseph comfortably and padded on behind her as she swept along the corridor, the gleaming folds of her ivory gown rustling, her jewels catching and tossing back a million points of light.

Well insured, she was thinking. So typical of him. He took enormous risks when necessary, but his motto might have been 'What I have, I hold,' for once he had acquired a thing, it was protected by every device known to man. She wondered cynically how he had guarded against losing her. She had heard it said that if you pay a high enough premium you can insure against any eventuality.

Two men watched her closely for the rest of that evening, which became night and almost morning before there was any sign of the party breaking up.

Garry Prosper's eyes were amused, as cynical as were her own whenever he caught their glance, which was many times, too many for her entire comfort. What a superb actress she was! What a hostess! Did any of them guess, as he did, that she despised them all, knew them for what they were, sycophants and parasites most of them, fawning on her for what they could get or hoped to get?

Well, wasn't that why he himself had come, uninvited? He did not know what, if anything, he did hope to get, but he had been intrigued by the knowledge that she had intentionally refused him an invitation. Why? Was she afraid of him? And again, why?

The other man who watched her, with brooding unrest that was not actual suspicion, was Joseph Bloggett, purchaser and nominal owner of this lovely woman. He, too, recognized the difference in the quality of the man Prosper, with whom she had been shut up in the Chinese room. Why had they gone there? It must have been her idea because he had never, within Joseph's knowledge, been to the villa before. But then, she had sent a servant to find him and ask him to go there. She would not have done that if there had been anything in it. Or would she?

Had she been warning him by sending for him to see her in the Chinese room with that man Prosper, the writing feller?

By the time the last, guest departed it was full daylight outside. Clementine gave an order to Louis, the majordomo, of whom Joseph was secretly in awe, and went upstairs to her room, a grandiose apartment with a great gilt, satin-canopied bed, satin curtains, and furniture which was a medley of genuine museum pieces and very indifferent fakes.

The enormous, elaborate dressing-table was spread with tortoise-shell inlaid with gold, her entwined initials, C. B., on everything. Even if the room had been simple when Joseph had rented it, it would have been heavily expensively elaborate by the time she reached it.

She stood looking round it with eyes which saw it as if for the first time again. She smiled as she thought what a pity it was that Garry Prosper could never see it. How he would have enjoyed it! And to be able to laugh at it with someone instead of only secretly within herself might have taken away some of the nauseated dislike she had for the room and its purpose.

She heard Joseph's feet padding along the corridor. He had a heavy tread which not even thick carpets could entirely deaden. He stopped outside the door, and she had to exert considerable self-control to keep herself from rushing to lock it. Instead, she stood quite still, her hands limp at her sides.

Not tonight – oh, surely not tonight?

He turned the knob cautiously, saw her standing there and entered the room, closing the door again with that extreme caution which always irritated her. After all, they were married. Why all the fuss to try to hide from the servants that they slept together?

'I just came to—to say thank you for giving such a successful party, my dear,' he said.

She was the only person in the world who could make him feel diffident and hesitate in his speech.

'Yes, it was successful, I suppose,' she said, 'if by success one means that everybody has had too much to eat and drink, won or lost too much at the tables, and will brag about having been here tomorrow.'

'Don't you like parties, Clem—Clementine?'

She shrugged her shoulders.

'Oh, I suppose so. What's the use of having this great place, and all these,' beginning to strip off her jewellery on to the dressing-table, 'if one doesn't show them off?'

He crossed the room and began to finger the jewels as she took them off.

'You'd better lock them in the safe tonight,' she said. 'I don't want to have them lying in my room all right—though it's daylight. Five o'clock!'

'Are you tired, sweetheart?' he asked cautiously.

'Yes.'

'Too tired, darling?'

'Oh, Joseph—yes,' she said with a sigh of impatience.

He waited in silence whilst she took the last of her jewels off, the magnificent parure from her hair, and something in his look suddenly touched her. Poor, common little man with his money!

She laid her hand on his.

'Stay if you want to, Joseph,' she said.

He lifted his head, his eyes brightening. Then, very gently, he reached for her lips and kissed them.

'Not if you're tired, my darling,' he said and tiptoed away.

She took off the ivory gown and the one tailored garment she had worn under it, put on the lace nightdress the maid had laid out for her, and crept into bed.

'Oh, Piers, Piers!' she whispered into her pillow, and wept for what could never come again.

# Chapter Nine

Although Diana told herself a hundred times that she did not intend to go to London on that Monday to meet Paul Esterre, she knew in the depths of her that she would go.

She persuaded herself at last to the belief that if she did not go Paul would trace her to Joan's house and present himself in person.

When the Monday morning came the Fates seemed determined to conspire against what she knew to be the right thing to do, for Joan had discovered that she was out of some wool she needed to finish a garment for the expected baby.

'If you've still got some bits of shopping to do, Diana,' she begged, 'do go today and get me two more ounces of that blue wool, will you? I wouldn't ask you to go specially for that, but if you *are* going, I'd be glad.'

Diana, who had almost persuaded herself by this time that she was not going, was haunted by a vision of Paul waiting and waiting for the girl who did not come, and she threw her better impulses to the wind when Joan spoke.

'I'll go this morning,' she said, and all the way up to Town she felt, too late, that it was madness to go.

Paul was waiting expectantly at the ticket barrier, and her heart gave a leap. It was quite useless to pretend otherwise.

'You have come, *chérie*,' he said, in his voice that warm note that was like a caress, and when she had given up her ticket and joined him he slipped a hand under her arm and walked her away from the crowds.

'You look so sweet, *ma mie*,' he said.

'Do I Paul? This is new. I haven't worn it before,' looking down at the suit of fine blue tweed, the blue of her eyes, which had really been intended for her going-away outfit.

To her dismay, it had started to rain and she had no umbrella.

'A taxi will answer that,' he said. 'You wait here one little moment and I find one.'

'We have to wait in a queue for them here,' she told him, but he only laughed, left her, and returned very quickly with a cab.

'How did you get one so quickly?' she asked, and he winked at her.

'By being so clever,' he said.

She knew it was not quite playing the game. With Andrew she would have waited for their fair turn. Paul had found some other way, but he did it with such a merry enjoyment of having outwitted other people that she had to laugh even contrary to her conscience.

'Where can we go, in the rain?' she asked.

'You have some shopping to do?'

'Oh yes, Joan's wool. I must get that before I forget it.'

With a lordly disregard of the cost, he took her to the shop and kept the taxi waiting.

'I thought you told me you were a poor, struggling artist,' she objected.

'I am having a holiday,' he said. 'Also, it is not every day that I have my Diane with me. For her the best always, isn't it?'

He was a delightful companion. He was as she remembered him, but now she was a woman and not a schoolgirl, and their comradeship had a new flavour and an excitement which had been lacking.

When she had finished her shopping and they had had lunch, it was still raining hard, but she resolutely refused to let him spend any more money on her.

'I know,' she said. 'We'll go to one of the picture galleries, or the British Museum.'

They went to the Tate Gallery, and she knew at once that she had lost him. He remembered she was with him, but only as someone to whom he could speak his thoughts aloud, with nothing personal behind it. She was unable to follow his thoughts. She could only make a show of listening and understanding as he raved about colours and light and form, dragging her from one room to another and back again to illustrate a point he was making, in which she had no real interest.

At last it dawned on him that she was very quiet.

'*Chérie, chérie*, you're tired!' he said, full of contrition. 'I am like a thing that is mad. We go at once, but at once! *Ma pauvre petite, elle est épuisée!* Come. We rest here not one moment more.'

He put an arm about her. It seemed only the most natural of movements, but at the almost unconscious touch they both stopped, their faces turned towards each other, their eyes grave with revelation.

There was no one else in the room, with the exception of one of the uniformed attendants, who was taking no notice of them. They were not the first young couple to seek the quiet and comparative seclusion of the Gallery on a wet afternoon.

'*Chérie*,' Paul whispered. '*Ma douce, ma bien-aimée.*'

Still her eyes looked into his, starry and wide. The breath came softly from her parted lips.

'Oh, Paul!' she whispered back to him. 'Paul!'

His lips came down to hers, firm and hard and compelling and everything in her responded wildly. There was no thought of or for anyone at that moment but Paul. Her whole being seemed filled and completed. He felt her tremble in his arms and gathered her more closely to him.

'Do you love me, my Diane?' he asked.

'More than the whole world,' she told him quiveringly, and again they kissed and were swept into that world which was for them alone.

Presently she drew away from him.

She was suddenly stricken by the memory of Andrew.

'Paul, we must go. I ought not to have done that. We mustn't meet again.'

Her voice was low and shocked. She was really horrified, though her body still glowed from the contact of his and her mind was filled with the realization of love.

He took her hand and led her to one of the seats placed in the centre of the room for the better observation of the pictures.

'Let us sit here a little and talk. There is much to say, yes?'

There was a new quality in his voice. It was gentle and tender, the voice of a lover, and she began to quiver again.

'No. Paul. I must go. I can't stay here with you. You know I can't. It's wrong.'

'Wrong that we love, *ma douce?* No, that cannot be wrong.'

'It is—because I love Andrew and I'm going to marry him,' she said wildly. 'You must let me go, Paul.'

But she stayed. His hand on hers was light and gentle. She could have broken away quite easily from its hold, and yet it seemed like a cord binding her to him.

'You will, then, marry this André?' he asked her when they had sat almost in silence for some minutes.

'Yes, Paul. I must. You see, he has been endlessly good to me ...'

'I would be good to you, Diane.'

'I have promised, Paul.'

'But you do not love him.'

'I do love him. No one could help it. He's so good and kind.'

She was troubled and unhappy, knowing that life had changed so much within the last few minutes that it would never be the same again. And she had thought that, with her decision to marry Andrew, all her life was now calmly set!

'But you do not love,' repeated Paul. 'You love me, Diane.'

'Oh, I'm all confused! I don't know what's happened to me,' she cried. 'I do love Andrew. He's everything that anyone would love, and— Paul, don't say these things to me or try to keep me here. Don't you see that I don't want things to be different? I want to go on as I was before I met you. I want to marry Andrew.'

He said nothing, but kept his eyes on hers. His expression was tender, amused, mocking; a complete denial, she knew, of everything she was saying.

'Don't look at me like that,' she whispered shakenly. 'I can't bear it. It isn't being fair to me. I want to do the right thing.'

'And you think, my little so foolish Diane, that it is the right thing for you that you marry this André? And you think you can forget your Paul?'

'I must. I will.'

He shrugged his shoulders.

'*Eh bien!* The poor Paul, he is *expulse*—sent out into the cold and the alone. *Hélas*, the poor, poor Paul!'

In spite of her distress and unhappiness, she could not help a little smile. His face and voice were intentionally comical and it was always easy for them to laugh together.

'You'll get over it. And sooner than I shall,' she said, the last words drawn from her almost before she knew she was uttering them.

He rose. His timing was perfect. To detain her any longer now would, he knew, be folly.

'Then you go? And to see me again, when?'

'Never, Paul.'

'Ah, but that is too hard! I am in England one week now. I go back the next Saturday. Is that never to see you again, Diane?'

'Not again,' said Diana with firmer decision, though the very thought that she would never see him again was tearing her in two.

Rather to her surprise, he offered no further resistance.

She picked up her bag from the seat beside her and rose.

'Take me to the station now, Paul, please,' she said shakily, not looking at him.

'Who would believe that my Diane, *ma douce petite*, could be so—without relent, you say?'

'Relentless,' she corrected him automatically.

His English was now so good, except for occasional lapses in construction which were endearing to her, that not even the language bar stood between them.

She hurried away from him and he followed her. It had stopped raining. The evening was fresh and sweet even in the unlovely purlieu of the Tate Gallery, and Diana stopped and unconsciously drew deep breaths of it. She longed to be away from the city sights and sounds and smells and back in her beloved country.

True, she would be going back to Maidstone, but the Hursts lived on the outskirts of the town and it was easy to get into the country. When she and Andrew were married they would be in the real country again. Even at the dreadful moment of parting from Paul, that thought had an uplifting calm. Nothing had ever been so bad for her if she could get amongst the grass and the trees and into the silence broken only by the sounds of sheep and cattle, perhaps a barking dog or a hen proclaiming a fresh delivery.

She was now in a frenzy of haste to get the parting over. She had always been like that over difficult or unpleasant jobs.

But forget Paul?

That thought brought a swift stab at her heart and she thrust it away and hurried on, too impatient to wait for a bus, too much afraid of the intimacy of the taxi which Paul would have called.

'It isn't far,' she told him, nor was it far to feet used to long trudges through the countryside or over the downs, though to Paul it was sheer torture and akin to madness to walk where one could ride, especially in a town.

Up Millbank, across Parliament Square, up Whitehall – he wondered that she knew her way about London so well, but she had been about a lot with Andrew, and he had taught her the main geography of the Victoria, Westminster, Kensington and shopping areas, liking as much as she did to walk whenever possible.

Paul arrived in a more or less exhausted condition at Charing Cross and wanted to go into the hotel for a rest and a drink or some coffee, but Diana consulted the table of train departures and found that she was just in time to catch one.

'You go and get your coffee, Paul,' she said. 'I know the number of the platform and I have my ticket.'

'*Chérie*, as if I should! No, to the end I will be martyr,' and he bought a platform ticket and hurried after her as she went to the waiting train.

'Now,' thought Diana wretchedly, 'now it will soon be over. Then the pain will begin again. Now I feel nothing, nothing,' and she leaned her head back and closed her eyes, only to open them again with the realization that she would miss this last glimpse of him.

He was looking at her with his dark, expressive eyes which could say so much. Just now they were saying unbearable things which she knew she must forget but would always remember. He was smiling a little, too, and she conjured up the ghost of a smile in response.

'It's been—wonderful, Paul,' she whispered, leaning forward to be near him as he stood on the other side of the open window.

She had not been able to find a compartment in which she would be alone. There were two women in the far corners.

'Wonderful, my Diane,' he agreed. 'But you can still go back and marry this André!'

'Don't, Paul.'

'You think you are going to be happy, *ma pauvre petite!*'

'I know I am,' she said defiantly, and then with a jolt the train started, and Paul stood back and it was over.

She darted to her feet and put her head out.

'Darling, goodbye,' she called, but she could not see his tall form because her eyes were filled with tears.

She lay back again in her corner and fought with the tears, conscious of the curious glances of the other two women. She felt sick and spent. How was she to bear it? All her life, and she would never see him again.

'Never again—never again—never again,' said the train chugging along, taking her from him.

She knew now beyond the shadow of a doubt that she did not love Andrew Shawn, never had loved him. Lonely and bereft and frightened of the future, she had given him the gratitude and deep affection which had seemed to her to be love, though all the time she had known there was something in her which he could not reach. There was still the gratitude and the affection, with shamed contrition added to it, but now she knew what it was that he had not and could not touch. Paul Esterre held her in the hollow of his hand.

Yet she was going to marry Andrew. He knew, surely must know, that he would never possess her wholly so he was losing nothing by her new knowledge of herself and she was determined that she would be a satisfactory wife to him and make him happy. As for herself, once she had recovered from the first shock and pain of being torn from Paul she would be happier with Andrew. She would not know the heights of bliss with him, but neither would she know the agony of the depths.

So she argued with and against herself, glad that she would at any rate not have to see Andrew tonight, and probably not tomorrow. He had gone to Northampton to see Blaize Merrimayne about some of the remaining snags over her grandfather's administration of the estate, and would stay overnight.

By the time she reached the Hursts' home she had almost persuaded herself that she had accepted the parting from Paul, especially as she found Joan in a state of acid-tongued misery over a quarrel she had had with Ian. The quarrel would not last, Diana knew. The two were such definite personalities that disagreements were inevitable, and because they were deeply in love the quarrels were correspondingly bitter. She and Andrew would be spared such things, thought Diana numbly.

She offered what consolation she could.

Joan scoffed.

'Don't ever let yourself get too much wrapped up in a man,' she said. 'It isn't worth it. You're wise not to go all haywire over Andrew. You quiet, gentle people get the best of it. You'll never wish you hadn't been born, the way I do now. And I feel so disgusting with this great lump to carry about, and who should know what a pregnant woman feels if not a doctor?' and Joan, who was as a rule so self-possessed and serene, began to cry.

Diana held her in her arms and tried to comfort her, but Joan sat up, pulling away from her at the sound of Ian's step in the hall. What would happen now? thought Diana anxiously, for Joan had said she would not speak to him or even look at him until he had apologized abjectly. Ian was not the sort to be abject about anything.

He came into the room and Diana prepared to flee, leaving them alone, but she need not have troubled, for a moment later they would not have known if a cup-tie crowd had been in the room. They merely looked at each other and went straight into each other's arms. Diana just caught the look in their eyes before their faces were hidden from her.

She went up to her room. Yes, she and Andrew would be spared the bitterness, but they would also lack the sweetness. She thrust back the thought. There must be no regrets, no looking back. She would never see Paul again, so that presently he would be again that vague figure in her past which could not affect her future.

Yet two days later she was with him again.

Robin and Simon were being looked after by some friends who had a house in the country, two miles from Maidstone, and it was Diana's habit on fine mornings to get up early and cycle there to give them a run over the fields.

On the Wednesday morning, wheeling her bicycle out of Ian's garage, careful not to wake anyone in the house, she came face to face with Paul.

She stopped abruptly, one hand going instinctively to her mouth to stop the half-uttered cry. Then she spoke in a shaken, uncertain whisper.

'You—but—oh, why have you come? What are you doing here?'

He gave a little chuckle, took the bicycle from her and wheeled it out of the drive and away from the house, Diana having no option but to follow him. She was fighting with the mad surge of joy that would not be checked.

It was not quite seven o'clock, and most of the houses were still shuttered and silent, though a few people were hurrying to their work. They had no time to bother with Diana and Paul, going the other way towards the open country.

'When you told me you jump from your bed so soon, it was hard to think it. Do you remember, my Diane?' asked Paul.

She remembered. He had been horrified and had told her there was no such time as six in the morning, yet here he was not much later than that, and in Maidstone when she had believed him to be in London.

'Paul, what are you doing here?' she asked him again.

'*Eh bien?* You ask that, Diane? But how could I not come? I am in London and you are here, so I am here too. Where can we now go, Diane? I want to hold you close in my arms again and kiss away the little frown. It cannot be that you are not glad? Glad to be with me again?'

'You ought not to have come,' she repeated wretchedly. 'It isn't fair, Paul.'

'To who is it not fair, Diane? I know what you think. To this André. But to us, Diane? We cannot part. You know that. We belong, *l'un á l'autre.* Is it not so, *ma mie?*'

Yes, she knew that it was so. They did belong to each other.

She still fought against herself and him, but when they reached a quiet side street where nothing moved but a prowling cat, and he propped the bicycle against the hedge and took her in his arms, she could fight no more. Back came the surging tide of her passion, engulfing her with its irresistible force.

And then, inevitably, came the reaction and she pushed him away.

'Paul, no! No! I don't want to feel like this. I don't want you to do this to my life. I have made up my mind. I didn't want you to come back. You mustn't come back.'

But she knew herself to be weak as a child.

'We cannot talk here, Diane,' was all he said. 'Let us walk along past the houses. This machine of yours! Why do we have to take her with us?'

'We can leave her at the end of the road.' she said, and only then realized that she was concurring with his plan.

The road led to a stretch of common land dotted with gorse and blackberry bushes, and they walked there, his arm holding hers.

'You cannot marry this André,' he said with decision. 'It is to me you must come, to Paul that you love. Isn't it, *chérie!* I have not the things to offer you of Andre. We shall be poor, Diane. I am artist, you know, and since the war people have not money, also not the sentiment, the sense, which sees beautiful things. Sometimes I sell my picture. Then we are rich and we spend and are very gay. We go perhaps to the best hotels, to the Meurice, and we take an *appartement* of the best and you wear your beautiful clothes—'

'I haven't any,' interrupted Diana, playing with the idea as she had played in the past with him, making up fairy tales in which neither believed.

'Then that is the first thing we buy. We live, we laugh, we play, and then the money is gone and we go back to the *atelier*—how you call it, *atelier?'*

'Studio?' suggested Diana.

He made a wry face.

'Studio. So ugly. You will learn French, *ma mie.* Good French for when we are rich and grand at the Meurice, and *argot* for when we are poor in the *atelier* and you do the shopping in Montmartre, the basket on the arm, and I paint—I paint—but no! When I paint, I paint you, always you, *ma belle, ma mie*, with the face so beautiful—'

She laughed tenderly. She had loved the picture he was painting.

'That's where you slip up,' she said. 'I am not beautiful.'

He turned and took her in his arms and kissed her with slow, lingering tenderness, her eyes, her shining, uncovered hair, her throat, her young, eager, passionate mouth.

'We shall he happy, Diane—so happy.'

But still she remembered Andrew. She could not betray him like this. It was too late. He had done too much for her. She belonged to him by all the ties of decency, of gratitude.

'It's no use, Paul,' she said stubbornly, though the colour drained from her face. 'I can't marry you. I'm going to marry Andrew.'

He lifted his arms in a hopeless gesture.

'Always, always this André! How can you be so *obstiné*? How can you think to be happy with one man but you love another? You do love me, Diane?'

'You know I do.' she said in a low voice.

Oh why, why had he to come?

'Paul, I'm going back now and I can't see you again. I do beg of you, *beg* of you, to go away and not try to see me again. Go back, please, and don't come down here again.'

'I am not now resting in London. I rest here, in Maidstone. I have a room at the Woodside Hotel. I say to them that I rest there until Saturday, when I return to France.'

'Oh no, Paul! You mustn't stay here,' she cried, dismayed.

'I rest,' he said.

She had never been able to persuade him not to translate the French '*rester*' literally and had often laughed at him.

'Then I shall go away,' she said wildly.

'Where will you go?'

That was the question. Where would she go? She had friends who would take her in for a few days, but how on earth would she explain the position to the Hursts? To Andrew? What possible excuse or reason could she give?

'Paul, please go. Please,' she besought him, but for answer he only took her in his arms again and made her forget everything but that she was in them and that she loved him with her whole awakened, passionate heart.

Now she knew why she had never mattered to her father and mother, why she had always been, outside the charmed and secret circle which enclosed just the two of them, Piers and Clementine, why Piers, in dying, had killed the real Clementine.

They had this wonderful thing, she and Paul – and yet she must marry Andrew. She must. She must.

Yet during the days until Saturday, only two of them, she spent furtive, stolen hours with Paul, unhappy with him, lost and miserable without him, longing for him to go and leave her to readjust herself and find again her lost peace, dreading the moment when she must say her last goodbye to him.

During those hours he was the tenderest, most gentle of lovers aware of the extreme innocence and purity which were still hers in spite of the passionate awakening of herself in her love for him He could have adopted no other attitude better to his avowed purpose, which was that she should leave England with him on Saturday. She had a valid passport, and there was nothing but her determined loyalty to Andrew to keep her from doing so.

White-faced, her eyes strained and deep-shadowed from her sleepless nights and hectic days, she was a source of anxiety to the Hursts and to Andrew, though she shied away from their affectionate concern and declared, with uncharacteristic brusqueness, that there was nothing the matter with her and they were not to bother her.

And then, lying awake in the grey morning hours of the day which was to take Paul from her, she knew suddenly that she could not go through with it, that she could not marry Andrew and lose Paul and all the lovely delight which would be theirs.

For the first time in her life she wanted her mother, not because she needed mothering but because, of all people, Clementine would understand and surely approve. Would she not have counted any price worth paying to have Piers when they were young?

She dare not wait until the daylight. Something would be sure to happen to deter her. Explanations would have to be given; she might have to leave without even the small case she had packed with essentials; there might even be a scene through suspicion, or discovery.

With the heavy knowledge of betrayal upon her, she crept out like a thief in the chilly September dawn, making for the station and the early train to Folkestone. She would be there long before Paul was likely to arrive, but she could wait for him.

It was Christopher who first discovered that she had gone.

He had formed a habit of padding along to her room as soon as his mother released him from his barred cot, and, encouraging him, Diana had got into the way of slipping out of bed early to leave the door ajar for him. This morning she had left it shut, and the child's knocking at the door and demands to 'Auntie Di' to open it brought Joan along the landing.

'Auntie may be asleep,' she told him, but as Diana was never known to be asleep at seven in the morning, she opened the door and Christopher trotted in happily, only to come running back to his mother.

'Auntie Di all gone,' he said.

'I expect she's taking the dogs out,' said Joan, but when a few minutes later she went to open the garage for Ian, she saw the bicycle leaning in its usual place.

'Auntie Di all gone,' chanted the little boy.

'She may have been hiding from you,' said Joan, and went up to Diana's room to find that she had really gone, her bedclothes neatly folded, her suitcase missing, a note addressed to Joan lying on the dressing-table. She tore it open.

*Darling Joan* [Diana had written, and there were tears smudging the ink],

*I hate doing this to you and inside me I feel dreadful, but I can't marry Andrew and I'm running away. Please tell him I'm too dreadfully sorry and ashamed of myself to write to him, though I've tried. I've gone away with Paul. Andrew will understand. I met him in London a week ago and we just know we've got to be together.*
*Diana.*

# Chapter Ten

The time of waiting for Paul to arrive at the entrance to the harbour seemed interminable and Diana, still in an agony of distress about her betrayal of Andrew, began to wonder wildly what she should do if Paul did not come, or if she missed him.

The channel steamer was there, and people were arriving at the harbour entrance to go on her, but still there was no sign of Paul, and at last she went to one of the officials in uniform who had been eyeing her with some interest. She had been there so long.

'Oh, if he's coming from London, miss, he'll go right through in the train and on to the boat,' he told her. 'He won't have to pass this barrier. Do you just want to see him off, or are you going across yourself?' – looking at her case.

'I'm going myself,' she said, and was now in a frenzy in case the boat left without her. 'I haven't a ticket. Please tell me what to do. Please help me.'

'I'll see you get on all right,' he said, and he went with her, helped her to get her ticket and saw her on to the boat. After all her hours of waiting, the gangways were just being drawn up when she made her dash up them.

Once on the boat, she was seized by a fresh panic. What if Paul had not come after all? What if he were still in Maidstone waiting for her, at last in desperation going to Joan's for her?

It takes a long time to search even a small channel steamer, and she wandered about, still clutching her suitcase and causing a good deal of interested comment.

And then she saw him. He was at the bar, a place which for a long time she was too nervous to penetrate. He had a glass in his hand, and the inevitable little knot of people about him. Wherever he went, people seemed to be drawn to him as by a magnet.

He did not at first see her, and she watched him with a little pain at her heart. He was a man and she could not expect him to feel as a woman did, but had he really forgotten so soon their parting of yesterday?

And suddenly something seemed to stop him, to check the laughter and draw his eyes to where she stood, on the outer fringe of the circle, pale and nervous and hesitant.

For a brief moment he stared at her, unable to believe his eyes. Then he set down his glass and pushed his way through the people and came to her, both hands outstretched, love in his eyes and his voice.

'Diane! *Chérie!*'

She could not even speak his name. She could only gulp down the lump in her throat and smile at him.

'Diane,' he said again, wonderingly, and took her case from her and set it down and drew her away from the curious eyes that followed them.

'You have come, Diane,' he said, and his dark eyes, whose every expression she felt she knew so well, travelled over her as if still unable to take it in and to believe she was really there.

'Do you—want me, Paul?' she asked him in a difficult whisper.

'Want you? *Want* you? Oh, my darling, *ma mie, ma bien-aimée*—if I want you!' and she was content, filled again with the happiness of being with him. It was the only thing that mattered or could ever matter again, she told herself.

'How did you come? Why did you not let me know?' he asked, taking her away from the bar and out into the open deck, where they could lean on the rail and watch the sea, the English Channel which she remembered was never so called by the French, to whom it was la Manche. It was odd to think that soon she, too, would be French, though she could not imagine herself ever calling the English Channel anything else.

She told him of her early start from the house, the hours of waiting at the barrier, and how she had almost missed the boat.

'Why did you not come to me at the hotel?' he asked.

'I don't know. I didn't think of it,' she said, confused. 'Anyway, it was too early. You would have been in bed.'

'Well?' he asked, and the way he looked at her, the tender mischief in his eyes, brought the blood rushing to her cheeks. He had never looked at her in that way before. It showed her how completely she had burnt her boats, that now she was his, his own.

He saw the expression in her own eyes and laughed and drew her arm more closely to his body.

'My small, frightened bird,' he said.

'I'm not really afraid, Paul.'

'You must not be afraid, ever. See, it is Paul, who is your *bien-aimé*. Isn't it?' he asked, and she nodded.

'I suppose you came away without any breakfast?' he asked her next, when they had leaned there in silent happiness at being together, the fight and struggles over.

'I wouldn't have dared to rattle about in the kitchen, even if I could have thought of food,' she told him.

'Come then. We go below and find something. Tea or your so terrible English coffee. I will teach you how to make real coffee, *ma mie*, though sometimes the gas he is out and then it is the oil-stove which has an *odeur*—but an *odeur*!'

'But why sometimes the gas he is out?' she asked him, teasing him about the vagaries of his construction.

'Because, *ma mie*, the *monnaie*, she is out too!' he explained, and they laughed together until he became suddenly serious.

'Diane, will you be happy, to be poor?' he asked.

'With you, poor or rich is all the same,' she said in her sweet way, and then, 'Paul, when I am your wife, shall I be French, or shall I still be English?'

'Oh, I—I expect you'll still be English,' he told her uncertainly, 'but you will learn to talk French and to be a little Frenchwoman, yes?'

'With my basket on my arm? Remember?'

That is for when we are poor,' he reminded her.

'Paul, never make me stay at the Meurice and be grand, will you? I like much better the sound of your studio in Montmartre.'

He had ordered food for her, but after a few sips of typical Channel-crossing tea, she pushed it aside.

'I'm frightfully sorry, Paul, but—I feel groggy,' she said. 'I hope I'm not going to be seasick.'

But alas, she was. Very, very seasick.

It was no consolation to her that nearly everybody else was sick too. After leaving the harbour, they had run into a heavy swell.

But it was then that she knew Paul's tenderness. Though she begged him to leave her and let her die alone, he stayed with her, giving her sips of brandy, wiping her face and bathing her head with handkerchiefs soaked in *eau-de-Cologne*, and at Boulogne almost carrying her off the boat, though as soon as the motion of the boat had stopped she felt miraculously well again, if washed out and weary.

He would not hear of going through to Paris that day.

'You have had enough of travel for one day, *ma mie*,' he told her. 'We stay in a small hotel just out of the town where I have stayed before, and tomorrow, if you are well enough, we go on to Paris, yes?'

She had never wanted to choose her own course and she was content to let him plan for them. After all, was she not his now for all time?

She saw him for the first time in his own country, so gay, so amusing, so quick-witted in his own tongue that wherever he went people laughed and were glad to make friends with him.

The hotel he wanted was a small, friendly-looking house above the town, and he helped the driver of the taxi to carry their luggage in and paid him and then entered into a lively and, to Diana, unintelligible conversation in which there were many shrugs, many exclamations, some smiles, frowns which seemed to have brought them to the verge of a duel, and then smiles again and more shrugs.

Paul came back to the plush seat on which she waited.

'*Bien-aimée*,' he said very tenderly, 'what would you? There is but one room, and I have had to tell the proprietor that you are already my wife.'

She coloured painfully and looked at him and then away again.

'We—isn't there somewhere else?' she asked.

'Perhaps, though I do not know the town well and always stay here,' he said. 'Will you that I go to find somewhere, *petite?*'

She nodded her head, and her eyes besought him.

He smiled and patted her shoulder.

'You stay, *petite?* Madame will bring you coffee and something, an omelette, perhaps. And presently I return.'

She could see he was amused, probably thinking her the complete prude, but there was that inherent something in her which would not let her do what he evidently thought nothing of. The French are different, she told herself, but Paul understands how I feel. He knows that I must wait until we are really married.

She did not know how long it would be before the marriage could take place, nor what arrangements Paul would make for her until then. She had a little money with her, just enough to pay a modest hotel bill for two or three weeks, she thought, so she would not have to take money from Paul until they were really married.

He came back to tell her that he had not been able to find two rooms in another hotel, but he had found one, so she could have the room in the house where they were, and he would take his case to the other one.

She was nervous.

'I didn't want to be left alone,' she said. 'You know what my French is like, so completely inadequate.'

It seemed that she would have to be left alone, with Paul at another hotel.

After they had eaten in an odd little dining-room with marble-topped tables, many aspidistras, an ancient knife and fork which had to be wiped on the bread at the end of each course and used again, but with excellent food and a wine carefully chosen for her, Paul tucked her up on her bed to sleep for an hour.

'And me, I go out into the rain, alone,' he said, commiserating with himself.

'It isn't raining,' said Diana.

'But it soon will rain, and then I shall get very wet, and I shall catch *la pneumonie* and I shall die, and when you stand weeping at my tomb, you will not be happy to remember that you sent me out to die.'

She laughed drowsily. She was tired, but very happy, almost too happy to sleep, she thought, but within two minutes she was sleeping and did not even hear Paul leave the room and softly close the door.

He walked about, his head bent in thought, his brow furrowed, though every now and then he smiled.

How like a child she was! He was astonished at her complete innocence, which was innocence without ignorance. She knew the meaning of life. She was a woman, warm and emotional. She had trembled in his arms and her lips had been eagerly responsive. She was a woman, ready for love and with all a woman's instincts both to flee and to surrender. Yet there was that disarming, almost frightening, innocence. It roused his protective sense, making an appeal to him which he was not sure he had wanted.

But he loved her. She was deeply in his heart, entwined with his very being. He had not dreamed that she would come to him as she had done, though he had urged her to do so. Now that she had come, she was a responsibility with which, in the calmer moments spent out of her presence, he did not know how to cope.

When he returned to her hotel she was up and waiting for him in the small bare foyer with its red plush and inevitable aspidistras. His passion for her rushed back at the sight of her and he hurried to her, taking her hands in his and gathering them to his breast. She looked sweet and shy and yet in her eyes was a new and enchanting awareness of herself.

'Have you slept well?' he asked her.

'Like a top.'

'Now what is that? A top?'

She laughed and explained.

'Ah, *une toupie*,' he said, 'but how is that asleep?'

'It's just a silly English expression. You will have to teach me the French ones. I want to learn everything French now that I'm going to be your little French wife! Oh, Paul, can you believe it? That we are going to belong to each other?'

Regardless of the curious but smilingly sympathetic interest of the *concierge*, he pulled her into his arms and kissed her.

'*Si douce, si douce, ma mie*,' he murmured. '*Je t'aime. Je t'adore.*'

'Paul, the porter's terribly interested,' she told him, smiling and blushing and drawing herself away.

'Well, what would you? Is it in England that a man must not embrace his wife? But we are not in England, *ma belle. Vive la France!*'

'We will, nevertheless, reserve that for the times we're alone,' she said with a quaint, adorable assumption of authority.

They went down into Boulogne and had a gay meal, strange and new to Diana, in a small restaurant facing the harbour, and Paul was enchanted by her naive interest in everything that was un-English. She had been out of England only once before, when she and Gramp had treated themselves to a very short holiday in Belgium.

'Why have you not rested with your mother, if she lives in Cannes?' asked Paul.

Diane's tell-tale face expressed disgust.

'You wouldn't ask that if you'd seen what she's married to,' she said. 'And she's so lovely, Paul. She could have married anybody, *anybody*, but she had to marry Joseph Bloggett! Imagine the name, to begin with! From Merrimayne to Bloggett! I shall have a lovely name, Diane Esterre,' she said with that touch of shyness that was so engaging. 'How long do you think it will be before we can be married, Paul?'

'I have to discover that, darling,' he said. 'When we get to Paris we will see.'

'It won't be very long, will it?'

'What is it that makes you afraid, *ma mie?*'

'I'm not exactly afraid, but—I think I shall always feel a stranger, not belonging, until we're married.'

In actual fact, she was beginning to feel frightened of what she had done, frightened but not sorry she had done it. Here with Paul lay her happiness, the sort of happiness Clementine had known, the sort that surely comes so seldom and for most people never. To think that she should be one of the lucky ones! But she wanted quickly, quickly, to belong to Paul, really belong.

'I will do everything that can be done, *petite*,' he said.

He made no attempt to persuade her to let him stay with her when night came. In fact, to her agonized distress, he spoke of the possibility of her returning home.

'Paul! You can't mean that!' she cried. 'You can't possibly mean it. Go *home?* Leave you?'

They were in her room. She had become used now to his being there.

He paced the floor, head bent.

'*Ma mie*, you can't think that is really what I want? But for you, is it not the best? This André, he is rich with all to give you and I am poor artist and have nothing—'

She flung herself into his arms and held him.

'I don't want to be rich. I don't want Andrew,' she said passionately. 'It is you I want, Paul darling, only you. Don't send me away from you. If you do, I shall die. I shall kill myself. I can't live without you. Darling, darling Paul, you didn't mean it!'

He was shaken by the strength of her passion. His arms came about her to hold her closely. She was like a being distraught by the very suggestion of leaving him.

'No, *petite*, no,' he said, soothing her. 'You shall rest with Paul. He is the so great *imbecile* to think it, but it was for you, *ma douce*, for that you be happy.'

'How could I be happy away from you, Paul?' she asked hysterically. 'You will not send me away? You won't leave me?'

'No, *ma douce.*'

'You promise me? I shan't find that tomorrow you have gone away?'

'Diane, do you think that of me? That I should leave you, here in France, alone?'

She managed a distracted smile.

'No, I know you wouldn't do that. I know it. But I was so frightened that you could even suggest my going back. Paul, you do love me?'

He took her face between his sensitive artist's hands and let her look into his eyes.

'What do you see there, Diane? That I hate you? That I want you not? That when the morning comes, I shall be gone away and you rest alone?'

His tone was gently rallying, and what she saw in his eyes brought happiness and peace to her heart again.

'You do love me,' she said, and closed her eyes and leaned against him, her soft hair brushing his lips, the fragrance of her sweet youth like perfume in his nostrils.

In his heart he swore he would protect her and give her happiness.

'And now," he said in that moment when to leave her was possible, 'I go away and you sleep, *ma mie.* In the morning I come and we go to Paris, isn't it?'

She nodded happily, and he kissed her and let her go.

Paul need not have feared to take Diana to his studio, for she was enchanted with everything she saw.

It was a poor enough place, merely one very large room with dormer windows looking straight up to the Sacré Coeur, and a high glass roof looking up to heaven. Across one end was a crazy partition, the flimsy wood covered with drawings and sketches of all sorts and shutting away the sight, but not the odours, of a sink and a disreputable gas grill. Tipped up against the wall was a shallow tin bath. The toilet, which he showed her with a Frenchman's entire lack of mock modesty on such matters, was approached from the landing outside and shared with all the other tenants of the old house with its narrow, winding, bare wooden staircases which could not have been cleaned, Diana thought, for a very long time if ever.

After the first interested glances at the drawings on the walls of the staircase, she had looked away, her face flaming. Then, conscious that Paul was watching her, she had resolutely swallowed and smiled. After all, if she was going to be an artist's wife, and a French artist's at that, she would have to get over being childish and insular, which was what she decided to call her natural modesty.

Paul had surreptitiously torn from the wooden partition one or two of the drawings whilst she looked about her with fascinated eyes and little burbles of laughter.

'Oh, Paul, it's a heavenly place! I've never seen anything like it, but then I've never been in an artist's studio before. I'd no idea they were like this. Oh, that funny person in the chair!' – catching sight of his lay figure, which someone (had it been Fifi?) had posed there, draped in a length of moth-eaten red velvet, a wreath of flowers, long dead, at a rakish angle on its hairless wooden head.

Paul laughed.

'That? That is a friend who live with us. I present you to her. Diane, Mademoiselle Silvie—Silvie, this is my Diane.'

Diana swept a deep curtsey and Paul, making the figure bow to her, let it fall in a clattering awkward heap on the floor, the wreath of dead flowers falling off, the jointed legs asprawl at all angles.

Diana gave a little cry and ran to pick it up.

'Oh, poor Silvie!' she cried, and he laughed at her as she replaced it carefully in the chair and rearranged in decency the moth-eaten robe.

'She won't be able to rest there,' he said. 'That is the only chair. Come on, Silvie. In your box,' and he opened the lid of a wooden chest, shabby and scarred like everything else, and pushed in the figure and the velvet and shut the lid.

Diana had a queer, ridiculous feeling of pity for Silvie. How awful to be tossed aside like that!

She looked about her again. Paul was right. The crazy chair in which Silvie had been sitting was the only one in the room, except for a wooden chair covered, like everything else, with a mass of papers and painting paraphernalia.

'But where do you sleep?' she asked, for he had told her this was the whole domain.

'*Voilà.*' said Paul, and indicated what she had taken to be a heap of draperies and old clothes but which, when some of these had been removed, showed itself to be a narrow divan.

'Then where—?' she began and stopped, flushing.

'Where will you sleep?' he asked. 'Now I become the *magician. Preste!*' and he flung the blankets on the floor and operated some mechanism which turned the divan into one twice its width.

She was watching with her wide, fascinated eyes, enchanted but a little afraid. It was all so new, so utterly different from anything she had known before. She could scarcely believe that it was she, Diana Merrimayne, with her life set in such surroundings and to be lived henceforth as people like Paul lived.

She took refuge in other things than that double bed.

'It's most awfully untidy, Paul,' she said, not liking to hurt his feelings by using the applicable word 'dirty', which it certainly was.

'I told you, *ma douce*, that it was not the place to bring Mademoiselle Merrimayne! We go, *chérie*. We find some nice small hotel for you, isn't it?' persuasively.

'Only until we're married, Paul,' she said firmly. 'Then of course I shall live here with you, though you will see it will be different. It will be clean and tidy, for one thing.'

'But, *petite*, I am artist. I must have a place where I can be not tidy.'

'All right. You shall have one part that I'll never touch, heaven help us, and it can be as not tidy as you like. The rest, you will see,' nodding her head.

'I thought I was bringing a sweet little *amie* to my home, not *un dragon de femme*!' he complained.

'You may not mind living in this mess, but I should,' she said, indicating the litter everywhere, and running her finger along a window-sill. She showed him the result. It was not merely the dust of a fortnight but the black, greasy grime of months, possibly years!

'You shall clean us up as you like if you will love me and let me love you when you are not making a so great cleaning,' he told her, and she was in his arms again, warm and yielding.

She was learning from his love-making how very near it is possible to get to such things as she had dismissed as unthinkable for 'people like us'. She was finding that 'people like us' were no different from the rest of the world when in love. Nothing seemed to matter when she was in Paul's arms? She had grown up quite a lot during her brief association with him. She knew that she was very ready for marriage.

'Where am I going to live until we can be married?' she asked him rather anxiously, seeing herself about to be cast out again, alone and in Paris and amongst people to whom she could not even talk. She thought of the hours of 'French' at school and bitterly regretted that she had not used the opportunity of really learning it instead of lightheartedly joining the customary ragging of 'Mam'selle', that poor, distracted, unhappy woman.

The pen of my aunt!

Paul applied his mind to the solution of that question. Where in Montmartre could he deposit her? Yet where, outside that queer, polyglot, haphazard community could he afford to keep her? The obvious solution never seemed to occur to her, and he lacked the courage, for all his experience, to suggest it to her. Had he ever properly considered this aspect of it when he had urged her to come to him, never believing that she would? Then he looked at her, sweet and desirable, and could not regret anything.

He remembered a small place, lodging-house rather than hotel, and took her there apologetically. Diana went inside with secret dismay. It was dingy and uninviting.

'You will hate it very much,' said Paul with a frown.

Even the modicum of furniture made the tiny room look crowded, the narrow bed, the chest of drawers and chair, a few hooks on the wall for wardrobe, the tiny mirror nailed to the back of the door.

Still, it was clean, and she told herself it would not be for long, and once she and Paul were married she would make a real home for them in the studio, with new curtains, some gay chintz, a rug or two, some pots of paint.

But when he had left her in the dreary little room she felt utterly forlorn and homesick, her thoughts going back to Joan's bright, neat little house, to all the other familiar places and people, to the two dogs she missed so badly and who would know that she had forsaken them – and to Andrew.

She knew beyond all doubt now that she had not really loved him, for the whole, passionate love of her heart was Paul's. Yet she could not think without a certain nostalgia of the ease and comfort of her association with Andrew, of the dignity of life with him.

She crossed to the small and slightly grimy window and looked out. The street was so narrow that she could almost have linked hands with anyone in the house opposite, or so it seemed to her, country born and bred. There were narrow pavements at either side of the cobbled street, but no one heeded them. The crowd flowed over the whole width of the street, and cars and a few horse-drawn vehicles had to nose and push, hoot and shout, to make their way amongst the people. There were people of all sorts, but all of them looked unfamiliar to Diana, and the sound of their voices came up to her as a confused babble of which not one word was intelligible.

She lay awake until, in the early hours of the morning, the noise gradually died down to only one or two voices, the clatter of only one or two pairs of feet on the cobbles. She seemed to have slept for only a few minutes before the sounds of the new day started, hard on the heels of the old one. Milkcarts came rattling along, not the quiet, rubber-tyred vans and trolleys familiar to her but little ramshackle carts with iron wheels that rattled and clattered on the stones, cans and churns adding to the din. Dogs barked, women came out of their houses to shake rugs, or flung up windows.

Paris.

Montmartre.

It was incredible that this was to be her home now, these her people, her friends, this her way of life.

She fought back the tears. Surely when she had freely chosen this, she was not going to indulge in self-pity?

She found about a pint of cold water in the cracked jug, washed as well as she could and dressed carefully.

Her heart began to sing again.

She was dressing for Paul – possibly for her wedding day too!

# Chapter Eleven

If Diana had slept but little, the Prune d'Or seemed never to sleep at all. People had been running up and down the uncarpeted stairs, shouting to one another, all night, but when Blanche, the chamber-maid, came rattling in with Diana's *café complet* ordered over-night by Paul, she seemed as brisk and bright as ever. 'Perhaps one gets used to not sleeping in France,' thought Diana.

She ventured on a little conversation with Blanche, both of them laughing at the other's efforts to understand and to be understood, and Diana was bright and cheerful when Paul called for her.

'The only thing I really do miss is my bath,' she told him. 'I asked about it, but the maid didn't understand.'

He laughed.

'She probably thought you were still looking for the pen of your aunt,' he said.

She nodded, flushing. She could not so quickly get used to the French attitude to the natural functions of the body, brought up as she had been to the modesty of the English in such matters.

'She did,' she said. 'She kept escorting me there, though I told her it was a *chambre de bain* I was looking for.'

'I doubt if there is one,' said Paul.

'No bathroom? In an hotel?' asked Diana, aghast.

'French people haven't the passion to wash the body that you English have, and the Prune d'Or is not a very large hotel.'

A hideous thought struck her.

'Haven't you got a bathroom, Paul? I mean, isn't there one in the house?'

'I think now there is perhaps one,' he told her, 'but it is used by someone who—how do you call *tisser*? Ah yes, to wove. She woves some cloth and she makes her colours in the bath. One cannot wash the body there any more.'

'But I have a bath every day,' said Diana blankly. 'I have done all my life.'

'Then it shall be made for you, *ma reine*. Everything that my lady wants she must have! I read that in a book sometime. It is for you, *petite*. Everything that my lady wants she must have. I shall make it. You will see.'

She noticed that as soon as Paul was in his own country again his English deteriorated and she was the more determined that she would learn to speak French fluently and quickly. Whilst he worked at his painting, she would work at her French and surprise him.

They spent a day that was for ever memorable to her, her first day in Paris, and spent with a Parisian who knew every stick and stone of his beloved city and showed it off as if it were a lovely woman. Diana was happy but utterly confused, not only by all he tried to show her but also by what seemed to her the inextricable and hideously dangerous traffic. Standing on the great pavement surrounding the Arc de Triomphe, with vehicles of all descriptions surging round her, hooting all the time and having apparently no regard for human safety, she told Paul she would have to spend the rest of her life there, but he only laughed, took her firmly by the elbow and brought her, by a sheer miracle, to safety on the other side.

He did not take her to the Louvre.

'We go there one day when we do nothing else. We walk in the galleries slowly, with our minds filled with no other thing.'

She was more than content. She was worn out with the rush and bustle of the streets and the many things she had seen. Her feet, which could walk for many miles in the country, were tired and aching from the hard pavements, and when at last they climbed the stairs to Paul's studio she threw herself down thankfully on the piled divan.

Paul took off her shoes and stockings and massaged her feet, teasing her tenderly but blaming himself for having made her so tired.

'We eat here this evening,' he said. 'You lie here and rest, perhaps to sleep a little, yes? And I go out to buy many things so that we make a little feast,' and, lapped in his tenderness and the sense of his protecting love, she did actually sleep, there on his bed, waking to find him looking down at her, the table behind him loaded with all sorts of familiar and unfamiliar food.

'Oh, Paul, our first meal here together, and I've let you do it all!' she cried, and sprang up to exclaim at and admire his purchases.

'But it's a feast!' she cried, looking at the *salmis* of small partridges with an elaborate salad, an ornate sweet with cream and sugar icing on it, biscuits, several kinds of cheese, an assortment of tiny savouries, and two bottles of wine.

'Paul, you must have spent the earth on all this!' she said.

'Well, most of it is black market, of course,' he admitted, 'but it is not every day that I have a lovely lady to supper with me, and the very first time it has been you, *ma mie.*'

They made a gay feast, sitting opposite each other at one end of the long refectory table, the other end still piled up with the equipment of his profession, a stack of canvases, tubes of paint, brushes stuck in jampots, and a litter of many less recognizable things. Paul was host, servant and lover. At the last minute he had rushed out without an explanation and returned with an armful of glorious chrysanthemums, tawny brown and yellow, and laid them in her lap.

'Salute to my lovely lady,' he said, and as he put them down, some of them spilt on the floor all about her and lay in glowing, fragrant loveliness.

Her eyes filled with sudden tears and she lifted her face to his.

'Oh, Paul, I do love you!' she said shakily, and he gathered her into his arms and crushed her until she cried out.

They decorated the table, the flowers standing in such pots and jars as she could find, and transforming the room's dusty untidiness into a bower.

When at last she felt she must go, as it was now very late, she realized that nothing had been said about their marriage and no arrangements begun.

'Paul, could we go—tomorrow—or quite soon, to—to the Marie?' she asked with some hesitation.

He had already told her that formal application would have to be made somewhere or other.

'Of course we will,' he said at once.

'Do you know yet how long it will be?'

'I don't know, *chérie*, but there will be little troubles, little complications, you understand, since we are not both French.'

'Yes, of course,' she agreed, and went back to her meagre room in the Prune d'Or, determined to be reasonable and patient, though she felt she could never be really happy until she was married to Paul and belonged wholly to him. She could not rid herself of the forlorn feeling of being cast adrift, and her mind returned again and again to the memory of the security she had left.

She wanted, too, to write to Joan, to be able to tell her where she was and that she was married. She knew how worried both Joan and Ian would be if she told them she was living in Paris under her present conditions, yet she would have to write to them soon. She had never spoken to Joan about Paul, but she supposed that by now Andrew would have told her who Paul was.

Her faint hope that the previous night had been exceptional was soon dashed. There were the same sounds from the street below, though tonight she slept from sheer exhaustion, and was still asleep when Blanche brought in her tray, with its shabby and not too clean cloth, though everything else was forgotten at the sight of the single, beautiful red rosebud which lay beside her plate.

Blanche nodded and smiled and managed to convey the information that the Monsieur had called early and brought the rose for her.

When the woman had gone, Diana lifted the fragrant flower to her lips. Darling Paul! Was not everything worth his love?

They spent that day in his studio, Paul unpacking the many materials he had brought from England whilst Diana made a raid on the dust and dirt and general untidiness. Wearing an old pair of the blue jean slacks Paul used when he was working, with a length of gaily patterned silk wound like a turban round her head, she was busy and happy, though never in her sheltered life before had she had to wrestle

141

with actual dirt, with grimed woodwork and old tins in which remains of food had gone bad, with a stopped-up sink and a floor off which she could literally scrape the layers of grime and grease.

Paul told her lightheartedly to leave it, that he did not mind in the least, but she retorted that she minded very much and finally told him to go out and find something to do for about three hours whilst she got on with the work. He had constantly interrupted it by picking her up bodily to hug her, by bending to kiss the nape of her neck, by calling her to see this or that purchase which thrilled him but had little meaning for her, though she professed interest.

The work was unbelievably hard for her, since she had neither knowledge nor experience, nor had she the soaps and powders and household tools which would have made it lighter. Still she struggled on, and by the time Paul came back there was at least some suggestion of what the place would look like when it was as clean and fresh and tidy as she intended it to be.

Paul took her hands in his and looked at them with concern, kissed the reddened palms and the rough, sore fingers remorsefully.

'They were the hands of a princess,' he said. 'You must not do such work ever again, *ma mie.*'

'I shall never let it get so dirty again,' she told him, 'but gosh, I am tired!'

'I hope you haven't hidden things where I can't find them,' he said, looking round with an appreciation of the transformation she had made, at the shining windows, curtained with some lengths of blue and white material she had found amongst a pile of clothing and rubbish, at the clean floor and the scrubbed table.

'I put a whole lot of your pictures in that corner,' she said.

He laughed at her expression and ruffled her hair with his hand.

'You were shocked by some, little one?' he asked.

'Well, if I'm going to be a French artist's wife, I'll have to learn not to be shocked, I suppose,' she told him, laughing a little, though the sight of the many nudes certainly had offended her. 'Do they come here, those girls?'

'But of course. This one,' crossing to the corner and producing a half-finished sketch, 'is Fifi. She is very good girl, Fifi.'

'Very good, and yet she lets a man see her like that?' asked Diana with disdain.

'Ah, you will understand later but not at once perhaps. Fifi is very good girl. She is married and also she dances at the Bal Tabarin, but if I touched her she would scratch me out the eyes!'

'Do you want to touch her, Paul?' said Diana curiously, trying to complete her picture of him which she felt always to be incomplete, so much of him still a deep mystery to her.

He shrugged his shoulders, dismissing Fifi.

'No. She is just a model to me, nothing besides. She is a very good model, very expensive. I cannot afford her often.'

'Do you have other models then? For the—the—like that?'

'Yes. It is my work, though now not many people buy and it is not always easy to sell pictures. I make other things, to advertise, and for the magazines. I do not like to do such things, but they are well paid, and what would you? We must eat, my little one.'

'Paul, there's another girl you've drawn and painted a lot, a girl with red hair,' and Diana pulled away some of the stacked canvases and brought out one she had looked at for a long time.

Though there had been some charcoal and pencil sketches of the same girl nude or very lightly draped, the picture she was showing him was of the red-haired girl in a flowered green frock, her feet bare, her toenails and her long, pointed fingernails matching the vivid scarlet of her mouth. She was extremely pretty, and the artist had caught the spirit of her in a mouth which had a faintly ironical twist and eyes that both smiled and mocked.

'Who is she, Paul?' asked Diana, as he sat staring at the picture, and she was sorry, with a stab of quick fear, that she had brought it to him.

'She was ... a girl I knew—once,' he said slowly. 'An English girl.'

'What was her name?'

'Sally.'

'Paul, did you—love her?' she asked fearfully.

He took the picture from her and thrust it, face hidden, against the wall and took Diana into his arms and kissed her long and satisfyingly.

'*Petite*,' he said, the deep tones of his voice able as always to turn the heart in her breast, 'I am artist, and I am twenty-seven. I am also

Frenchman. If I tell you there have never been any other woman for me, you would not believe it. Do you ask me then to tell you what is not so?'

'No. Of course there must have been others. It was silly of me to ask. Forgive me, Paul. There will never be others now, will there?'

'Never, *bien aimée*. Never,' he told her fervently. 'These others, they have come and gone, but you—you are my only love, *ma douce, ma petite reine*.'

Presently she stirred in his arms.

'Paul, did you go to see about our marriage today?' she asked.

'It can be in about three weeks, darling,' he said.

She sighed with mingled relief and impatience.

'In three weeks of the Prune d'Or I shall be a prune myself,' she told him, 'though not of gold!' with a rueful grimace. 'I—I feel simply awful about saying this, Paul, but I—I don't think I can afford to stay even there for a whole three weeks.'

It took a good deal of courage to say that to him, but she had been worrying about it.

'But dar-r-r-ling, you do not think that I allow you to pay such bills?' he said.

'I shall hate you to be paying for me before we're married.'

He kissed her. How young and sweet she was! How different from all other women he had known!

'Then come and live here,' he said, half in jest, though she heard the faint hopefulness behind the jest.

She shook her head.

'I couldn't do that. It would spoil things for us,' she said.

But again Fate decided to take a hand and was soon in control of the game again, for as she went down the bare, uneven stairs later she slipped and fell, and when Paul picked her up she was deathly pale, her weight heavy on him.

'You are hurt, *ma mie?*' he asked with passionate anxiety.

'My—foot—I—I ...' and she slumped in his arms in a faint.

When she recovered consciousness she was lying on his divan with Paul anxiously bending over her. He had taken the shoe and stocking from her foot, and when she instinctively tried to move it she gave a gasp of pain.

'I've hurt it,' she said in a surprised voice, 'and I must have fainted. But I never faint! Ooh!' as she tried again to move the injured foot. 'Paul, what have I done to it?' – looking at him anxiously.

'I don't know yet, *ma mie*, but one has gone for the doctor and he will say us what is it.'

He fussed over her in passionate contrition until the doctor came, pronounced it a bad sprain and said that for the present he would come in every day. With Paul's help, the foot and ankle were encased in plaster and, rendered immobile, gave her little pain. Paul would not, however, hear of her going back to the Prune d'Or.

'How could I look after you there?' he asked her. 'To be alone, it is not to be thought for one moment. You rest here, *petite*. All will be *comme il faut*. I will do so—and so ...' – showing her by the expressive French gestures which she had come to know so well just how he intended to safeguard her privacy.

The ancient red velvet which had served Silvie, the lay figure, as a robe was suspended from two hooks between the wall and the rickety wooden screen which shut off the 'kitchen', and presently Paul came back into the room with a tubby, bald-headed little man in corduroy trousers and blue smock, the two men carrying between them a small camp bed with a palliasse which looked to her most uncomfortable but which he assured her would be as soft as down.

He presented the little bald man to her. It was the first of Paul's friends she had met, though she had been aware of teeming life all about her, much coming and going on the staircase, the banging of doors, voices and laughter.

'*Chérie*, this is Poucet who out of the kind heart lends me his bed,' and the two men became involved in one of the rapid, energetic conversations which made her laugh and close her ears with her hands. It was still difficult to believe that they were not having a fierce quarrel which would end in a fight.

Whilst Paul went out to fetch her belongings from the Prune d'Or, Poucet (a nickname which she learned later was short for the French equivalent of Hop-o'-my-thumb) stayed to entertain her, and as he did not possess a word of English but was enchanted with her schoolgirl French, they soon became the merriest of friends. He called her

Madame and she called him Monsieur Poucet, to his great delight, and to the delight of several other people, of both sexes and varying ages and types, who seemed to materialize out of nothing. They seemed to have odd names – le Barbier, Brouette, Remi, Chaton, Etincelle. Some of their real names remained a mystery to her for ever, just as she never quite fathomed who belonged to whom.

There was a ravishing blonde, Susette, and a tiny dark-haired imp of a girl, Fifi, whom Diana recognized. They had been models for some of Paul's sketches. It gave her a queer feeling to know that they had posed like that for Paul, and for Poucet and Remi and probably a lot more men. Yet they seemed like any other girls.

Paul came back to find the studio full, and it was very late before, becoming aware of her look of white exhaustion, he drove them all out and came back to her with contrition.

'I have let you get too tired, *ma mie.* I will make you a hot drink now, and then you will sleep, yes? I tell them that if they make one sound, I kill them.'

The doctor had left a sedative for her, and when she had drunk it she lay back on the pillows in a state between sleeping and waking, her body quiescent, her mind refusing unconsciousness. She heard Paul moving softly about behind the old red curtain, pretended in sudden shyness to be asleep when he crept across the room for a last look at her, and then could not keep back the little gust of laughter at his expletive as the legs of the camp bed collapsed and sent him cascading to the floor.

The days that followed were strange and unreal, with a charm and a dangerous excitement of which both were aware. At first she remained in some pain, and Soeur Marie-Marthe, a nursing sister in rustling black gown and starched white headdress, came every day, kind, efficient but completely without any individuality. She did not understand English, and Diana's painstaking attempts to talk to her in French produced little or no response, though in Paul's friends they evoked hilarious but never unkind laughter. If Paul remained in the room when she came, Soeur Marie-Marthe studiously refrained from looking at him, never met his eyes and returned only the essential monosyllables to his questions.

Diana was learning French with a rapidity that amazed her, though she had so many and such lighthearted teachers always ready to sit with her, to bring their work in, to entertain and amuse her. She had quickly become Diane to them, and though it was clear that Paul had represented her to be his wife, she felt that to no one in that haphazard company did it matter in the least.

Paul had to leave her a good deal, as he was executing a commission he had undertaken before his visit to England, the cleaning and repair of some murals damaged by the Germans during their occupation. She was seldom alone, however, and as the door was never locked, one or another was always popping a head in to see if she wanted to sleep or if she would enjoy their company. Her most frequent visitor was little Poucet, who did charming pen-and-ink sketches for which Paul told her he was paid the merest fragment of their worth, but what would you? People now had the souls of *marchands* and Le Petit Poucet's work was of a delicacy, of a rarity, which now meant nothing to those who had no eyes.

With her rather embarrassed consent, Diana let him use her for a model for some exquisite little drawings he was making to illustrate a children's book of fairy tales. Idealized, but still unmistakably Diana, she appeared as a captive princess or the fairy queen, and she was enchanted when he gave her a delicate little sketch of herself as she was in reality, a sketch which revealed a knowledge and understanding of her which was greater than she had of herself.

It was Poucet who was her chief French teacher, too. The others, teasing her, taught her all sorts of phrases which Paul said would horrify far more worldly people than Soeur Marie-Marthe, on whom they had urged her to try them. She could trust little Poucet, who often reminded her, with a guilty stab, of Andrew Shawn.

Andrew whom she had treated so shamefully, after all his kindness and generosity to her!

She preferred not to think of him, and deliberately shut her mind to those things in Poucet which recalled him.

Each morning there had to be a little ceremony of taking down the red curtain which Paul called Cerbère – Cerberus, the guardian at the entrance to Hades. He lifted it down from its hooks and put it away so that it should not appear to the doctor, or to Soeur Marie-Marthe, or to any of the miscellaneous assortment of their visitors, that it was an overmodest provision by a husband.

Then there came a night when one of the hooks gave way, and the curtain hung forlornly by one corner, and the next night it did not go up at all.

Diana lay in the pale autumn dawn, so soon to slip into winter, and realized that Paul had not put up the curtain. She could see the long line of his body in the camp bed, a line that could not be quite straight because the bed was too short and he must lie curled up.

Actually it made no difference at all, that old red curtain, but it had been a symbol. Now that it no longer hung between them she felt as if some other, more intangible and yet far stronger barrier had been removed. During the last few days, when the plaster had been taken off her foot and she was able to walk a very little, no more than a few steps at a time, she had become increasingly aware of the ephemeral nature of that barrier, and that a word, a gesture, a touch might destroy it entirely and for ever.

Her love for Paul had become different, more conscious of the demands of her body. He had been wonderful to her whilst she had lain there helpless, needing to have everything done for her. He had been as tender as a woman, showing understanding and delicacy which had drawn from her a passionate gratitude to him, a longing to be everything to him, that longing the deeper and more insistent for his very reticence and reserve.

No more had been said about their marriage, though the three weeks had lengthened into four and then into five, but whilst she had lain there helpless she had not wanted to speak of it. What sort of bride would she be?

But she knew, from the way he held her, from her own ardent response and the urgency of her young, awakened body, that neither of them could go on as they were doing once she was squarely on her two feet again, and that time could not now be far distant. The doctor came now only every two or three days, and she had told Soeur Marie-Marthe that she did not really need any nursing care now. With the aid of a stick, she could hobble about the studio, though she could not yet go down the stairs.

Lying awake on the morning she discovered the absence of 'Cerbère', she watched Paul come to life and sit up in his narrow, short camp bed, stretching his cramped legs with a groan.

'I was wondering how long you were going to lie watching me without speaking,' he said.

It was a new joy to her to be able to understand him and to answer him in his own tongue, and already she found herself able to think in French.

'You didn't put Cerbère up last night,' she said.

'No. Did you mind?'

'Well—it's not much good minding now, is it?'

'No. After all—it doesn't make any difference, does it, *petite?*'

'Not really,' she said slowly, and lay very still until she became aware that he had left his uncomfortable little bed and was padding across the floor, barefooted, to sit on the side of hers.

She had a moment's unreasoning panic, but the next moment his arms were about her and she was filled again with that wild, frightening but exultant joy which he alone had ever been able to evoke in her.

'I'm not the right length for that little bed,' he told her pathetically. 'I sleep all doubled up and in the morning I am not like man any more but like an S.'

'You have this bed tonight, and I'll sleep in the little one,' she said.

'No,' said Paul, kissing her with little teasing kisses, on her chin, on the end of her nose, nibbling at her cheek. '*La belle dame sans merci,*' he said. 'Let us give back his little bed to Poucet, yes?'

'Not yet, Paul,' she said, her eyes troubled. 'Please don't ask me—that. When I am quite well, able to walk properly—'

He kissed her lips into silence again.

'All right, *chérie.* I will be *bon garçon,*' he said, and went to the other end of the room and began to busy himself heating water for shaving, and putting on the coffee.

No more was said about it, and the camp bed stayed there, but later in the day Susette strolled in, big and blonde and in some indefinable way insolent. She was the only one amongst Paul's friends whom Diana disliked, and it could not be only because she had posed for him for the figure, for Fifi had done that too, yet she found Fifi amusing and liked her gay *insouciance*, her impudence which had none of the insolence of Susette.

Diana, fiddling about with the knobs of the radio set in a fit of nostalgic longing to hear the familiar 'This is the B.B.C. Home Service', turned with a glance of enquiry as Susette came in without knocking and sauntered across to the bed, on which she flung, uninvited, her coat and her bag. Though the door was not kept locked, no one ever came in without knocking first, even if a visitor occasionally came in without waiting for her 'Come in', which was usually a glad one. The time would have hung heavily on her hands whilst she was tied to her couch had it not been for these casual, friendly, amusing visitors.

But Susette had not been a frequent and never a solitary visitor, and she could not help seeing the surprised expression on Diana's face when she threw down her coat.

'Good afternoon,' said Diana on an enquiring note.

'Paul not back?' asked the girl without replying to the polite salutation.

'I'm not expecting him yet,' said Diana, still enquiringly.

'He wants me to model. He told me to come,' was the cool, laconic reply, and to Diana's outraged affront, she threw herself down in the one easy chair, which Diana had been occupying a few moments ago, and picked up a magazine to turn through its pages.

Diana hesitated and then decided she could do nothing but accept the position, though she thought Paul might have warned her. She turned off the wireless and limped across to the table, taking with her some of Paul's mending which was beside the easy chair and on which she had quite obviously been engaged.

Susette gave her an amused glance.

'Quite domesticated,' she said, and though Diana did not understand the word, for of course they had to converse in French, she could not mistake her meaning.

'Naturally I do such things for my husband,' said Diana proudly.

Susette's smile deepened.

'But yes—your husband,' she repeated, and Diana's face flamed. It was obvious that Susette knew that Paul was not her husband. She felt cheap at having let her pride betray her into claiming him as such.

A minute later the door opened and Paul came in, glanced at the two girls and then went to kiss Diana, who averted her head so that his lips met her cheek.

'You said half past two,' said Susette sulkily.

'All right. I will pay you from half past two,' retorted Paul. 'I'm not sure I want you at all now.'

He was already regretting that in a moment of pique against Diana's determined virginity he had told Susette to come.

'There's plenty of light,' said Susette, and to Diana's speechless confusion, she proceeded to divest herself of her clothes and sauntered across to the model throne completely nude, a cigarette between her lips. Paul, not looking in Diana's direction, turned through a stack of canvases, put an unfinished one on his easel and began to prepare a palette.

'I shall be some time,' he said to Susette curtly. 'Wrap something round you.'

'I'm not cold,' she said, sitting in a chair and crossing her legs, glancing at Diana with contemptuous amusement.

For answer, Paul marched across the room, picked up his own dressing-gown and flung it at her.

'Cover yourself up,' he growled, and Susette, with a laugh, tossed the gown round her shoulders in a quite ineffectual manner.

For another few minutes he made a pretence at making up the palette. Then he flung it from him and walked away.

'I'm not in the mood. You can go,' he told Susette.

'You'll have to pay me,' she said shrilly.

'I've told you I'll pay you. Here,' and he pushed a handful of paper money at her, not caring whether she caught them or not. Some fell on the floor and she made a grab at them, spitting out an expletive which Diana was glad she could not understand the girl's malevolent expression was enough.

'Be quick,' said Paul as she put her clothes on in a leisurely fashion.

Diana sat quite still, her eyes cast down at the sock she had been darning, the beating of her heart loud and fast. She knew, needing no telling, that Susette had once been Paul's mistress, and it was obvious that the girl believed that she, Diana, now occupied that position. Why, why did not Paul marry her? Why did he now not even speak of marriage?

When Susette had gone he went across the room and locked the door and came back to where Diana still sat motionless, knelt at her feet and rested his head on her folded hands.

'I'm sorry, darling,' he said.

'Did you mean to hurt me like that? To—insult me?' she asked in a shaky voice.

'Yes. Yes, I did mean it, but when it happened I felt ashamed and mean. Diane, do you understand? Do you see how things are with us? That we cannot go on like this?'

'Yes, I do understand,' she said slowly. 'It means that I must—go away, Paul.'

Now, she thought, now he must speak of our marriage, must tell me that everything is going to be all right, and she waited, her heart contracting at his long silence.

'Not that, *chérie*. Not that,' he said at last, and rose to his feet and went across to the unfinished picture of Susette and drew a brushful of paint across and across it with savage pleasure.

Then he picked up his coat and the leather case he carried with him when he went to work at the murals.

'I'll go and do another hour's work whilst the light lasts,' he muttered and left her without any other explanation.

The light had long gone when Diana went to bed, but he had not come back, and though she slept only fitfully, never entirely unconscious, he did not return. It was the first time he had left her. She was frightened and unhappy. If only her foot was well enough for her to get down the stairs, she was in a mood to run away, she had no idea where nor to whom.

During the morning, whilst still Paul had neither come nor sent a message, to her relief Poucet came in.

'Am I welcome?' he asked.

She lifted her woebegone face. He saw she had been crying.

'Oh yes, Poucet, very welcome,' she said. 'I'm so worried. Paul hasn't been home all night and I don't know what to do. He may have had an accident and I—I don't know what to do,' she repeated.

He put down the books he had brought with him to amuse her and stood looking at her, a funny, fat, bald-headed little man with the eyes of a spaniel.

'We artists are queer people,' he said consolingly. 'Don't worry. He may have met some old friends, become very gay over a little wine and has overslept somewhere,' with a vague gesture which embraced all Paris.

'That isn't like Paul. He knows I would worry. Something has happened to him. Oh, Poucet, I know it has!'

'Poucet will go to look for him,' he told her reassuringly. 'Will that make you less sad, Diane?'

'Do you know where to look?' she asked anxiously, and he nodded his head.

'First I telephone to the house where he is working on the murals, yes?' he asked, and bustled out on his little feet, leaving her a prey to all the horrors which had been accumulating during the wakeful night and the fruitless morning.

When Poucet returned to tell her beamingly that yes, it was all right, that Paul himself spoke to him, that he was quite well but very busy, she did not know what she felt, relieved or miserably angry.

'But, Poucet, why did he not come home?' she asked.

Instinctively she knew there was no need for her to make any pretences with Poucet nor to be proud.

He took her hands in his own short-fingered, pudgy, clever hands.

'Diane, it is not well that you love too much,' he said gravely. 'For a man, yes, but for a woman to love so much, no.'

'I can't help it. Paul is all my life to me.'

'No, Diane. Your life belongs to you. You must not give it away for someone else to live. Paul's life, that is his own too. A little love, a little laughter, but not so much, never so much or there are too many tears.'

'Poucet, you know that Paul and I are not really married?' she said.

'Yes, *ma chérie.*'

'We have not been—anything else, either. Do you believe that?'

'If you tell me so, Diane.'

'It's true. I want to be his wife, not—the other thing,' she said painfully. 'I love him too much to make things cheap and beastly between us,' faltering over the unaccustomed words but grateful to him that his face did not tell her whether she was finding the right ones or using funny ones.

He took her hands in his and lifted them to his lips, that funny little bald, fat man who in that moment was not funny at all.

'You are most beautiful, Diane,' he said gently. 'Listen now. If I help you, do you think it would be possible for you to go down the stairs? And then we will take a taxi and go somewhere for a lunch, a very good, nice lunch that will make you feel better, and some very special wine that is—ah!' and he kissed his fingers in the air, saluting the very memory of that wine.

Diana conjured up a smile but shook her head.

'I wouldn't want not to be here when Paul comes home.'

'That is unwise, *ma chérie*, to be here, the patient little one. If you are not here, then he begins to wonder and to ask himself who has taken you away and to want his blood, until presently he knows that it is only the blood of old Poucet.'

But though deep down in her heart she knew he was right, and that she had always been too accessible to Paul, who, it seemed, did not so greatly want her, she could not bring herself to risk a further breach between them, and presently Poucet went sadly away to eat his lunch and drink the delectable wine alone.

Diana made herself an omelette. In these days she was very grateful to Joan, who had taught her at least the rudiments of good cooking, and Paul, who was no mean cook himself, had shown her how to prepare and cook that most French of French dishes.

She had just finished, and put away the clean dishes neatly, when the door opened.

She snatched off her apron and limped as quickly as she could to the other side of the wooden screen, ready to fling herself into Paul's arms, to promise anything, give anything, if only he would never leave her again.

But it was not Paul.

It was a girl, a lovely redhead, exquisitely dressed, a look of amusement on her face at sight of Diana.

'Hullo,' she said. 'Who are you? A model?'

'No,' said Diana, wondering who the unannounced visitor was and why she felt she had seen her before. 'I am Madame Esterre.'

To her surprise, the other girl chuckled delightedly.

'No, are you really?' she asked. 'By the way, aren't you English?' asking the question in that language.

'Yes,' said Diana wonderingly.

'Well, so am I, so we can be comfortable, can't we? Though as a matter of fact, nowadays I hardly know whether I'm talking in English or French. What's your name, by the way? Mine's Sally,' and then Diana remembered.

This girl, too, had been one of Paul's models, and many times his model, to judge from the number of sketches in addition to the finished portrait she had found. She had asked Paul about her, and he had said, rather as if he had not wanted to speak of her, that she had been an English girl called Sally.

'You know Paul, don't you?' she asked shyly.

The other girl was looking round the studio as if she saw a good many things that interested and amused her – the new curtains, fresh flowers in a tall blue jar, bright cushions on the neatly covered divan, and the lay figure which, in a fit of light-hearted frivolity, Diana had dressed in some garments of her own.

'I see you've reformed poor old Sylvie,' she said. 'When I lived with her she was always lying about in the most indecent attitudes. By the way, perhaps I'd better clear the air a bit more. My name really *is* Esterre. I'm Paul's wife.'

# Chapter Twelve

Diana stared at her visitor for a moment of shock. Then she felt her way to a chair and sat down, her face parchment white.

Sally looked at her in some concern.

'You didn't know, did you?' she asked.

'No,' Diana forced herself to answer.

'Bad luck. I suppose he hasn't actually married you, has he?'

'No.'

'He'd draw the line at that, of course. Have you hurt your foot?'

'Yes.'

'Nuisance for you. You're quite different from what I expected, you know.'

'Then you—knew about me?'

'Only that there was a girl here. How on earth did you get yourself mixed up with anything like this?' looking round the shabby studio disparagingly. 'You're not out of this drawer at all. You're what I believe used to be termed a lady, aren't you?'

Diana swallowed but did not answer.

'You're quite a kid too. Rotten of Paul. Are you in love with him?'

'I—I don't have to answer questions.'

Sally shrugged her shoulders.

'No. Perhaps I shouldn't have asked. After all, it's self-evident, isn't it? He hasn't anything to offer a girl like you except his fatal fascination,' with a hard little laugh. 'What are you going to do about it now you know I'm in existence? I really am his wife, you know. Bell, book and candle and all that.'

'I don't know,' said Diana painfully.

'I don't want him back, if that's what you're wondering. To be quite honest with you, I thought you were a different sort of girl and I came here to do you a bit of no good, just petty spite, call it what you will, though not against you. I've nothing on you, but Paul treated me badly and when I was told he was living here with a girl he seemed to be fond of I behaved like a rotten little skunk and came to do him a bad turn.'

'I'm glad you came,' said Diana slowly and with difficulty. 'I have to know, haven't I?'

Her world had collapsed. In her heart perhaps she had known that there was something like this, but she had been afraid of it, too much afraid to let the actual thought form in her mind. She could not yet think clearly or even coherently.

And then the door opened and Paul came in, Paul with an armful of flowers and a paper carrier bulging with parcels.

At sight of Sally he stopped, his face grey and stricken. Then he set down his parcels, laid the flowers on the table and went back to close the door. The two women looked at him and waited, Diana white and intense, Sally with a speculative smile on her vividly lovely face.

When Paul could bring himself to speak, it was to Diana.

'You know, then?' he asked.

She nodded her head, tears suddenly blinding her eyes, and at the look in his, that stricken, defeated look, she laid her arms on the table and her bright head down on them.

'You're proud of yourself, aren't you?' asked Sally.

'Not very,' he said.

'Why didn't you stick to one kind? My kind? Or, better still, Susette's kind?'

She had gone into French that was obviously as easy to her as English. Diana listened, trying to follow them with a mind, bruised and aching.

'So it was Susette?' asked Paul harshly.

'Yes. I see her sometimes. I ran into her yesterday, and when she told me there was another Madame Esterre living here, I was naturally interested. I didn't expect to find her like that, though,' with a gesture towards Diana, whose face was still hidden in her arms. 'She's quite a kid too.'

'She's twenty-two,' said Paul.

'I'm not thinking of years.'

'Would you believe me if I told you she is not my mistress?' asked Paul, and Diana, at least understanding that, gave a little shiver and an involuntary in drawing of her breath.

'*Allez counter á d'autres,*' said Sally derisively. 'Tell that to the marines.'

'It is true, nevertheless,' said Paul doggedly.

'Then you must have lost your touch,' and her laugh told him how little she believed him.

'What are you going to do about it?' she asked.

'Nothing. Why should I?'

Suddenly Diana got up. Her face looked like that of the dead thing she felt. She started to drag herself across the room.

'Where are you going, Diane?' asked Paul, his voice changing as he spoke to her rather than to Sally.

'I don't know, but—I can't stay here. I must go—go—just anywhere,' she said bleakly.

He had hurried to her and now, though she made no response and even tried to repulse him, he held her arm firmly with his hand.

'You can't go, Diane, not like that. You can't even get down the stairs. Don't go, *chérie.* Please stay and let me talk to you.'

She shook her head.

'No. No,' she said dully.

'Then will you go to Poucet? Let me take you to him.'

Behind them, Sally laughed.

'Good old Hop-o'-my-thumb,' she said. 'Is he still going strong? Still the universal confidant?'

They took no notice of her.

'Please go to him, Diane, will you? And stay with him at least until we can talk?'

She hesitated and then, because she had no idea what to do or where to go, nodded her head slowly.

'I can go alone,' she said as he opened the door for her and held her arm again.

'You promise you will go to Poucet?'

'Oh yes,' she said in a hopeless voice, and he let her go, standing at the open door until he had watched her out of sight, round the corner of the landing in the direction of Poucet's room, a studio similar to his own. He and Diana had been there many times to the little parties Poucet loved to give.

When he came back into the room Sally's expression had changed. The mocking amusement had given place to anger.

'You're a skunk, Paul,' she said. 'The girl had no idea you were married. Have you promised to marry her?'

'I suppose so. I never meant any of this to happen, having her here and all this. I'm not very proud of myself, but at least there's one thing. I love her, Sally.'

Her lip curled.

'The way you loved me?'

'You left me.'

'Because I was sick and tired of your women.'

'*You* should talk!' he told her bitterly.

'Well, let's say we were birds of a feather.'

'Our marriage was a mistake,' said Paul.

'I don't agree. If people of our sort get married at all, it should be to one another. We understand each other. Anyway, it was fun whilst it lasted,' with a reminiscent smile.

There was no answering smile on his face.

'What are you going to do about it, Sally?' he asked.

'Do? Why, nothing. What is there for me to do?'

'Will you divorce me?'

'On what grounds? You say you and this girl are living in beautiful Platonism.'

'I would give you grounds,' said Paul doggedly.

'Don't forget we were married in England and would have to be divorced under English law.'

'I know. If necessary, I'll go to England and produce the evidence there.'

She was eyeing him with speculative interest, but he could still sense her anger.

'I'll have to think it over,' she said at last.

'For how long?'

'I don't know. I'm not sure that would be the best thing.'

'Best for whom?'

'Chiefly for the girl.'

'She's in love with me.'

'You mean she was, until she discovered my existence. Even if she is still so misguided as to go on loving you, are you sure it's going to be a good thing for her to be able to marry you? I ought to know better than most people just what it involves, being married to you, Paul.'

He was silent, remembering the madness that had been theirs for so brief a time, their delirious happiness and their bitter quarrels which had ended in their parting.

'Do you seriously want to marry this girl, Paul?'

'I wish you wouldn't keep calling her "this girl",' he said testily. 'Her name is Diana.'

'Odd, the fancy you have to marry English girls. Do you want to marry her?'

'Yes.'

'And if I set you free, would you marry her?'

'Yes.'

She walked about the room, taking note of everything, the new cleanliness and neatness, the polished windows, one or two bits of shining brass, the neat divan with its pillows cased to look like cushions.

'She's not your sort, Paul,' she said at last. 'She wants to make a home of this, but you don't want a home any more than I did. We were perfectly happy living in a pigsty, so long as we had other amusing pigs about us. Diana will want little white woolly lambs or perhaps bleating sheep—with nice clean fur, of course. I should give up the idea if I were you, Paul. It wouldn't last.'

'I've told you I love her. You wouldn't understand that,' he said harshly.

She laughed. He remembered with a sudden pang that delightful, joyous laughter of hers.

'Oh, Paul, Paul! To have grown so serious over your little English miss! What is it about love that I don't understand? That there is one name for two quite different things? And that you think you have both these things for your Diana? I wonder.'

'Sally, will you divorce me?' he asked abruptly, cutting her short.

'I've told you. I don't know—yet. I'll think it over.'

'When will you decide?'

She gave a shrug.

'Oh—some time. I'll let you know when I've thought it out.'

'How shall I find you?'

'I've got an apartment,' and she looked in her handbag and gave him a card.

He read the address – a good one – and looked at her enquiringly.

'Don't get ideas,' she said. 'It may surprise you to learn that I earn every penny I spend, both as regards my domestic affairs and my clothes. If I take a lover, it is for fun and not for money. When I left you, I made a lucky discovery. I found I could design clothes and that they were the sort that will sell. I have a little shop, a tiny affair with a slip of a workroom behind it, and I'm getting known and doing quite well. So you see, Paul, *mon cher*, that I am quite independent. You would be amused to see me, the complete *vendeuse*. I would make special prices for your Diane if you wanted me to dress her. She would pay for dressing. She has a charming figure and her colouring is exquisite. Also as she will never be living like a pig here in our sty, she could always look charming. You should not let her wear those old slacks and jersey, and you an artist!'

He knew she was deliberately goading him. She had always done that. There was no sweetness in her.

'We need not discuss that,' he said coldly, refusing to be drawn into one of the old flaming rows which had stimulated her and seemed essential to her.

'No,' she agreed. 'Well, I will leave you, *chéri.*'

'And you'll think about the divorce?'

'Oh yes, I'll think about it,' she said, and there was that well-remembered mocking gleam in her eyes.

'I can't trust you,' he said irritably. 'I never could.'

'No, we couldn't trust each other, could we, *bien-aimé?*' she said mockingly and left him.

Slowly he went to Poucet's studio. It was like its tenant; small and neat and comfortable, and Diana was sitting on a sofa with her foot up, coffee and biscuits at her elbow, little Poucet fussing round her like a hen with one chick and, also like a hen, ready to fluff out his feathers at the first hint of danger.

He was ready to fluff them now, and Paul knew that Diana had told him of the advent of Sally. Poucet knew, as all the others knew, that he was married to Sally, but none of them had told her. That, he knew, was one of the things that must be bitter to Diana – that they had all known whilst she was keeping up her pitiful pretence of being Paul's wife.

'Will you come back and let me talk to you, Diane?'

Poucet busied himself at the farther end of the room.

'There's nothing to talk about, is there?' she asked, and he saw that she had regained control of herself. She was still pale, but quite calm.

'Yes, a lot,' he said, speaking in English out of consideration for her, though lately they had used French to each other.

'I don't want to talk to you, Paul. I don't want ever to see you again.'

'I can understand that you feel like that, Diane,' he said, 'and there are not enough words to tell you that I am sorry and—full of shame. I have wanted for all the time to tell you about Sally, but I had not courage. I was afraid to lose you, and now—it is not that I have lost you, Diane?'

'How can I ever feel anything for you again?' she asked, her voice a cry of bitter disappointment and despair.

Poucet came back to them.

'I will leave you for a little while,' he said gravely, but they scarcely heard him, though with the closing of the door they realized they were alone.

Paul went on his knees beside the sofa, one arm laid across her.

'Diane, once you tell me that you have much fear,' he said, and she knew by his awkward English construction that he was deeply concerned with his meaning rather than his words. 'You remember that? Much fear of many things, you tell me. It is not then that you understand I also have fear? Much fear to tell you about Sally, because

I think that if I tell, then you go away from me, isn't it? Always I have fear of that—that you go away.'

'But to deceive me like that, Paul! To let me stay with you in the belief that we could be married—that makes it all so dreadful.'

'The greatest thing of them was true, *bien-aimée*, that is that I love you. You still believe that?'

'How can I, when everything is different and—wrong? You knew that I was not like that, Paul, that I should not have come to you at all if I had known you were—married,' speaking the word with difficulty. 'I came with you to be your wife, not—not what they all think I am,' her mouth quivering and her hands gripping the sides of the couch.

Except for that protecting arm over her, he was making no attempt to touch her, but she was aware as she had never failed to be of his nearness. One of the things she was beginning to realize was that, whatever he had done to her, whatever he was, she must still love and want him. That thought was humiliating, but she could not rid her mind of it. All she could do was to keep him from knowing it.

'Diane, Sally has said she will set me free,' he told her.

She did not reply, lying back with her eyes closed, not only so that she should not see him but also so that he could not see what lay in them. She had been trying to readjust herself ever since she had known the truth about him. Since she could not be his wife, she could not stay with him. But what was she to do? Where could she go? She felt lost and alone and desperate. Poucet, she thought, would help her to get back to England if she asked him for money, but he might not have any. She had already learnt that none of this little colony of cheerful, haphazard people had any money.

And if she got to England, what could she do then? It was out of the question for her to go to the Hursts, or anywhere where she might meet Andrew, and at the thought of her mother she had to remember Sir Joseph. She could never, never go to him.

If only she had been trained to do something useful at which she could earn a living! It may have been assumed that she would marry, or that Gramp would leave her enough to live on, but whatever the cause or the idea, the fact remained that she was useless as a wage-earner.

Besides, how was she going to live whilst she learnt? Her knowledge of the labour market was nil. It never occurred to her that she could have gone on the land, or, with her knowledge and skill with animals, found employment with a veterinary surgeon or in kennels.

She heard Paul's voice talking to her and gradually brought his voice into focus again.

'—until then. I promise you, Diane. Please believe me.'

'What are you promising me, Paul?' she asked drearily.

'To look after you, and, as soon as ever I can, to marry you. Haven't you understood, *mignonne?*'

She passed a hand wearily over her forehead.

'I don't think I was listening,' she said with her native honesty. 'I'm trying to see my way through. You see—I don't know what to do, Paul. I don't know what to do, nor even where to go.'

His arm tightened until it held her and, as she made no resistance, he slid the other one beneath her and gathered her to him. She lay against his breast like a dead thing.

'Diane, don't leave me. I know I don't deserve it, but stay with me. Please stay with me. Whatever I have done, it's been because I love you. Truly, I love you. You are in my heart even closer than in my arms. Can you look at me and not believe me? Open your eyes and look at me, *ma douce, ma petite,*' setting a hand beneath her chin to tilt her face up so that at last, unwillingly but irresistibly, she opened her eyes to meet the look she knew would be in his, a look which could sap all her will-power and make her utterly his.

'Oh, Paul,' she whispered sadly, 'why didn't you tell me?'

'It is what I have said, Diane. I had fear, too much fear.'

'Everything is spoilt for us now. It can never be the same.'

'I will make it the same. I will make it better. Come to me, Diane. Come back to me.'

She shook her head and moved restlessly in his arms and he released her. She raised herself and finally slid her feet to the floor, wincing as her weight came down on the injured foot. How could she go anywhere or do anything, like that?

'I can't Paul,' she said.

'Then what will you do, *chérie?*' he asked anxiously.

'I don't know. I don't know,' with another of those weary gestures of her hand across her aching forehead. 'I don't seem able to think any more.'

'Will you go back to the Prune d'Or?' he asked her, though he dreaded the break with her which he felt might well be final.

'I won't be able to go up and down the stairs,' she said drearily.

'Then stay in the studio and let me go to the Prune d'Or.'

'You couldn't do that because of your work.'

'Darling, come back to me, then. Let me take care of you. Let me love you, Diane.'

Again she shook her head. She scarcely knew what he was suggesting. Her whole mind was still occupied with its problem of how to get out of the morass of difficulties she had created for herself by her precipitate flight from the safety of England and of Andrew; safety which now was a haven irretrievably lost to her.

'Will you at least sit down and let me tell you about things? About Sally and our marriage?'

'All right, though it won't make any difference.'

She sat down on the sofa, her hands folded listlessly in her lap, and let him talk to her. Her face was so expressionless that he could not be sure that she was even listening, but he felt he must try to show her how things had been, how different in every way was that brief madness with Sally.

'We met just after D-Day. She had been working for the Secret Service, one of the people specially trained for work in occupied France. She had been brought up in this country and she speaks French without any accent. She was dropped by parachute just before the Normandy landings and we worked on the same job. You know how she looks, and she was so courageous, so gay. We fell in love but it didn't endure. We became *ennuzi*—there were many quarrels. We did not love, do you understand, but only to *courtiser*—make the love. Can you understand that, *petite?*'

She nodded, her eyes distant and unhappy. She wanted at least to believe that. It made her position seem less humiliating. But could she believe that he loved her better than he had loved Sally, with her loveliness, her radiance, her clever brain and hands? And if he did, what difference did it make?

'Go away now, please, Paul,' she asked him at last, and he could see by her white exhaustion that she had reached the limit of her endurance.

'You will tell me what you want to do, *petite?*' he asked, almost humbly.

'I don't know yet, but—please go away.'

After he had gone, and before Poucet returned, she must see just how much she could do with her foot still very weak and, the doctor had warned her, liable to be damaged very easily for some time yet.

No stairs, he had said, but now, without any very clear idea of what she meant to do, she began slowly and carefully to go down the narrow staircase whose sloping, uneven treads had been the original cause of the accident.

At the bottom of each flight she stood panting, and with beads of perspiration on her forehead, but she got down the whole four flights and was at last in the street. She had undertaken the task of getting down the stairs as a test of her powers. Now her whole body and mind revolted from the thought of going back, to be tortured with every step. Yet she had no money, no coat even, and it was December. It was madness not to go back, and yet she began with no concrete plan to limp along the pavement, going instinctively the way she knew best, to the street market where, before her accident, she had gone with her basket and her halting French and a gay sense of adventure and of at last being alive, to shop for herself and Paul.

It was still the quiet hour in the middle of the day when many people remained indoors, or lingered in the restaurants, or sat outside the cafés over their coffee or tall glasses of wine or of *strops*. The women behind their stalls also rested, sitting on upturned boxes, talking, laughing, shouting to each other in a babel of cheerful sound which lessened when Diana appeared, limping aimlessly along in her old slacks and jersey, hatless and coatless on the December afternoon.

The woman they all called Rosine, a fat, cheerful, loud-voiced woman from whom Diana was accustomed to buy whatever dairy produce was obtainable, stopped talking to stare and pulled her ungainly body to its feet when Diana paused in front of her stall.

'You wish something, madame?' she asked.

'I—do you know—any place, very cheap, where I could perhaps have a room, just for a little while?' asked Diana, first unconsciously in English, and then in her careful French.

Rosine consulted her next-door neighbour, who in turn called across the street to another stallholder, until a dozen or so were engaged in vociferous discussion of the matter, at the conclusion of which Rosine, leaving her but poorly stocked stall to a friend for 'minding', waddled off down the street with Diana limping beside her. Rosine, it appeared, had been told of a friend who would perhaps let her have a room in her house, which was, you well understand, small but cheap.

It was certainly small, but Diana, with only a hazy idea of how much remained of the little stock of money she had been able to bring from England, did not agree that it was cheap. The proprietress of what was no more than a third-rate *estaminet* with a few poor rooms above it mentioned a figure which Rosine, on Diana's behalf, vigorously refused, and the two women embarked on a wordy battle with much waving of hands and shrugging of shoulders, apparently on the verge of getting at each other's throats, and then suddenly became all smiles and friendliness again. They had agreed on a price that Diana should pay for the tiny bare room over part of the café, its walls thin match-boarding, its uncovered floor made of boards between the spaces of which floated up the sounds and odours from below. A narrow truckle-bed, a wooden chair and an ancient washstand fitted with chipped, unmatched toiletware completed the furnishing. There was neither drawer nor cupboard, but a shelf was screwed to the wall and there were two hooks behind the flimsy door. Diana had never been in such a room before, but she was cold and exhausted, and felt that all she wanted just then was to be left alone and in privacy. She knew that somehow she would have to go back to the studio to collect her clothes and her money, but first she must rest and think.

'Thank you, madame. You have been most kind,' she said to Rosine, and to the proprietress, 'I will take the room, madame, for a few days.'

She was always punctiliously polite to Rosine and her kind, brought up from earliest years to be so.

Left alone, she sat on the edge of the bed and knew that never in her life had she felt so utterly forlorn and helpless, suffering great pain in her foot but scarcely aware of physical pain for the agony of spirit.

Paul – Paul – wept her heart, her eyes dry and burning.

She was hungry and thirsty, but as she could not bring herself to undertake the journey to the studio, especially as Paul would almost certainly be there at this time, she could not pay for even a cup of coffee. She drank the brackish water in the carafe on the washstand and lay down on the bed, pulling over her the two thin blankets and the lumpy flock quilt for warmth.

She dropped into an uneasy series of dozes, waking to the sounds from below, laughter, loud voices, the banging of a piano and the singing of raucous songs which seemed to go on all night.

In the morning, faint from want of food, she ventured down into the disordered restaurant where a slatternly potboy was making a pretence at cleaning up. She asked for coffee and a roll, and when she had finished them ravenously told Madame Gante that she must go back to the place where her clothes and other belongings were 'stored', though she could not think of the French for 'store' and hoped Madame would understand.

Madame seemed to understand with much suspicion, and in fact, when the girl limped downstairs again, having decided to go to the studio for her money, Madame was standing foursquare in front of the door, obviously barring her way.

'*L'addition, Mademoiselle,*' she said, firmly placing the bill in her hand.

Diana tried to explain that she was going to fetch her money, but Madame shook her head.

She was a small, beady-eyed woman with the beak of a bird of prey in the middle of a leathery face.

'*D'abord l'addition. Mademoiselle,*' she said inflexibly, and when Diana again tried to explain the woman shrugged her shoulders, spread out her hands and then conducted her into her private office and shut both the door and the sliding windows opening on the restaurant.

'Now, Mademoiselle,' she said, 'let us understand each other. You have no money, no?'

Diana explained again. Madame pushed aside the explanation.

'You have no money, no. Then you want to earn some?'

'Yes, I do,' said Diana painfully.

'Good. Then you work for me, yes?'

'Here?' asked Diana shrinkingly, looking round with wide eyes. 'But I am afraid I cannot walk very well yet. I injured my foot. I might not be able to do this sort of work. I thought I could perhaps find some sewing to do.'

Madame gave another shrug.

'Me, I can find you work, good work,' she said, 'and it will not be so bad about your foot, though you must at first take care.'

'You mean I should not be working here?' asked Diana, relieved.

'No. For how long will it be that you find it hard to walk?'

'Only two or three days, I think, if I do not have to use it much.'

'Good. Then for three days you stay here. You will have meals. I will send them to your room. Here it is rough, with men who may not respect you, so you stay in your room and rest, rest all the time, until you say to me that now you can walk a little, yes?'

Diana agreed gratefully. Evidently Madame, for all her eyes and her beak and her thin lips, and her ruthless presentation of the bill, was not so bad after all.

'I shall have to go and get my clothes, though,' she said.

This Madame refused to permit.

'But no. You stay there and rest and make your foot quite well. I have clothes. They belong to my daughter who is not here now, good, nice clothes which will fit you if a little large. You go back to your room and I bring them to you.'

Seeing that she had no alternative, and catching at such a good excuse not to go back to the studio until she was forced to do so, Diana agreed and went up to the little room again, helped solicitously now by Madame. A can of hot water was brought for her at her request, and Madame reappeared with an armful of clothing, tawdry and much trimmed, but clean.

'Your daughter will not mind, Madame?'

'But no. She is not here any longer,' was the indifferent reply, and, urged by Madame, who now, it seemed, could not do enough for her, Diana undressed, put on one of the cheaply trimmed nightdresses and got into bed. It seemed it would be quieter in the day for sleeping than at night.

She supposed afterwards that she must have had a slight fever, for once she had got into bed, warm now and fed, she had no real wish to get up whilst Madame urged her to stay there. At intervals the beaky nose and beady eyes would appear round the door, and if she were awake Madame would shortly afterwards, and with her own hands, bring a tray of food, surprisingly well served and as appetizing as is every Frenchwoman's cooking. Fish with delicious sauces, cutlets, an unending variety of the ubiquitous omelette, appeared in procession, and though Diana began to wonder how she would ever pay the bill that must be mounting up, Madame waved aside her protests and insisted on her guest eating what was brought her.

'You pay me afterwards, when you work for me,' was all she would say, but the girl could not make out from Madame's flowery half-explanations exactly what work she was eventually to do. Yet since all that seemed to be required of her at present was to eat and rest, and in particular not to try to go downstairs, she could not complain, and Madame kept insisting that she should not be *inquiete* about her bill.

It was a strange, dreamlike interlude, but shut up here in this bare little room she was safe – safe from any chance of Paul's finding her, safe at the moment from any need to plan the future.

She stayed there for almost a week, at Madame's directions using her foot a little each day until she could walk without pain.

'Now,' said Madame, after she had brought Diana's evening meal and waited, watching her with an odd intensity whilst she ate it, 'we go.'

'Go?' asked Diana blankly. 'Where?'

'I think now you can begin to work. Come. Here is a coat of Louise. It is a little large, perhaps, but we shall not walk,' and when the girl, puzzled that she should be going to embark on her job, whatever it was, when most people were finishing theirs, put on the coat and followed Madame down the stairs and into a waiting taxi which whisked them off at the usual hazardous speed of the Parisian driver.

'Here you will work, and it is better too that you live here,' said Madame, and Diana, still bewildered, followed her into a house of considerable size and elegance, its wide hall well furnished, the staircase thickly carpeted so that, as she followed Madame, their footfalls were noiseless.

In fact, the noiselessness of the whole house struck Diana as unusual, accustomed though she was to large, softly carpeted, well-kept houses. From the lack of sound, it might be empty, and yet she had a strange, eerie feeling as of watching eyes, though every door was closed and nothing seemed to move. Not even the sounds from the street outside penetrated the silence.

Then, as Madame opened a door and ushered her into a room beyond it, she understood, suddenly and completely.

The room was a bedroom, luxuriously furnished, its long windows shrouded in heavy curtains, a fire burning in the grate, an open door admitting a view of an elegant bathroom with shining taps and folded towels.

Mad with rage and fear, the girl turned on Madame and began to speak in rapid, incoherent English before she realized it and had to change into quite inadequate French.

'I wish to go at once! I cannot stay here I Do you understand? It is necessary that you let me go at once, this minute!' she stormed.

Madame stood like a small graven image in front of the door and waited until Diana could find nothing else to say. Then she started to speak, coldly, slowly, choosing her words so that they could not fail to be understood.

How, she asked, had Mademoiselle imagined she would be able to earn money, enough money to pay the large bill which now she owed Madame? It had been quite understood by Mademoiselle from the first, and now that she was well again, and had been fed and even clothed by Madame, did she think it was possible that she could go away without paying? It was not to be believed for a moment.

Diana raged again, then pleaded, besought Madame with all the words at her disposal, even going on her knees to her and laying her face against the cold, unresponsive hand.

Madame was inflexible and Diana wondered how she could ever have been such a fool as to think her kind. She rose to her feet and rushed into the bathroom. There was no second door, and when she tried the window, it was to find it securely fastened with no visible means of opening it.

Back into the bedroom, Madame still mounting guard over the door, she tore aside one of the long, padded curtains, only to find that this window also apparently had no means by which it could be opened, and even if she could have opened it, the street lay sheerly below, some thirty feet.

She let the curtain fall into its place. She thought she would remember all her life the sound it made, shutting her in with that devilish old woman, shutting her in with a fate too awful to be contemplated.

'I will leave you to come to your senses,' said Madame when she had watched in silence the girl's frantic search for a means of escape. 'You cannot get out. There is no way. And if you scream, no one will hear you, and if anyone should hear you, no one would come. Later perhaps you will see that it is better to be sensible,' and she turned and went out of the door, which she locked behind her.

Diana was like one demented. She tried to shake the door, which was thick and unyielding, hammered on it with frenzied fists, banged on the windows with no more effect, and finally collapsed on the floor in a passion of angry, helpless, frightened tears.

No one came near her. Not a sound from the rest of the house reached her. It was like being shut in a tomb, though this was worse than a tomb to her, for in a tomb she would be dead and nothing could hurt her any more.

But at least no one came near her, and towards morning she got up, stiff and cold, from the floor and tried to think more clearly.

Obviously the only means of reaching the outside world was by means of the window. She pulled back the curtain, first switching off the light, and looked out as far as she could see.

The room was in the centre portion of the house, and near the window a wing jutted out at right angles. A foot or two below, on the wall of this projecting wing, was another window, and running down the corner between that window-sill and the one at which she was standing was a collection of drainpipes. She was active and strong, and if she could get to that other window-ledge, and if her injured foot would hold her, surely it would not be an impossible feat to climb into whatever lay below? It was too dark to see exactly what was below, but it must be a small courtyard or alley, and surely from there she could get into the street. Even if she killed herself, that was better than remaining in her present position.

But how to get out of an apparently solidly fixed window?

The panes of the window were very large. The ones in the bathroom were possibly too small, but she was slender and though that window was farther away from the ledge from which she hoped to get a grip of the pipes, she decided that was her best course.

Taking off her shoe and wrapping it in one of the bath-towels, she drew a deep breath and then, taking her courage in both hands, she struck hard at the panes she had selected. The glass broke and splintered in all directions, and she crouched down on the floor feeling sick with apprehension.

Nothing happened. There was not a sound from the rest of the house, and now that she could hear the faint hum of far-off traffic she already felt safer and a good deal braver.

She waited a few moments and then carefully pulled away from the frame the fragments of glass until that section of it was clear. She laid the glass carefully down on a towel so that none of it should fall down outside and betray her, or chink on the inlaid marble floor. Then, wishing devoutly that she had on her old slacks instead of a skirt, she started to squeeze her body through the aperture, knowing that once she got her shoulders through the rest of her would follow.

A minute later she was outside on the window-ledge, flattening herself against the window, taking deep gulps of the cold night air and persuading herself not to look down. Carefully she edged along to the end of the bathroom window-sill, bridged the two or three feet between it and the next ledge, felt her way along that and then, still with her back to the outside and an insane desire to laugh hysterically at the thought that from down below Madame or some other of her captors might be standing calmly watching her, she stretched her foot down to where she hoped the lower ledge would be.

Her foot found it, and a moment later she had firm hold of the pipes. They were not quite rigid and rattled a little as she caught hold of them, and she clung there, paralysed with fright, and then, as still nothing happened, she began the climb down. Before leaving the house she had taken off her shoes and tied them round her neck inside her blouse, and when she had reached the bottom she could drop soundlessly on the concrete of the little courtyard she had rightly decided would be there.

After that, it was easy.

An unlocked gate led into the street, and after a furtive look right and left, she stooped down, put on her shoes, and walked quietly to the end of the road, her heart hammering so loudly that she thought any passer-by could have heard it.

But there were no passers-by. The street, in a substantial and respectable suburb of Paris, was empty and silent save for a stray mongrel dog which sniffed at her heels for a moment and then went off.

She had no idea where she was, but a few minutes' walking brought her to one of the stations on the *metro*.

A gendarme on his beat looked at her suspiciously, and she decided that, without even a sou in her pocket, she could not hope to escape notice. Approaching the man, she told him that she was a visitor to Paris and had lost not only her friends but also her bag containing her money and that she did not know how to get to Paul's address in Montmartre. The officer was attentive and gallant, as is every Frenchman to a girl in distress. He asked her a few questions about herself and her papers, but she professed not to understand him and kept asking how she was to get to Montmartre, appearing to be in greater pain from her foot than she really was, and finally he found a taxi for her and put her into it, explaining what he understood of the position to the driver.

She did not know at what point she had decided to go back to Paul. She only knew that, even if she had had any alternative, still she would have gone back to him. Her whole being cried out for him. Whatever the cost, whatever the future, she belonged to him.

Keeping the taxi waiting, though the man regarded the procedure with suspicious grumbling, she mounted the stairs and passed the closed rooms which sheltered their sleeping tenants, and pushed open Paul's door, nervous now that the moment had come.

He was asleep on the bed that had been hers, one hand beneath his cheek, the other flung out in the careless abandon of a sleeping child. The sight touched something within her. In sleep it was he who was defenceless, very young. Did she only imagine that he looked thin and tired? Had he had sleepless nights because of her?

Below, the taxi-driver hooted his horn raucously, and she bent down to touch Paul on the shoulder.

'Paul,' she said in a low voice as if, against the need, she could not bear to wake him.

But he sat up at once at her touch, stared at her increduously, and then caught her fiercely in his arms.

'If you're a dream, don't go,' he said. 'Don't go yet, Diane.'

'I'm not a dream, but—please give me money for my taxi, Paul. Hark at him!' as the horn sounded furiously again.

'I'll go down,' he said, still not quite sure that he was awake but taking some money from his trousers' pocket and going towards the door. 'If I leave you for a moment, promise you won't vanish again?'

Her eyes filled with tears.

'Oh, Paul, I promise! I promise!' she said brokenly. 'I've come home!'

# Chapter Thirteen

When Paul returned from paying the taxi-driver, tipping him magnificently, he found Diana as he had left her, standing with a dazed look on her face, very still as if for the moment her universe had become static and she feared to start it into movement again.

He came to her and took her hands in his, felt them rough beneath his caressing fingers and looked at them. They were dirty, the nails broken, dried blood on some of the cuts and scratches.

'Diane!' he cried, startled. 'What has happened?'

She looked down at her hands. She had scarcely noticed their condition.

'I broke a window and climbed down a drainpipe,' she said, and tried to laugh at his look of amazement until the laughter turned to tears and she leaned her head against his breast and let them have their way.

Presently, when he asked her if she were hungry, she shook her head and clung to him, feeling she would never want to taste food again. The memory of Madame Gante was still too fresh, the feeding and cosseting with the one undreamed-of purpose.

Seeing that something shattering had happened to her, Paul did not try to get her story from her then but made her lie down on the bed, covering her warmly and sitting beside her since she seemed uneasy the moment he was out of reach.

When she woke, hours later, she found him lying on the outside of the bed, asleep, his head slipping uncomfortably off the end of her pillow. With passionate tenderness she pushed the pillow gently into a more comfortable position, and lay beside him, thinking and wondering but knowing now that she could not leave him again.

When he woke it was to full consciousness, his arms reaching at once for her to hold her closely, and, lying like that, she could tell him now of that strange week with its tragi-comic ending, herself doing a film stunt along window-ledges and down drainpipes to protect her virtue.

To protect her virtue! And here she was with Paul, knowing what it meant and what could be its only end and that her ardent mind and responsive body would no longer be held by the artificial barriers with which she had sought to restrain them.

At whatever cost, she belonged to Paul.

He felt the quivering delight of her body in his nearness. For one moment he saw in her eyes the last appeal of her untouched innocence, the last remnant of her childhood. The next moment she was all woman, the eternal Eve, eager and desirous.

Later, she did not know whether in minutes or in hours since it was an eternity, he told her that he had been to see Sally.

'She has promised me that she will give me my freedom, *chérie*,' he said. 'Then we can be married. You will not be entirely and completely happy until then, will you, Diane?'

She shook her head. She had been brought up that way, and though her body was still filled with the rapture of its final satisfaction, she knew that conscience would trouble her.

She would not plague him with questions, though. Some day she would belong to him legally as well as by every law of nature.

Meanwhile, in spite of that increasingly faint pricking of her conscience, she was happy as she had never known or dreamed of happiness. Paul was the perfect lover as he had always been the perfect companion, and for the first time in her life she knew what it was to be utterly and absorbingly loved just as she loved in return. She could think now of Andrew with a different mind. Remembering his calm affection, his restraint in their love-making, she saw his feeling for her as something too quiet and serene to be love as she now understood it, and therefore he could not have suffered by her desertion of him as she had been imagining he would have suffered. He had just been 'fond' of her. He had probably forgotten her already. Poor Andrew. Since this power to rush to the heights and know the last ecstasy of human delight had obviously not been given him, neither would he have had to suffer knowledge of the deep pit which waits for those same human beings.

From her new-found happiness and feeling of security she wrote to Joan. Since she had run away she had sent only one postcard, a view of the Arc de Triomph, on the reverse side of which she had written only that she was well and happy, giving no address.

Now she wrote at greater length, but again without giving an address.

Paris was wonderful, even in winter, she said, and she was becoming quite a Parisienne. Her French had long passed the stage of *la plume de ma tame*, and she could even laugh at French jokes, though some of them, especially those in Paul's studio, were such as would make well-behaved English hair stand on end, others being merely silly. For instance, quite a number of them were lavatory jokes, so humorous to the French.

> *I am terribly happy, Joan dearest* [she had added]. *Paul is wonderful to me, and though I still have the feeling that J treated you and Ian and Andrew badly, I'm too happy to make myself unhappy about it. Please tell Andrew I have written to you, if you think he would be interested. He probably hates the very thought of me by now, though,*
>
> and she signed herself Diana Estcrre.

Joan read the letter several times before deciding to put it in an envelope and send it to Andrew. Of the few people who knew him at all well she was the only one who realized how deep and fatal had been the wound Diana had dealt him.

Beneath the carefully considered calmness which had so deceived the girl he loved there had been the fire and passion of a man who, past his first youth, had found an object for that stored wealth. It was the intensity of his love which had insisted on that serenity, that care not to alarm or distress her, and it was in that that he showed his lack of complete understanding of her. His mind stressed too much her youth and innocence. She was far more ready for knowledge and experience than he believed, and if he had not so strongly held his own passions in leash, Paul would have lost half his power to lure her from him.

The blow was that of a two-edged sword. He suffered not only in his love for her but also in the shattering of the image he had had of her. Behind the facade of unsullied innocence, which he rather than she had erected before her real self, she had been a sham. That was the intolerable hurt, the bitterness.

He had sold his Sevenoaks home when he had anticipated living at Wayside with Diana, but it was unthinkable that he should retain the new house after she left him, and he sold it quickly and at a loss, and took a couple of rooms in Town. He felt he wanted to be as far away as possible from the things associated with her. All he wanted now was to keep away from all thought or mention of her so that in as short a time as possible he might forget her.

The sight of her writing told him how little that hope had been fulfilled. It was so characteristic of her, part hesitating, part boldly dashing. He read between the lines of the letter and realized that she had an inner happiness she had not known since the death of her grandfather, and yet there was also a faint nostalgia for the things she would not know again, the known, familiar things of home. The gardens at Versailles, she wrote, had reminded her of part of Mayne Downe, 'only not so beautiful'; that she supposed London as well as Paris was getting ready for Christmas.

Yes, there was nostalgia there clearly perceptible to anyone who knew Diana as he did. He corrected himself to 'as he thought he did', and his lips were compressed into a tight line.

Joan was to 'tell Andrew if she thought he would be interested', and Joan had replied to that request by sending him the letter.

Recently he had had a letter from Clementine, sent to him at his office. She had hesitated to write to him before, she said, as she thought he might prefer not to have any prods from outside sources, but she hoped by now he was feeling better about the disgraceful way in which Diana had treated him.

*I have had a postcard from her, sent from Paris but without an address* [wrote Clementine], *in which she says she hopes we shall all forgive her in time and that she is very happy. If she is, she doesn't deserve to be. She treated you very badly, and from the worldly point of view (which is probably the only one you would believe me interested in) she is a fool. I'd much rather bet on a stockbroker than an artist in these uncertain days. Joseph and I propose to come back to England soon after Christmas, and I'll look you up and see what can be done about the broken heart. I know of some quite good kinds of cement guaranteed to mend hearts in practically any state, so that the joins scarcely show at all.*

There had been quite a lot more of the letter. Clementine was a good, gossipy letter-writer and Andrew had realized that beneath the amusing style, the little anecdotes, was a genuine desire to show friendship and regret. There was an essential kindness in Clementine which he had not recognized in their former contacts.

And she was honest. She had never tried to pretend that she was marrying Joseph Bloggett for anything but his money.

But Diana had not been honest. She had pretended love for him and then had left him. Clementine, in her position, would have had the courage which would have made forgiveness possible and left a wound less deep and poignant. Deceit, treachery, dishonesty, these were things he could neither understand nor forgive.

Joan had asked him to send the letter on to Clementine.

'It's such a long time since Diana wrote that possibly she won't do it again for months and this may be the only letter she's brought herself to write. I don't suppose she feels very well in with her mother at the moment. I think you told me you know the Bloggetts' address.'

He put the now travelled letter into an envelope and sent it, with a brief covering note, to Clementine.

Clementine was sitting up in bed reading it, with the rest of her large morning mail, when her husband opened the door and walked in. He had never broken himself of the habit of early rising, acquired in the years when he had been making the nucleus of his fortune, and he was fully dressed and looked, as he always looked, spotlessly clean and immaculate, as if he had just emerged from a Turkish bath via Savile Row.

Clementine gave him an icy stare.

'I've told you to knock before you come into my room,' she said.

'And I've told you I'm not going to have any more of such nonsense,' retorted Joseph stoutly, though his heart quailed as it had never done before anything born until Clementine seized it in the hollow of her hand. 'You're my wife. I've got a right to come into your room. I've got a right to sleep here every night, like decent husbands and wives, if I've a mind to.'

'Oh yes, Joseph,' she purred, her words and her mouth sweet, but her eyes like points of steel, 'you have a *right* to me. I know that. You bought me, didn't you? I think that's what you're trying to say, isn't it?'

'You're my wife,' he repeated, but his eyes had dropped beneath that look of hers.

'I'm not denying it,' she said sweetly. 'If I were not your wife you would certainly not be in this room at all, as you know quite well. You've bought the right to come in here, but *not* the right to offend me by denying me the small courtesies to which I, at any rate, am accustomed. However, if you think it *wise*, Joseph, to insist on your rights, don't let me spoil the pleasures you've paid for. Do come into my bed, won't you?' and she pulled back the covers, pushing her letters aside and making a gesture of invitation, her words and smile like honey on a rapier.

His face turned a dull red and he shifted his feet awkwardly, but made no attempt to move nearer to her.

'I don't want to upset or offend you, lass,' he said after a pause. 'I know my ways are not your ways, though I've tried not to make it hard for you to live with me.'

Her heart softened as it did so surprisingly and so often towards him. Bully though he could be, in spite of his wealth and ability he was no more than a child when it came to a passage of arms with her. Her sarcasm, the delicate thrust of a wit too finely tempered for his experience, were weapons which never failed against him. He had learnt, during these months of their marriage, that the surest way to be pinked by those weapons was to show any sign that he regarded her as a possession. He had come to realize, too, that if she were allowed to give her favours when and how she pleased, she gave royally, and taught him exquisite pleasures of which he had never dreamed.

But Clementine knew better than to let herself soften and show him how easily he could touch her heart. He had despised his first wife because she was a poor, weak-willed thing and he had been able to bully her. The two children she had borne him had died in infancy, and this he had held against her too.

'Very well,' she said calmly, drawing the bedclothes about her again and sitting up more comfortably against her embroidered, lace-trimmed pillows. 'Now that you are here, you may stay, but if you really mean that you wish to respect my ways and make it comfortable living with you, don't come into my room again without knocking.'

'All right, m'dear,' said Joseph meekly, and she wanted desperately to laugh. How easy it was to control a man who was as desperately in love with her as Joseph was!

She passed him Diana's letter.

He read it through and handed it back.

'She should have written to you instead of Mrs. Hurst,' he said. 'You're her mother.'

'Not a very good one,' she said lightly. 'She seems to be happy with her French artist, though it's against all justice that she should be, letting Andrew Shawn down like that.'

'Well, you know, if she's really in love with this chap,' said Joseph slowly and ponderously, 'perhaps she couldn't help herself.'

'You think love is sufficient reason for—betrayal?' she asked him curiously.

'She hadn't married Shawn. I suppose she could change her mind. She was only going to marry him for his money.'

'So if I'd left you on the altar steps because I preferred someone else, it would have been all right?'

'Well—putting it that way—yes, I suppose it would. But you didn't, you know, m'dear,' with a faint warning note in his voice which was recognizable.

'No, I didn't, so now it would be too late, wouldn't it?' she asked, her eyes regarding him with that inscrutable expression which never failed to make him feel uncomfortable, unsure of what she was getting at.

'Yes,' he said bluntly, 'it would be too late, much too late.'

'Because you can change your mind about goods before they've been paid for, but not after?'

He came and sat on the side of the bed.

'Now look here, Clemmie—Clementine,' he said, 'what's all this about? Have you changed your mind? Is that what you're wanting to tell me?'

She narrowed her eyes between their lids. Her mouth smiled mockingly. To him she never looked more alluring, even in her loveliest clothes and her diamonds, than as she was now, her face only lightly made up, her hair still ruffled from her sleeping-net, a lace nightdress barely covered by a transparent wrap.

'Would you mind very much?' she teased him.

'I'd kill with my bare hands any man who tried to take you from me,' he said, his lower lip jutting out, his voice a threatening growl.

She laughed.

'Nobody *takes* me, darling,' she said softly. 'I give myself if I want to.'

He glared at her.

'And do you want to?' he demanded.

'Maybe,' she said, nodding her head and laughing a little.

His hands came down with a cruel strength on her shoulders.

'What's all this? Is there another man? Eh? Eh? I'll have the truth if I have to shake the life out of you.'

She laughed. Though he was fifty-seven, he was strong and virile and with none of the inhibitions of her own social class. It was exciting to know that he could, and might, actually kill her.

'I shouldn't be much good to you dead,' she told him.

'I'd rather see you dead than in another man's arms.'

'Darling, I'd never be so careless as to let you see me,' she mocked him.

'I warn you. You're driving me mad, and when I get mad, things happen. I could easily kill you, Clementine. I could throttle you with these hands' – taking them from her shoulders and putting them round her throat. They were large, powerful hands for all their stubby fingers, and she knew he spoke the plain truth.

She put her own hands over his, not pulling them away but pressing them against her.

'I know you could, you brute,' she said with a laugh that was infinitely provocative.

'Is there a man? Tell me. Is there a man you want?'

'If you'll let me breathe, I might tell you,' she said, and he took his hands away but sat leaning over her still, glowering down at her.

'Now,' he said, 'is there a man you want?'

'Yes, there is,' she said sweetly, and her eyes mocked him.

She knew she was playing with fire, but it was life to her only if she were living it dangerously. This was part of the fun of being married to a man like Joseph Bloggett, part master, part slave, strings in her hands for her to pull this way or that.

His eyes bulged. The veins stood out on his forehead.

'Tell me,' he said. 'Tell me.'

She laughed again, softly, tantalizingly.

'Then lock the door, my sweet,' she said in a voice he had come to recognize.

'Clem!' he said hoarsely, and bent down to kiss her.

She avoided his lips.

'Lock the door first, darling,' she said. 'Husbands aren't the only ones that come in uninvited.'

One of the surprising things she had forced him to learn was that making love was not a thing to be indulged in only at night and in the dark. The whole business, with Clementine, was so different from any previous conception and practice of love-making that she had made him feel young again, an ignorant and curious boy almost. At first he had told her that it didn't seem quite right somehow, but she had laughed, told him he had a common mind, and shown him new delights into which, after that first reluctance and surprise, he had thrown himself with a vigour as eager as it had been unexpected. In marrying her he had acquired something he had never dreamed of, never even known to exist. She was not only something superlatively beautiful to show off and to dress up and to bejewel; she was an amazing and ecstatic delight, and the love he had felt for her when he married her, a love which was more the desire to possess, had become an overmastering passion.

When he had left her, and she lay languid and serene with half her letters still unopened, the telephone bell beside her bed called her reluctant attention to the rest of the world.

It was, as she had guessed it would be, the voice of Garry Prosper, slightly hectoring.

'What's the idea?' he asked.

'What idea?'

'You were going to ride with me.'

'Oh yes. Yes, I remember,' she said lazily.

'Why didn't you come?'

'I was busy,' she said.

'Doing what?' he asked scornfully.

'As a matter of fact, my husband was making love to me.'

'You're disgusting.'

'Am I? Perhaps.'

'I suppose if it had been I who was making love to you, you'd tell the world of that too?' he demanded furiously.

'Too many suppositions on too slight foundations.'

'Are you lunching with me?'

'No, I don't think so. I'm deliciously tired. You know how one feels?'

'You're filthily disgusting, Clementine.'

'Do you really think so? Anyway, I'm having lunch brought to me here.'

'May I join you then?'

She gurgled with laughter.

'Darling, I'm in bed,' she told him. 'I don't think Joseph would like that.'

'You're impossible,' and she heard the furious click of his receiver, put back her own and lay like a cat, curled and purring. She knew he would ring again in a few minutes. Garry Prosper was in love with her and furious with himself for being so. He could not leave her alone, though she felt that by this time he surely knew he would never get her. His pride was pricked constantly by the knowledge that her middle-aged husband had something he could not acquire, though he had had women by the dozen and could have them again.

For a very short time she had wondered if he would succeed in seducing her. He was attractive in a special way, not only because of his clever tongue and quick mind, not only because his experience with women gave him power, but also because of that indefinable likeness he had to Piers, a sudden turn of the head, a way of looking at her, his laugh, something crinkly about his smile. These things could catch at her heart and set her reeling as if from a blow. She resented that power he had over her, but she had never told him of it. If she had done, she knew he would exaggerate that intangible resemblance until her immortal longing for Piers might send her into Garry Prosper's arms.

Piers, her beloved, the unforgettable.

Nearly always after she had lost herself in shared physical experience with Joseph she had this sick grief for him, a hatred of herself because for that brief time she had forgotten him. She could not live with the dead. Gramp had told her that when he saw that her first grief, instead of being assuaged by time, was still gnawing at the very core of her being. But neither could she live without her dead, for he was always with her, gently mocking her, at other times seeming to share with her her own mockery of herself. Dressed in her finery, overloaded with jewels, ostentatious and, she knew, a little vulgar, she would turn her head suddenly, as if she had heard his very laugh, would see his face.

It was that constant reminder of him which made it impossible for her to do what she knew would be more prudent, and refuse Garry's constant invitations – invitations which could usually be accepted without Joseph's knowledge. Joseph was a creature of habit, and even though he had ostensibly retired from business he was incapable of doing so in actual fact. His secretary, Richard Bent, travelled and lived with them, an earnest, sober young man who could efface himself so completely as not to appear to be there at all. Every morning, and all the morning, he and Joseph would be shut up together in a room kept as an office, and it was very rare indeed for the financier to be seen outside that room until after lunch. Lunch was served to the two men there, and though they might be busy until two or half past, work was then finished for the day and only on matters of the greatest urgency would Bent consult or interrupt his employer for the rest of the day.

Clementine wondered what it was that had made Joseph break that almost inviolable rule and come to her room that morning. It was amusing to think it might have been an overwhelming desire to see and speak to her; it was more reasonable to think that he came with a less pleasurable purpose; to find out, for instance, how she was going to spend her morning, and with whom. He might have had a hint from some source of her arrangement to ride with Garry Prosper. She had ridden with him several mornings lately, had lunched with him openly at one of the smart restaurants.

It was annoying to think of him getting suspicious and perhaps having her watched, and yet the idea amused her. It was something new, anyway, and some perverse devil in her, born of her resentment against Joseph for taking Piers' rightful place, enjoyed the prospect of being able to torment and bait him.

Garry came through again.

'We got cut off,' he said, and she laughed.

'Well, what is it this time?' she asked.

'Are you meeting me for lunch?'

'No, I don't think so,' she said.

'Why not?'

'Because you bore me,' she told him mendaciously.

'Sorry,' he said grimly. 'Have you found someone more entertaining?'

'Someone whose company I prefer,' she amended.

'Very well. I'm glad you're so well escorted,' he said with the pettishness of a spoilt child, and she laughed again and rang off.

She lunched quite alone at one of the restaurants they frequented together and he saw her there, stared at her for a moment incredulously and then sauntered across to her.

'Don't tell me you've been what I think the young call being stood up?' he asked, pleased at the thought.

'Not at all, I told you I was lunching in company which I prefer at the moment to yours—my own,' said Clementine sweetly.

Out of the tail of her eye she had caught sight of Richard Bent's inconspicuous, sandy head. She was both annoyed and delighted that

Joseph had sent his faithful hound to follow her. She had either seen, or imagined she had seen, the secretary at a distance soon after she had left the villa, but had not been sure until she saw him through the window near which she was sitting. Poor Bent! she hoped he was going to get his lunch all right.

Garry Prosper stared at her, his colour rising.

'Do you mean that?' he asked angrily.

'Entirely. It's so restful,' she said, and he marched away in high dudgeon.

She paid her bill and sauntered out, made sure that little Bent was following her and proceeded to lead him a rare dance, in and out of the shops, along the front, half-way back to the villa and down to the sea again. She met a number of people to whom she stopped to gossip but accepted none of the invitations to join them, and eventually she took a taxi for a drive round Cannes and then back to the villa.

A second taxi deposited the secretary at the side door which the servants used.

Clementine strolled into the warm, glass-walled winter garden where, as she had expected, she found her husband. He was reading the latest English newspapers, but put them down when he saw her.

'Been for a walk, my dear?' he asked.

'Yes,' she said, and then, 'Joseph, I do hope you've seen that Bent gets his lunch,' in a solicitous tone.

'Bent? Why shouldn't he get his lunch?' he asked, but she could see that he was a little disturbed.

'Because he hasn't been able to do so since I went out—unless, of course, he had it before then?'

'What are you talking about? And what's all this sudden interest in Bent?' he asked, attempting to bluster.

She sat down in one of the chairs near him. For once she felt he had enough on hand without being reprimanded for not rising when she came into the room.

'Don't you mean what is his interest in me?' she asked. 'Look, Joseph. If you want to know what I'm doing, where I'm going and who I'm meeting, why not ask me? It would be so much easier, and I'm sure it must have been very irritating to you to be so long without Bent.'

He did not know what to say, but kept shuffling and sorting the newspapers. He liked directness himself and was fond of referring to himself as John Blunt, but this attack of Clem's was a bit too direct, straight from the shoulder.

'Sorry,' he muttered at last.

'May I take that as an apology?'

'Yes, I suppose so. Clem, I—I arranged that with Bent yesterday, before—before this morning'

'I'm glad of that, anyway,' she said crisply.

'He had some other jobs to do for me, and I'd clean forgotten what I'd told him to do until it was too late.'

'It's a very delightful position for me to be in, Joseph, with one of the servants told off to watch and follow me and report to you on my activities.'

'Bent isn't exactly a servant, dear.'

'To me he is. What possible reason could you have had for doing such a thing?'

'I'm an old fool, and a jealous old fool, and it's still hard for me to believe that—that you're really mine,' he said almost humbly. 'To be frank with you, it's that fellow Prosper. I know you've been seeing a lot of him and—he's young—'

'Joseph, he's forty-five!' she said.

'Well, even forty-five's young compared with me, and I'm not such a fool as not to know that I'm not attractive to a woman like you except for what I can buy you.'

For a moment she was silent. He made her angry. She was still torn between humiliation and amusement at the morning's escapade and the dance she had led poor, helpless Bent.

'Oh, Joseph, how right you are to call yourself a fool! Nobody with any sense quarrels with their bread and butter, and you're so much more to me than bread and butter. You're cake, rich cake, with lashings of cream and icing and so on. You don't think I'd risk losing that for any number of Garry Prospers, do you?'

He gave her a doglike look of fidelity and appeal.

'Is that how you feel about me, darling? No more than that?'

She gave him a long, lovely look.

'Don't you know? Even yet?' she asked him.

He looked into her eyes and at last gave a deep sigh.

'I'm such an old fool that I'm downright afraid to believe you,' he said.

She rose and kissed the top of his head. It was bald and pink. Seeing him as he was now, she was surprised and rather disgusted with herself that he could give her even brief rapture.

'All right. You're forgiven, so long as it doesn't happen again. I'm going to change my dress. Then you can take me out somewhere amusing and tonight we'll have a little flutter at the tables.'

Joseph was no gambler either with cards or the roulette wheel, though he had played for high stakes in other ways when he was making his fortune. It amused him, however, to watch Clementine play. She was so unmoved, so completely mistress of herself. No one could ever tell from her face whether she was winning or losing. At such times he was immensely proud of her, told himself that she was a thoroughbred if ever there was one, and she was his, his own property, bought *and* paid for, by gum!

But he didn't begrudge a penny of what she cost him. She was worth it, and he'd got far more than he'd bargained for.

No other man was going to poach on his preserves, though, and at even the thought of Garry Prosper his jaw jutted out in its bulldog fashion and his little eyes grew smaller until the pupils were mere pinheads.

# Chapter Fourteen

Spring in Paris! Spring in the boulevards with their trees and their flowers, spring in the shops with new frocks, new hats. Spring, too, in Montmartre, with the flowers, the fruit, even the cheeses and the delicatessen taking on new, brave colours, the sun filtering through the narrow streets and touching the cobbles till they seemed tipped with gold. Spring in hearts and bodies reaching up for the warmth again, spring in the reappearance of striped awnings over the tables of the pavement cafés.

And spring in the heart of Diana, caring for the place that had become home for her, taking her basket to the market where she could now drive as shrewd a bargain as any. At first she had avoided going anywhere within range of old Rosine, terrified of any retribution which Madame Gante might levy on her, though Paul had told her again and again that, far from seeking her out, both these women would be only too anxious not to be discovered by her.

'It's the money I owe for staying there all that time,' she said anxiously.

'That's nothing to her fear of the law,' said Paul. 'She doesn't know that you haven't an idea where this place is that she took you to. I wouldn't mind betting that if you go along there in a few weeks you'll find that both old Rosine and the hag herself have departed,' which she found was quite true.

The *estaminet* was in different hands, and someone else was in charge of Rosine's stall.

But Diana never quite forgot the horror and the fear, and she would wake sometimes in the night, wet through with perspiration after a dream in which she was again trying to escape from that house. Only

191

in Paul's arms could she find comfort again, just as all other of life's new and wonderful joys culminated there.

To outward seeming she no longer cared whether people knew she was not his wife. She felt secure in the world they had created for themselves. They could not belong more utterly to each other. Deep within herself she longed to be his legally as well as every other way, but he told her he was doing everything in his power to get his freedom and with that she tried to be as content as she seemed.

Paul, too, was happy. There could be no mistake about that. It showed, too, in his work, which had become livelier and more colourful, though all the artists they knew were sharing the same depression of their profession.

Paul, who could produce gay little studies of Parisian life, was more fortunate than the more serious artists, since his little pictures were such as the tourists would buy, especially the wealthy Americans looking for souvenirs. Paul was 'in' with some of the agencies which organized sight-seeing tours, and his was one of the studios which tourists were brought to visit. He had to pay a large commission to the conductor of the tours on sales which he made through such visits, but as he could not otherwise have found such a ready market, he had to put up with it. Diana was a great asset on these occasions, since she could talk to them in English.

These visitors had fallen off during the winter, but now, with Easter just ahead and the long, light days to come, things would look up again and Diana sang at her work.

She came staggering in one morning with a heavy basket and a bunch of primroses perched on top, to find Paul working with a model, a thing he had not done for a long time. He had become something of a specialist in his outdoor sketches.

The model was a girl she had not seen before, small, fair as a lily and with something lily-like in her pale, fragile delicacy. He was making studies of her arms and hands, the rest of her modestly covered by a long, old-fashioned robe of dark blue which was one of the studio 'props'. The model throne was facing the door, and the girl lifted her eyes without moving her body, to glance at Diana as she came in.

'It's wonderful out,' Diana said to Paul, filled with a sudden unreasonable desire to announce herself.

'Yes,' was all he said, absently, and still staring at his model – and not only at the hands and arms, Diana felt.

She stood just within the doorway, setting the basket down slowly, fascinated in spite of herself by the sight of the small, pale girl, so different from the type which suited Paul's love of colour.

There was hardly any colour about this girl. Her hair was almost silver, her eyes a pale, washed blue, her skin creamy, her mouth coral, the fingernails of her small, perfect hands painted with the merest rose-flush of colour. Against the dark blue velvet robe, she looked almost transparent.

Diana looked from the girl to Paul. He was painting again, absorbed, eager, his face wearing the look which she knew meant that his work was going well. After that brief monosyllable he took no notice of her, and she picked up the basket again and went across to the screened 'kitchen' which she had transformed with gay yellow paint and a series of bright blue tins and jars.

When Paul was working in the studio she prepared their lunch and called him when it was ready. This morning, since it was their usual lunch hour, she made an omelette, filled with tiny button mushrooms and chives, and carried it out, creamy and piping hot, to the end of the long table. On the blue-checked cloth she had set a brown honey-jar filled with the primroses and beside it the carafe of *vin ordinaire* which glowed deep red. The table was an unconscious challenge to the pale, colourless girl on the model stand.

'Ready, *chéri*,' she called out gaily.

Paul went on working and she called to him again, and then, as he still did not answer, went close to him.

'Lunch, Paul, and it's an omelette,' she said.

He lifted his brush with a little sound of irritation.

'I can't leave this now,' he said.

'But Paul, it will spoil!'

'Never mind. Don't bother me now.'

'But—'

He turned to her and spoke in a tone he had never used to her before.

'Go away, Diane. Don't bother me, I told you,' and he went on with his work.

Something impelled her to look at the model. For a brief instant she saw, or perhaps only imagined she saw, a look of triumph in the pale eyes, but the next moment it was gone and there was no expression at all in their translucent blue.

Swallowing her annoyance, she walked back to the table and in silence ate her own lunch, knowing that by the time Paul came his omelette would be uneatable.

She did not mind the work of preparing another for him, but money was not plentiful just now, and she had to use considerable ingenuity to produce palatable meals and satisfy Paul's big appetite. Wasting the omelette meant wasting three eggs, to say nothing of the mushrooms which she had been so delighted to get, and she had put almost the whole of the small quantity in Paul's omelette, keeping only a taste for herself.

He worked on without speaking again until, half an hour later, the girl on the model stand spoke.

'I am tired,' she said, her voice as colourless as the rest of her, a mere thread of sound.

At once Paul threw down his brushes.

'I am sorry, Victoire. Forgive me. I am so happy working with such loveliness that I have forgotten,' and crossed to the model stand to help her as she rose from the chair. With one hand carefully holding the blue robe about her, she gave him the other one and smiled a small, enigmatical smile.

'I will come again,' she said.

'Of course,' said Paul fervently, and watched her as she trailed across to the screened corner to dress.

Diana said nothing until the girl had gone. Then she made her voice even and pleasant.

'I'm afraid your omelette is spoilt and uneatable now, Paul, but I'll make you another.'

He was contrite at once, coming to her and putting his arm about her shoulders and kissing her cheek with little nibbling movements of his lips.

'I'm so sorry, *petite*,' he said. 'Can you forgive me? But I know you always do. Wasn't she ravishing? The skin texture—oh, but impossible, impossible!' running his fingers through his thick, dark hair till it stood up in fantastic points. 'Like a pearl! And a perfect model, never moving and not wanting to talk. No, don't make another omelette for me, *chérie*. I will eat this.'

He enjoyed his food so much as a rule that it was obvious his new model, with skin like a pearl, was greatly in occupation of his mind.

'Where did you find her?' asked Diana, trying not to be silly over a mere model.

'Remi found her, but she's no use to him because she won't model for the figure, only face, arms and hands. I saw her in his studio the other day and persuaded her to come to me, though I shall never get those exquisite tints,' with another gesture of despair.

'She's not your usual style,' said Diana. 'Not enough colour.'

'No, but one gets tired of the reds and blues and all the orange and brown and green. Victoire is just all the whites there are, white and cream and silver—exquisite! Did you not think so, Diane?'

Suddenly it dawned on him that she was having to make an effort to talk and listen about Victoire, and with one of his great laughs he swept her into his arms and began to kiss her, talking to her in extravagant love-language, teasing her until the very memory of the pale Victoire seemed to have vanished from the studio.

Later, happy and at peace again, she stood before the canvas on which he had been working and looked at the pearl-like arms of the girl, the slender fingers with their pink tips. It was fairly good, but it lacked Paul's distinctive style. Flesh tints like these had to be too restrained, too delicate for his strong colour work.

He came behind her and laid an arm about her shoulders and drew her head back against him, looking at the canvas with her.

'Shocking,' he said at last.

'Oh no, Paul, not as bad as that,' she protested, 'but it isn't you.'

'It was just a fancy. How very clever I thought I was! Remi's crazy to paint a nude of her, but if all her skin is like that, not even he will make much of it—not that she'll agree to pose for him.'

'If she's a model she'll have to, won't she?'

'She's not entirely a model. She has money of her own and does not need to work, but she sits sometimes, just for hands and face. Remi is mad about her.'

'You sound a bit mad yourself,' said Diana dryly.

He laughed and kissed the top of her head.

'Not mad enough to think I can paint her,' he said, and leaned forward and slashed a brushful of paint across the pale painted arms, to Diana's horror.

'Oh, Paul, all that work!'

'*And* an omelette,' he said. 'I shan't try it again.'

'You might get those tints next time.'

He shook his head.

'Not because of the tints, *chérie*, but because of you.'

'Because of me, Paul?'

'Yes. You thought I perhaps did not know, but I do. You didn't like me to have another model, even for the arms. So—I shall not have another model. I have my model, my own, and so beautiful, here.'

It had taken a good deal of persuasion on his part to get Diana to sit for him, but she had done so rather than have Susette, whom Paul rudely called *vieille vache*, flaunting her charms on the model stand.

Since she had come into the full knowledge and satisfaction of her womanhood, Diana had lost the slight awkwardness of her girlhood, had matured in body as well as in mind without losing any of the young, eager grace. He had made many studies of her, and laughed at her because she insisted that they be kept turned face to the wall when there were any visitors in the studio.

She crushed down the slight feeling of guilt at his giving up using Victoire as a model merely because she did not like it, but as the days went by and nothing further was said about her, she accepted the position and was glad she had not made more fuss.

But the little episode had raised in her mind again the longing to be Paul's wife, and she gathered up courage to speak about it.

'Do you mind so much?' he asked her, frowning a little.

'I know you don't feel that it does, but it's perhaps because I'm a woman, or perhaps because I'm English, that I feel different about it. Have you seen Sally lately, Paul? Has she started proceedings?'

'These things take a long time, sweet,' he said casually, 'and as you know, there is a big hold-up in your English courts and a long time to wait.'

'You don't think that if you went to England, to London, to see a lawyer there, Paul—'

'It is not in our hands, darling, but in Sally's,' he said. 'Have patience a little longer, *ma mie*. It will come right in the end.'

She had to appear to be satisfied. She could not keep 'at him' and, as he said, in what way would things alter for them by marrying? They could not love each other more, and they needed no legal bond to keep them tied together when all they desired was to remain close to each other.

A few days later Paul strolled into Sally's discreet little shop in the Rue de Rivoli, a shop in whose windows was displayed one grey gown, and one grey hat with a brilliant blue ostrich feather sweeping from its brim.

Sally herself was in the shop.

'Why, Paul!' she cried in pleased surprise. 'What an honour indeed!'

'I thought perhaps you'd lunch with me,' he said.

'Why not? But somewhere *chic*. I do not now eat in miserable little places. I am arriving, *mon cher*. People begin to know Sallee l'Anglaise.'

'So long as it isn't too expensive. I am not arriving,' he said with a touch of bitterness.

'Your little pictures sell. I have seen them in very smart shops.'

'Oh those, yes,' he said, dismissing them with a shrug.

He was thinking of Victoire's pearl tints, so fascinating to his artist's eye, so unattainable to his artist's hand. He had abandoned lightly his attempt to transfer that wonder of flesh and blood to canvas, but he had done so at the moment of his dissatisfaction at himself. It had been easy then to promise Diana he would not use Victoire as his model again. Now, after a few days, the impulse to try again had returned and he was finding no savour in his other work which had to be done so that they could live.

'What is it, Paul?' asked Sally. 'What's gone wrong in the love nest?'

'Nothing,' he said, and was silent again for a moment-Then he burst into rapid, almost incoherent speech.

'It's myself I'm sick of, my limitations, the fact that I want to do so much and yet what do I achieve? Pretty little pictures to give away like calendars, Christmas card designs which could be reproduced by the three-colour printing process! You say you are arriving and they call you Sally l'Anglaise. Well, it seems I have already arrived where I am going to get, and these little pretty nothings, they are called Paul Esterres!'

She nodded, understanding. Perhaps she understood him better than anybody else ever had or ever would, the complex nature that could make him tender as a loving woman and cruel as a devil, exalted to the heavens one minute and in the lowest depths the next. She had found him impossible to live with. She liked him a great deal more now that she did not live with him.

'What does Diane feel about the pretty nothings?' she asked.

His fingers burrowed savagely into a roll of bread, tore it apart.

'She thinks everything I do is wonderful,' he growled.

'Well, isn't that what a man likes?'

'She doesn't understand that I aim at other things, that I'm not content just doing *calendars*,' with scornful emphasis.

'Poor Diane,' said Sally quietly.

'Why do you say that? She's perfectly happy,' he said, instantly on the defence.

'Is she? Paul, do you know why I haven't divorced you?'

'I thought one had to wait one's turn.'

'That, yes, but I have not hurried.'

'Why not?'

'Because I can't make up my mind that it would be good for you to marry Diane—good for her, I mean. It isn't comfortable being married to you, Paul.'

'She wants it. She's different from you. She doesn't like the way we live. She's *bien élevée.*'

'I ought to feel insulted,' she said. 'I also was *bien élevée*, finishing school and all that.'

'Yes, but you're by nature free, just as I am. Diane isn't. She likes to be tied.'

'Poor Diane,' she said again, thoughtfully, and then, 'Paul, if I set you free, would you marry her?'

'But of course!'

'You give me your word?'

'Of course,' he said again, but with a frown. It was unlike Sally to be insistent and make demands.

'All right. Then I'll tell you. It's come through.'

'What has?'

'The divorce. Last week. I flew to London and back. It's simple, though I admit that it felt very odd to be standing there, in an English court of law, looking very virtuous about having left you when I discovered that you had been sleeping with Veronique. Remember Veronique?' with her lovely red head cocked on one side, her eyes regarding him merrily.

'Good heavens! Veronique. So you pulled her out of the bag, did you? Nice of you not to bring Diana into it.'

'I shouldn't have liked doing that.'

'How did you manage Veronique?'

He was tickled at the idea. The affair of Veronique had been so slight, just one of those things, and Sally, then living with him, had laughed at it.

Sally tapped her handbag.

'That manages most of the Veroniques,' she said.

He frowned.

'You mean you had to pay her to be the—what is it you call it? I don't know the name for it.'

'The co-respondent, your partner in sin,' said Sally with a laugh. 'It didn't cost me much. Poor old Veronique is down on her luck. She was glad to pick up a few dishonest francs.'

'She doesn't think I'm going to make an honest woman of her, does she?'

'Heavens, no! Nothing like that. I advised her to use it on going somewhere to have her figure restored so that she can model again, but I expect it'll go down her throat. Poor Veronique.'

Paul, thinking of Veronique, felt he was recalling someone else's life rather than an episode in his own. Everything had been so different since the coming of Diana, and although he censured himself, he could not help a feeling of faint regret for the old haphazard existence with people like Veronique and like Sally, who expected so little of one and could always be relied on to understand.

His marriage to Sally had been the affair of youthful exuberance and ignorance, soon to be regretted, and when she left him there was no scene, no angry quarrel or recrimination. She had just told him she was tired of married life and preferred to go her own way, and he had shrugged his shoulders and turned back to his work. A week later they had met over a drink, sitting companionably at a bar, and for a short time they had met like that frequently, gradually drifting apart until she surprised him by walking into the studio.

When they parted after this lunch together she held out her hand to him.

'Well, I suppose this is the end?' she said.

'You don't really mind, do you?'

'No. Do you?'

'No.'

'And you'll marry Diane?'

'Yes.'

But he found he could not immediately go back to her with the news he knew she was waiting anxiously to hear. What a nuisance this marriage business could be! He and Diana were entirely happy – at least, he was – but as soon as they were legally married, each would feel the bonds, and it is an essential part of human nature to resist any restraint as soon as it is known to exist.

Instead of going back to Montmartre, he walked for a little while in the gardens of the Louvre, and then was drawn irresistibly inside the building, to stand as he had stood so many times before the Mona Lisa with her baffling, seductive smile, the prototype of all women, unknowable, unpredictable.

Where had he seen that very smile? On a woman's face? On the face of Victoire! Busy as he had been painting her exquisite hands and arms he found he remembered what he had scarcely noticed – her face, with its pale purity, its other worldliness and, yes, the smile of La Giaconda!

He had promised Diane that he would not use a model again, a rather foolish promise for a painter to make and one which he did not imagine he would keep forever, but that did not mean that he must not even feast his eyes and feed his imagination on that elusive pearliness which was enough to drive any artist mad.

She had told him where she lived, and he remembered it. It was in a small street leading off the Rue Royale and probably expensive, for she had never given any impression of being in any need of money. She allowed artists to paint her because it amused her, and also because she was vain as a peacock.

He found the place where she lived, a small apartment above a shop, reached by a noisy flight of stairs which terminated at a white-painted door bearing her name on a framed card:

Mlle. Victoire Laimant

He had not known her name until then. He smiled at the thought that it was singularly inapt. Anything less loving than Victoire appeared to be was hard to conceive.

An elderly maid in old-fashioned black, with white cap and frilled white apron, opened the door to him. Behind her he glimpsed a narrow passage, panelled in polished oak and softly carpeted, several doors opening on it but now closed.

'Monsieur?' asked the maid, as Paul stood for a moment adjusting his mind to the change from the rough uncovered staircase to the vista beyond the door.

'Mademoiselle Victoire? Will she receive me?' he asked in a formal tone. 'Monsieur Paul Esterre.'

'I will enquire, if Monsieur will wait,' and she admitted him to the passage and rustled starchily away, firmly closing behind her a door which she had opened farther along.

She returned a few moments later.

'Mademoiselle will receive you, Monsieur. Please come,' she said and conducted him into a surprisingly large room where half a dozen people were scattered about, most of them men, Victoire herself the centrepiece, seated in a high-backed chair, her utter lack of colour accentuated by the perfectly plain grey dress, high-necked and long-sleeved, which she wore. There was only one note of colour about her – an immense ruby which she wore on one hand and which drew, as possibly it was intended to do, the eye of the beholder to her perfect hands.

Paul bowed profoundly, and she smiled faintly and held out her hand to him. He had to resist the absurd impulse to raise it to his lips. The setting and her gesture seemed irresistibly to invite it.

'Monsieur Esterre, an unexpected pleasure,' she said in her light, clear voice, thin and cold as water. 'May I present Monsieur Paul Esterre, the artist?' naming one after another of the little company, two of them well-known writers, one a sculptor of some repute, none of them of the type which would, or could, live the haphazard, hand-to-mouth existence of him and his fellow artists.

Paul was entertained and amused at himself for behaving exactly as they did, drinking coffee and cognac from fragile little cups and discoursing learnedly on various subjects, on some of which he had expert knowledge, on others none at all.

It was Victoire herself who intrigued him. He felt that she held a string tied to each of them, and was interested to see the way they behaved, giving now one string a tiny jerk, now another. There was no need for her to say anything. It was sufficient that she should sit there and look as she did – unique, exquisite, baffling.

One by one the guests drifted away, but Paul felt she still held his string in her hand, willing him to stay, and when the last of them had gone, leaving him alone with her, she gave him a smile that was infinitesimally warmer and more personal.

'Why did you come, Paul?' she asked him.

'I don't know. You tell me, Victoire.'

'But how should I know? Not, I think, to paint me again?'

'No.'

'You are not going to paint me again?'

'No.'

'Why not?'

How could he tell this remote, ethereal creature that he had had to promise Diane not to do so?

He shrugged his shoulders, took her hand and looked at it.

'You are too exquisite,' he said. 'It is not in my power.'

'Monsieur is too modest,' she told him, and he caught the faint mockery in her voice, saw its shadow in her strange, light eyes.

He laughed.

It was the first loud sound that had penetrated the room since he had entered it. It seemed to splinter something brittle in the atmosphere, make it less rare and more human.

'It's the first time I have been accused of that,' he said. 'Surely other artists have despaired of being able to paint you, too?'

'Am I then so extraordinary, Monsieur?'

'You called me Paul just now.'

'Am I then so extraordinary, Paul?'

'You're fascinating because you're so different. The way you dress, this jewel, the room, your friends, even your maid—everything. Who are you? What are you, Victoire?'

'You find me different, Paul? Yes, perhaps I am different. I have come back from the grave—or rather, I have only just been born. I have spent all my life, but all my life from the very beginning, out of the world. I was born in a convent in the Swiss Alps, and my mother, who died at my birth, wanted me dedicated to the religious life. I never knew anything else, never knew there was anything else, until I was grown up and old enough to take my vows. The Mother Superior was wise, and though I was so sure that I wanted to embrace the life of a religious, she sent me with two of the lay sisters to stay in Lucerne for six months. I was to see everything, to know everything. One thing I knew then was that the religious life was not for me, and when we returned to the convent and I told the Mother Superior, she sent me away with one of the lay sisters who wanted to go with me as my maid.'

'Your maid?'

'Yes, Lucine. We came to Paris after travelling about in France, Italy, Spain. I liked Paris best and we took this little *apartement* and I think perhaps I shall remain in Paris. I am French. My father was a soldier in the First Great War, and he went into the Alps to die of a disease they had not been able to cure, so it was there I was born.'

Her voice right through the recital had not varied in its thin clarity, in the lack of emotion which gave everything about her that strange effect of being translucent, unsubstantial. He found it both attractive and repellent. Had she been right, he wondered, not to adopt the religious life? Surely she was of the stuff of which nuns are made?

And yet she had let Remi paint her, had sat for him, Paul, and for other artists, and he remembered that in his studio she had looked at herself in his long mirror, and that on her face had been that strangely exciting, unfathomable smile of the Mona Lisa.

'And now? What do you want of life?' he asked.

She spread out her lovely hands.

'I don't know. What is there to have, Paul?'

'You have riches already?'

'Not riches, but enough.'

'Then—love?'

'I don't know. I don't like to talk of it.'

'Nor to think of it, Victoire?'

She let her eyes rest on his for a moment. He knew that, deny it as she might, she did think of it. And in connection with him? That thought was vaguely disturbing.

'Nor to think of it, Paul,' she said, and rose from her chair and rang a little silver bell. He thought the sound partook of her own quality, clear, cold and yet oddly compelling.

'May I come again, Victoire?' he asked, rising as well.

'If you wish. And if you wish to paint me again, my arms, my hands, my face perhaps, I am willing.'

'Thank you,' he said. How could he refuse what was obviously meant as an honour paid to him?

'Is there a good light here, Paul?' she asked, moving across to one of the long windows and drawing back further the curtains of grey brocaded satin.

'You mean I could paint you here?'

'I should prefer that. At first it amused me, or I thought it would amuse me, to be with the artists in the Latin quarter, but it does not amuse me,' she said regally.

Lucine had entered the room and stood by the open door, waiting for him to go.

'I should be honoured,' said Paul in a low voice.

'Then—tomorrow?'

'Earlier than this because of the light.'

She smiled.

'I always rise at six,' she said in her cool voice.

Paul laughed.

'I shan't be here quite as early as that, I am afraid.'

'Lucine and I keep our old customs,' she said, and he knew she was letting the maid know that he had been told her strange story, and Lucine's part in it.

'Then—nine o'clock?'

'We shall be quite ready for you,' said Victoire gravely.

Once outside, and so near the heart of Paris with its crowds, its gaiety, a new life beginning as the spring day began to die, he could almost have believed that fantastic visit a dream. Nothing about it now seemed real and possible and yet, looking up, he caught a glimpse of the grey-curtained windows and, as he looked, fancied that one of them moved.

He realized that he had committed himself to being there again, to doing the very thing he had promised Diane he would not do.

But what right had she to exact any such promise from him? It was not as if he were painting a nude of Victoire, though even then she had no right to object. It was part of his work.

The mere thought of Victoire posing for him like that sent the blood hammering through his veins. How exquisite she must be. He imagined her curled up in a great open shell, or standing against a background of black velvet, or floating in blue, moonlit water.

He forced his mind away. Victoire would never pose for him or any man like that; nor, he told himself, did he want her to do so. He wanted her to remain as she was: remote, mysterious, unknowable.

# Chapter Fifteen

'You are going out again today, Paul?'

He frowned at the faint touch of criticism in Diana's voice, and became busy with the fastenings of the portfolio he was carrying.

'It is necessary, *ma chére.*'

'The light is good. If you could finish the market pieces I could take them to Gavel's tomorrow.'

'I promised to let Macaire have the studies for the frieze today,' he said, indicating the portfolio.

'Let me take the studies whilst you make the most of the light and finish the other things.'

'Thank you, *petite*, but I think it is better that I take the studies myself. I will finish the market pieces tomorrow perhaps.'

'Tomorrow the light may be wrong.'

'*Chérie*, I know what is best,' said Paul, kissed her with the calm kiss of the long-married, and left the studio.

She stood there for a full minute, trying not to feel there was something wrong, trying not to resent things being as they were, trying to make herself believe that Paul really did know best and was doing all that was possible.

The summer had come and gone, but it had not been a good one. Either something vital had gone out of Paul's work or else the taste of former buyers of his 'Life in Paris' series had changed.

Diana herself, unknown to Paul, had been to Gavel's, had seen Monsieur Gavel himself, taking with her some of the gay, colourful little pictures which Paul had thrown aside as not worth offering him.

'I am sorry, Madame,' he told her, and she felt his regret was genuine, 'but there is something—something one feels but cannot describe. You see it yourself? There is not the *joie de vivre* that made them live. They are good, but not good enough. Paul should not try to alter his style if he wishes to live by his painting.'

'But has he altered it, Monsieur Gavel?' asked Diana, her head on one side, trying to see Paul's work with the eyes of a man like Gavel but knowing she could not do so. To her eyes these little pictures looked exactly the same as they had always looked. Yet why did not people buy them? Why would Monsieur Gavel himself not buy them as he had once done, but if he accepted them, would do so only on a commission basis?

And now, during the last few weeks, Paul seemed to have lost heart, for he spent more and more time away from the studio, giving her only vague ideas of where he was and what he had been doing, and a faint unease had sprung up in her mind.

She never even asked now whether anything had yet been done to set him free to marry her. She was afraid to speak of that. The last time she had done so Paul had almost snapped at her, though afterwards he had been extravagant in his apologies and had gone out and bought her an armful of flowers out of season and a huge box of chocolates, and it had been quite beyond her power to tell him that she needed desperately, for their ordinary household essentials, the money he had spent on those presents to her.

That was one of the most worrying things just now – money. He had always been a gay spender, generous and open-handed, not only to her but to all his friends, and he teased her about what he called her parsimony and what she considered the merest common sense.

'Let me have it to put by, Paul,' she would beg him when he had made some good business deal over a picture. 'I can make it last such a long time that way, much longer than you ever will.'

'When that is gone I can earn more,' he would reply airily. 'Come along, *chérie*. First I am going to buy you a new dress and then we will go to all the newest and gayest places to show it off.'

'But, Paul, I don't need a new dress,' she might protest.

She had learnt, however, that that was a dangerous line to take with him. Part of his love for her lay in his pride of her, in liking to show her off, in knowing that other men envied him his possession of her, and in her deep, unchanging love for him she was not able to assess the value of this pride nor realize what danger lay in its mitigation, though she humoured him to the extent of letting him spend at least some of that precious money on her.

She liked it best when she could persuade him to spend it on taking her out of Paris even just for a day. Living in a city, especially in the crowded Latin quarter, she felt stifled, and longed for green fields and hedgerows. Now and then he would humour her and after a few days away from Paris, with Diana a completely different person, gay and young and happy-hearted again and passionate in her gratitude to him, he would swear that they would do this again, and often, that some day they would even move out of Montmartre, find a little house with a garden, even perhaps in the real country.

Diana would laugh a little sadly at this last suggestion, knowing him for the inveterate city-dweller that he was, loving every cobble, every paving-stone, even every gutter of his beloved Paris.

But today, though she lacked the courage to tell him so, was a day of crisis.

If she had been able to take just one of the little market studies to Gavel, even the promise of one the next day, she knew she could persuade him to advance something to her, and though it was a shattering experience to her to ask for it, it would not be the first time, and she was helped by the knowledge that all the other artists whom she knew did the same.

But for some reason Paul could not be persuaded to finish the little pictures and day after day he went off, presumably to find new material, leaving them standing there. At first she had accepted his excuse of the artistic temperament.

'I'm not in the mood, *chérie*. The eyes they will not see and the hands they will not work because the mind does not make the right atmosphere for them. Another day, but not today.'

She had waited for that other day, for the right mood, but meantime there was no money coming in and she hated to ask him for it and surreptitiously she sold anything saleable which he gave her from time to time; trinkets, a gay scarf which she wore once or twice to please him and then carefully ironed and put away, even boxes of chocolates which she made some excuse for not opening at the time. Such things she smuggled out to the girl they called, for some never explained reason, Brouette. Brouette worked in one of the big stores as a sales girl, and with considerable ingenuity she could sell to customers articles which, not being a part of the legitimate stock, had not to be accounted for so that she could slip the money into her own pocket. She charged a commission on such transactions and at first Diana had been horrified at the very idea, but in the end she had come to it.

Now she had nothing left to sell, only a few francs in her purse and the rent in arrears. Paul had got into the habit of leaving everything to her, saying truthfully that she managed the money better than he did, and so far she had been able to meet the landlord with smiling ease. Now she had not been able to pay for two weeks, but Paul had shrugged his shoulders.

'Everybody owes him rent, *petite*,' he told her.

'Not us, Paul.'

'Many times before you came,' he assured her. 'He will wait.'

She knew, shrinkingly, what she must do. She had put it off as long as she could, but now she must face it.

Brouette had told her she would be able to get a job at the store where she worked, not perhaps a regular one but one which would bring her in a little money now and then, walking about the store to show off clothes. It was the last sort of job Diana would have chosen, for though she was now perfectly at her ease with the sort of people she met in her daily life, she had never been able to conquer her self-consciousness amongst strangers. To have to parade before them for the express purpose of making them look at her would be an exquisite torture, but she did not know any other way in which she could earn money in Paris, and Brouette had assured her she could get such a job.

'There are so many Americans, and they'll be glad to speak English to you, and you're their style, taller and slimmer than most of the model girls at the store.'

The woman she had to interview terrified her, as Brouette had warned her she might; a hard-faced, tight-lipped, full-bosomed martinet whom the girls referred to in strict privacy as '*La Guerrière*', the virago, the old war-horse.

She gave Diana the job, however. She was to go to the store every afternoon for the 'five o'clock', and parade through the restaurant and through certain of the departments in whatever garments were given to her to show off. She would receive a small retainer, and commission on any sales made through her.

She wondered how she was going to explain her regular absence at this hour to Paul, but in these days he seemed so much occupied that it seemed providential she should have to be at the store at that particular time.

She hated it, but had to steel herself to it. In the tiny, airless dressing-room where she and several other girls had to dress, a bird-like woman with clever hands would arrange their hair to suit the style of dress, make up their faces, give a few rearranging dabs at their dresses and shoo them out again to make their smiling rounds. There was fierce and bitter rivalry amongst these girls, much jealousy if one seemed to be given more attractive and saleable clothes than another, and Diana, who for sheer nervousness kept aloof from these arguments and quarrels, merely accepting without comment the clothes she was given to wear, was disliked and distrusted by the French girls.

In spite of her unceasing hatred of the work, she was fairly successful at it. The grace of movement which had always been hers and some indefinable quality which was the result of many generations of good breeding, gave her a charm which set her apart from the French girls, and her hair of corn-gold, which little Mlle. Jeanne made her wear in loose waves, attracted as much attention as the clothes she was exhibiting. She became as expert as the other girls at catching a look of interest in a customer's eye almost before the lady herself knew she was interested, and her pretty broken French gave her an advantage which she was quick to exploit.

La Guerrière condescended to be pleased with her and the amount she earned in commission kept things going at home, though there were times when she was astonished that Paul should never wonder how she managed. And then, one day, it suddenly dawned on him that it was a fortnight since he had given her any money, and yet there was always a meal for him and the landlord smiled and greeted him if they happened to meet.

'How are you managing, Diane?' he asked. 'You must have been a very clever girl to make the money last so long.'

She gave him a rueful smile.

'You don't really think it has lasted, Paul, do you?' she asked, and then told him what she had been doing, minimizing the loathing she still had for the job, even making him laugh by her descriptions.

He pulled her down on his knee and laid his cheek against hers.

'Darling, you have to work for me!' he said with a sigh. 'You know that I try to make enough money for us?'

'Yes, of course. Don't worry, *bien aimé.* When we get over Christmas and it is spring again they will want your pictures again.'

'I haven't been a very good provider, have I?' he asked, but it was not in his nature to feel as badly about that as many men would have felt. She rubbed her cheek against his, smiling as she reflected that she understood him, and with understanding there could be no bitterness or thought of blame. So long as they had their love, nothing else mattered very much.

And then, to her horror, one afternoon she found she had been chosen to display lingerie, to walk in the flimsiest of intimate garments amongst the customers as they drank their 'five o'clock'.

'Oh, Jeanne, I can't!' she told the little dresser, scarlet-faced and ready to cry. 'I simply couldn't walk about like that!'

A snigger from the other girls, who had obviously waited for her arrival, told her that the suggestion to display lingerie had come from them, and they had worked it so that the choice should fall on her.

'Madame has said so, Diane,' said Jeanne, who liked the English girl and would have spared her this had she been able. 'It will soon be over, just this one set and then a nightdress.'

Diana looked with horror at the wisps of cobwebby chiffon and lace, turned round and went at once to La Guerrière.

'Madame,' she said, 'please do not ask me to display the lingerie. I could not do it. Please do not ask me.'

It happened to be a particularly bad day for that bad-tempered woman who enjoyed taking out on the staff the pains of indigestion she suffered almost continuously.

'What is this? Of course you will show the lingerie. What is it you are here for then? Tell me that.'

'I did not agree to show lingerie,' said Diane, quailing. 'I will show anything else, Madame, truly, but I cannot walk about in public in these things,' offering the garments for her inspection.

La Guerrière took them from her and flung them aside.

'Very well, Madame,' she said with angry emphasis on the title she had not so far accorded her. 'I shall not require your services again.'

'But, Madame—'

'Either you display the lingerie or you go.'

Diane turned away, leaving the garments there.

She was hot with anger at the way she had been treated, knowing that sales in the stores were falling off, and that the manageress was seizing on the excuse to get rid of one of the mannequins without the necessity of paying her a week's wages.

But beneath the anger was the sheer misery of losing her job, which for the past few weeks had been keeping both her and Paul. This week she had been obliged to buy herself new shoes and stockings to wear in the store, since these were not provided. With the loss of two days' commission she did not know how she was going to pay the rent, and she hated to have to worry Paul, who had not been at all well lately.

Still, it was unthinkable that she should do what had been asked of her, and she went slowly back to the dressing-room, collected the few toilet articles she kept there and went to the cashier's office to find that La Guerrière had already informed him that she was to be paid off without the usual week's money in lieu of notice.

When she reached the studio it was to find Paul there, stretched on the bed and moodily turning over the pages of some magazines.

She thought he looked ill. He was pale and there were deep circles under his eyes.

'You're back early,' he said listlessly.

'Yes, they—they didn't want me today,' she said, but she was too transparently honest to be able to deceive him.

'Have you lost the job, *petite?*' he asked her.

She told him what had happened, nestling up beside him on the bed, grateful for the comfort of his nearness and drawing courage from the feeling that he needed her and depended on her.

She realized that he was really ill when, the hours dragging on, he lay on the bed tossing and turning, refusing the food she brought him but asking constantly for water, which as a rule he would not drink.

By nightfall she ran along for Poucet, and between them they got him into bed, and whilst he stayed with Paul she went for the doctor.

One of the many virulent forms of influenza was sweeping France at the time just as it was sweeping England, and Paul took it badly, with a very high temperature.

Poucet, sitting up with Diana and insisting on taking from her as much of the burden of nursing Paul as she would allow, told her in those quiet night watches many things at which her heart filled with pride in Paul. She had never been able to get him to say much about his war experiences, but according to Poucet he had been one of the most daring of the Free French members who had been dropped by parachute into occupied France prior to the day of liberation.

Diana loved to hear of these escapades. The tale of them, seemed to take her back beyond the last few months when there had been strain and a vague feeling of uncertainty in her relations with Paul. She was the young Diana on the rocks of the Welsh coast again, adoring her hero.

When the fever abated, Paul grew rapidly stronger, and then, with the same swiftness, Diana herself went down with it.

It was on a day when Paul had insisted on going out, though she was anxious about him and had tried to prevent him from going.

'Then at least let me come with you,' she urged.

Paul laughed.

'I'm sorry, *ma vie*, but to get you to cross the roads is more than just yet I have the strength to do!' for she had never conquered her terror of the Paris traffic.

'You will be careful, Paul? And keep wrapped up?'

'Oh yes, yes,' he told her, and she could see with a little stab that her insistent care of him was becoming an irritation.

Still, she was not sorry to be spared the necessity of going out. She had made several journeys to see Monsieur Gavel whilst Paul had been ill, and the little man, in the kindness of his heart and of his very real affection for her, had given her good prices for some of Paul's work which, though she did not know it, he had already refused to buy from Paul himself. On that money they had contrived to live, and she had no suspicion of the truth, which was that Gavel knew the pictures were very unlikely to find a buyer.

It was only after she was alone and had decided to take down the curtains to wash them that she realized that she felt ill. She clung to the step-ladder before she could nerve herself to get down to the ground again, and once there, she collapsed.

It was Poucet who found her there, calling in to see Paul and discovering Diana huddled on the floor, barely conscious.

When Paul arrived, having been gone some hours, it was to find Diana in bed, with Poucet in attendance and Brouette, hastily summoned, helping him to prepare the hot fomentations prescribed by the doctor.

For several days her life seemed to hang by a thread and Paul nursed her with tender care, never leaving her side until, when she was over the danger period, he began feverishly to work again.

When she was able to get up she was a mere wraith of herself, and she could not hide from him her deep longing for the healing and comforting calm of the countryside.

'If we could go away, Paul, just for a little while,' she said, 'I should soon get strong again. I know I should—and you could work in the country. I've always remembered what you used to tell me about the place where you lived as a little boy, Sept Saules, with the little river, and the old inn where they have all the celebrations.'

His face grew dreamy.

'Sept Saules,' he repeated. 'Yes. Yes, let's go there, *petite*,' and in a moment he was all eagerness, all terrific activity, making plans, altering them a dozen times, even starting to pack.

It was not difficult to let the studio for a good rental, so that they had something to live on, and Paul said it would not cost them much.

'Just the one room, *petite*, and we shall eat simply, the food of the country people, live like peasants, and you will get well and strong again and I—I shall paint a masterpiece!'

Within a week it was all settled up and they had gone, Paul driving a crazy old car which someone had lent him and which might or might not hold together for the journey. Diana, wrapped in a multitude of coats and rugs, sat beside him in a state of utter contentment, and in the short December evening, with Christmas only a few days off, they arrived at the inn, the only building of any size in the little village which sprawled away from it in two directions and was intersected by the small, peaceful, grey river.

People who remembered Paul made a fuss of him and took Diana to their hearts. They were given a large, peaceful room, with polished wooden floor, old rugs of peasant craft on the floor, great quilts on the enormous bed, a log fire burning in the open grate.

They ate their meal in the red-floored kitchen. All along one side of the kitchen was the gleaming range, with huge pots and casseroles and the inevitable earthenware coffee-pot sending out savoury smells. The proprietress and her bustling, cheerful staff ate with them, and the service straight from fire to table was a simple and homely thing, the many courses piping hot.

'It's going to be so wonderful here, Paul,' said Diana with a happy sigh as they climbed the stairs to their room. 'You can simply *hear* the silence! No more shouting, or those terrible motorhorns, or the city that never sleeps!'

'My Paris,' said Paul with a grimace which told her that the silence and the ways of this remote country village reacted on him in a very different fashion.

Yet he had to admit that for a time he was happy there, happy and busy. They went one day to find his old home, though they knew already that it was in ruins, and Paul made a sketch of it as it had been in his childhood. Diana hoped with all her heart that Sept Saules would lay its spell upon him to keep him there, but she soon saw that her hopes were vain. He was becoming bored and restless, and it did not surprise her when, after nearly a month of what was to her heaven's own peace, he was talking of going back.

There had been a wedding party at the inn, and they had been invited to it as honoured guests. The bride had been amongst Paul's childhood friends and he and Diana were made much of, eating, drinking, dancing, the fun growing more and more boisterous as the night wore on. Paul seemed tireless, always the centre of the fun, still fresh when Diana felt tired out, and at last she slipped away, intending to go to bed.

But it was a wonderful night of clear, bright stars, the air like a draught of cold water to a fevered man. She actually swayed for a moment after leaving the fetid air of the room in which seventy or eighty people had been shut in for many hours. Instead of going across the courtyard to their room, she wandered out into the empty village (everyone was at the party) and down to the river's edge. There was magic in the air tonight, the sheer loveliness of star-sown sky and placid water and dim lace of bare-branched trees catching the breath. An old, friendly dog came from somewhere, and then walked companionably beside her, but nothing else seemed astir. Even the sounds of revelry from the inn had become a low murmur to blend unnoticed with the gentle lapping of the stream.

If only they need not go back to Paris! Here she and Paul had recaptured something of the essence of their first loving, something she had known they were losing in the teeming life of the city. She could not give it a name, even in her thoughts, but she was more than ever conscious that in Paris they had lost it and here they had found it again.

Presently Paul missed her and guessed where she had gone.

She heard the crackling of the fallen twigs beneath his feet and turned to meet him.

'Oh, Paul, did you feel me calling you? It's all I wanted in the world to make this perfect,' and she slid an arm beneath his and held him closely to her.

They stood quite still, the old dog after a preliminary sniff at Paul's heels lying down contentedly. There was hardly a breath of wind to stir the dry leaves at their' feet. A twig fell without a sound from an overhanging willow into the water. In the concentric circles of the ripples, a thousand mirrored stars were awash. Somewhere in the leafless trees an owl hooted.

Diana put a hand up to her throat. All the dear familiar things she had known and loved all her life seemed to rise to accuse her to call her back, to tell her that all this frenzy of living and of loving of the past seventeen months had not been life at all but a fevered dream, unsubstantial, unenduring.

'It's so wonderful, Paul,' she whispered, as if she feared to break the enchantment.

'All this? Yes—but cold,' he said.

'Oh, Paul!'

'Oh, Diane!' he mocked her gaily.

'And you an artist.'

'But of the cities, *ma mie*. Paris is my medium.'

'And your love,' she said slowly, and he did not answer.

'Paul.'

'What is it, *ma mie*?'

'Paul, is it that you are tired of being here?

'*Mon ange*, we have been here already nearly two months.'

'Then you mean you really do want to go back?'

'And you mean that you don't?'

'Not much.'

They were silent again, his arm about her, her head resting against him. At such a moment he was so wholly hers.

'I love you so much,' she whispered.

'Still? After so long?' he asked her tenderly, and they kissed as lovers, the silent night all about them, its peace and serenity in their hearts.

But for Paul it was a passing phase, and she knew it and withdrew herself from his embrace with a sigh.

'I know you want to go back, Paul,' she said.

'Would you not stay here, *ma mie*? A little while without me?'

At first she would not think of such a thing, but gradually he persuaded her. After all, he told her laughingly, he had managed to exist by himself in the studio before she came to him, and why not again? In fact, he might enjoy being a bachelor again, he added with tender raillery and she tried not to think there had been any real meaning behind that.

For that, she told herself, was the simple truth. Paul *was*, to all intents and purposes, a bachelor. She had no real claim on him. She was not his wife. She was still, after all, only his – mistress.

She had long ago forced her mind to use that word, though her lips could never utter it. She had not mentioned the divorce for a long time now. Her pride kept the words back. She could not believe it possible that, if Sally had applied for a divorce, they were still waiting for the petition to go to the English courts. Sally must have had some reason for not applying for it, but she could imagine none and believed that it was just negligence which surely Paul could by this time have overcome.

It was an insistent, galling bitterness corroding her mind and her love, but at such an hour as this, when she seemed one with him and could not doubt his love, she thrust such thoughts from her. As he himself had said, in what way would anything be altered for them by the mere fact of legal marriage?

Eventually she agreed that he should go back to the studio and she should stay in Sept Saules. The very first touch of spring was on the land, imperceptible to all but those to whom, like Diana, there was meaning in the lightest breath, the faint swelling of the buds which as yet showed no colour, the song of the birds who also knew that spring was near. On the farms, poor sullen things compared with those she had known, there was that same expectancy, the first stirring of new life.

She did not want to be parted from Paul, and yet her whole being shrank from the return to city life. Her illness had taken heavy toll of her strength, which had already been devitalized by the long months that had preceded it when food had been scarce because of its high cost on the free market, and she had fed Paul on anything she had the means to buy, existing herself largely on potatoes and milkless coffee with 'black bread' baked into hard rusks to make it slightly less unpalatable. Paul had no idea that she was not eating the sort of food she contrived to give him, the eggs and cheese, tiny portions of meat, an occasional tin of milk. She was not hungry, or she had had a meal out. He accepted without thought or question the various things she told him to account for the frequent meals she did not share.

But these months of loving foolishness had taken their toll, and in spite of her delight in being in the country again, she did not pick up as quickly as Paul had done.

So in the end he went back to Paris with a portfolio full of studies for his new country series, and Diana remained at the inn, to the delight of Madame, who had conceived a great affection for the English Madame. Diana, who could not be idle, worked with the buxom French girls in the house and on the farm, learning French ways and teaching English ones and, except for her hunger for Paul, she was happier than she had been for a long time.

Paul, having regained possession of the studio from his temporary tenants, found it difficult to work. He missed Diana, disliked looking after himself again, and with Poucet away on one of his visits to his mysterious 'family' whose actual components not even Paul and Diana knew, he was finding life dull even in his beloved Paris.

Finally, on an evening which followed a day of futile beginnings, he went to see Victoire Laimant. Deep in his mind he had been aware of her all this time, but had refused to recognize the awareness. Now with his steps set towards her *apartement* he found his blood running more warmly. For the first time for days he was doing something he was really eager to do.

Victoire was resting, Lucine told him primly, and he was put to wait in a little ante-room and given some extremely dull magazines to look at. He looked instead at the room itself, which, like the rest of the flat, he thought so typical of Victoire. Everything was in pastel shades or in white, extremely good and quite plain, its pure lines and beautiful fabrics unmarred by decoration. Also it had the same strangely exciting quality he divined in Victoire, in that it looked cold and yet was warmed from some hidden source so that warmth permeated the whole without having any focal point.

When at length he was brought to her in the sitting-room he found her seated at a needlework frame, the silks lying in orderly lines beside her, the work itself a splash of colour against which her pale, exquisite hands found their perfect background.

He tossed aside as without real value his first impression that she had been sitting there, peacefully sewing, whilst he had been kept waiting. The moment of pique was lost in his delight in her, as man and as artist.

'I want to paint you like that,' he said without any preliminaries, 'exactly as you are, and in this room.'

She gave him her slow, strange smile which was neither a refusal nor a promise.

'Look at my work, Paul,' she said, moving along on the long, low stool so that he could sit beside her. 'Tell me if you think the colours are good or if they are perhaps too bright. This one,' showing him the flower she was working on, a brilliant splash of blue and scarlet.

'They are perfect,' he said, and he lifted her fingers from the linen and looked at them and then bent his lips to them.

'You are a courtier, Paul,' she said.

His eyes held by the sheer force of his will the gaze of her strange, pale, clear eyes.

'You're beautiful,' he said.

'Is that why you want to paint me? There are many women in Paris, everywhere, with far more beauty to paint.'

'Not to me. Are you going to let me paint you again?'

'Here?'

'If you will.'

'Like this?' indicating by one of her slow, effortless gestures her gown of pale greenish blue and the needlework.

'In this, in everything,' said Paul, and she made no resistance when he gathered her into his arms, though equally she offered no response.

Her mouth was soft and full and cool against his lips. The subtle fragrance of some perfume she used, of her pale hair, of herself, was in his nostrils. He touched her hair. It was like silk with none of the springing vitality of Diana's.

Diana!

He let his arms drop. Victoire remained as she was, cool and untouched and – untouchable?

He rose and walked restlessly about the peaceful room. He felt that she was watching him, but when he wheeled round suddenly she was occupied with her needlework again, her eyes on her work. It was difficult to believe that he had just held her in his arms and kissed her mouth. What was she, angel or devil?

The next time he came he brought with him a sketch book and painting materials, set his easel up incongruously in the quiet room, working with a fever which he had not known for many months, knowing that the work that he did was good though the essence of her still escaped him and he found himself staring into her eyes, unable to read their riddle or to find the woman herself.

Victoire was a perfect model, and as he did not require her to keep still all the time for the many studies he made of her she sat peacefully sewing, her fingers moving amongst the silks and her head bent to her embroidery frame like some medieval lady.

He came now every day, and soon was making no pretence at studying the changing light or the time of day. If he did not work (and work with Victoire as a model had become a passion) he sat talking to her, listening to her cool, unhurried voice, finding her well informed, even erudite, and able to converse on a great range of subjects. She had acquired a circle of friends in Paris, interesting people with a variety of tastes and experiences, and Paul met them in her house and, later in their own houses. It was a circle to which he had not formerly had the *entrée*, one to which both her birth and her high standard of education admitted her as an honoured member. It was a new experience to him.

It was Victoire's setting, and yet he could always divine in her that mixture of devilry springing from some secret source, something to which he could give no name but which kept her mysterious, exciting.

Once he got her to sit for him in an Empire gown which he had amongst his studio properties; dark wine-red, its neckline leaving bare her shoulders and the hollow between her pearly breasts. His fruitless attempts adequately to portray that gleaming loveliness of her skin angered him, but with the anger of the artist was mingled the frustration of the man, and at last he threw down his brush and strode across to her and seized her by those smooth shoulders, his fingers digging into the flesh, his eyes like hot coals.

'You're infuriating,' he told her angrily. 'You sit there with your damned smile, knowing all the time that no man ever has or ever will get what I'm trying to get.'

Her smile deepened and changed in quality. His fingers hurt her but she made no protest. It was only afterwards, when he saw the bruises, that he knew how hard he had gripped her.

'What are you trying to get, Paul,' she asked him in her cool, thin voice.

He stopped speaking to stare at her, excited beyond measure at the change in her, unable to know what it portended.

'You,' he said thickly. 'I want you,' admitting it to himself for the first time.

'What of me, Paul?'

He gave her a savage little shake.

'You know. You must know. All of you.'

'Do you mean that you want to marry me, Paul?' she asked slowly, and it seemed she mocked him with the question.

He released her, but still stood staring down at her.

'Aren't you forgetting Diane?' he asked at length, passing his tongue over his dry lips.

'Aren't you, Paul?'

He tore his gaze from hers, suddenly ashamed. It was as if with the speaking of her name Diana herself had come into the room.

'I'm going,' he said, and turned and left her, his palette and brushes flung aside uncleaned, tubes of paint scattered.

Victoire rose and collected them and did as she had watched him do many times, cleaning everything and putting it away and finally standing in front of the easel to look with appraising eyes at his unfinished portrait. She knew that it was not good, and yet he had caught something of the secret essence of her. With the red dress he had been more successful, as he always was with the strong, deep colours.

She looked at those colours, the highlights of brilliant crimson, the shadows of wine and purple and black. They expressed him to her mind, his vigour, his sudden ardours, his equally sudden depression. He had few half-tones. It was impossible for the artist in him to reproduce the undertones of colour in which outwardly she was made.

Paul rushed back to the studio and began a letter to Diana, loving, demonstrative, demanding. She was to come back at once. She must never leave him again.

Half-way through it his pen faltered until he let it fall from his fingers. Part of him meant all he had written. Part of him longed for Diana, for her faithful loving, her clarity of mind, her honesty which had a translucent quality. He wanted to have her in his arms, warm, eager, passionately yielding, knowing no reserves in the fullness of her giving. With her was safety, peace. He had behaved badly to her though she did not know it. He would atone for it. When she came back to him they would be married and then Victoire would cease to matter. He would never see her again.

Yes, that was the only way. He must never see Victoire again, never try to make immortal her skin and her pale hair, her eyes that made him mad by denying him understanding of what lay within them, her snowy coolness beneath which there might lie an infinity of ice, or a raging fire. He would never know which of them, now.

He remembered that he had left his materials there.

That was infuriating.

Could he possibly ask her to send them to him? No, of course not, with her portrait still unfinished. He would have to offer some sort of explanation.

Neither could he send anyone for them. He had kept hidden from all his friends this association with Victoire, and Poucet was still away – though Poucet was the last in whom he could have confided. His friendship and admiration for Diana would forbid it.

He must go himself, just this once – tomorrow, and get it over. His mind began to revolve about what he was going to say, how explain to Victoire. He would tell her, of course, that he was finding the task impossible, that he was not good enough, that he would never be able to achieve it – and she would sit there with that enigmatical, maddening smile behind her eyes ...

He screwed up the letter to Diana and flung it away. He could not possibly write to her whilst he still had the interview with Victoire to face.

He would write the letter again tomorrow – no, after tomorrow.

# Chapter Sixteen

Diana was restless and was beginning to recognize that restlessness as unhappiness.

She was missing Paul badly. It was two months since he had gone back to Paris, leaving her there, and the charm of the countryside could not compensate her for being without him.

If he had been a good correspondent and written to her – well, not every day perhaps – she could have been reasonably content. But he was so bad at writing letters, and the intervals between them had grown longer until now it was a fortnight since she had heard from him, though she wrote nearly every day, letters in which she let him know that she was missing him but which did not in any way complain or whine at his absence. They were a picture of her life at Sept Saules, uneventful and dull in its monotony but infused with life and interest by her colourful phrases, her sense of humour and of values. She imagined what Paul's life at the studio would be, working there in his special place, leaving off for hasty meals, perhaps making a spasmodic effort now and then to keep the place tidy in case she returned suddenly ...

Returned suddenly?

The idea began to germinate, fed by her longing for him, watered by the tears which she shed at night in the big bed, his pillow clasped in her arms in a vain attempt to believe he was there. She ought to be with him, looking after him, seeing that he had proper meals. In his last letter he had told her of the use he was making of the studies of country life which he had taken back with him.

That was it. He was working too hard, probably went to bed exhausted. He would be ill again.

She wrote again to him, suggesting more or less playfully that one day she would stroll into the studio and surprise him, though when she was writing she knew she did not really intend to do this. Even at this distance he still dominated her and she was reluctant to go against his expressed wish that she should stay there until he came back to fetch her.

*I shall be working so hard, chérie* [he had told her]. *It is best that I am alone just until I have caught up with all this lost time, whilst I was ill, whilst you were ill, and now at Sept Saules.*

But after another week she became worried, and in yet another one really anxious. Her letters, which had grown more insistent in their request to be allowed to return to Paris, remained unanswered, and she decided at last, frenzied, that he must be ill – ill and alone, perhaps dying ...

She made up her mind.

Madame Taquet, who knew that she was worried and anxious and without letters, was sympathetic, agreed that she must go, insisted on lending her money which Diana hesitated to take and yet knew she would be foolish to refuse. She had just enough to get her back to Paris, carefully husbanded out of what Paul had been able to leave with her since the Taquets had refused to let her pay for her board, saying that she more than earned it by her work.

'I will send it to you as soon as I reach Paris, dear Madame Taquet,' said Diana.

'Do not trouble yourself at all, *ma chére,*' insisted the kindly woman. 'After all you have done here, working so hard and so long, it is we who owe it to you, not you to us.'

Now that she was really on her way to Paul she found the journey intolerably long. The train service was bad, and it was evening before she was at last in Paris, hurrying by *metro* and then on foot, her heart filled with mingled joy and fear.

She looked up at the studio windows. They were dark, and her apprehension increased as she ran up the flights of stairs, arriving out of breath at the studio door.

She turned the handle. The door was locked! That was an astonishing and disturbing thing, for they scarcely ever locked the door when they went out.

She remembered where Paul had put the key on the only occasion when she had seen him lock the door, which was the day they had left Paris for Sept Saules, the man to whom the studio had been let not having arrived.

She had to stand on tiptoe and stretch up as far as she could to reach the top of the high door, where she was thankful to find the key, but before she could fit it in the lock she had to stand leaning against the wall for a minute. Her heart was still pumping painfully after her run up the long flights of stairs, and she felt faint and giddy. She knew she had not been feeling quite herself for some weeks now. It seemed her illness had taken even greater toll of her than she had known. After all these weeks in the country, she should not feel like death just through a run up a few stairs.

When she had recovered, though still swaying a little, she unlocked the door and went in. It was a moonless night, and the room was in pitch darkness, and when she found the light switch it clicked without producing light.

She fumbled in her bag for a coin for the slot meter, thankful to be lucky enough to find one, and felt her way across the room. Papers or books or something of the sort rustled at her feet and she trod carefully, smiling a little in spite of her puzzled apprehension. Untidy Paul, always flinging things on the floor and without her to pick them up!

Then the light came on, and she saw with a stab of real fear what the papers were.

They were her own letters, unopened, some half-dozen of them.

She snatched them up and looked at the dates on the postmarks. The oldest of them was dated three weeks ago.

She looked frantically round for some sign by which she could discover what had happened, where Paul had gone, why he had not been in the studio for three weeks.

There was nothing to tell her. Everything seemed much as it would have been left by the vacating tenant, with little of the mess and litter Paul would have made by his occupation of it, though in the little kitchen space there was a pan with fat congealed in it, some unwashed plates, the remains of coffee in the big stone pot.

She had left the door open when she had felt her way in in the dark, and as footsteps came up the stairs and paused outside she went hurrying out.

It was Brouette, whose usually cheerful face expressed a concern and a hint of embarrassment which increased Diana's feeling that something was wrong, very badly wrong.

'Oh, Brouette, I'm so glad it's you!' she cried. 'I've just come back, but I don't know where Paul is.'

The girl came slowly into the studio, frowning and obviously trying to avoid Diana's eyes.

'Why—hullo, Diane,' she said slowly. 'I don't think—Paul's here now.'

'Not here?' echoed Diana incredulously. 'You mean, he's not living here! But—'

Her knees gave way suddenly, and she dropped down on the edge of the model throne, staring blankly at Brouette, her mind in a whirl.

'He—he—he didn't say anything about—going away ...'

Brouette, after a vain look round for someone else to relieve her of the task which she saw had been thrust upon her, closed the door and came slowly to sit beside Diana, dropping her bag and her parcels on the floor to put an arm about her.

'Brouette, something's happened to Paul. Something terrible has happened. Tell me. Please tell me.'

'It doesn't seem possible—that you—don't even know,' said Brouette with difficulty, wishing with all her heart that it had been someone else who had come up the stairs just then.

Diana clutched at her arm with her two hands.

'Brouette, tell me. He's ill, isn't he? He isn't—he's—Brouette, is Paul *dead!*'

'No, *chérie*, no! Of course he isn't dead. He's not even ill, as far as I know,' said Brouette quickly.

*Nom d'un nom*, how did one tell things like this? Her anger against Paul was hot and fierce. They all loved Diana, and Brouette had even more reason than most to know the gallant fight she had put up to keep things going when Paul was down on his luck.

'Then tell me, Brouette. *Tell me!*' insisted Diana, tortured.

'Oh, *chérie*, how can I? You see—he's gone away,' began Brouette helplessly.

'Yes, I know. You've told me that. But where? What for?'

'I don't know where, but—he isn't alone, Diane. He's—with someone.'

'Someone? Whom? You mean—some woman?'

Diana felt terribly sick again. She hoped she was not going to do anything so idiotic as to faint. She summoned all her reserve strength. She managed to remain upright, to sit still.

Brouette nodded unhappily. It was horrible that Paul should have left anyone else to tell Diane. The very least he should have done was to tell her himself, to write to her, not to let her come back like this, knowing nothing.

'What woman?' Diana managed to articulate.

'Victoire Laimant.'

'Victoire? *Victoire?*' echoed Diana incredulously. 'You mean the model?'

'She isn't actually a model, though she's sat once or twice just to amuse herself. She is a rich woman, they say.'

Brouette spoke pityingly, filled with disgust at Paul's treatment of Diana and wondering if she had really taken in all the implications of the affair.

'But—to go off with—Victoire,' said Diana in the same puzzled, astonished fashion. 'Oh why? *Why?*'

'Diane, *chérie*, he is married,' she said gently.

Diana knitted her brows.

'I know, Brouette. I didn't know at the beginning,' flushing and looking away, 'but I did afterwards. She—Sally—said she would divorce him, and when she does, we—of course, Paul and I shall be married,' lifting her head proudly and meeting Brouette's pitying gaze.

'Diane, *ma chére*, you do not understand, and I do not at all like telling you, but—it is to Victoire that Paul is married. Sally divorced him a long time ago. There has been, of course, much trouble over the marriage because Victoire has been brought up as a Catholic, but she and Paul have been married by civil law.'

Diana sat as if turned to stone. Though her impulse was to deny it, to say that such a thing was quite impossible, could not have happened, she knew that Brouette told her the truth. Very soon, when the first stunned numbness had worn off, she would feel the agony of the pain. Just now, just at first, the thing was hammering, hammering at her brain without gaining entry. She said the words over to herself, but they were without reality.

Paul is married to someone else, married to someone else, married to Victoire.

Brouette grew frightened at this silence and stillness.

'Are you all right, Diane?' she asked anxiously. 'You're not going to faint or anything? You look so pale.'

'No, I shan't faint,' she said. 'I'm all right.' And then, 'I think I'd like to be alone for a little, Brouette. No, I shan't do anything like that,' as she saw Brouette's eyes go in the direction of the kitchen, and knew she was remembering there was gas there.

'You are really sure you want to be alone, *ma chére?* I would stay with you.'

Thank you, Brouette. You are very kind,' she said with careful courtesy, and at last the Frenchwoman left her, still reluctantly, and with a promise to look in later.

When she had gone Diana stumbled to the bed and threw herself down on it. She had no tears. The terrible wound was too deep.

Not to tell her – not to tell her! That was one of the worst things to bear. Why could he not have explained to her what had happened to him? That he had stopped loving her, that he had fallen so terribly in love with Victoire that he could not help himself? It would have been bitter for her, but she would have understood. Did he think she would have tried to hold him? Wept all over him and moaned at his feet or what? Could he not have known that she had her pride?

It was in the dust now. The farther her mind groped about in that holocaust of all that had made her life happy, the more agonizing were its revelations. Paul had been free 'a long time', Brouette had said, and she could not doubt that. There had been trouble over Victoire's marriage to him because of it. That in itself had been sufficient to prove that Brouette was right, though Diana did not need that proof. Things which at the time had seemed insignificant came back to her mind. Paul's easy acceptance of the extreme slowness of the English courts, his glossing over of her comments on the apparent lack of interest Sally was taking in it after giving her promise, the adroit way in which he had contrived not to give her Sally's address when she had suggested going herself to see if she could persuade her to hurry things.

Oh yes, it was quite true. Paul had been free to marry her long ago, but he had not done so. Was it because he was already tired of her, or because the affair with Victoire had started even before he was free and she, Diana, poor fool, had never suspected it?

She was seeing Victoire much more clearly than she had believed she could remember her; pale, colourless, silent, still, and yet it had been impossible to think of her as stupid. Even Diana had been aware of the dynamic force behind that studied facade.

Gradually as acceptance of the fact became part of her mind came the inevitable thought of the material future for her, though this mattered little as yet. If only she did not feel so sick and as if at any moment she might faint, she would be able to get her mind clearer. She thought vaguely she must have eaten something that disagreed with her, though they had had very plain, well-cooked food at the inn when there was no party to cater for.

Perhaps she ...

And suddenly, blindingly, chokingly, she knew.

She was going to have a child.

It needed only that, only that.

When Brouette came in later, bringing groceries and milk for her, she was still lying face downwards on the bed, one arm curved over her head, the other dangling to the floor, her attitude one of utter desolation.

Brouette touched her and spoke cheerfully, though her heart was wrung with pity.

'Still tired, aren't you?' she asked. 'I've brought you in some food because I thought you wouldn't get any for yourself, and I'm going to have it with you if you don't mind. Something's gone wrong with the lights in my room and I shall not be able to find anybody to put them right tonight. Will you show me where you keep the coffee-pot and the plates and things?'

Diana roused herself. Brouette was shocked at the wreckage of her youth, at the grey, drawn face and expressionless eyes.

She went on talking, and slowly she seemed to be returning to some semblance of life. She even forced herself to drink some coffee when Brouette had made it, though she could not swallow more than a few mouthfuls of food.

Brouette wondered whether she had begun to make any plans yet, since it seemed obvious she would not be able to stay on in Paul's studio even if she could bear to do so. Paul, married to a rich woman who would certainly be ostracized by the better-class Parisian circles for marrying a divorced man, was unlikely to live in the city at all, and there were always people, not only artists, clamouring for these studios. If he had not already let it, he would certainly do so.

When she said good night to Diana, extracting a promise from her that she would go to bed and try to sleep, she still felt anxious and returned later, tapping softly at the door.

Diana started up with a wild hope – but of course it would not be Paul. Why should it be? And he certainly would not knock.

'*Entrez!*' she called wearily, switching on the light.

'*Ma chére*, I am desolated to disturb you again, but all is dark in my room and I fall over everything. I hate the dark so much! Could I remain here with you tonight?'

Diana tried to smile.

'Dear Brouette,' she said, knowing quite well what was her kind reason for coming.

'I shall not be in the way?'

'No, I shall be glad,' said Diana, and drew some small comfort from her presence so that she dropped off to sleep before morning, but woke with a new agony because in her dreams she had been with Paul and none of this had happened.

Over their breakfast Brouette persuaded her to talk about what she would do.

'I daresay I could get your old job back if you liked. La Guerrière's left, as I told you. The others would like to have you, and until we can find you a little *apartement* of your own, you could live with me.'

'It's lovely of you, Brouette, but I couldn't do that sort of job again. Besides, with all that time on heaps of food, I've got fat,' a faint flush colouring her pallor as she realized the truth.

It was agonizing to think that Brouette, or anybody else, might be able to guess what had happened to her. Somehow she must get away before that could happen.

Brouette laughed.

'Yes, you have certainly put on weight, but you were like a shadow before you went away. Well, we must think of something else.'

But Diana had already decided she would go back to England. She had no clear idea of what she meant to do there nor even where she could go, but, like a wounded animal crawling back to its lair, she knew she must get back to her own country.

Brouette agreed sadly, for she was fond of the girl and would have been glad had she stayed.

'Diane, forgive me, but—have you any money?' she asked gently.

'Enough,' said Diana, thinking with gratitude of the money the Taquets had forced her to accept from them. Some day she would pay them back, though at the moment that seemed a vague dream.

Having made up her mind what to do, she could not accomplish it soon enough. She was filled now with a frenzy of fear lest she should see Paul again and every minute spent in his studio was fraught with that danger.

Methodically, her heart like a stone, she left everything clean, the crocks put away, the blankets folded, the divan neatly covered. Then, her face grimly set, she turned through his stack of canvases, his portfolio, his sketch books, a drawer filled with rough studies, and took from them everything that he had drawn or painted with her as his model. They made a formidable pile, but they burnt easily in the iron stove in the centre of the room, and she stood with the poker forcing them in, ramming them down viciously, as if by destroying them she could destroy their part in her life.

At the last moment she took the first painting he had made of Victoire. There were no others there, though she had searched with jealous anger for them. The face and head had merely been roughed in. He had been concentrating on the arms and hands, and afterwards had slashed his brush across them, partly because their beauty had so maddeningly eluded him, partly because he had seen that Diana was jealous.

She dragged out an easel and set the ruined picture on it and left it facing the door, dominating the room, so that it must be the first thing Paul would see.

It was a childish gesture, even a little vulgar, like a thumb to her nose, and she sometimes remembered it afterwards with a bitter little smile at herself. It was the last gesture of the child in her. She was never to be a child again, scarcely even a girl.

It seemed fitting that the journey to England should be about as uncomfortable as it could be. For economy's sake she travelled third class on the train and she had to endure one of the worst Channel crossings of the year.

She was sick the whole way across, lying down on the hard sofa where a kindly stewardess had put her, clinging with both hands to the railing beside it, scarcely conscious that already she was instinctively protecting the child in her womb.

She had not thought much about that yet, though it was always waiting in the background of her mind, ready to come forward and be one of the greatest of her problems.

When she reached England, having changed on the boat what little French money she had, she found she had not enough to get her to London. She had had to give half-a-crown to the stewardess and a shilling to the man who carried all her worldly possessions off the boat and saw her through the customs. He looked down disparagingly at the shilling in his hand.

'Sure you can afford it?' he asked her witheringly, and turned to a colleague with a shrug and a pointing thumb.

Diana hurried away, her suitcase in her hand, her cheeks hot. She went into the little waiting room at the entrance to the quay and sat down whilst she considered what to do. Unpalatable though it was, she had made up her mind to go first to her mother. She did not delude herself that Clementine would be glad to see her, but she did not intend to plant herself on her and Joseph Bloggett, and would relieve them of her company as soon as she could work out her future. For one thing, she would do everything in her power to avoid the discovery by them of her condition. On a rough computation she had decided she would have the baby in December. In the intervening seven months she must have established herself in some way and have contrived to earn enough money to see her through the final stages and the confinement.

It had occurred to her only fleetingly to try to get rid of the baby. She had no idea how to set about such a thing, and also there was, in spite of everything, a longing to have the child, to have something of her very own, something on which she could lavish care and love all her life, the final satisfaction of the instinct which had made her gather about her mongrel puppies and unwanted kittens, the motherless lamb.

Her eyes caught a framed notice offering advice and help to 'friendless girls'. Heaven knew she was friendless enough at the moment, but a girl?

With a bitter smile curving her lips she set off on foot to the address given on the framed notice, dragging the case with her. There was very little in it, for she had left behind everything she possibly could which had either been given her by Paul or would remind her of him. The trinkets, none of them very valuable, which had been gifts from him at various times had been left rolled up in paper on the studio table, and the clothes neatly packed in a box. It was the case itself which was heavy, the one with which she had made her escape from England more than two years ago, a case which had been Clementine's and therefore an expensive leather affair. Its original owner had certainly never been obliged to carry it!

She found two females of the dragoon kind at the address she had sought. They listened to her story that she had just returned from a holiday in France with insufficient money to pay her fare to London, but she found it was not as simple as all that.

She was a bad liar at any time and was soon tied up in knots by the forthright questions put to her, humiliated by their obvious disbelief, the more so because her story was not entirely true. At last, in desperation and no longer able to avoid it, she gave her mother's name.

'My mother is Lady Bloggett,' she said. 'She married again, which is the reason why my name is different from hers.'

'*Lady* Bloggett?' asked one of the dragoons, and Diana's lip curled. 'You say your mother is *Lady* Bloggett?'

'Yes,' said Diana briefly.

'And her address in London?'

Diana gave the only one she knew, that of the flat which her mother had occupied prior to her second marriage and which she had said they were going to retain as a *pied a terre* in London.

One of the women went away after a whispered colloquy with the other, to return presently with smiles on her face. Presumably she had made enquiries at some source or other and had ascertained that a Lady Bloggett did indeed exist and at that address.

Diana was given a pound note, signing a receipt for it and undertaking to repay it as soon as she had rejoined her mother.

She had fourteen shillings and threepence of it left when she reached Victoria, and thankfully depositing her bag in the Left Luggage Office, she went outside the station and took a bus. In spite of her unhappiness, she could not help a feeling of comfort steal into her mind at being in her own country again. Even London was dear to her in her forlorn state.

She rang the bell at Clementine's flat several times before accepting the melancholy fact that there was no one in, and she went slowly down to the hall again and found the porter.

'Do you know if Lady Bloggett still lives at number seven?' she asked. 'I've rung the bell but there's no one in.'

'Sir Joseph and Lady Bloggett are away,' said the man. 'They only use the flat for odd nights now and then.'

Diana felt chilled with fear. Though she had kept telling herself Clementine would not be there, she had not really believed it.

'Do you know where they are?' she asked. 'I am Lady Bloggett's daughter and I have been away from England for some time.'

'I think they're just travelling round,' said the man vaguely. 'I keep her ladyship's letters till she sends me an address, and all Sir Joseph's go to his office in the City. The last time I had to forward Lady Bloggett's letters was about ten days ago when they were in Bermuda.'

Bermuda – and she had thirteen shillings and sevenpence!

She thanked the man and turned away.

What was she to do now? She could not bring herself to go to the Hursts, nor, indeed, to any of her few friends. She shrank from the inevitable revelation of this outcome of her 'romantic' flight with her French lover. She felt cheap and bitterly humiliated in her own eyes. What, then, would she be in theirs?'

Besides, if she went to Maidstone she ran the risk of meeting Andrew.

The very thought of him was like the sight of a rock to the drowning man who cannot hope to reach it. Andrew, so safe, so sure, whom she had deserted for Paul!

Yet she could not make up her mind utterly to repudiate Paul, nor regret the magic of her life with him, magic which she could never know again because she would never again be that eager, ignorant, trustful, romantic girl again.

Yet where was she to go? What did one do, stranded in London and in her condition, with thirteen and sevenpence in her purse?

She went back to Victoria, since at some time or other she must reclaim her suitcase. It was nearly nine o'clock, and a cold drizzle had set in. All about her people seemed to have somewhere to go and something to do. One or two porters began to look curiously at her, and she got up and walked outside the station again. For the moment the rain had stopped, and she decided she had better get herself something to eat, since she had not eaten since early morning and had been seasick.

She went into a tea-shop and ordered hot coffee and a roll. It was one of the shops that remain open all night, and the girl who served her stopped to speak to her.

'You look tired and cold,' she said in a friendly voice which almost brought the tears to Diana's eyes. It seemed so long since anyone had spoken like that to her, though it was only this morning, on the Channel boat.

'Why don't you try a hot-dog sandwich instead of that roll?' the girl went on. 'It's sixpence, but it's a meal, and the rolls they use for them are new. These are like old boots,' indicating the roll she had brought her.

Diana agreed, and whilst she sat munching the sandwich, the waitress talked to her. There were very few customers just then.

'People come in a bit later when the picture palaces and the Victoria come out. Seen the show at the Victoria? I'd like to go again. Wish I could change this shift, but we're short-handed and they're pretty decent to the staff and I don't like to chuck it up.'

Surely it should not be very difficult to serve in a tea-shop? Thrust on by the thought of that thirteen and sevenpence, and even that a debt, she took her courage in both hands.

'Do you have to have experience to work here?' she asked.

'You're supposed to, but they want people so bad that they take anyone. A bit hard on us having to teach them, but what can you do?'

'Do you think they'd take me?' asked Diana, the flush deepening.

The girl stared at her in surprise.

'You? But you're a lady!' she said.

'Believe me, I want a job pretty badly. Look, this is all the money I've got in the world, and I don't know how to do anything that will earn me a living. I came to London expecting to find my mother here,' she added, seeing that some sort of explanation would have to be given, 'but she's away and until she comes back I'm flat broke. The only job I can do is being a mannequin in a dress shop and I wouldn't know how to get that sort of work in London.'

'Well, they'd take you, but do you reely think you could stick the work, with all the standing? My pore feet!' lifting one and then the other, her round, homely face screwed up.

She was in her late twenties, Diana thought, one of the thousands of such unassuming, undemanding women who, with little hope of ever finding anyone who would see beneath and beyond the homely exterior, went about doing a dull job cheerfully and well, truly the salt of the earth.

Her name was Thelma, she told Diana, Thelma Breeze, and she lived with her family at Herne Hill.

'Tell you what,' she said, when Diana had asked her if she knew somewhere cheap and clean where she could spend the night. She was to come to the shop the next day to be interviewed, on Thelma's recommendation, by the manageress, who was not on duty at night. 'Tell you what. We got a spare bed. Young Sis is staying at my aunt's a few days, and Mum would make you welcome, honest.'

After some demur, Diana accepted the kindly offer, and as it meant waiting until Thelma came off duty at midnight and it was raining again, she sat at the table in a quiet corner and made a second cup of coffee last until it was time for Thelma to go.

The two girls crept into the house near Herne Hill Station. They didn't wait up for her, Thelma explained, but Mum always left her a snack, and she made herself a cup of cocoa.

This they had in the small, crowded kitchen and then, their shoes in their hands, they crept upstairs, Diana warned of the fifth stair, which creaked, and into a room at the back, with two beds.

It did not occur to Thelma to put clean sheets on her sister's bed for the visitor, but Diana forced herself to overcome the offence to her fastidiousness and indeed found herself so tired that she soon forgot that the sheets were smeared with chocolate and unaired. There were even crumbs in the bed.

She woke with a start to a thunderous knock at the door.

'Thelm! You going to stay there all day?' demanded a rather harsh woman's voice, and the door opened to admit a curl-papered head and then the rest of a middle-aged woman.

Mrs. Breeze stopped short at seeing the second bed occupied.

'Well, I never!' she said. 'How did you get here?'

Diana sat up.

'I—I'm terribly sorry. I'm Diana Merrimayne,' she said. 'Your daughter said I might sleep here for the night.'

Mrs. Breeze advanced into the room to stand looking hard at the guest. She had a thin, lined face, not unkind but certainly not gentle or smiling.

'She did, did she? And how come you hadn't a home of your own to go to?' suspiciously.

'I've been living in France for the past two years,' she said, wishing it had occurred to her to make up a good and likely story which would have sounded better than the truth. 'I only came back yesterday, and I found that my mother is away and—your daughter thought I might be able to get a job where she works and—she said I could sleep here for the night.'

Mrs. Breeze grunted in a non-committal fashion and went to the other bed to shake Thelma into consciousness.

'Wake up, Thelm. Come on now. Open your eyes and look lively. What's all this about you bringing a strange girl home with you and putting her into Sissie's bed, eh?'

'What?' asked Thelma sleepily and then, awake at last, sat up and smiled across at her visitor.

'That's O.K., Mum,' she said. 'No need to carry on. Where did you want her to sleep? On the Embankment?'

Her mother sniffed.

'Funny thing. Girl like that and nowhere to sleep,' she said. 'Well, get up, both of you, if you want any breakfast.'

'Oh, Thelma, I feel dreadful! I ought not to have come,' said Diana, getting out of bed and sitting on the edge of it for a few moments to combat the sickness she felt most mornings.

'Oh, don't take any notice of Mum,' said Thelma, stretching and yawning. 'Her bark's worse than her bite. You'll see. You going to get dressed? The bathroom's just across the landing. Everybody else'll have gone by now so it's sure to be empty. I'll wait till you've finished.'

Diana went to the bathroom, which looked as though a tornado had swept it. On the wet floor damp towels were flung in disorder, shaving materials were on the chair and window-sill, some of them fallen to the floor.

Diana cleared a space on which to stand, cleaned up the basin, found there was no hot water in the tap so labelled, but made shift with cold.

Thelma, following her when she had finished, commented on the fact that she had 'done a spot of charring'.

'We're rather an untidy lot,' she said easily, 'but folks have to take us as they find us.'

Breakfast, which she and Thelma took alone in a small dining-room leading off the kitchen, was plentiful and well cooked, out the used dishes of the rest of the family were still on the table, and Diana was invited to 'push 'em on one side' to make room for herself. She found she was not hungry enough to relish a meal in such circumstances, but Thelma was genuinely kind and Mrs. Breeze thawed out and she told herself she was ungrateful to feel as she did about their slipshod ways.

In spite of that, she remained more than two months at 3 Aspen Villas.

As Thelma had assured her she would, she got the job as waitress and undertook the night shift so that she could work in the company of and under the guidance of the girl who seemed to be her only friend in London. It was Mrs. Breeze who had surprisingly suggested that she remain with them.

'Sissie's staying with her aunt and she can go to school from there, so I've said she can stay on if she likes. They haven't any children and mine have always made a second home of it, so if you like to stay on, share and share alike with the rest of us and put up with our ways, you're welcome.'

Somewhat appalled at the prospect of actually living in the incredible muddle of the Breezes' home, Diana did not know how to refuse so kindly an offer; also the friendly kindness not only of Thelma but of the rest of the family warmed her cold and aching heart.

The father was a taciturn man, a gas fitter by trade, of whom none of them took much notice, seldom speaking to him, though when they did they received such mumbled, grudging replies that Diana soon realized he preferred to be left alone. When he came home he removed his coat and his shirt collar, rolled up his sleeves and sat in his own armchair by the fire and read the newspaper or a book until he was called for supper. After the meal he returned to the chair and his reading, and the family life surged about him, with arguments, quarrels, plans, violent comings and goings.

At half past ten he would rise from his chair, wind up the clock and, his book still under his arm, depart for bed. Diana discovered that he was reading Gibbons' *Decline and Fall.*

'He always reads stuff like that,' Thelma told her.

Diana wondered why he was a gas fitter, but in the two months she was there she never found an opportunity to ask him.

Sissie, who was thirteen, called in occasionally, leaving the house a little more untidy than before, but the life of the family seemed to have closed over her departure and no one appeared to miss her. Diana felt it would be like that with any of them. They lived their separate lives, the home the one meeting-place, their mother the only thing they had in common. Their father seemed not to count at all, though presumably he maintained the house. They all paid in something according to their means, and Mrs. Breeze fed them well, but otherwise left them to their own devices.

Vi, the eldest, was a typist in the City, cheaply smart and possessing a young man called Jos, who appeared now and then to fetch or to deliver Vi, a very hearty young man whose practical jokes were a private terror to Diana. She found it difficult to roar with laughter when her chair was drawn from under her, or when a covered plate on the table was found to be hiding a small frog.

'Jos is a rare one for a joke,' Mrs. Breeze would observe.

After Vi and Thelma came Gus, who was apprenticed at a local garage and lived, moved, and had his being in and with cars.

Diana's whole existence just then seemed a nightmare of things she hated – the work at the shop, which she found exhausting and difficult, the constant uproar and turmoil in the Breezes' home, Jos with his jokes, Gus with his cars and Vi with her trail of powder, her smears of lipstick over everything, her loud laughter and her airs and graces. Thelma, whom nobody regarded as important, and to whom they referred as 'poor old Thelm', was the best of the bunch, the only one who tried to do anything to help her mother, whose favourite was undoubtedly the synthetically pretty Vi – who never did a hand's turn for anyone but expected to be waited on.

And then one afternoon, when Thelma had gone shopping but Diana had decided to stay in and lie down with a book, Mrs. Breeze came into the bedroom and stood beside her, looking down at her with a mixture of concern and disgust.

'I think you and me had better have a few words, Diana,' she said. 'Hadn't you better tell me something about yourself?'

Diana put her book aside and lay there with a sick knowledge of what was coming. She had seen Vi's rather spiteful glance considering her, and she knew that the other girls in the shop had begun to look at her, though Thelma had never said anything.

She did not know what to say, and Mrs. Breeze went on.

'You might as well tell me,' she said. 'You're going to have a baby, aren't you?'

Diana nodded and turned her head on the pillow and closed her eyes. The thought had been with her day and night ever since her first discovery of the truth, but she had let things drift on, doing nothing because she had no idea what to do, nor what she ought to do.

Mrs. Breeze grunted.

'Well, it's what I thought,' she said. 'Not married, I suppose?'

'No,' whispered Diana, her face still turned away.

'Who's the man? Some Frenchman?'

'Yes,' said Diana faintly, whilst her heart cried, 'Oh, Paul!'

'Married, is he?'

'Yes.'

'H'm. Well, you're in a fine mess. Your mother doesn't know?'

'No, she's still away. I don't know when she's coming back.'

'Any idea what you're going to do?'

Diana shook her head.

'Well, I'm sorry for you, but you've been a fool, as I expect you know without me telling you, and you can't stay here. Breeze spoke to me about you last night and says you're to go, and when Breeze says a thing he means it.'

So Mr. Breeze did occasionally talk, thought Diana dully, and presumably when he did it was to some purpose.

She dragged herself to her feet. Before lying down she had taken off her dress and loosened the tight belt and brassiere she wore. She was conscious that even without her admission her condition would have been obvious to an experienced woman at that moment.

'Of course I won't stay, Mrs. Breeze,' she said. 'It's been more than kind of you to have me so long. I—I'll go now before Thelma comes back.'

'Oh, you can stay out the week,' said Mrs. Breeze, and paused in the doorway to turn back for a moment.

'I don't like turning you out, Diana,' she said, 'but Breeze is most particular about things like that, and he says with three girls of our own, and young Sissie beginning to notice things—'

'Please don't trouble to explain, Mrs. Breeze,' said Diana, interrupting her with that little touch of dignity which all the family had felt distinguished her from the rest of their associates.

Alone, Diana dressed rapidly, threw her few belongings into her case and was down the stairs and out of the house before Thelma could possibly return from her shopping.

Mrs. Breeze heard the soft closing of the front door and stood at the window to watch her go, the heavy case dragging at her hand, her whole body sagging with the weight of it and with the burden of her own body.

She was not a cruel woman, but life had not been easy for her and she had always lived in mortal dread of one of her daughters getting 'into trouble'.

Not that poor Thelm was likely to get a chance to do so, but the sooner she had Vi married the better she would like it, and to have Diana about the house, getting perceptibly bigger, would be simply asking for trouble, with young Sissie getting so knowing and thinking her parents thought it was quite O.K. for a girl to be in Diana's condition.

Diana, feeling utterly humiliated and longing to have some corner into which she could creep and die, went into a telephone box and rang up the manageress of the tea-shop.

'I'm sorry but I'm not well,' she said, 'and I'm afraid I shan't be able to come in again. Will you please let me go without notice?'

'Of course you won't expect to collect any wages for this week, will you?' she asked.

'No, of course not,' said Diana meekly, and put up the receiver and walked away.

She could not see any of them again, not now that they knew. She could not even see Thelma again, though some day, if she ever got out of this mess and there were any real life for her again, perhaps she could repay her somehow for her kindness and atone for her desertion.

And where was she to go now?

# Chapter Seventeen

Clementine, cool wet pads over her eyes, her hair protected by a towel, lay back in the chair in the beauty parlour and surrendered her face to the soothing hands of the masseuse.

'Don't talk,' she said as the girl started to chatter about sunburn and open air. 'When I come here I want to relax.'

But Clementine had not gone there to relax, but to think.

'I'm in a mess,' she thought. 'I'm in the sort of mess I thought I should never get into, an idiotic and stupid and revolting mess, and what am I going to do about it?'

The 'mess' had started at Cannes, had continued throughout a London season, had enjoyed a slight respite whilst she and Joseph took their long, lazy world tour, but had caught up with her again when they had returned to London, which was only a few days ago.

She had definitely parted from Garry Prosper when they had left Cannes, and yet to her mingled amusement and annoyance he had followed the Bloggetts to London and she had not been able to shake him off. Well known, and a welcome guest in almost any house, he had found it easy to meet her constantly, not so easy to avoid contacts with Joseph Bloggett, but the more exciting for that very fact.

It was partly to avoid Prosper that she had suggested the world tour. Her husband had been delighted.

'I didn't think you'd care for anything like that,' he said, 'but it's right up my street. I've always fancied one of those trips but didn't care to go alone, but if you'll come with me it'll be just grand.'

It had been pathetic to see the pleasure it gave him, the hours of unadulterated happiness poring over guide books and timetables, telephone calls to shipping offices, agents coming and going. Meantime she was ordered to get herself a 'proper rig-out', no expense to be spared, this being right up 'her ladyship's' street.

But she had not shopped alone, for it seemed that everywhere she went she ran into Prosper, the mocking light in his grey eyes telling her what she already knew, which was that he was taking unusual trouble not to let her escape him. He went with her to the dress shows, which Joseph would never have done, and his impeccable taste helped to make her what her husband intended her to be, the best-dressed and most-talked-of women in their circle. Her photograph was constantly in the illustrated papers, and to her annoyance and alarm it was frequently he who was and 'friend' thus briefly described in such photographs.

'I'm not going to see you when we come back,' she told him firmly when they were saying goodbye the day before she went.

He smiled his lazy smile.

'And how do you propose to avoid me?' he asked.

She had a momentary feeling as of an animal caught in a trap, she, Clementine, the clever and self-sufficient!

'If you're a gentleman, you won't force your attentions on a lady who doesn't want them,' she said, trying to carry it off lightly.

'But I'm not a gentleman,' said Prosper.

'And I suppose you're also implying that I'm no lady?"

'*You* no lady, Lady Bloggett? he asked with his malicious grin.

He knew exactly why she had married Joseph and admitted that he would have done exactly the same. The only difference was, he told her, that now he would consider he had carried out his share of the bargain and might have a little private relaxation.

'Garry, listen. You know you attract me. We attract each other inevitably as we are alike in so many ways. We have the same rather mordant sense of humour and we know each other's worst failings. In other circumstances we might have what you call a little private relaxation, by which you mean hopping into some bed together. Well, I want you to understand quite clearly that I am not a bed-hopper and never shall be one. You're wasting your time and exposing me to risks which are not fair. You know as well as I do that we're being talked about, and the only reason, I think, why Joseph doesn't know that we are is because at the moment he is absorbed in preparations for being so long away from England. He would be a dangerous man to arouse, and what's more, I have no wish for him to be aroused. I am quite happy with him. We suit each other, and I'm not going to let you jeopardize my happiness in an attempt to get something you'll never get.'

His answering smile left her irritated and apprehensive. He was disturbingly attractive, and that elusive resemblance to Piers had increased rather than decreased – or perhaps he had acquired an attractiveness of his own which had superimposed itself on what she believed was the memory of Piers. She was afraid, and he knew it.

She had come back from the long voyage with a feeling of immense relief, for however well she got on with her husband, his too close proximity for all these months had become a bore and she longed for other people, for movement and variety. Also she had put on a little weight, and this horrified her. At forty-two she could certainly not afford to gain an ounce. She was, she felt, the sort who would age rapidly once she let herself go, and she was not prepared yet to lose her reputation for beauty and forgo the admiration which had always been her meed.

It may have been that first premonition of the loss of these things that had made her quicken in spite of herself the first time she saw Prosper again after her return. She had missed him at one or two welcome-home parties which had been given for her, and had not sent him a card for the restaurant dinner and dance she and Joseph had given, a very splendid and elaborate affair, but a day or two later she returned to the flat to find him lounging comfortably in her sitting-room.

He rose as she came into the room, and there was no mistaking the glad light in her eyes, a light which she instantly extinguished but which he knew had been there.

'You, Garry?' she said, hating herself for being so glad.

'I indeed,' he said, and took her handbag from her and laid it down and held both her gloved hands in his, his smile deepening.

'I asked you not to see me again,' she said.

'I don't often do the things I'm asked—unless, of course they're pleasant things. Be sensible, darling. Why do you try to pretend with me? You know quite well that it isn't any good, that you wanted to see me as much as I wanted to see you.'

It was the first time he had used any endearment to her, and she knew that it was an endearment. He was not given to using such words in the light, foolish fashion of the day.

'I don't want to see you,' said Clementine.

'You mean you know you ought not to want to,' he corrected her. 'Why fight against it, my dear? We're not young. I'm forty-six and you have somewhere a grown-up daughter, and time is passing for us both. Don't try to by-pass the issue,' he said. 'You know we're in love with each other. Where is the sense of trying to escape it? Why should you want to? I've got quite a good technique.'

'I'm not in love with you,' she said sharply, 'and your technique is at fault for once. It doesn't interest me.'

He smiled, turned the gloves back over her hands and kissed her wrists. It had the effect of a much more intimate caress and she drew her hands away sharply.

'Don't,' she said.

'Why not?'

'I dislike being touched.'

'You mean you're afraid—not of just being touched, but by being touched by me. Own up. Let's be honest with each other. You're a supremely attractive woman, but it isn't only that. I've known other attractive women. But I haven't fallen for a woman for years, and I've fallen for you, Clementine, hook, line and sinker, whatever that means. I'm completely and entirely yours, my beautiful. What are you proposing to do with me?'

'Don't be absurd, Garry. I don't want to do anything with you.'

'But you do. You want to sleep with me—using the word sleep in a modern sense, of course. It would be quite revolting actually to sleep with anyone, don't you think? I believe I snore and you, my precious, probably like to use cold cream and a net for your hair.'

She had to smile. That was the worst of Garry. He could be so amusingly direct. He had no inhibitions.

'Since I have no intention of sleeping with you, in either the modern or the old-fashioned way, that need not be answered.'

'You'll change that intention,' he told her calmly. 'I can wait, though not too long. As I have told you—'

'Yes, I know,' she interrupted him. '"Make the most of what we yet may spend." I'm making the most of it already. With my husband.'

His smile told her what he thought of that, and she found herself colouring. She looked away, furious with herself and with him.

'Please go, and don't come again. I don't want to be obliged to give my maid orders not to admit you,' she said.

'Flora? Oh, Flora and I are quite good friends. She was much more pleased to see me today than her mistress was—or was she? She said so, anyway. You only looked it, Clementine.'

'I've asked you to go.'

'I know. If I don't, I suppose you ring the bell and in your best lordly fashion—or can one say ladily?—you'll have me thrown out. By whom? Flora?' with a jeer.

'Garry—please go.'

Her voice was low and frankly troubled.

He took her hands in his again.

'Why fight against it any longer?' he asked quietly, the mockery gone. 'It isn't just the fun of a liaison I'm asking you to share, Clementine. I love you. I want you for keeps.'

'I suppose you mean marriage, by two divorces. No, never anything like that, Garry. Please leave me alone and accept my decision. I've made my life as I want it to be.'

'And being the wife of a rich, vulgar old man satisfies you?'

'Quite,' she said, lifting her head to meet his eyes steadily. 'I happen to like my rich, vulgar old man.'

'I'm not quite as rich and nothing like as old, but I can be quite vulgar and common—and you do more than like me, don't you? You're on the very brink of being in love with me.'

'No,' she said calmly. 'I'm not in the least in love with you, Garry. I've loved only one man in my whole life, my first husband, and when he died all that part of me died too. I've nothing to give you and you've nothing that I want.'

He had left her with that mocking smile of his and refusing to give her any promise that he would not return, and after he had gone she had found, laid on her bag, a card with an address on it.

Lying back for her 'facial', having had every intention of completely relaxing, she found herself unable to clear her mind of troublesome thoughts.

If only he would leave her alone! It was disturbing to know not only that he intended to pursue her, but also that her fleeing feet had a tendency to drag in her flight from him. She had told Garry Prosper that she did not and never could love him, but it was not the truth. She could love him, not in the same degree as she had loved Piers, but at least with love that was not mere physical desire.

The thing was that she did not want to know such love again. She had set her life as, in her sanest moments, she knew she wanted it to be set. She did not want it disturbed.

Her mind veered round again. She might not want to love, but was she content to let all that pass out of her life and be satisfied with Joseph? Never to know anything else but his rather clumsy and inarticulate love-making and what she herself had taught him?

And that was the mess she told herself she was in, the mess of wanting Garry and determining not to have him, of trying to keep him from her and being afraid he would eventually go.

If she had met him when they were both free she would almost certainly have married him, but he had a wife and she a husband, and the thought of divorce was too distasteful for her to consider for a moment, even if she thought Joseph would ever have set her free.

She was going to meet Garry tonight. It was unavoidable, a send-off party being given to an American family who, after being resident in England some years, were going back to their own country. Clementine and Garry Prosper were amongst the half-dozen people who, having received much hospitality from their American friends, had hit on this idea of combining in an elaborate and amusing send-off party.

At the last minute, when she was almost dressed, Joseph rang up, to her great annoyance, to say he could not be there.

'I'm sorry, girlie, but I'm at Dreward's place and we've got Sennit here and we simply must get this thing settled before another day's business,' he said.

'Oh, Joseph, how irritating!' she said. 'I'd simply counted on your being there. I don't want to go without you.'

She could almost hear him preen himself, but she was not talking for effect, merely to please him.

'That's nice to know, darling, but tonight it can't be helped. It means a lot to me, a cool ten thou or more.'

'Joseph, we don't want any more money!'

'That can never be true, poppet,' he said. 'If it goes through I'll buy you the biggest diamond you've ever seen.'

'I'd rather have you with me this evening,' said Clementine crossly, as she put up the receiver.

When, as a hostess, she arrived early at the hotel where they were holding the party, it was to find Prosper already there.

His eyebrows went up enquiringly when she entered the room alone, and she knew that he was listening to her explanations and apologies.

'You know what men are when it's a case of completing a deal,' she said lightly.

'Perhaps he will drop in later,' said Mrs. Tarlton – *dear* Lucy, as Clementine called her mentally, with irony.

Lucy Tarlton had an unassailable position and a tongue like a razor – except that it did not always cut quite so cleanly but sometimes left jagged edges ready for infection.

Inevitably Clementine and Garry drifted together during the evening. It was unavoidable and anything else would have caused more notice and comment than their dances together.

'What did you really do with him?' he asked, holding her closely, but only, he explained to her, because he was a perfect dancing partner.

'You mean Joseph? That was the truth. He's doing a deal which, if it comes off, will bring in "a cool ten thou". You would not expect him to abandon that for a mere party?'

'Do you expect him to turn up later?'

'It depends on how cool the ten thou is.'

'Come and have a drink somewhere quiet. I don't want to hold you in my arms without being able to kiss you. I've never kissed you yet, have I?'

'Should we remember?' she asked lightly.

'You would.'

'But you, kissing so many women, might not?'

'Who says I kiss many women?'

'I merely assume it by the agility of your mind about kissing me. I shall go down to history as the woman Garry Prosper didn't kiss.'

'I wonder? Anyway, here's our quiet spot—for a drink, I mean,' having edged her towards the door and out to a broad landing from which several doors opened, one of them leading to a small room set with small tables and low, leather-covered chairs.

He settled her in one of the latter and left her to find someone to whom to give his order.

Clementine felt a rising excitement which was only faintly unpleasant. She was still angry with Joseph because he had not abandoned his money-making conference when he knew she wanted him to be with her.

She had a faintly derisive smile still on her face when Prosper returned, followed by a waiter with a tray of drinks which he set down, casually closing the door as he departed.

'Have a drink?'

'What is it?'

'A bitser. You know, a little bit of this and a little bit of that.'

'Guaranteed to knock anybody over in one?'

'In two perhaps. Do you want to be knocked over, Clementine?'

'I don't know what I want.'

'I can tell you.'

'I don't think I want you to,' she said.

'Because you know? I can give it you. You want to have fun, to know you're young still and not merely an old man's darling—'

'I'm not young still, Garry.'

'Young enough, my sweet. Drink up. There's some more in the shaker.'

It was very potent but she didn't care. Why go on denying herself something she now knew she wanted? Did Joseph deny himself anything? This money, for instance, which neither of them wanted but which he must grab for the moment's satisfaction?

She drank the second 'bitser'.

'Your guests have gone,' he said. 'No need for the hostess to stay, or even to say good night. Can I get your coat?'

'No. I'll get it.'

She knew she was going with him. She knew what might, what probably would, happen. She was in a mood not to care.

He was waiting for her when she found her coat.

'You look beautiful enough without that,' he told her, his eyes on her reddened mouth, his expression and the tone of his voice something new in her knowledge of him. Did he really love her then?

In the taxi he was silent and she was glad it was not far. She did not want her mood to break. Tomorrow she might regret it passionately, but she had today, and just now he was more than ever like Piers, who could have said the things he had said, could have looked with just that look compounded of love and lust.

His rooms were on the second floor of an old house converted into bachelor suites. He unlocked the door which led to them and she went in, realizing how odd an experience this was for her. She was not at all the sort of woman to go to a man's rooms at night. For a moment she turned in a panic. He closed the door behind him and put an arm about her and propelled her gently forward.

'You can see my whole domain,' he told her, opening the door to his bathroom, and, next to it, his sitting-room. 'My bedroom opens out of this. There's no kitchen. The couple in the basement look after all of us and food comes up in a lift.'

She went into the sitting-room, a comfortable, male place of deep leather-covered chairs, a substantial table, adequate bookshelves at a comfortable height, a few good prints, an electric clock and a couple of good bronzes the only decoration.

'It's elegantly masculine,' said Clementine.

'It's comfortable with the comfort only men can produce,' he said. 'Like to take off your coat in there?' nodding towards the open door to his bedroom.

'I can leave it here,' she said with a ridiculous touch of nervousness. She might be in the twenties instead of in the forties.

'Afraid to enter the unhallowed precincts of my bedroom?'

She threw back her head and walked into the room.

Again it was a man's room, large, comfortable, without trimmings. Plain silver-backed brushes bearing his monogram lay on the uncovered dressing-table. On the table beside the bed were a few books and a pad with a pencil attached. Within easy reach was a telephone extension.

She laid her coat down on the dark blue eiderdown and made a few ineffectual dabs at her hair in front of the mirror.

He crossed behind her and drew back the heavy dark blue curtains from the long windows.

'This is the *piece de resistance*,' he said, and went out on the small, iron-railed balcony which overlooked miles of London rooftops and, below them, the traffic of a busy street.

Clementine followed him and stood beside him, looking down.

'It's wonderful,' she said, fascinated.

She felt that it was typical of Garry Prosper that he, amongst millions of his less fortunate fellows, should have acquired that balcony and that view.

He pointed out to her many well-known landmarks, seen now at such different angles, and then, shivering a little though it was July, she turned and went back into the bedroom.

He came behind her and caught her by the shoulders and drew her back against him.

'So you're here, my sweet, at last!' he said, and bent his head to kiss her shoulder and her throat and then, as she turned her head to him, her mouth.

The old thrill, loved and hated, ran through her. Whatever her heart dictated or her mind forbade, her body would always be the rebel, its unquenchable ardour her master. Nor was Garry an old man catching at the skirts of her passionate desire for his own delight. He was young still, and eager and virile with a vitality that matched her own.

The result was inevitable, as she had known it must be.

Just as inevitable was the reaction, her horror at herself which was almost a hatred of him.

She dragged on the taffeta dress again and instinctively went across to the windows and flung them wide and stepped out on the balcony, drawing deep breaths of the clear, cold air. It blew on her hot cheeks, and her bare shoulders, but it could not blow away that feeling she had of defilement and degradation.

She heard Garry come out and stand beside her, felt his arms about her and herself draw back against him, her cheek against the roughness of his dressing-gown.

'Is it going to worry you, sweetheart?' he asked her.

'I hate myself.'

He turned her so that she was facing him, set a hand beneath her chin and tilted her face up to his.

And at that precise moment Joseph Bloggett struck.

# Chapter Eighteen

Joseph had returned to his wife's flat, which they had kept on as a temporary convenience, filled with intense satisfaction at the deal he had just completed.

He had hoped Clementine might have returned, but had not expected that she would.

He telephoned to the hotel where the party was being held, but it was Lucy Tarlton who answered him.

'I really wanted to speak to Lady Bloggett,' he told her, never quite comfortable with this particular type of woman.

'Clementine? Oh, but she's left,' she said. 'She left some time ago, quite an hour.'

Mrs. Tarlton had not been pleased when she had been left to carry on the party after the chief guests had gone, and she considered, quite reasonably, that Clementine Bloggett should have stayed. She had ascertained from someone who had seen them that she had gone off in a taxi with Garry Prosper.

Apparently she had not gone home, however! Lucy Tarlton loved a bit of scandal so long as she were not one of the parties involved, and she was jealous of Clementine's effortless acquisition of most of the amusing and desirable men. Mrs. Tarlton was a widow who had cherished ideas about Garry Prosper, not being aware of the existence of his wife.

'Left? Do you know where she went?' asked Joseph, who knew no finesse about such matters.

'I've no idea, but I think she went somewhere with Mr. Prosper,' cooed Mrs. Tarlton, 'though I can't imagine where they would be going at that hour. I mean, London's so dead now, isn't it?'

He put up the receiver, breathing heavily.

Garry Prosper.

He had never quite got over his fear of the man. He knew that he was of Clementine's world rather than of his, Joseph's. They understood each other's language, laughed at things which did not appear funny even when they tried to explain them to him.

And she had gone off, at almost midnight, with him and had not returned. It was five minutes to one.

He wandered about the flat.

He wondered where the chap lived – not that he really cared, of course. His name was not in the telephone book, and he rang up the supervisor and demanded to know if 'Garry Prosper, the writing chap', had a telephone number in London.

The supervisor was polite but firm.

Yes, Mr. Prosper had a telephone number, but it was ex-directory and it was quite impossible for the number to be divulged. She could not even be prevailed upon to give Mr. Prosper's address.

He slammed back the receiver, unaccustomed to not getting his own way and fuming inwardly about the absurdity of a man being able to go gallivanting about with another man's wife in the middle of the night and actually being protected by the Telephone Authority!

He wandered into Clementine's bedroom. At least he felt she was nearer to him in there.

She had a habit of writing her letters in there. Her writing-desk was set in one of the window bays. The lid had been closed on a projecting paper and automatically he pulled down the flap to push the paper in.

Lying on top of her address book, as if she had been going to enter an address but had been interrupted, was a card with something scribbled on it.

It was Garry Prosper's card with a West End address, and the scribbling on it was his telephone number.

Why, if he made such a secret of his number, should he give it to Sir Joseph Bloggett's wife?

Joseph saw red. He did not know what prompted him to act as he did. He only knew that something impelled him to go down into the street, to hail a taxi which by the merest chance was passing, to give the address that was on that card.

Paying off the taxi, he found that the main door of the converted house was ajar and he pushed it open and walked in.

There was no one about, but on a board in the hall he read four names, amongst them that of Garry Prosper. Still impelled by the smouldering anger within him he marched up the stairs and paused outside a door which again bore Prosper's name.

Almost without thinking, he put his hand to turn the knob and to his surprise the door yielded. It was one of the original interior doors and had no automatic latch on it, and Garry, in the emotional moment of Clementine's first being in his rooms, had neglected to relock the door.

Sir Joseph advanced gingerly into the small hall. In front of him was the lighted, empty sitting-room and on the far side of it a closed door. He stood for a moment hesitating. After all, he was walking uninvited and unannounced into another man's home, a procedure which he himself would greatly resent.

Then he caught sight of Clementine's bag lying on the table, an extravagant trifle with a gold jewelled clasp.

He entered the sitting-room and walked across to the closed door. He must know. At all costs now, he must know.

As he crossed the room he heard the sound of a curtain drawn back, and he opened the door. It made no sound, but in any case the man, pulling on a dressing-gown as he followed whoever had opened the french window, would not have heard, for he knocked against a chair in the darkness and uttered a man's expletive. In the shaft of light Sir Joseph caught sight of the tumbled bed and of a woman's fur coat fallen to the floor.

Again the uninvited guest hesitated. After all, it might not have been Clementine's bag, and in such circumstances his intrusion would be unpardonable.

A man's voice came to him from the balcony, softly, a lover's voice.

'Is it going to worry you, sweetheart?'

'I hate myself,' said Clementine, and with the agility of a much younger man Joseph Bloggett was across the room and on the balcony and hitting out with all his force at the man in whose arms she had just turned, her face uplifted.

Prosper gave a cry, clutched, unavailingly at anything that might save him, and fell headlong over the rail and down onto the pavement below.

Clementine, with a scream, was at the railing in an instant, looking over. Her husband pulled her back and held her by main force.

'Don't look,' he said hoarsely. 'I expect I've killed him.'

She stood motionless in his strong grip, transfixed with horror, her lips moving but unable to utter a sound after that one terrified scream.

Joseph dragged her back into the bedroom, closed the french window and pulled the curtains across.

'Put your coat on,' he said, picking it up and thrusting it at her. 'We're going.'

He half pushed, half dragged her across the other room, pausing to put her bag into the pocket of his overcoat and to look round for anything else belonging to her.

'Gloves?' he asked.

She shook her head.

'Nothing else but your bag?'

'No.'

On his way up the stairs he had noticed, without at the time realizing it, a glazed door with 'Fire Escape' painted on it. Reaching this he opened it, thrust Clementine through it, followed her and closed the door behind him. A flight of iron steps led down into an area. The door from that might be locked. On the other hand it might still be open.

Stumbling, Clementine found herself at the bottom of the staircase and in the area. Some stone steps led up into the street, and the door at the top of them was not locked.

'Come along,' said Sir Joseph impatiently.

They were in a side street at the back of the building. All activity at the moment was concentrated on the front of it where Prosper must be lying, a mangled heap. With his hand firmly holding her elbow, Sir Joseph propelled her along, away from the main road and into an

Underground station, where he pushed her back against a wall and spoke to her in a low tone of authority.

'Pull yourself together,' he said. 'You've got to behave as if nothing has happened. We've got to get away from this neighbourhood. It doesn't matter where. Once we're away from it I'll get a taxi and take you home, but you've got to help me. Understand?'

She nodded, made a supreme effort to control the trembling of her limbs, and a few minutes later was able to walk with him to the booking office. He screened her with his body whilst he bought tickets to some place of which she had never heard and took her into the lift, supporting and screening her as best he could.

The liftman gave her a curious stare which turned to a sly grin as he met the knowing look in her escort's eyes.

'Bit of a gay night?' asked the man and Sir Joseph nodded and winked. Clementine took no notice of either of them. Her face was like a death mask, her eyes fixed and staring, her whole mind turned inwards on the horror of what had happened.

'He's killed him,' she kept saying to herself over and over again. 'He's killed him. Joseph's killed him.'

She did not know where they went in the train, for which they had to wait an endless time. She obeyed his voice and his guiding hand into the train, out of it and into another, out of that and up into the dawn, into a taxi and at last back in her own bedroom.

Then Joseph released his grip on her and let her sink down on the bed.

Neither of them spoke until the maddening repetition of her thoughts found speech.

'You killed him,' she whispered.

He had been staring out of the window, from which he had drawn aside the curtain.

'Yes,' he said without turning.

'You—killed him! Will they—know?'

He turned at that and came to stand beside her as she crouched on the bed, half sitting, half lying.

'Nobody saw me go in. I took a taxi but stopped him before I got there. Who knows that you were there?'

'Nobody,' she whispered.

'You're sure?'

She nodded and then remembered that she and Garry had taken a taxi.

She told him, haltingly.

'Let's hope the driver didn't take special note of you, though that poisonous Tarlton woman knew you had gone off with him.'

'How do you know?'

'She told me,' he said grimly, and Clementine shrank down further on the bed.

He looked at her, at the white mask of her face and her dry, stricken eyes.

'You're not crying,' he said.

'No.'

'Who are you sorry for? Him? Or yourself?'

'For you, I think,' she whispered, not looking at him.

Now that the first shock was over and she had had time to think, she was becoming aware of the implications of what had happened, Joseph, her husband, had killed a man. That was more important to her just now than that it had been Garry Prosper he had killed. He had killed someone!

When they found him, they would – take him – take him ...

Her mind boggled at the rest of it. They must not find him.

'Why are you sorry for me?' asked Joseph grimly.

'If they find you—if they know—'

'They'll hang me for murder? Yes, I suppose so. It doesn't matter all that to me—now. You've done worse to me, my girl, than any hangman can do. You know that, don't you?'

His voice was slow and heavy. She knew that for him life had already ended. It was the bitterest moment of her life, more bitter even than the one in which she had known that Piers was dead. With him, her love and her heart had died. Now her very self was dead because of what she had done, her betrayal of the man who had loved and trusted her, her act whereby another man who also, in his fashion, had loved her, was dead.

'Is it any use my saying I am sorry, Joseph?'

261

'Not much,' he said, and went back to his sombre gazing out at the dawn sky.

'You'd better go to bed,' he said, and went out of the room.

A few moments later she came running out again.

'Joseph!'

There was unbearable anguish in the cry and he came quickly to her. She was standing in the hall, her back against the wall, her hands opened out against it, the anguish that had been in her cry reflected in her white face and horrified eyes.

'What is it?' he asked harshly.

'Joseph, my jewels! I left them there—the emerald and diamond necklace and—my bracelets!'

They were silent, staring into each other's eyes, knowing what this meant.

When he spoke it was on a low note of terrible bitterness.

'So all I did was no use? We might as well have stayed,' and he turned back into the sitting-room.

Automatically she followed him and saw him go towards the telephone.

'No, Joseph, no! What are you going to do?' she cried, clutching at his arm to deter him.

He shook her off.

'Telephone to the police, of course,' he said grimly.

'The—police? Oh no—no, Joseph!'

'Don't be stupid. They'll have found the things already and the insurance company have photographs of the necklace.'

She watched, terrified, as he dialled a number and waited for the reply.

When it came he began to speak heavily but clearly.

'This is Sir Joseph Bloggett. *Bloggett!* ... Yes, that's it. You'd better send someone to Preston Square; 7 Goring Court. I've got a statement to make ... About a man who fell from a balcony in Merion Street ... yes ... yes.'

He put up the receiver and then dialled another number.

'Templar? Bloggett here. I want you ... I know what the time is ... Then you'll have to get up ... No, not money. Something more serious ...

You didn't know there was anything more serious? There is. I've killed someone, Templar. A man. Chucked him over a balcony into the street ... I've rung up the police ... All right. But quick. I'll send a taxi ... No, I know that.'

Clementine had stood motionless by the telephone after he had thrust her aside, feeling like death. Whilst Joseph was speaking to his solicitor the knowledge had swept over her that though Garry Prosper was dead she had scarcely thought of him, only of herself and Joseph, more than anyone of Joseph.

What was going to happen now? She was filled with a nameless horror which she dare not try to put into words even in her own mind. Garry was dead. That seemed to matter so little beside the awful fact that Joseph had killed someone.

'Oh, why did you? Why did you?' she asked, clasping and unclasping her hands, the nails biting into her flesh.

'Why did I what? Kill Prosper?' he asked her roughly.

'No, I know—why you did that—but—the police—there might have been some way—'

'There's no other way,' he told her in the same rough, harsh voice. 'Just at first there might have been, though probably you left your tracks everywhere even without the jewels.'

'*My* tracks?' she asked, wide-eyed.

'You don't suppose I was trying to run away because of what I'd done, do you? It was because of you, because I didn't want the world to know what *you* are—*Lady Bloggett*,' with bitter irony.

She caught her breath but could find nothing to say. Her humiliation was the more intolerable because she condemned herself so profoundly. How could she have stooped so low? And because she had, Joseph had become a murderer!

He gave her a brief glance and then looked away again as if he hated even to look at her.

'Go and change into something,' he said gruffly. 'No use going to bed now. That'll be the police,' as a car stopped outside.

He went into the hall, opened the front door and stood by it.

'Joseph, you—you won't say—'

'Go and get dressed. I shan't say anything at all until Templar gets here.'

Flora, who had been in bed and asleep, having been told earlier in the evening she need not wait up, had heard the noise by this time and come out, dressing-gowned, to see what was the matter, but Clementine sent her back to bed.

'It's nothing, Flora. Nothing you can help in,' she said, and went into her room. She could hear the whirr of the electric lift that was bringing the police up to arrest Joseph.

To arrest Joseph!

Fumblingly she got out of the taffeta gown and took a day dress from her wardrobe at random. She thought of Jeffrey Templar with a faint shadow of comfort. The middle-aged north-country solicitor who managed all her husband's legal affairs was not only shrewd and knowledgeable, he was also kindly, a rock to which she could cling if nothing could avert this awful thing.

Mechanically she smoothed her hair and put on fresh make-up, with a little colour on her ashen cheeks, and composed herself determinedly to walk into the room where her husband sat with two men in plain clothes who, to her momentary relief, did not look in the least like policemen.

'My wife,' said Sir Joseph briefly as they rose. 'Don't ask her any questions until my solicitor arrives. He should be here any minute.'

'May I—have a drink?' asked Clementine.

Joseph rose to go to the cocktail cabinet, but one of the two men forestalled him.

'Allow me,' he said. 'What would you like, Lady Bloggett? There seems to be everything here.'

'Brandy,' said Clementine, and he put aside the half-full decanter and opened a new bottle, pouring out a generous portion for her.

She drank it neat and felt a false courage so that she could sit down and wait for Jeffrey Templar.

He came after what seemed an interminable half-hour, his round, fresh-complexioned face and his kind blue eyes seeming to offer comfort even before he said a word. He nodded to Sir Joseph, smiled in friendly fashion at Clementine and scrutinized the two police officers.

'Now what's all this?' he asked. 'Getting a body out of bed at this hour!'

'This is my solicitor, Mr. Jeffrey Templar,' said Sir Joseph.

'I think we know Mr. Templar,' said one of the men with a slight smile.

'That's right,' said Templar. 'How d'you do, Chaffin, Arkell. Now, Sir Joseph. There's no need for you to say anything at all now unless you want to.'

'Sir Joseph himself gave us certain information over the telephone, which is why we're here, Mr. Templar.'

'That's right,' said Joseph Bloggett heavily. 'I've killed a man, Templar. Man called Prosper. Lived in Merion Street. I had occasion to go there and I hit him and he went over the balcony into the street.'

'It was an accident—' put in Clementine swiftly, and three of the men turned to her. The fourth, her husband, looked down at the floor.

'So you were there, Lady Bloggett?' asked Chaffin smoothly.

'Better not to say anything at all,' warned Templar quickly.

'That's right. Don't say owt, lass,' said Sir Joseph.

She glanced at him in swift gratitude for that last word, which so many times she had objected to his using. Coming now, it was like a hand laid on her in blessing, though he still did not look at her.

Guided and warned by the solicitor, Sir Joseph told the bare facts, that he had gone to Garry Prosper's room, had found Lady Bloggett there with him, had lost his temper and struck at him, that Prosper had overbalanced and fallen to the street over the balcony rail, that he and his wife had gone out by another door and had reached their home about an hour ago.

'You did not then go to to see if you could do anything for Mr. Prosper?' asked Chaffin.

'Sir Joseph—' began Mr. Templar hastily, but Sir Joseph pushed aside the warning.

'I know. I know,' he said. 'There was no need to go. We could hear people running, and the police whistles. There was nothing we could have done.'

'Yet later you decided to let us know what you had done?' asked Chaffin in his smooth, expressionless voice. 'Why?'

'I must definitely refuse to let my client answer that or any other question,' said Mr. Templar with authority, and Sir Joseph remained silent.

The two men rose.

'Thank you for what you have told us, Sir Joseph, and for being helpful. You will be glad to know that Mr. Prosper is not dead, though he is badly injured, and it is impossible, of course, to say now what will be the outcome.'

'Not dead?' cried Joseph, and Clementine drew a sharp, sobbing breath of relief.

'No, by a miracle. It seems that the builders who are about to rebuild part of the house next door shot a load of sand on the path late last night, and this broke the fall. Mr. Prosper is in hospital and badly injured, but we received information before coming here that he is alive. May I use your telephone?'

'Scotland Yard speaking. I want the latest information about a man named Garrick Prosper, brought into the hospital as a casualty an hour or so ago ... He is? ... Thank you. That's all.'

'He is unconscious, but still alive,' he told the others, who had listened with strained attention. 'I must ask you to come along with us, Sir Joseph.'

'You don't mean you're arresting him?' cried Clementine.

'Not formally at the moment until we see what happens to Mr. Prosper.'

'Better come with me, Templar,' grunted Sir Joseph, and he stumped out without another glance at his wife.

Jeffrey Templar paused to let the other three go out of the room.

'Try not to worry too much,' he said to her in his kindly fashion, gentle with every woman, though Clementine wondered what his thoughts of her were just now. Her presence in Garry's rooms in the middle of the night admitted of only one explanation, the true one.

'How long will they keep him there?' she asked.

'They'll probably let him come straight back, as he rang them up to give them the information unasked. They won't charge him with anything until Prosper—until there's a definite outcome.'

'And if he—doesn't recover, then they'll charge him with—with—killing him, Mr. Templar?'

'They're not likely to 'call it murder, considering the circumstances. There's no need to worry yet, anyway. Prosper may recover.'

'Coming, Templar?' called Sir Joseph from the hall, and with a reassuring pat on her arm the solicitor left her.

When the door had closed behind them Flora came from her room again, fully dressed now.

'Oh, Flora, I told you not to bother,' said Clementine, white and exhausted.

Flora took no notice of the protest.

'Was that a police car outside? Has something happened to the master, my lady?' she asked anxiously.

'You'll have to know. I suppose everybody will know in the morning. It's all my fault. I went back with Mr. Prosper instead of coming home after last night's party, and Sir Joseph came and—there was an accident and—Mr. Prosper may die.'

The words came out in jerks, her voice as expressionless as her white face. The maid caught her breath in a long half-sobbing sigh.

'Oh—my lady! And the police have found out?'

'Sir Joseph rang up and told them. Mr. Templar is with him. He doesn't think they'll—keep him.'

The maid stood looking anxiously at her mistress for a moment and then turned to leave her.

'I'd better get you something to eat,' she said. 'No good ringing down to the service at this time o' night.'

'I couldn't eat anything,' she said. 'What time is it?'

'Just gone four, my lady.'

'Four? Four in the morning?' asked Clementine vaguely.

'You get into bed,' said Flora comfortingly. 'I'l bring you a hot-water bottle, and if you're sure you can't eat anything, I'll beat up an egg in milk for you with a spot of brandy.'

'Those detectives—I suppose that's what they were—opened a fresh bottle,' said Clementine vaguely. 'Did they think the other was poisoned or something? Odd things they do.'

Flora's 'spot' of brandy was large enough to send Clementine off to sleep so that it was after nine when she woke and at once remembered and went to her husband's room. It was empty, the bed not slept in, and Flora, coming to her, told her Sir Joseph had not been home.

'Then they've—arrested him!' she whispered with horror. 'Arrested—Joseph!'

'I should get back to bed for a little, my lady. There's nothing you can do,' advised Flora soothingly, but Clementine pushed past her.

'I must dress,' she said. 'I've got to go—got to tell them—'

She rang up Jeffrey Templar and was told that he had already gone to the police court, where Sir Joseph was to be formally charged.

'Get me a taxi,' she told Flora, and waited in a fever of impatience until one arrived. It was not until afterwards that for the first time since she was a schoolgirl she went out without make-up.

At the court a wooden-faced policeman offered her no help and told her it was quite impossible for her to see the magistrate, whatever she said.

'But it's most important. It's absolutely imperative for me to see him. He's going to try my husband for something that I did, and I've got to tell him about it and stop him,' she said, distraught.

The whole atmosphere of the place appalled her. It must be such degradation for Joseph, who had always been so proud of himself, so childishly and pathetically proud of his title and his wealth.

Other people who were standing about waiting for their cases to be heard, or sitting on the wooden benches arranged around the dreary entrance to the court itself, were looking at her and listening avidly, glad of a diversion, but she was only vaguely aware of them. She must get Joseph out of this horrible place.

To her infinite relief she saw Mr. Templar come in, and hurried to him.

'Lady Bloggett, there's really no need for you to have come,' he told her with a touch of acerbity.

She guessed rather than knew that she was the type of woman this sturdy, good-living man most disliked. She had met him when the marriage settlement was made, and he must have known that she was marrying Sir Joseph Bloggett for his money; now, having taken her price, she could not even be faithful to her own bargain, but had been indulging in an affair behind his back, and it was Joseph who was going to be called upon to foot the bill again, possibly with his life.

Yet his solicitor's manner to her was faultless in its courtesy and attentiveness, with that faint touch which told her what his opinion of her really was.

She held her head high and looked at him steadily.

'There is every need, Mr. Templar. Sir Joseph is trying to take the blame for what I did. It was not he who caused Garry Prosper to fall over the balcony. It was I. I pushed him, and he lost his footing and overbalanced. It was not Sir Joseph.'

Mr. Templar looked grave, his small, piercing blue eyes narrowed by his frown of uncertainty.

'Have you told this to anyone else?' he asked.

'No. That policeman wouldn't even listen. I want to see the magistrate. I must see him. You can understand now, can't you, why I came?'

'Suppose we sit down for a minute, Lady Bloggett?' he said, piloting her to an unoccupied bench where they would not be overheard. 'You really want to make me, and the magistrate, believe that it was you and not your husband?'

'Yes.'

His lips smiled faintly and there was a slightly kinder look in his eyes as he shook his head.

'I'm afraid it won't do,' he said. 'You're trying to take the blame, but you know that he really did cause the accident, and you know that I know it, don't you?'

She looked away. It was difficult to go on lying, even with such good intent, under the regard of those keen blue eyes.

'You know that the whole thing was my fault and that I should take the blame and pay the penalty, not my husband,' she said.

'I appreciate your motive, Lady Bloggett, but believe me, it will be better to leave things as they are. Nothing is going to happen to your husband. Not today, anyway, and perhaps not at all.'

'But he's got to answer a charge today, hasn't he?'

'No. It will be purely formal, and I shall apply for bail; and he will be at home with you within an hour or so.'

'And then what?'

'Well, that will depend largely on whether Mr. Prosper recovers, and then again on whether he will prefer a charge against your husband for assault. In the meantime I am quite sure bail will be accepted, so that Sir Joseph will remain quite free until he is asked to surrender to it.'

'And then?'

'Suppose we take one step at a time? I have spoken to the hospital this morning, and their reply is reasonably hopeful, though of course they won't commit themselves. Now I advise you to go home, Lady Bloggett, and wait until Sir Joseph joins you. Please believe me that at the moment there is no need to worry unduly—and I wouldn't try to tell that tale again about having pushed him over the balcony if I were you!—' with a little smile flickering at the corners of his mouth.

Her attempt to take her husband's place in the dock was quite absurd, of course, as all the evidence was against any such possibility and there was no motive, but he liked her better for having made the attempt.

Clementine took his advice and returned to the flat, where she wandered miserably about, refusing comfort or food, unable to believe that Joseph would be set free as Mr. Templar had said, her mind producing unimaginable horrors until she heard his key in the lock and his step in the hall.

She remained where she was, in her bedroom, not daring to go and face him. She heard Flora telling him that her ladyship was in her own room. 'You look all in, sir,' the maid added with compassion. She had never liked him, and tolerated him only because he had been the means of making Clementine into 'my lady' and thus raising her maid's prestige. At such a moment, however, one could not feel anything but sorry for him.

'I suppose you know what's happened?' he asked.

'Yes, sir,'

'I'll have a bath,' he said, 'and then some food. Couldn't eat the stuff they brought me this morning,' and Clementine heard him go into the bathroom and turn on the bath.

He had acquired from her the habit of taking baths at all sorts of odd times instead of only on Saturday nights, though he still had a sneaking feeling that he ought to stay at home on Saturday evenings.

'I'll have breakfast in my room,' he told Flora, and when he had finished his bath he stumped along past Clementine's half-open door to find an appetizing meal set for him. As he ate it his thoughts were bitter, his heart heavy.

He was not afraid of what man could and might do to him. He did not care whether Prosper lived or died. The one thing filling his mind was the knowledge of what Clementine had done to herself and to him. Not even she had known the worship he had given her, something far deeper and stronger than the admiring desire for her which had made him marry her. When she had given herself to him with such abandon, when she had shown herself a woman of emotion and passion, he had conceived for her a love which consumed and utterly destroyed the taint of his knowledge that she had married him for his money. He did not expect her to love him as if they were both young, or even as if he were her own age and sort, but he had been passionately appreciative of her generous giving of herself, her gay companionship, her loyalty. He had known many women, had countless sordid little affairs, one or two of them not so sordid because there had been affection in them. But Clementine had been a woman apart. He had felt he could lay bare his very soul to her, sure of her understanding. He had counted on her loyalty, would have staked his whole fortune on her good faith.

And she had pulled herself down from the high pinnacle, had smashed her image, his idol, to pieces as he had hurled her fancy man off that balcony, though Prosper might recover, they said, whereas nothing could ever mend his precious porcelain for him. She was no porcelain, no delicate, flawless ivory, but just an empty shell, cheap trash that had looked genuine.

It bit into his very soul.

Templar had told him that she had been to the court that morning, had tried to take the blame on herself by telling some cock-and-bull story about having pushed Prosper over the edge of the balcony herself. Nobody would believe such a crazy thing, of course, but he tried to draw what small, vague comfort he could from the knowledge that she had been prepared to take the guilt on herself in order to spare him.

Presently the door opened and she came in and closed it. She was very pale, her eyes deeply ringed, her lips ashen without their make-up. In spite of himself he felt his pity quicken. She was suffering badly. Then he asked himself bitterly for whom she was suffering, herself or Prosper, and the face he turned to her was grim.

'Well?' he asked.

She came nearer. He remained seated and for once she did not even notice his lack of good manners, though ever since their marriage she had painstakingly and without his resentment, been teaching him the code of manners of her own world.

'Could we talk, Joseph?'

'I don't know that there's aught to say,' he told her heavily. 'Yon chap's still alive but not conscious yet, if that's what you want to know.'

'I suppose one ought to be thinking about him, but somehow I can't,' she said drearily. 'He doesn't matter, does he?'

'He ought to, to you,' grunted Joseph.

'I don't expect it's any good saying this to you, and you probably won't believe it, but he doesn't mean very much to me. He never has.'

'Then why did you go to his place with him? Is that all you are? A whore? Not going to ask me to believe you didn't go there to go to bed with him, are you? Are you? Eh?' with withering contempt and anger.

The tide of colour receded from her face, leaving it very white.

'No,' she said slowly. 'I'm not asking you to believe that, but—that was the only occasion. I have never done it before. I should never have done it again. I'm bitterly sorry.'

'Because you've been found out and I've half killed him?'

'No. Even if that hadn't happened to Garry I should have felt just the same—hateful in my own eyes.'

It hurt him to see her so humbled, even though with part of him he wanted to humble her further. Had she been a woman of the class into which he had been born, amongst whom he had spent his young days, he knew he would have knocked her down, probably half beaten the life out of her, after which he could possibly have forgiven her and taken her back. But with Clementine that was not possible. He knew he would never lay a finger on her, and so the wound would fester and gall him, probably for ever.

'You want me to believe that last night was the first time you've committed adultery? You can flinch, but I'm a plain man, and I call a spade a spade.'

'It was the first time, Joseph,' she said in a low voice.

'You say you don't love the fellow. Then why the heck did you go with him? What had he got to give you that you can't get from me? Eh? Eh?'

How could she tell the truth, which was that Garry's only attraction for her was that he reminded her of Piers? That she had had some sort of crazy notion that, in Garry's arms, she would be able to recapture in the darkness something of that old, thrilling, rapturous delight, that ecstasy, which she had known only with Piers? Joseph had never admitted jealousy of her first husband and yet she had known instinctively that that was the one sore spot with him, the one thing she must never allow to intrude into their relationship. Joseph must never know that the memory of Piers, the longing for him, was ever-present and everlasting.

So now what was she to say?

'I didn't love him. I don't know why I did it, except that I've always been restless, that I like excitement, things happening to me, even dangerous things. And I suppose it was that he amused me—'

'So you went to bed with him for a good laugh?' asked Joseph with bitter scorn.

She flinched and drew back. He saw by the convulsive movements of her hands that she had been stung, but she made no attempt at defence or retaliation and he wished he had not said that.

'Have you any idea what will—happen next?'

'If he recovers and makes a charge they'll arrest me. If he doesn't make a charge the police will probably have to, as the affair's been given a good deal of publicity.'

She knew how he was hating that.

'And if—he doesn't—get better?' she forced herself to ask.

'Then I suppose I shall be tried for murder,' he said curtly.

She drew a sharp, sobbing breath.

'Oh, Joseph, no!'

He looked at her reflectively, wishing he could see her again as she had been; proud, laughing, autocratic – her ladyship. Would she ever be like that again?

'Templar says you went to the court this morning to try to get them to believe you did it,' he said. 'Why did you do that?'

'Because it's so unfair that you should be bearing the brunt of it when it was my fault, all my fault.'

'Well, don't try to start up anything like that again. For one thing, nobody in their right senses would believe it, especially with your jewels found on the table by the bed and your powder all over the dressing-table. And for another thing, leave me to manage this for myself. My back's broad enough. I don't want any interference.'

'I wanted to help you, Joseph.'

His face softened by an infinitesimal degree.

'Well, you can't. Only person that can help me is myself, and when it comes to the point, Templar. You keep out of it. I'm going into the City now. If folks think I'm going to skulk in a hole because of what they're saying about me, they're mistaken.'

'I'm the one they'll be saying things about, Joseph,' she said in a small, dull voice.

'Happen they are, but that's your funeral. I've told Templar to let you know when he gets any more news from the hospital,' and he stumped out of the room, and she heard the shutting of the front door and the clang of the lift gates.

That was the moment at which Diana presented herself.

# Chapter Nineteen

Miserable, frightened, Diana had left the haven of Mrs. Breeze's untidy house with no idea what she was going to do.

She was feeling physically ill, too, which made it the more difficult to make plans. Where, indeed, could she go? It was useless to think of getting another job since it was already obvious what was the matter with her. Also she could not go on doing the standing, the trudging about with heavy trays, which a waitress's job demanded.

She left her case at Victoria Station, and bought a newspaper to study the advertisements. It was an early edition of an evening paper and as she turned the pages her eye caught a familiar name. Under the caption 'Assaulted By City Knight' she read that Mr. Garrick Prosper, the well-known novelist and dramatist, had met with an accident through an assault by Sir Joseph Bloggett, who had appeared before the magistrates' court that morning and been released on bail.

Diana did not take it in fully. The main feature of it for her was that her mother was in London again. She could not understand why Sir Joseph should be going about assaulting people, but she could believe anything of him, and anyway it could have nothing to do with Clementine.

It was really the last thing she wanted to do, to present herself before her mother in her condition and with so sorry a tale, but at least Clementine would tell her what to do, give her money.

Flora's greeting of her was surprising.

'Oh, Miss Diana, thank goodness you've come!' she said. 'I didn't know you were even in London. Her ladyship is in her room, poor soul. Sir Joseph's just gone,' and Flora went along the passage, knocked at a door, and opened it.

'Here's Miss Diana, my lady,' she said, and ushered her in.

Clementine, coming through the communicating doorway from her husband's room, stopped short at sight of her daughter.

'Diana! What on earth are you doing here? And where have you come from?' she asked. 'I suppose you've heard about this foul business?'

'Not—not really,' said Diana. 'You mean—Sir Joseph?'

'And Garry Prosper, yes. How do you know about it?'

'It's in the newspaper.'

Clementine flung herself down on the bed, her face in the pillow.

Diana stood watching her, bewildered and helpless. There must be more in this than she had supposed. She had never seen her mother like this in her life. Even when the news of her father's death had come, Clementine was quite calm, ice-cold, silent, stony-faced. This writhing, sobbing woman was a stranger to her.

She sat down on the edge of the bed and tried to make the distraught woman look at her.

'Mummy, what's happened? What is all the trouble about?'

Clementine sat up, pushing her disordered hair away from eyes red with weeping. All her beauty had fled. She looked an old, sick woman. Diana was profoundly shocked.

'What is it?' she asked again.

'I thought you knew?' said Clementine sharply.

'Only what is says in the paper, that Sir Joseph assaulted someone and had to appear at the magistrates' court.'

'It'll soon say more. He's killed him. Joseph did it. He killed Garry Prosper, and if they find him guilty they'll—hang him!' and she collapsed on the bed again and refused any comfort.

Diana went to fetch Flora and between them they soothed Clementine to some measure of composure, but Diana knew that she could not possibly tell her what she had come there to say. Her mother had quite enough to bear, and neither Diana nor Flora was in any position to refute what Clementine was saying about the possibility of Sir Joseph having to stand his trial for murder. It was horrifying, and Diana did not know whether to go or to stay.

When her mother had regained control of herself and lay back quiet but exhausted, Diana, at a respectful touch from the maid, tiptoed out of the room.

Flora closed the bedroom door softly.

'I'm glad you've come, Miss Diana,' she said. 'I'm so worried about her. I've never seen her like this before, not even when the master died, but then that was different.'

To Flora, Piers was always 'the master'.

'It was much worse,' said Diana, frowning. 'You don't really think that—*that* will happen to Sir Joseph? Has he really killed this Mr. Prosper, Flora?'

'No, he's not dead, Miss Diana, but they think he's going to die. The police were here and they took Sir Joseph away and he had to spend the night in the cells, but they've let him out on bail.'

Diana was as ignorant of legal procedure as Flora, but it seemed to her to augur well for Sir Joseph if they let him go.

'But what was it all about?' she asked. 'I shouldn't have thought he was at all the sort of man to attack anybody.'

Flora looked uncomfortable and hesitated.

'Well,' she said at last, 'I expect everybody's got to know, if they don't already. You see—her ladyship was there, Miss Diana.'

Diana stared aghast, realizing at once the implication.

'I see,' she said at last. 'That's why she's so upset. It's pretty frightful, isn't it? Where is Sir Joseph now?'

'Gone to the City. He didn't say when he would be back.'

'I suppose there's trouble between them over it?' and the maid nodded.

'I don't know what to do, whether to go or not. My mother and I have never been very close friends, and I don't know what to say to her.'

'I'll order you some lunch, Miss Diana,' said Flora the practical, in whose opinion nothing ever looked so black with a full stomach as with an empty one. 'Maybe I can get her to eat something too, and then you'll see how she is.'

Diana went into the bathroom and looked critically at herself in the first full-length mirror she had seen for several months. She realized that no observant eye could fail to detect her pregnancy, and her own alarm and fears returned a hundredfold. What was she to do? Where could she go? Above all, where was she to get money on which to live until she could work again? And even when that happened, what was she to do about the baby? She had come to Clementine with a vague idea of asking 'help', relying on her mother to know and suggest the form it should take, though her one resolve had been that she would not be persuaded, even if it were still possible, to get rid of the baby. Fiercely, in spite of all that it had cost her and would still cost her, the child was hers, her own, the first thing that had ever been completely hers, for even her dogs she had had to share, and in the end had had to abandon. She knew Joan would have looked after them, found them good homes. This child she would not abandon, not because it was Paul's, of whom, strangely, she now rarely thought, but because it was her own.

If her mother would give her some money – and then she paused on a sickening thought. It was not Clementine's money but Sir Joseph's, and how, in the circumstances, could she give her any? Diana did not know about the marriage settlement and that Sir Joseph had been generous and had made it all right for his bride, whatever happened. She saw the money as still his, and could not assess the position now that Clementine had been such a fool, as to have an affair with another man and let Sir Joseph find her out.

After she had forced herself to eat what might be her last good meal for a long, time, she went back to her mother.

Clementine was looking more like herself, had changed her dress and made up her face, though she had not touched the dainty tray Flora had brought her, especially sent up from the service kitchen.

'Do you feel better, Mummy?' asked Diana nervously.

She had dressed for the street again so that she could wear the long coat which still successfully hid her figure.

'Sorry I was such a drip,' said Clementine. 'I'm not very good company at the moment.'

Diana need not have worried, for her mother barely glanced at her.

'Would you—would you like me to stay?' she asked.

'Good heavens, no! Where would you sleep, for one thing? There are only the three bedrooms, and my own tenure here is rather slight at the moment,' with a bitter little smile of self-derision. 'Why was I such a fool?'

There was no answer to that, and Diana realized that already her mother was absorbed in herself again and wanted to be alone.

'All right,' she said bleakly. 'I—I just thought—'

Clementine turned to her for a brief moment of contrition.

'I'm sorry, Di. It's ages since we've met, isn't it? How's your husband? Is he with you? I can never think what possessed you to go off like that and marry a Frenchman, but then what does possess women when they do idiotic things? I hope you're happy and take a lesson from what's happened to me,' her thoughts turning inward again.

It had been a shock to have her 'husband' referred to like that. Of course that was what everybody thought.

'If I can't do anything for you, perhaps I'd better go now.'

'Leave your address. I'll let you know what happens—though it'll be plastered all over the newspapers, I suppose,' said Clementine bitterly.

Diana slipped away and let herself out of the flat.

She wondered blankly what to do now. She had been idiotic not to ask her mother for the loan of even ten pounds, which surely Clementine would have had, notwithstanding the circumstances.

During her two months as a waitress she had managed to save three pounds, a considerable feat since she had had to pay Mrs. Breeze for her keep, and her wages had been low in consideration of the tips she was expected to receive but which, in that part of London, were small. Three pounds between her and – what?

She knew now with a sick feeling that she had at last reached the lowest depths of humiliation, what she was going to do. She was going to write to Andrew.

She took a room in the cheapest-looking hotel she could find, a shoddy little place off Vauxhall Bridge Road, bought a writing-pad and some envelopes and composed that letter, tearing up so many attempts that she used up most of the pad in the process.

*Dear Andrew* (she wrote at last),
*You will be surprised to have this letter and I know I have no earthly right to ask you to read it, but I am in desperate straits and I don't*

*know who to go to nor where to turn. Is it possible for you to lend me a little money, perhaps fifty pounds? I know it is a most terrible thing for me to be asking, but you will realize I am desperate or I wouldn't be doing it. I don't know when I can pay you back, but it will be paid back, every penny, however long it takes. Please, Andrew, will you help me?*

*Diana.*

She enclosed an envelope addressed to herself, not knowing how else to tell him that she was still Miss Merrimayne.

The hotel was, she discovered, even worse than she had thought from the outside. There were comings and goings all night, whisperings and laughter, the babblings of a drunken man, the shrill voice of a woman urging him.

She had posted her letter to Andrew's office in the City, but he might not be there. He might have retired, as he had intended to do soon after they were married. He might even be married. That thought made her swallow a lump in her throat.

Andrew, so safe, so kind, so badly served by her when she had owed him everything that now seemed so utterly desirable.

He might be out of the country. He might even be – dead.

In any case she could not get an answer from him, even if he were at his office and wrote at once, before the next night. She might have to stay in this awful place another night. She dare not go away until he had had time to write to her – or until she could be sure he' was not going to reply to her letter!

She would not let herself think of that. It was too frightening.

She had taken the room for the night only, and in the morning she tidied it, locked her door and went to get a frugal breakfast. As she left the unsavoury house she was remembering that house of ill fame in which she had found herself the first time she ran away from Paul. What an ignorant child she had been then! She could scarcely believe it possible that she had ever been so innocent, so trusting. How terrified she had been, fleeing from that place after her hazardous climb out of the window!

280

'I seem to do a lot of running away,' she thought mockingly. 'I've been running away from people and from things all my life. This is something I can't run away from,' and instinctively she leaned a little forward at the table where she was having her breakfast, cradling with her arms the precious burden within her.

In spite of everything, the thought of her child lying there brought her a strange exaltation and peace. She had fulfilled herself, brought her womanhood full circle.

It was a fine day, soft and warm, and she walked in the direction of Westminster, seeking to put as far behind her as possible the sordidness of her surroundings. She walked along the Embankment, unconsciously turning her steps in the direction of Andrew until at last, tired, she decided she would go back to the hotel, there to wait for the afternoon post, which was the earliest by which she had decided she could possibly hear from Andrew.

She went up the unwashed steps and opened the door, and found herself face to face with him. He had risen from a chair in the entrance hall as she came in.

'Andrew!'

To see him was the last thing she had expected.

Yet here he was, and not changed by so much as a hair or a line, when she herself felt she had lived for a century since their parting.

'Where can we talk?' he asked, with no other greeting, and she wondered if he were too much shocked by her appearance to greet her.

'I've got a room here,' she said.

'Here?' looking round with unmistakable recognition, of the surroundings, the frowsy woman behind the office desk, the furtive silence.

'I don't live here, but I didn't know where else to go,' said Diana, and led the way up the stairs and into the tawdry room dominated by the black-and-brass double bed.

'I'm not living this way,' she said with a hard note in her voice which told him how very far she had gone from the Diana he had known.

Poor, foolish, betrayed Diana!

She kept her coat on, and sat on the edge of the bed, leaving the one chair for him.

'This is a dreadful place for you to be in,' he said.

'I haven't any money—at least, I've got a bit less than three pounds,' she told him stonily, knowing that that hard matter-of-factness was her only protection against herself, and that if she let herself go she could easily have flung herself into his arms, or at his feet, and implored his compassion and his help.

'Have you left—the man?' asked Andrew.

'Paul? He married someone else,' she told him tonelessly.

Strangely, it did not hurt as much to say his name as she had believed it would. The whole thing had changed for her with the coming of Andrew, had shifted on its base, though she did not recognize with any clarity of thought that it had done so.

'You're not married, then?'

'No.'

There was a long silence in which she sat on the edge of the bed and he sat opposite her on the one thing which had seemed to her to miss being sinister, the straight-backed chair.

'Would you like to tell me everything?' he asked at last, and though his voice had none of the old gentleness which would have brought her to his feet, it was not unkind, not even judicial.

She nodded her head and then, not looking at him, told him the bare bones of her story.

'I didn't know he was married when I went away with him. When he told me, he said his wife had promised to divorce him, as the marriage had taken place in England and she was English. I kept waiting for him to be able to marry me, and then he—married someone else and I—came back here.'

Only someone who knew her as well as Andrew Shawn had known her could have filled in that outline, could have guessed at the fears, the shame, the heartbreak, which had turned her from an eager, affectionate girl to this quiet-voiced, self-possessed woman who, he knew, would never be a girl again. In his heart he cursed the unknown Paul with all the invective his lips would never have uttered. To take all the joyousness of her, which he had loved so much, and give her nothing in return but this.

She sat motionless and silent. Her whole attitude of patient waiting hurt him intolerably – Diana who could never bear to wait but must rush forward with open arms to greet life.

When he spoke again she saw that he had put the past behind him.

'You asked me to let you have fifty pounds. What did you propose to do with it?' he asked her gravely.

For a moment she did not reply, but he saw a strange look come into her eyes, of appeal, of despair. Then she rose slowly to her feet and threw off the coat she had been wearing and stood before him.

'Look at me, Andrew,' she said bitterly, and turned her head away so that she should not see his face.

He saw what she had intended him to see and drew a long, broken breath. So that was it? Oh, Diana, my bright star! his heart mourned.

'You understand?' she asked presently, when he did not speak. 'I am going to have a child.'

'And he let you go? Like that?'

'He didn't know. I didn't realize it myself until after I had—after I found out he had—left me.'

'Couldn't you have found him?'

'What was the use? He'd married—her, by then. Besides, I wouldn't want to have tied him to me just by that,' with a touch of the old pride which survived her bitter humiliation.

'And the fifty pounds was to help you through?'

'Yes. I know I have not the slightest right to ask it, Andrew. You of all people. But—I don't know what else to do. I went to my mother, but—do you know the trouble there?'

'Yes, I've heard something about it.'

'She was in such a state about it that I couldn't tell her—about me, or ask her for anything. So I—came away again. I don't want you to give it to me, Andrew. I want to feel I can pay it back—some day,' speaking painfully and without looking at him.

'You won't do much with fifty pounds,' he said grimly. 'When is it?'

'December, I think.'

He got up and paced the room, his hands behind him, his head bent. She sat and watched him. It was like a cold hand over her heart that Andrew should consider so thoughtfully and for so long whether he would let her have the money. If he didn't, what was she to do? She could think of no way out but the river, and on top of that came absurdly the thought that she was too good a swimmer to be able to drown before someone came to fish her out.

When he ceased his pacing and stood in front of her, his next words took her breath away.

'Diana, will you marry me?' he asked her gravely.

She could not answer. She stood staring at him, wide-eyed, her breast heaving, her hands working at the folds of her skirt.

'Well?' he asked as she did not answer. 'Will you?'

'Oh, Andrew—Andrew!' she whispered.

'There is only one thing I am going to ask you to tell me, Diana, and that is how you still feel about this man; whether at any time and in any circumstances you could go back to him.'

She let her hands drop. Her eyes besought him.

'Go back to Paul? *Paul?*' she asked incredulously. 'Oh no, never. Never! I don't want ever to see him again,' shivering away from the thought.

'And what will you feel about his child?'

'Andrew, I don't think I could make you understand. I don't think any man could understand,' she said with difficulty, trying to feel her way through her confused mist of thought. 'A child is something that can be quite apart from—the man. It's mine, my own, a part of me, growing inside me, and Paul doesn't even know it exists. It doesn't seem to matter any more whose it is since it is mine. I suppose if—if I were still with him, still—loving him and being loved, it would seem a part of him too, but not now, not any longer. It's mine, Andrew—mine.'

'So that if I married you I should not feel all the time that you were hankering after this man? Living with him again in the child?'

'No. No, Andrew, you would never feel that. It could never be true,' she said steadily and he drew a deep breath. He knew he could believe her.

'Then you will marry me, Diana?'

The trouble returned to her face.

'Andrew, it wouldn't be fair to you.'

'Leave me to decide that.'

284

'Why—do you want to marry me? You can't possibly still love me.'

'I'm not going to pretend that, or anything. If you marry me, Diana, let's always be quite honest with each other. It was terrible to me when you went as you did, not trusting me to understand, as I should have done. I knew you cared for me, but that I did not possess the whole of you. I believed that once you were my wife that would come naturally. It was the way you left me as much as the actual leaving which—killed something in me that I know will never live again. I loved you very much, Diana.'

'Andrew, I'm so sorry, so—ashamed,' she said in a low voice.

For the first time she was beginning to realize what she had done in throwing aside Andrew for the glittering tinsel of Paul – gold for dross. And yet she had known intense happiness with Paul, something which she would never have known with Andrew.

'If we marry, all that must be put aside and never spoken of again,' he said firmly.

'And the child, Andrew?' she asked fearfully. 'I could never give it up.'

'I wouldn't ask it of you. If I marry you, I take the child as well.'

'You make me so—so humble, Andrew,' she whispered.

'I'm not trying to humiliate you, Diana.'

'Andrew, why are you doing this for me?'

'We won't go into that too deeply. Perhaps I don't know the answer myself, but I have a certain feeling of responsibility towards you. If it hadn't been that you were engaged to me you wouldn't have gone off with him like that, without proper investigations. It would have been discovered that he was a married man.'

'I loved him. I don't think at that time anything would have held me back.'

'Well, we'll put it behind us and face the future. To begin with, of course, you can't possibly stay here. Get your things together whilst I go down and pay the bill and find a taxi. I'll meet you in the hall.'

He took her to a quiet, ultra-respectable and very dull hotel in Bayswater and left her there until he could arrange for a special licence. Before leaving her he took her left hand and replaced on it the ring he had given her over two years ago and which she had left behind at Joan's. He showed no emotion whatsoever in doing so.

'You had better wear this,' was all he said. 'It regularizes your position,' and at the hotel he said, 'This is my fiancée, Miss Merrimayne. Please look after her well.'

Quiet, respectable, dull – she realized that this hotel was typical of what her life was to be, and she was glad. She had had enough of adventuring. All she wanted now was to be safe and sheltered, and she knew that with him she would be utterly secure.

She remained as far as possible in her room, going in and out of the dining-room unobtrusively, doing a little essential shopping with the money Andrew had given her, though she disliked spending his money before she was actually his wife. She did not know what his plans were for her. She asked him nothing and was very quiet with him.

A fortnight later they were married.

It was an unreal ceremony to Diana, taking place in a registrar's office with two clerks as witnesses and no friends of either of them present. He had asked her if she would like to have anybody there – her mother perhaps, but she had refused.

'I haven't any friends in London now,' she said, 'and Clementine wouldn't be interested. She's too much taken up with this business of Sir Joseph and Garrick Prosper.'

So she stood alone with Andrew before the registrar and in a few minutes with a few short sentences and the writing of her name she became Diana Shawn.

'Where now?' she asked him, coming out into the street again with the shining new ring on her finger.

He smiled at her, looking at her for almost the first time since he had fetched her from the hotel that morning. He had seemed cold and distant, chilling her by the practical way he was dealing with everything, and the smile warmed a little her sad heart, sad because of all the bright hopes and happy anticipation that had once been hers and the contrasting reality of her wedding day.

'I think we could have at least a mild celebration, don't you?' he asked her, and exerted himself to entertain and amuse her over a perfectly chosen lunch *à deux* with champagne in an ice bucket.

They went down by train to the quiet Sussex village where she was to live until the baby was born. Andrew had taken a furnished house and had found a married couple, the Barretts, who would look after the house and garden.

'I thought the train journey would be better for you than going by road,' he said, 'so I left the car down there. Barrett will have it at Playndon Station for us. We'll look for a small, reliable car for you, though I don't want you to drive it yet. Barrett is a careful driver. By the way, nobody at Playndon knows that we have only just been married, so be careful not to give it away.'

She had listened with a mixture of passionate gratitude and shame. It was all wrong that Andrew should be mixed up with lies and deceit, and yet he took it all so calmly and with no hint of resentment or embarrassment.

'You're so good to me,' she murmured.

'You're my wife,' he said, and she swallowed a lump in her throat and looked down at the narrow platinum ring on her finger.

It was true. She was actually Andrew's wife, for good or ill, and passionately she vowed to herself that it should be for good, for him. He should never regret this wonderful thing he had done for her. She had destroyed his love for her and lost forever for him the magic that should have been theirs today, but at least she would give him everything that lay in her power to atone.

Her secret worry over the basis on which they would live together was settled when Mrs. Barrett, a capable, middle-aged woman, took charge of her whilst Andrew saw to the luggage and discussed with Barrett some cars he had been told to look at.

'This is your room, madam,' said Mrs. Barrett. 'It's not quite as large as the front room but Mr. Shawn thought you would like it better with a view over the garden. I hope you have quite recovered, madam?'

'Thank you, I'm much better,' said Diana, taking her cue from that speech and looking gratefully round the pleasant room with its old-fashioned furniture and frilled white muslin curtains.

'The master is having the front room across the landing, madam, so he won't be very far away if you feel poorly or anything, but Barrett and

I have the room just along here, and I am a very light sleeper, so don't hesitate to call me at any time.'

'Thank you,' said Diana gratefully, looking in dutifully at Andrew's room, larger than hers but not, she agreed, nearly as pleasant. She felt mingled relief and sadness that they should be embarking on the perilous sea of married life like this, and for the first time knew regret that the child was not Andrew's. Were not his steadfast qualities so much better worth perpetuating than Paul's charm? The thought was bewildering. What was happening to her conception of Paul and her feeling for Andrew?

She went downstairs to find him waiting for her.

'Do you like the house?' he asked with a smile.

'So very much, Andrew.'

'Then come and see something else I've got for you,' linking an arm with hers to lead her through the house into the garden.

'It's rather a wilderness at present,' he said, 'but time and care will put that right. This is what I wanted to show you,' taking her to the end of the large, neglected garden to a substantial brick building with a stable door to it.

He opened the upper half and stood back, and she looked in wonderingly and then gave a cry.

'Andrew! Oh—*Andrew!*'

'Don't let them jump up at you,' he warned her, but she was blind and deaf to anything but those leaping bodies.

She was down on her knees with them – no longer puppies but still Robin and Simon. She had her arms about them, the golden cocker wagging his whole body, the magnificent bull mastiff towering over her, calmer, more dignified, but licking her face with his great rough tongue and laying one huge paw on her shoulder.

'Oh, my darlings, my darlings!' she said, and laid her head against the smooth, satiny flank of the mastiff and wept.

'Don't let them be rough with you,' warned Andrew's voice again, and then he went away and left her with them.

# Chapter Twenty

Though Garry Prosper regained consciousness within a few days of Sir Joseph Bloggett's attack, it was a month before he was able to leave hospital, and he had declined to say whether or not he intended to prefer a charge of assault against Clementine's husband.

Sir Joseph went about his ordinary life a changed man, and no one was more acutely aware of the change than Clementine herself. It was not merely that the life had gone out of him, but something else had entered to take the place of the affectionate, generous, happy man he had been. When he spoke to her it was merely on the practical arrangements of their life, whether he would be in for dinner, whether to accept a weekend invitation.

Presently she did not ask him about invitations which would involve their being away for a night. She realized that he would always refuse them, that he did not intend to risk being obliged to share her room again. He was shut closely within himself and she heard from other people of the phenomenal deals he was making in the City. He was making money fast, and though the bulk of it went in taxes, he seemed not to care. The thing was to make the money, to take it from other men, to get the better of other men.

He increased his allowance to her, leaving her bank to notify her of the fact.

'I don't need this, Joseph,' she told him.

'That's rather a new line, isn't it?' he asked grimly.

'You've always been so generous to me.'

'Well, it's what you married me for, isn't it? It takes two to make a bargain, but only one to break it. In my case, I prefer to keep my part of the bargain even though you've broken yours.'

She could find nothing to say. She had never known him like this, and it was ironical that she should find her wish to stand well in his eyes increasing as they drifted further apart.

They never mentioned Prosper, but one day, when she answered a telephone call, she was electrified to hear his voice.

'Clementine? I want to see you. You know who's speaking?'

'You Garry? I don't want to see you. I never want to see you again,' she told him violently.

'I'm afraid you'll have to.'

'Why?'

'Because it depends on you whether I charge your husband with assault.'

'How can it depend on me? You can do what you like,' she said.

'I don't think you mean that. You'd better see me. I'll be at the Haymarket entrance to Piccadilly tube station at three this afternoon.'

There was a threat in his voice, and hating the necessity she kept the appointment. He looked thin and pale, and walked with a stick with difficulty. His fall had resulted in multiple injuries, and it was a miracle that he had lived at all.

'Ought you to be walking about?' she asked.

'No. We'll get a taxi to the park and find some chairs there,' he said, and again she was torn with pity and remorse when she saw the extreme difficulty with which, with the help of the driver, he got in and out of the taxi.

He saw the look on her face and laughed harshly, beginning to limp into the park.

'Nice, isn't it?' he asked. 'The world's hero, the great lover, Romeo without his balcony.'

'Don't, Garry,' she said, wincing.

'I'm sorry, m'dear,' he said, his tone altering a little. 'I didn't mean to make a scene. Where are the nearest chairs? Over there? I think I can hobble. I suppose you wouldn't give me your arm?"

She let him lean on her, and they reached the chairs he had indicated, two chairs which stood apart in the sunshine.

'Better drag them back under the trees a bit,' he suggested. 'We don't exactly want to advertise. A newspaper photographer would consider us a find just now. I wonder what the caption would read? They have to be so careful over contempt of court. Lady Bloggett and friend, probably. Or perhaps Garrick Prosper, the well-known author and dramatist, takes an airing with a friend. Wonder which of us would make the better front-page news?'

'Don't be so bitter, Garry,' she said in a low voice.

'Well, I haven't much reason for feeling particularly sweet. What about coming away with me, Clementine?'

She stared at him, scarcely able to believe her ears.

'Coming away with you?' she echoed blankly.

'Oh, we could get married eventually. It's quite an honourable proposal, even though it started with such a fracas.'

'I haven't any wish to marry you. I never have had. You know that. There was never anything like that between us.'

'Not on your side perhaps, but I had toyed with the idea quite a lot. I thought that eventually you would come to the same way of thinking.'

'Well, I haven't and I never should,' said Clementine.

'You're beautifully frank, anyway. What's the matter with me? Quite apart from my present somewhat dilapidated condition?'

'Nothing, except that I'm not in love with you.'

'Oh—love? My dear, surely you aren't still playing about with that time-honoured, man-made idea? Analyse it and look honestly at what it is. Nothing but the primitive urge to copulate, and we've got that—or rather, we had it, and as soon as I'm fit we shall have it again. We've only to be together for half an hour or so to want to go to bed together. Well, there you have what is miscalled love. What about the rest of this glorification of the sex urge? We speak the same language, we laugh at the same things. I haven't as much money as old Joe Bloggett, but I can earn as much as we need and pretty nearly as much as you want. Also we've both got enough sense not to expect perfection of each other, and to go our own ways when it suits us without making absurdly possessive demands on each other. What else could anyone possibly need to form a pleasant and lasting union?'

'Things aren't just like that, Garry. I know it's smart and good form to mock at love and call it ugly names, but it exists for all that. I know it because—I've had it.'

'Not, oh tell me *not*, for honest Joe?' he asked her mockingly.

'No. For my first husband, Piers.'

'Oh yes. You told me once I reminded you of him, didn't you? Well, isn't that another proof that we should make a good pair? I suppose Joe would divorce you?'

'I'm not going to ask him to, though of course I wouldn't need to do that. He's got the evidence if he wants it.'

'Us, you mean? Not at all. He's what they call "condoned" that by taking you back to live with him. One can only assume that he doesn't mind your having cannoned off another man since he could do the real he-man stuff and half kill the other man.'

'He didn't mean to hurt you so much. You know that. You fell over the balcony rail.'

'I know. Lucky for him that that pile of sand was there, and for you, too. You'd have lost both your lover *and* your husband. Wonder if they'd have hanged him for killing me? Or if he would successfully have pleaded what they call "extreme provocation"?'

'This conversation is most unpleasant, Garry, and quite pointless, as far as I can see. Was that all you brought me here for?'

'In my present state I regret I can't take you anywhere for anything but conversation,' he said. 'I'm asking you if you'll come away with me, Clementine.'

'And I've said I won't, so shall we go? '

'No. Sit down again. There's more to it than that, quite a bit more. You see, unless you come away with me I shall prefer a charge of assault against Sir Joseph, and even if he manages to justify it, there'll be the hell of a stink in the papers about you, my sweet.'

'It's blackmail,' said Clementine angrily. 'Is it? Well, I want you and I'm prepared to fight for you, and naturally I shall use the weapon put right into my hand.'

'You mean you'll do your best to injure me horribly?'

'If I have to, my darling.'

She had spoken of herself, but she was thinking of Joseph, picturing to herself the position he would be in if such a case were brought against him. He would fight it. He would have to fight it, since Garry was in no mood to be bought off when it was publicity he was seeking.

Jeffrey Templar had said that if a case were brought, in his opinion Joseph would get away with a plea of extreme provocation, so that he would be set free after the nominal sentence of one day's imprisonment, which he had already actually served before being granted bail. The damage to Joseph would be the public dragging of her name through the mire so that he would never be able to hold up his head again. There had, of course, been rumours of what had happened, but until these were dragged out and confirmed in a court of law few people would dare to act as though they believed them. Some people had cold-shouldered her. All had appeared curious and interested, and most of her friends had dropped hints and invited confidences, which she had never given.

After such a case as Garry could bring, all that would be altered. Her own life would be ruined, but what did she care about that? It had ended for her with the death of Piers, and since then she had merely been existing. The damage he could do was through her to Joseph, so proud of his frightful name, so careful of it and of everything connected with it.

Yes, for Joseph it would mean utter degradation, annihilation.

'You couldn't do anything so horrible,' she said at last.

'Oh, but believe me, I could,' he said.

'But why? What good would it do you if you did get me? I'm not worth much to anybody,' bitterly.

'Oh, but that's where you're wrong. You're life to me. You're the remains of my youth and its dreams. You're excitement. I actually believe I'm in love with you, Clementine, in spite of all I've said.'

'Life together would be beastly for us both, with this for a background.'

'Not so. In a little time we should forget and be able to laugh at it. We don't have to stay in England. I can live and work anywhere. We need never have a home unless and until you felt the need of one, and we both love wandering. Come to me, Clementine. I know I've threatened you, but I also entreat you.'

'I don't want to, Garry. Strange though it may seem to you, I want to stay with Joseph.'

He gave her a look of mock admiring wonder.

'O admirable lady! O faithful wife!'

She coloured and rose to her feet.

'Shall we go?' she asked.

'You mean you've decided to put poor old Joseph through the mangle?'

'He'd rather have it that way than for me to leave him,' she said, looking at him steadily and wondering whether she were really deceiving him. She could not deceive herself, nor be at all sure that Joseph even wanted her to stay with him. She could come to no conclusion about his feeling for her, now that their lives lay so widely separated even though they occupied the same small flat.

Garry rose to his feet and stood steadying himself for a moment before embarking on the short walk to the gates.

'I'll give you a little while to think it over,' he said, 'though not too long. It will be much more effective if I can appear in court like this. Say—a week?'

'I shan't change my mind,' she said.

'I wonder? Well, if you do you know where to find me. I'm back in Merion Street. Can I get you a taxi?'

'No. I'll find one for myself. You take the first one that comes.'

'How gallant of you! There's one coming along. Would you signal him? I find it a bit difficult to balance.'

After he had left her she walked back to Preston Square to give herself time to think before taking a risk of meeting Joseph. She wished she knew exactly how Joseph now regarded her, whether he would not be actually relieved to get rid of her altogether.

She came back to the question of how he would react to the publicity which would surround their name if Garry did actually bring his case. Joseph would hate it beyond words. He had always told her he believed in advertisement. How would he take that sort of advertisement? And was not her own life with him, any possibility of happiness, over in any case?

She would hate the publicity for her own sake, but not as he would hate it. Of all his possessions, his wife had been the one of whose value he was most sure and most proud. She knew that he was suffering horribly over his discovery that she, too, was a fake, was neither genuine nor unique as he had believed her to be. She told herself this with bitter self-contempt. How cheap she had been! How utterly she had lowered herself in her own eyes!

Yet she was thinking most of Joseph. It was strange to her to realize that that was so. She wanted her private happiness with him, and it was gone for all time. She was remembering his kindness, his generosity. What poor measure she had given him in return! And the only thing she could do for him now was to leave him, though the only thing she wanted to do for herself was to remain with him, not for the material gain but because she had come to know and to appreciate the man beneath the unlovely exterior.

How strange that he should have grown so deeply into her life, the private and personal life of her mind!

Within the week which Prosper had given her she told him she was ready to go away with him.

'I don't love you, Garry. I shall never love you. Through you I've done myself too much harm, because the thing I really want is to stay with Joseph. Oh, not for his money,' she said quickly, interpreting the smile he gave her at that. 'Money doesn't enter into it and in any case I've got my marriage settlement which ethically I should renounce but which practically I intend to keep.'

'Because you don't trust me to be able to provide for you?'

'Because I don't trust you at all,' she told him calmly.

For a moment he was angry. Then he laughed and presently she laughed a little herself, in spite of her sick misery.

'You see?' he asked. 'We find amusement in the same things, and we can be absolutely honest with each other because we don't think each other angelic. What better basis for a reasonably happy future together? As for what is called love—we're both getting on, and in the normal course of nature, in a few years we shan't be slaves to the sex urge any more.'

'Then why do you want to break up my life like this?'

'That's not a flattering way of putting it.'

'It's the way I feel about it.'

'Well, I know I shall feel the damned urge again, and towards you once I'm fit, and by then it will be too late to go for your husband. But

I thought all that argument was over? I thought you'd decided to come to me?'

'Yes,' said Clementine simply. 'Yes, I have.'

'Tell me quite honestly why.'

'I have told you. You've blackmailed me into it. I'm doing it to save Joseph that kind of publicity. The alternative is bad enough for him. but not as bad as the things he would be asked and have to say in a public court about that night. You won't be generous, Garry, and drop the case and let me stay with Joseph?'

'No. Why should I?'

'No reason except decency.'

'I haven't got that sort of decency. I want you on any terms.'

'All right. When do we start and where do we go?'

'I've booked seats on the 'plane to Dublin tomorrow morning. Will you go back to Preston Square or to an hotel for the night? I'm not going to ask you to share any sort of privacy with me whilst I'm like this.'

'I'll go to an hotel,' said Clementine, stony-faced.

But when she got back to the flat to prepare for her departure, dreading in case she might have to see Joseph again before she left, she found a letter from Diana with the surprising and belated news that she was married to Andrew Shawn and living at Playndon.

*If you can come down to see me, perhaps to stay a few days, I should be very glad. Andrew joins me in the invitation. Please come.*

The letter came as an unintended reproach, and she recalled the brief visit Diana had paid her on the day after Joseph's attack on Garry Prosper. She had been distraught and had taken little or no interest in her daughter's reappearance. Quite suddenly her indifference smote her. Diana was Piers' daughter! The one living thing in this world which had something of himself in it, and yet always she had seemed remote, inaccessible, even as a child.

She wanted desperately to see her again, scarcely knowing why.

And what was the story still untold which perhaps Diana had come to tell her? The story which had ended (or was it beginning?) in Andrew Shawn's arms.

'I'm going down to a place called Playndon, somewhere in Sussex,' she told Flora. 'Pack just for tonight, and I shan't want you to come with me. I'm going down to see Miss Diana. She seems to have married Mr. Shawn after all.'

'My lady!' cried the maid, as much surprised as Clementine had been, but keeping her thoughts to herself, as she had done ever since that visit of Diana's, which had told Flora so much more than Clementine had observed.

'Mr. Shawn,' thought the maid. 'Well, I never! Who would have thought it of *Mr. Shawn?*'

Clementine spoke to Garry Prosper on the telephone.

'I've had a letter from my daughter. She is in England and wants to see me. As it may be difficult later, I'd like to go there tonight. Is that all right with you?'

She disliked the necessity for asking him. Her present position was opposed to her nature in every way.

'All right. I don't mind. Will you meet me at Northolt?'

'Yes.'

'O.K. Don't overdo the luggage,' he said and rang off.

She sent Diana a telegram, and found her at the station to meet her, Barrett driving the car.

'Don't you drive yourself any longer?' she asked, surprised, for Diana loved driving.

'Not just now,' said her daughter, and Clementine looked at her and realization dawned on her with a staggering impetus.

'Please—not now,' said Diana in a low voice, and they talked of other things on the short journey to the house.

Once in the pleasant guest-room, the door shut, Clementine turned to her.

'How on earth has all this happened?' she asked. 'Is it true?'

'That I'm going to have a baby? Yes. I want to tell you about it. Andrew thinks I ought to.'

'You mean you don't want to yourself?' asked Clementine with a somewhat wry smile. 'I really am your mother, you know, though you're to be forgiven for forgetting it.'

'I haven't forgotten it, but—we've never been very close, have we? It's probably been as much my fault as yours, but—I want to tell you, and not just because Andrew wants me to. I think perhaps I feel—different now that I'm going to be a mother myself, though I still find it—not very easy to talk to you. I expect you feel that way about me.'

'Yes. Yes, I do,' admitted Clementine thoughtfully. 'I wonder if there's always this barrier between parents and children, or if it's just us? I haven't been a great success as a mother, have I?'

'Well, I don't know that I'd get a medal as a daughter,' said Diana. She was suddenly finding her mother more approachable.

'Let's call it quits then. How long have you been married, Di?'

'Only three weeks, though the Barretts don't know. It—it isn't Andrew's, Mother,' looking away, her cheeks hot.

Clementine could not remember that Diana had ever called her that before. It seemed to mark the change in their relationship. Clementine had become a mother, and Diana had grown up.

Sitting on the edge of the bed, Diana told the whole story: of her meeting with Paul so long ago, of the Knight in Shining Armour which her young imagination had made of him; of the dulling of the armour and the final revelation of the man himself, and as she listened, Clementine's hand stole into Diana's and their two hands clung together, bridging the years.

'You loved him?' she said when the story was told.

'Yes,' said Diana simply.

'I can understand better than a good many people could. Nothing, nobody, could have kept me from your father. I was luckier than you because he was good right through, and love lasted. Yours won't, Diana. We don't go on loving what has proved itself to be base, though just at first we may think we do. You're not actually in love with Paul any longer even now, but only with your memory of what you believed him to be. Isn't that so?'

'Perhaps it is,' said Diana with a sigh. 'I'm still so confused, and with Andrew so kind to me—the contrast is always there. It's such a marvellous thing that he's done, especially after the way I treated him. That rather disproves your theory that we don't go on loving what we know to be unworthy.'

'Andrew evidently doesn't think you are unworthy,' said her mother grimly. 'Well, let us hope you don't produce an obvious little Frenchman when you ought to be producing a little Scot! You look very fit, by the way.'

'I ought to, with all the care Andrew and Mrs. Barrett take of me. You don't look well yourself, or do you hate my saying that?'

'No, I don't mind. I feel like death and I'm tired of chasing my youth and have decided to let it escape me. Oh, Di, never mind about your youth when you grow older but hang on to Andrew, hang on with all your might and never let him go.'

'Why—Mother!'

'Surprised at that passionate advice? I'm leaving Joseph.'

'Whatever for? You mean—he wants you to?'

'I don't know what Joseph wants, but he is the living proof of what I said about not going on loving. He's found out what I'm really like and—well, that's rather that. I'm going to Garry Prosper. I'm flying to Dublin with him tomorrow.'

'What does Sir Joseph think about it?' asked Diana, worried.

She had a vivid memory of his adoration of her.

'He doesn't know yet. I'm going back to the flat before I meet Garry at Northolt. I suppose I shall have to leave the traditional note on the pin-cushion. Got a pin-cushion to lend me?'

Diana was anxious. She realized that Clementine was desperately unhappy. What had Garry Prosper to offer her as a panacea for the unhappiness? She knew that her mother was greatly changed. Or was it that she had never before known her as she was? It was difficult to reconcile this lonely, embittered, ageing woman with the lovely and happy wife of Piers Merrimayne, or even with the self-assured woman who had married Joseph Bloggett.

Impulsively Diana put an arm about her. It was the first spontaneous embrace either could remember.

'Mother, don't do it! You don't really want to leave him. You're not in love with Garrick Prosper, are you?'

'Love? Can one love a man who refers to it as the primitive urge to copulate?' asked Clementine bitterly, and she laid her head down on her daughter's shoulder and wept heartbrokenly.

Gradually Diana discovered the truth, and that she had decided to go away with Prosper only because it would save Joseph the worse of two evils. He could divorce her for going off with another man, whereas if she stayed he would stand his trial for assault and Garry would see to it that the whole story was told in detail. Clementine, the proud, had been caught almost *in flagrante delicto*. The elderly man, with his bald head and his money-bags, would be made an object of derision and would know it. She could save him the worst of that by going quietly away with Garry.

'But if you don't love him, Mother?' asked Diana, when the storm of tears had subsided and Clementine had gone through force of habit to the mirror to start repairing the damage.

'Love? What does that matter at my age? I'm nearly forty-three and ought to know better. Besides—I've had love, and nobody gets it twice, not like that. Heck, what a fright I look! Is there hot water in your taps or do they only say hot?'

'There's hot water if you let it run for a bit,' said Diana, and she knew that the discussion was over.

She was desperately worried, however, and that evening after they had all gone to their rooms she tiptoed out of her own and, rather diffidently, knocked at Andrew's door.

He opened it, surprised to see her there, and she flushed hotly.

'Could I talk to you a minute, Andrew? About Mother? It was difficult downstairs.'

'Of course. Won't you come in? That's a fairly comfortable chair. Are you cold? Shall I light the gas fire?'

'No. I'm quite warm. I've got two much more comfortable chairs than this in my room. Why don't you have one of them?'

'That one's all right for me, and I like you to have the others,' he said, pulling up a chair to sit opposite her. 'Now what's it all about? Not been upsetting you, has she?' looking at her keenly.

When she had told him the story he sat silent for a few moments looking at her with that inscrutable look in his eyes which she had come to know so well but never to understand. He was hidden behind it. She wondered if she would ever know the man himself.

'Can't we do something, Andrew?' she besought him. 'Can't you think of anything? Seeing Sir Joseph or—or something?'

'I don't think we can interfere, my dear,' he said.

'But Andrew, to stand aside and do nothing!'

'Your mother will go her own way, Diana, and even if she could be dissuaded from her purpose of going away with Prosper, what would be left to her? Bloggett will never forgive her—though I don't think it's so much a case of forgiveness as—as of having had the thing he cared for smashed to bits. I don't think he'll even care now whether she goes or stays. As a matter of fact, I saw him in the City and went to have a drink with him and I realized from the little he said that was how he felt. He worshipped her, Diana—largely, I think, because she was so far above him. At heart he's an idealist, but he can't idealize her any longer.'

'Yet she seems to think he would suffer badly if she let Prosper drag him into court and the whole story had to be told.'

'Because of his pride, which is all he has left. I think she's right.'

'Right to go, you mean?' asked Diana, astonished.

'Yes, in the circumstances. It will give him his only chance to forget her and make the best of what remains of life.'

'How hard you sound when you say that, Andrew! And yet—you forgave me and—took me back.'

Had she not been looking down she might have seen the flash of tenderness in his eyes, of the love that had never died, though kept so rigidly in check that she never guessed at its existence. He wanted to win her back, intended to do so, but knew that he must give her time, win her gradually and in his own way.

'The circumstances are different. For one thing, you were not my wife, and for another you loved Paul Esterre.'

Purposely he spoke the name which, since their talk on that first day, had not been spoken between them. He saw her flinch.

She was silent, thinking of what he had said both about Clementine and Sir Joseph, and about themselves. She was going back in her mind to her mother's happiness with her first husband, realizing how different Clementine would be now had not the war taken him from her and left her purposeless. What if she herself should lose Andrew? The thought pierced her sharply though the next moment she told herself that there was no parallel there, since she and Andrew were not in love with each other – at least ...

Clementine slid from her thoughts, which became wholly of herself and Andrew. What was this relationship between them? It could not be happiness – or could it? It was peace, a calm haven, a blessed sense of belonging which she had never known before.

'She's going to be so unhappy,' she said at last, forcing her mind back to Clementine since she could not speak to him of what lay closest in her thoughts.

'Won't she be that anyway, for a time? My dear, I think perhaps you don't know your mother very well. She will find compensations. Eventually I suppose she'll marry Prosper. He's a celebrity. All this will die down. He'll probably produce something quite brilliant on the crest of the new wave. She'll like that. She'll make a tremendously successful come-back when the present turmoil has died down. I think she'll be perfectly happy again, unless happiness is too strong a word for the sort of satisfaction she'll find in life. You'd never really find satisfaction in that way. You need to—have other and less spectacular things for your contentment, the quiet things of life, serenity, stability.'

He did not say love, but that, she knew with profound conviction, was what she needed for happiness, and she had thrown it away when she had it, tossed it aside to take the counterfeit that Paul had dangled before her eyes, making it glitter like tinsel.

Andrew rose and took her hand and drew her gently to her feet.

'It's very late,' he said, 'and you should be in bed. Have you got everything you want? A book, though I hope you won't have to read? Your flask of hot milk?'

He went with her, opened the door of her room and waited whilst she took off her dressing-gown and got into bed, an intimate thing he had never yet done, though when she glanced momentarily at his face she could see no sign of any reaction.

He switched the bedside light on for her.

'Good night, my dear,' he said gently. 'I'll turn off the other one for you,' and left her.

She lay with her thoughts turning about like a kaleidoscope, revealing this and that unexpected pattern and combination of colours. Several times that evening he had called her 'my dear'. Was she dear to him? And if she were not now, would she ever be? She remembered that someone had once said – (was it Brouette?) – that the more a man has to do for you and give you, the more he thinks of you, because you're giving him a sense of responsibility towards you. She had never pursued those tactics with Paul, who had done almost nothing for her and who had certainly had no feeling of responsibility towards her. How impossible it was to imagine Andrew evading any obligation like that!

The next morning Clementine, ready to go, came into Diana's room. Mrs. Barrett always brought breakfast to her there, and she was sitting up in bed with her tray.

'Are you going already?' she asked, her pity for her mother catching at her heart.

Clementine gave her a bright, hard smile.

'When you've made up your mind to do something, you might as well get on with it,' she said, a gay recklessness in her voice which did not deceive her daughter. 'I've got to go back to the flat to collect one or two things. Flora amongst them, but I won't leave any note. I'll just send poor Joseph a wire from Dublin.'

'Mother, *must* you do this?' asked Diana desperately.

'Yes, darling, positively and definitely. Don't look so tragic about it. It'll soon pass, and when Garry's quite fit again we'll have fun. It hasn't been all that fun being Lady Bloggett. What a name! It'll be quite nice to be Prosper, I think. Goodbye, Diana, my dear, and—I'm very glad that you're married to Andrew. Don't make a mess of it, will you?' and for a moment the mask slipped and Diana saw that this was by no means the fun to Clementine that she intended it to appear. There was a look of bleak loss in her eyes, the note of it in her voice.

'Not if I can help it,' said Diana, swallowing a sudden lump in her throat. 'Oh. Mother, I'm so sorry—about you, I mean.'

Clementine bent down to kiss her lightly. The two clung impulsively to each other.

'Pity we've never known each other before,' said Clementine.

'Don't let's get so far apart again, Mother.'

'My dear. Andrew may not relish his notorious mother-in-law!'

303

'Andrew likes you and—understands you, I think.'

'Does he? Well, he's cleverer than I am if he does. Look after my grandchild, my sweet. Heavens, I wish I hadn't said that! Doesn't it sound awful? But I bet there are not many grand mothers who elope! Bye-bye, darling. I'll let you know,' and she was gone, leaving behind her with her perfume and the echo of her voice a world of regrets for what might have been, for the mother she had never known, probably never would know.

When Sir Joseph Bloggett put his key in the door at his usual time that evening he knew at once that Clementine had gone. It was not only the silence, nor the fact that Flora was not there to take his hat and coat. It was something more intangible, as if the spirit which had infused the place had vanished.

He went into the sitting-room and into the bedroom. There was no note, no message of any kind, but a sealed envelope in a drawer contained the key of the small safe in which she kept such of her jewels as were in constant use. He went to the safe. Everything he had ever given her was there. He scarcely knew what he had expected, but not that she would have taken nothing. He could have imagined her justifying herself for taking everything by saying that she had given value for them.

He relocked the safe and went heavily into the empty sitting-room, empty as was his own life.

So she was gone. There was nothing left that he would even want to remember. His face grew hard, his mouth shut in a thin line, his hands gripped the chair until the knuckles showed white.

For an hour or more he sat there, motionless, his face grey and grim, his eyes' staring straight in front of him. It was his farewell to Clementine, whom he had loved.

Then he rose and went back into her bedroom, emptied the safe of its contents, took the jewels from their cases and made a rough parcel of them, leaving the cases piled on the dressing-table. He had a grim appreciation of his care of his inanimate treasures compared with the careless way he had let his one priceless treasure slip from his grasp, to be shattered into a thousand bits.

He left the flat with scarcely another glance round it. Bent would come and pack his clothes and get them away. He did not try to analyse his conviction that Clementine had left and would never return. He merely knew it, even without the corroboration of Flora's absence and the jewels in the safe.

He carried a small suitcase of necessities with him, took a taxi to his bank, where, with a grim appreciation of the clerk's feelings the next morning, he pushed and shoved the packet of jewels through the opening of the night safe. The paper broke, and he stuffed the last diamond bracelet loose into the box.

He got back into the taxi and gave his sister's address in Highgate. There was little love lost between them, but she was his only surviving relation, though he would have scorned the suggestion that there was pathos in his turning to his own kin in his hour of defeat.

As he paid off the taxi at the small surburban house which he had given Milly years ago he found his brother-in-law beside him. He was an inoffensive little man in the late fifties, with drooping sandy moustache, large spectacles and an umbrella. Joseph had always thought him a rather poor thing, content to sit all his life on an inconspicuous office stool and be bullied by his employer, his workmates and his wife and kids.

'Oh, hullo, Ed.' said Joseph gruffly.

'Bit stormy in there,' said Edward, inclining his bowler-hatted head towards the white steps of his wife's house.

'Oh? What's up?' asked Joseph.

'It's—it's me,' said his brother-in-law meekly. 'Fact is, I spent the other night in the lock-up and Milly's taken it hard, poor girl.'

'*You* spent the night in the lock-up?' he asked, astonished. 'Why, whatever could *you* have done?' repeating the unflattering emphasis on the pronoun.

'I—I happened to meet some of the boys—you know, the boys of the old mob,' and Joseph recognized the reference to the companions of the one glorious and memorable experience of his life, the 1914-1918 war in which the only enemies he ever saw or felt were lice and mud, but which was a memory which glowed the more brightly as dull year succeeded dull year.

'We met quite by chance in the Strand,' said Edward, and in spite of what had obviously succeeded that meeting his voice and eyes brightened at the mere mention of it. 'We went and had one or two. You know how it is, and perhaps I was a bit off colour or something, and Milly doesn't really like me to take anything. She doesn't like the smell of it, and then what with the taxis and everything, she thinks it's a waste of money, and I suppose it is in a way. I mean, there's nothing to show for it afterwards, is there?'

'I take it there was something to show for it that night though?' asked Joseph with a grim smile.

Edward took off his bowler and rubbed his head.

'You're right, Joe. I don't think I had more than three or four, and there's nothing much but water in it nowadays, but somehow when the boys had left me I couldn't find my way home. They seemed to have moved Tottenham Court Road Station.'

'Tottenham Court Road? I thought you were in the Strand.'

That's where we *started*, but I think it was Tottenham Court Road by then. Anyway, when I thought I'd found it, they wouldn't let me get on the platform, and I was going up and down the stairs until in the end a copper told me he'd take me home, but he took me to the police station and I spent the night in the cells! I felt awful, but nothing to what I felt the next morning when I woke up and thought of Milly! They sent me home about six and she was waiting for me. Oh, my golly!' swallowing hard and flinching at the mere memory. 'She told me a policeman had knocked her up at three o'clock to tell her where I was, so I didn't get a chance to make anything else up. I tell you, Joe, I'm in a proper hole with her. She won't speak to me. Hasn't ever since, only when she has to.'

'Well, I should think that'd be a relief,' said Joseph grimly, knowing Milly's capabilities in speech.

'I don't know. It's pretty—awful,' said Edward, with another of his scared-rabbit looks towards the house. It was a considerable relief to find his brother-in-law at hand at this moment. He could not imagine Joseph being scared of anything, even Milly.

'Well, come on,' said Joseph.

'I'm a bit late, too,' he muttered uneasily. 'Got kept late by old Tozer, but she'll never believe that. They'll be having tea.'

'Oh, come on, man!' said Joseph impatiently. 'She can't kill you. Got your key?'

'No, I don't have a key,' said Edward meekly. 'She—Milly—you see, it being her house—'

Joseph dismissed the explanation with a frown. He ought to have given the house to poor old Ed, not to Milly, but at the time he didn't realize what a martinet it'd make her to own her house. He thought of a house he owned in the Derbyshire hills, quite a small house with a big garden which he had bought a year or so ago in a moment of sentiment, his idea being that there might come a time when he would want to retire from business and when Clementine would feel able to leave London. Well, since business was all he had left, why should he ever retire from it? And Clementine would never live in the Derbyshire hills, or anywhere else with him again.

Why not turn it over to poor old Ed? It was let well, and it would give the poor old chap an income and keep Milly from crowing over him quite so much.

In spite of Edward's half-raised, protesting hand, Joseph gave a loud rat-tat-tat on the knocker, and after a suitable interval Milly flung the door open, the reprimand dying only half uttered.

'Oh! Oh, it's you, Joe! Come in. You can come in too,' with a withering look at her husband, who was concealing as much of himself as possible behind the other's bulk.

'I'm sorry I'm a little late, dear,' he said placatingly.

'I expect you've been doing the round of the pubs again with your disreputable friends. Your meal's in the oven. Do you want anything, Joe?'

She was only a shred of a woman, smaller than her husband, thin and taut as a wire, with grey-sprinkled light hair, small grey eyes, prim mouth, a worker; thrifty, honest, keeping her home, her children, her husband as clean and tidy as herself – the salt of the earth, though, like salt, with a sharp tang and scouring qualities.

'Not a meal,' said Joseph heavily, setting down his bag, 'though I don't mind a cup of tea,' as he walked into the living-room and saw his nephew and niece seated at a well-spread table.

He nodded at them and they murmured a greeting suitable to an uncle whom they disliked but to whom they were humiliatingly indebted, since he was paying for their good schooling, Marjorie fifteen, John two years younger.

'Thought I'd like to stay a couple of nights, Milly,' said her brother in the same heavy, depressed tone.

'Well, you can. Ed can have the sofa in the kitchen,' said Milly.

'What's wrong with the spare room?' asked Joseph.

'Ed's been sleeping in that, but you can have it now. He'll be all right on the sofa.'

'Yes, quite, quite,' said Edward hastily, shrivelling into silence again at the look his spouse gave him. It was for her to say where he was to sleep and whether she would receive him again into the marital double bed, but she was not going to allow any suggestion on his part that he would *prefer* the sofa in the kitchen.

'I'll get your supper, Dad,' said Marjorie, getting up.

Her mother waved her back peremptorily.

'He can get it himself,' she said. 'Sit here, Joe. Ed can get another cup and plate. I got some ham today. Pass your uncle the ham, John. No, not for you, Ed. You've got hash. It's in the oven, as I told you.'

Her tone, affable in the extreme to her brother, commanding towards her children, was one of withering contempt when she addressed her husband.

'Yes, dear,' he said meekly, and slid past her into the kitchen, returning with a plate of warmed-up stew which he ate with no more than a sidelong glance at the slices of pink ham.

'I suppose you've heard of his latest performance,' she went on acidly, addressing Joseph but indicating her husband. 'Put into jail for the night—in jail like a common drunk, charged before the magistrate with being drunk and disorderly, if you please! I don't know when I shall ever hold up my head before folks again.'

'Well, I've spent a night in custody too,' Joseph reminded her.

'That was different,' said Milly with another withering look at her meek little husband who was trying to make himself even smaller than nature had designed him. 'If you've finished, Marj and John, you can get down and do your homework.'

When the children had gone out Joseph spoke with an air of defiance.

'You might as well know, but Clementine's left me.'

Edward's face expressed sympathy and concern. Milly snorted.

'Well, that ought to teach you to marry into your own class,' she said. 'Let it be a lesson to you.'

'I'm not likely to need a lesson. I shan't want to marry again,' said Joseph shortly. 'Anyway, she's gone, and I don't want to talk about it or hear anything said about it.'

'Like daughter, like mother,' commented Milly hardily. 'Look what that Diana did, and engaged to a decent man too, running off almost at the altar as one might say. And now the mother's done the same—'

'Didn't I tell you I didn't want to hear any more about it?' thundered Joseph. 'Come along, Ed. We'll have one at the local. Oh yes, we will—*and* one more if we feel like it,' rising from the table and so dominating his little brother-in-law that almost without realizing it he was meekly walking out of the room and out of the house in the very face of the indignant Milly.

'If you both end up in the police court you needn't come back here, either of you.'

'You know, I didn't ought to go,' said Edward uneasily. 'She'll be that mad with me.'

'Well, if you're going to sleep in the kitchen anyway, what does it matter? Come on, man,' said his brother-in-law irritably.

Over their pint Joseph spoke heavily of Clementine, though he would not have referred to her again in his sister's hearing.

'You know, it's my own fault if Clem's gone. I didn't know properly how to treat a lady like her. Milly's right. It's better to marry in your own class, but—well, I was fond of her, Ed. Am still. Daresay I shall always be. Funny thing, being fond of a woman. Sort of sticks in yer gizzard, whatever they do to you.'

'Gone off with that chap Prosper, has she?' asked Ed.

'S'pose so. No letter nor anything. Just cleared out.'

'Bad job. Very bad job. Milly'd never do that,' said Edward with a sigh which was not untinged with regret. Of course Milly would never leave him. For one thing, it was her house. Then his thoughts brightened. There were the kids, too. Nice kids. He was fond of his kids. Always sorry he couldn't have done more for them, but there it was. He wasn't clever. Not a money-maker like Joe. Not even bright at a bargain like Milly – though she hadn't been very bright when she picked him, Edward.

He came back from his mental meanderings to catch something Joseph was saying.

'... put it into your name. It's a decent little house. People in it, of course, but you wouldn't want to live there, and you'd have the rent coming in. Couple o' hundred a year and they pay the rates. Just a bit for yourself, Ed.'

'You mean, you're—you're going to give me a house, Joe? *Me?*' he quavered, and when Joseph had made it clear that that was his intention, the little man buried his nose deep in his mug so that his brother-in-law should not see that his eyes were wet.

To own a house! To have two hundred a year of his own! In his wildest dreams nothing like this had ever happened to him. He could pay the kids' school bills with it, buy Marj that new tennis racquet she wanted, get Johnny a dynamo lighting set for his bike. He could buy Milly something, too; a new hat, perhaps.

'Oh, Joe,' he said, and again, 'Oh, Joe, I—I don't know what to say. I really don't know what to say.'

'That's O.K.,' said Sir Joseph, and rapped on the counter and ordered another pint each to cover the embarrassment of such unexpectedly touching gratitude. Dammit, one miserable little house, bringing in a potty little two hundred a year, and poor Ed hysterical about it. It made him feel unusually humble.

And it was the thought of that house, and not the effect of Government beer, which made little Edward Batten walk into his wife's house later, up the middle of the steps, with quite a strut.

He was a man of property now!

# Chapter Twenty-One

Paul Esterre's daughter was born on a gusty December morning and Diana, who had had an easy confinement, lay and looked at the scrap of humanity which was being put into her arms for the first time.

What she saw gave her a strange, tumultuous mingling of emotions, for though this was her child, born of her body and looked for through nine interminable months, it was beyond all possible doubt also Paul's. The tiny face, formless though it was as yet, was an absurd replica of his, and the line of dark hair grew exactly as his did, in a peak on his forehead.

'There! Isn't she a little beauty?' asked the nurse, laying the soft, powder-scented bundle gently down on Diana's curled arm.

'Please—leave her—with me a few minutes, 'she begged, and after the girl had gone she gazed into the face of the new being.

'Paul! Paul!' she whispered, and closed her eyes and saw him as she felt she would always see him to the end of her life, his dark eyes mischievous and yet loving, his mouth laughing, everything about him vibrant with life and the joy of living.

Then, blotting out that memory, came the thought of Andrew, her husband. Andrew had wanted the child to look like her. He had not said so in so many words. Yet she knew, from the way he had once or twice looked at her, from little references he had made to her hair, to the smoky blue of her eyes, that that was how he was envisioning her child.

And now he would know, must know, what Paul Esterre had looked like, would have to live with his very counterpart, perhaps watch the child grow into somebody who was like Paul in other ways as well, ways so different from Diana's that he would never be able to forget that she was not his child.

She longed for and yet dreaded his visit, and before it was time for him to come she rang to ask the nurse to take the baby away.

'But her daddy would like to see her,' the nurse protested.

'Another time. Take her now, please,' insisted Diana, and when Andrew came into the room it was to find her alone.

His eyes smiled at her above the great sheaf of late roses he had brought her. She felt something rise chokingly in her throat at the look he gave her. He must be hating this moment, hating her possibly, and yet he was smiling.

'Andrew—dear Andrew,' she said in a whisper, and half stretched out her hand to him and then drew it back.

But he had seen the gesture, and laid the flowers down and went to her and took her fingers in his.

'I'm so glad it's all over and that you're all right,' he said.

She nodded, unable to speak, her eyes bright with tears.

'Where is she?' he asked, looking round the room.

'I—I told them to—to take her out,' said Diana with difficulty.

'Let's have her back, shall we?' he suggested, and leaned forward and pressed the bell.

'Andrew she—she isn't a bit like me,' said Diana desperately.

'That's bad luck for her,' he said. 'Oh, nurse, what about bringing Miss Shawn in for me to have a look at?'

'I told Mrs. Shawn you'd want to see her,' she said. 'She's a real pet, and so good.'

Diana lay with closed eyes, longing for the moment to be over.

When she opened them again it was to see Andrew with the baby in his arms, looking with absorbed interest at the little face.

'How small she is,' he said, his voice almost a whisper as if he feared speech might shatter something infinitely delicate, and then he touched the baby's cheek. 'How soft her skin is!'

The baby stirred and opened her eyes, eyes of that unfocussing baby blueness which is so touching in its unawareness, and in that moment Andrew Shawn knew that this child was to be the best-loved thing in his life with the exception of Diana, his wife.

But Diana could not know the thoughts which lay in his mind as he held her child in his arms, thoughts that were bitter and sweet, tossed, uncertain, yet wholly tender.

The little thing, his mind was saying – the little thing.

'No, she isn't like you, is she?' was all he said, and gently laid the baby in the curve of her mother's arm and stood looking down at them.

She was seldom able to read his thoughts. His face was not expressive, nor did the calm gaze of his eyes ever reveal his mind.

'He hates her,' she was thinking dully, achingly. 'He hates her because he knows she's like Paul, because he will never be able to forget,' and unconsciously her arm closed more tightly around the unconscious baby as if in protest and protection.

'My baby. My own. My very own,' she thought.

'What are you going to call her?' asked Andrew, and though he had said 'you' by intent, so as not to seem to lay too much claim to the child, Diana misinterpreted that intention.

'He doesn't want me ever to regard her as his,' was her thought.

'I'd like to give her—rather an odd name,' she said. 'Brouette. It isn't really a name at all, but a sort of nickname of somebody who—a girl I knew—a girl who was kind to me.'

'All right,' he said indifferently. He had hoped Diana would appeal to him for his choice, perhaps to combine with hers, and ever since they had told him the child was a girl he had hoped they would be able to name her Teresa, after his mother.

But Brouette! Not even a name at all, but one which would always remind Diana of those years she had spent with Paul, for obviously the name was of French origin.

'What does it mean?' he asked.

'A silly thing, really. It means a wheelbarrow,' said Diana.

'And you're going to name your daughter Wheelbarrow?' he asked with a grim smile.

'It does sound rather idiotic, doesn't it?' agreed Diana regretfully. 'Well, we'll call her something else then.'

'Oh no.' He shrugged his shoulders. 'If that's what you want, let her be Brouette, so long as one forgets what it means.'

The nurse came back, gave Diana a professionally critical look and turned to her husband.

'I think perhaps Mrs. Shawn should be left to have a nap now, Mr. Shawn,' she said. 'Come along, poppet,' lifting up the baby again. 'Isn't your daughter a beauty? And all this dark hair may come off, you know. It often does, and she may be as fair as her mother then. You're neither of you dark, are you?' with a friendly smile. 'If I were you I'd take a look at the milkman, Mr. Shawn,' and she laughed and went off with the baby cuddled up to her.

Husband and wife were alone again, but neither could find anything to say and Andrew moved awkwardly, stooped to touch Diana's hand and then, as she did not open her eyes, softly left the room.

The slow, bitter tears forced themselves between her eyelids and trickled down saltily to her lips. Nothing was as it should have been. Whatever she had hoped would come about when the child had been born was different, broken, torn. Andrew, for all his tender care of her during these months, had not forgiven her, didn't love her, was merely performing what seemed to him a duty.

The years stretched endlessly ahead. Whilst she had been waiting for the birth of the baby there had been only vague shadows beyond. Now she was facing the actual future, with nothing to look forward to, nothing with which to fill it. She had been wrong, terribly wrong, to marry Andrew, not for herself, but for him.

Her thoughts were filled with him. After that first moment when Paul himself had come so strongly to her there had been scarcely a thought to spare for anyone but Andrew. Presently she would remember that, try to analyse it as she did analyse her thoughts. Just now everything was too confused, too hurtful.

Brouette.

It was perhaps silly of her. She should have chosen some quite ordinary name, Mary or Betty or Sarah. By choosing to call her after Brouette she had only added to all the other things that would remind him of Paris and of Paul, though actually she was scarcely thinking of Paul at all now.

When she left the nursing home and took up the new life, centring round the baby at Playndon, it was as if a wedge had been driven between Andrew and herself. During the months of waiting they seemed to have been establishing a friendship which she had believed was the basis for a life of understanding and sympathy, something which could not be love but which might in the end be much better than love. Now, however, she not only saw less of her husband, but when they were together he talked to her less and it was increasingly difficult for her to find topics of conversation.

She was surprised and not a little confused when, a week or two after Christmas, he made a suggestion to her.

'Diana, I've been thinking. We ought to have the child christened. I've been wondering if you are still in touch with the friend she's named after, and if so, whether you would like to ask her for a visit and to be the official godmother.'

Diana's eyes widened. They were having their after-dinner coffee in the sitting-room, everything looking the perfect picture of home life though never had she felt further away from him.

'Brouette? Ask Brouette?' She repeated, amazed.

'Wouldn't you like to? You must think a lot of her to call the child after her. You know how to get hold of her?'

'Yes,' said Diana, still feeling bewildered and yet beginning to picture Brouette here, the comfort of her friendly presence. 'Oh, Andrew, I'd like that very much, if you're sure you won't mind. She's— she's not your sort, you know.'

He smiled wryly.

'And what is my sort?' he asked.

'I mean—well, Brouette's French, and—she lives in the artists' quarter and—she may shock you.'

'Perhaps I'm more shockproof than you imagine.'

She managed a little embarrassed smile.

'I don't know. Sometimes I think—we don't know each other very well. Not as well as we did, even.'

'That's difficult to decide. I'm not very difficult to know.'

'I think you are, Andrew,' she said in a low voice and bent her head down to her needlework.

He let his eyes rest on her with a yearning hunger which, had she looked up, would instantly have vanished. He had never been able to forget the look that had been on her face the first time he had seen her with her child.

'She still loves him,' had been his thought, watching that look of brooding tenderness, of sadness, a lost look which held regret and a yearning for – what? Inescapably he believed it to be Paul Esterre, the father of her baby. Not for an instant did Andrew Shawn ever imagine that it was of him she was thinking with that look in her eyes; of him, her husband, and not of Paul Esterre.

So he had withdrawn as far from her life as he could, never obtruding himself nor making any possible claim on her time or her interest, or on the baby. No one knew of the times when he stole up to the nursery to stoop over the cot, delighted if he found the child awake so that, with infinite caution, he could pick her up and hold her in his arms, absurdly flattered if she smiled at him and refusing in his heart to believe that those smiles were a touch of the wind.

Brouette wrote delightedly about Diana's invitation, though she added the surprising information that she was going to bring Poucet with her.

*Believe, ma petite* (she had written in her flowing, so characteristic French), *that your Brouette has married the man! It is a true surprise, yes? To me also. It is so long that he has wanted me to, but always it was for me no, no, no. Now it has been yes and your Brouette is Madame Jacquot and my little Poucet wags all the time like a dog. So if it is not too difficult for you and your husband, I bring Poucet, Yes?*

Of course it was 'yes'.

Diana felt it was difficult to explain Poucet to Andrew, just as she had found it difficult to tell him anything of her life in Paris. It all seemed so remote, so impossible of explanation to anyone who lived as conventional a life as he did, and because of that difficulty she had not made much attempt at it, which was another of the many mistakes she made in her failure to understand her husband. He recognized the omission and that there was a great deal in her knowledge and experience which she had not tried to share with him. The knowledge was bitter as gall. It served to root ever more firmly his certainty that

Paul still held her heart, and that it was because of him she could not bring herself to speak of those years.

He thought Brouette and Poucet a queer pair; Brouette with 'her dashing, gallant ways and completely unreticent speech; little Poucet whose adoration of his wife seemed only a little more than what he felt for Diana – Diane, as they called her, thus appearing to link her up with them as a different, unfamiliar personality in whom Andrew could have no part.

He was present when they had their first glimpse of the baby, though Diana had not intended it and looked with swift concern when she saw him following them into the nursery after breakfast that first morning. He misinterpreted her glance, believing it to be resentment, but he could not make himself draw back.

The child had been bathed and fed and lay in her cot, kicking and waving her arms about, happy as she nearly always was.

'Oh, *la petite*!' cried Brouette delightedly, and then she paused. They both paused, she and Poucet, and stared down at the baby's face, full of vitality and expression even at so formless an age, when most babies are little more than expressionless and unmeaning creatures vaguely resembling human beings.

'Diane!'

It was Brouette who spoke after that pause and gasp, yet of course these friends of Diana's must have known that the child could not be Andrew's. Then he realized why they had gasped. They had seen the likeness to Paul Esterre.

He turned away, but heard Diana's quiet reply.

'Yes. Quite absurd, isn't it?'

'But fantastic! *Ma petite, ma douce*!' cooed Brouette, and stooped and lifted the child and held her against her breast.

Andrew turned away. They would not even realize he had gone, he thought bitterly.

But he was quite wrong.

Diana had seen the bitterness in his face and had watched him turn and leave the room.

'He hates my poor little baby,' she thought miserably. 'He can't forgive me. He tries not to remember she is even in the world, but he can't. He hates her. And me too. Me too.'

She watched Brouette, so unexpectedly maternal, cradling the baby in her arms, her vivid face lit with tenderness. Looking up, she caught Poucet's smile and knew he was thinking the same thing – that there were always fresh facets to Brouette's nature.

Diana thought they would make an ideal marriage, these two, neither of them very young, both, as Brouette herself said, a little battered by life, neither expecting too much nor possessive. Poucet had always had a mysterious source of income which had enabled him to live better than most of them without doing any apparent work, but since the death of an uncle whose sole heir he was, it was revealed that he had actually been a buyer of curios and antiques for a series of shops. Brouette had known of this, and made no secret of the fact that, though she was definitely fond of Poucet, she would not have married him but for his comparative affluence. As for Poucet himself, he had always been more or less in love with Brouette, but had never expected to marry her, so her decision had made him completely happy.

Diana recognized in little Poucet's smile a certain regret that he and Brouette would never have children of their own.

'Does Paul know?' asked Brouette, when she saw that Andrew had gone. It was obviously nothing to her that Diana should have produced another man's child.

'No. I wouldn't want him to know,' she said in a low voice. 'Do you— see him ever?'

'I don't, but Poucet saw him one day, didn't you, *mon gars*?'

'He still has the studio though I don't think he paints much now,' said Poucet. 'I met him on the stairs. We didn't say much.'

'And—Victoire?'

He shrugged his shoulders and dismissed Victoire.

'She is no good,' said Brouette scornfully. 'What made him want her? And after you, Diane? *Mon Dieu!* Such foolishness I do not understand.'

'Perhaps Diane does not wish to talk of him,' put in Poucet.

'Do you know that I don't mind any more?' asked Diana, her eyes and her voice filled with the wonder of that discovery which she had only just made. 'I thought that when I saw you both it would come rushing back, to make me miserable all over again, but there's just nothing there, nothing.'

Brouette laid the baby back in her cot.

'That is as it should be, Diane,' she said practically. 'The only thing, it is a pity this little one is like him and not at all like you. It makes it so that you cannot always forget, yes?'

Diana nodded but she was thinking of Andrew. It was Andrew who could never forget.

When the christening ceremony was triumphantly over and no suggestion on the face of any of the interested village guests that there was any reason why the baby in no way resembled either of her parents, Brouette and Poucet lay in bed talking in their friendly, comfortable fashion. They had been lovers years ago, and desultorily ever since, so that marriage had not been in any sense an excitement to them, scarcely even an adventure, and Poucet knew that she would quite calmly leave him if she were not happy.

'Diane is not happy with her marriage,' said Brouette.

'No,' agreed Poucet soberly and waited for her to tell him why.

Brouette's perceptions were at all times keener than his, except where some antique chair or cabinet were the point at issue.

'It is the little one, my little Brouette. If she did not so much resemble that Paul all might be well, but you see how her husband turns from the child and will not even regard it?'

'Yes,' agreed Poucet.

'Yet it is the sweetest thing,' she sighed.

Diana, with all the rest of the household asleep, had stolen into the nursery as she often did when she could not sleep. Here with her baby, the one thing in all the world which really belonged to her, she could draw some measure of peace and comfort.

Yet tonight she felt neither, and after a time she turned away from the cot with its placidly sleeping occupant and sat beside the stove. Her body in its padded satin dressing-gown, a present from Andrew to take with her to the nursing home, was warm but within herself she was ice-cold.

The revelation which had come to her when she had spoken of Paul and of Victoire was still with her, strengthened and deepened. She knew now beyond any doubt that that phase of her life was over. She did not try to deny or belittle her love for Paul. It had possessed her utterly. Had Paul remained faithful to her it would have lasted all her life. The shock of his betrayal had killed it, but things do not lose all their virtue and their beauty in memory because they are dead, and so she knew her love for Paul had been a lovely and a happy thing. It had been the love of her first awakening, a love in which all her dreams, all romance, all poetry and fairy-lore had been woven to make a magic web, enchanting and enchanted. She would perhaps never know the magic again, but she had something in its place which as yet she scarcely dared to recognize or to believe in. That something was so strangely intermixed with her thoughts of Andrew, her husband and yet a stranger still – Andrew who had never held her in his arms, never kissed her, since that far-off day when she had run away from him with Paul.

Andrew, her husband yet not her lover, perhaps never to be her lover.

Unconsciously she stretched out her arms, but they clasped only the empty air, and with a realization of her loneliness, her impotence, she laid her head down on her arms and wept softly, silently.

She went back to her bed but tossed and turned, sleepless until she could make up her mind to do the one thing which it seemed to her she must do.

For Andrew's sake she must part from her baby.

It was a decision which was all part and parcel of the makeup of Diana, impulsive, courageous, so often foolish but now so completely selfless. Brouette and Poucet would take her baby. Brouette was a born mother who would never have a child of her own. They would both love the little one, and the child herself would be far happier than in the divided household which Diana could visualize as inevitable if she remained in it, beloved by her mother but hated by the man she would have to regard as her father.

The only alternative, that of leaving Andrew herself, was unthinkable. Not a second time could she fling back his kindness and his generosity in his face and betray them. No, the only possible thing she could do for Andrew was to give up her baby. She owed him everything, both for herself and for the baby. She was ready to pay her debt and perhaps some day they would find some basis for mutual happiness, a friendship such as Brouette and Poucet shared. Would that be too much to ask? That Andrew should love her – that she never asked. She had thrown his love away. How should she hope that it could ever be picked up again?

So if she achieved peace for him, contentment, a serene sort of middle-aged happiness, surely she would in some measure have repaid her immense debt to him?

She slept at last, and in the morning did not wake until after Andrew had gone to town, which she felt was best for her purpose. He would have said goodbye to Brouette and Poucet, who were going back to Paris so that he could attend an important sale.

Diana, dry-eyed and perfectly calm, told Brouette what was in her mind, told the whole story of Andrew's rescue of her, and now of his obvious dislike of the child.

'You see that it is all I can do. It is for Andrew's happiness, and also for hers, my little baby's.'

Brouette was profoundly touched. Worried, too.

'Of course we will take her, and love her as if she were our own. We do that now. But you, Diane? You love her.'

Diana turned her face away. Not even to this friend would she show what must lie in her eyes at that moment.

'I want you to take her,' she said steadily. 'Please—not letting me see her go. Presently I will go out, up on the downs, very far away and I shall stay there until I know you must have gone. You will let me do that? So that I shall not see—my little baby go?'

'Of course, *chérie*. Of course,' said Brouette, but stood there looking frowningly after the girl who had let herself out of the house, forgetting even to say goodbye to Poucet. She had already spoken to Mrs. Barrett, telling her to her supreme astonishment that she had agreed to

'Madame's' proposal to take the baby to France with her for a short holiday.

'Madame thinks it will give me a rest,' Diana had said, and her stony face and uncompromising voice had silenced the very natural protests and questions. 'Please pack everything the baby will need. I can send some more when those are finished. I may not be back when they leave. Barrett knows the time of their train.'

Mrs. Barrett was stupefied with astonishment, as much by Diana's calm demeanour as by the situation itself, but when she had seen the girl actually leave the house, there was nothing for her to do but obey her instructions. She could not converse with Madame Jacquot, so that she could get no explanations there.

Diana, sick with misery and longing for the death which she knew never came to those who longed for it, trudged on up the familiar path. A snuffling at her heels told her that Simon, the cocker, had escaped and followed her joyously. She told him half-heartedly to go back, but she did not persist and even found a tiny grain of comfort in his presence. Later, however, he met a lady friend, named Heinz, whom he admired beyond even his loyalty to Diana. He cast an anguished look from soft, sad brown eyes at first one and then the other and gave a short, questioning bark.

Diana turned, saw the disreputable, engaging Heinz.

'All right. You can go,' she said, and Simon tore off.

Diana went on alone, her feet taking her along familiar paths without any conscious choice. Before her and around her lay trackless miles of the downs, bleak, unsheltered on this winter's day. It suited her mood, was the echo and shadow of her anguished heart.

Hour after hour, it seemed, she trudged on, afraid to look back in case she saw the road, afraid to listen in case she should hear the whistle of a train taking her darling from her for ever.

At last she stumbled, picked herself up, stumbled again, and knew for the time being she could walk no farther. She lay where she had fallen, exhausted, mindless now, unable even to weep any more.

She did not know whether she was struggling out of unconsciousness or out of sleep when, hours or minutes later, she became aware of the joyous snuffling which proclaimed Simon again.

She was so numb from cold that she could scarcely lift a hand to meet his eager welcome, when she became aware that he had not come alone.

'Good dog,' said a voice, and then it was not Simon touching her but someone else drawing her against the warmth of him.

Andrew.

She had her eyes still closed. She seemed to lack even the amount of strength required to open them. She rested against him, a dead weight, her face ashen with the cold, her hands lifeless as he tried to chafe them.

'Diana! Diana! Darling, open your eyes,' she heard him say.

Then she knew that of course it was not really happening, that it was just a dream. In real life he never called her that.

'Open them, Diana,' he told her urgently. 'Look at me. Please look at me, my darling,' she heard him say, and then slowly, wonderingly, fearing, she lifted the heavy lids.

'Andrew,' she whispered, and closed them again and let herself lean there against him, her mind as powerless and relaxed as her body.

'Thank God,' he said. 'I was so terribly afraid. Darling, I'm going to carry you. Can you put your arms round my neck? Like that? And hold on to me? There's a hut over there, only a queer little shack where I suppose they keep tools and things, though I can't think what for, up here on the downs. I can carry you as far as that if you can hold on to me.'

'I can walk,' she told him faintly, but he did not set her down.

'Let me, darling,' he said, and she locked her hands about his neck and with Simon scurrying joyously about they came to the little tumbledown hut which offered them shelter from the biting wind.

Andrew set her down, steadying her as he did so and looking round the hut. It was completely empty, nothing but four wooden walls, a broken door and half a roof. They could not stay there long, but at least it would give her a chance to get enough strength for the downward climb. He took off his overcoat and wrapped it round her, first taking from its pocket a flask with its encasing cup.

'I can't—take it,' whispered Diana through her chattering teeth, and trying to resist the offer of his overcoat, but he only wrapped it more firmly about her.

'Nonsense,' he told her briskly. 'I can't carry a corpse all that way down. Here. Drink this,' putting the cup half filled with brandy to her shaking lips and holding it there until she had emptied it.

The fiery liquid made her cough, but it sent its reviving warmth through her and in a few moments her face and lips had lost their bluish look which, at first sight, had struck such terror to his heart.

'Now,' he said, putting the flask away, 'that looks a bit better, so shall we talk? There's nothing for you to sit on, and it isn't exactly cosy here, but you can't start walking yet, and we've got a lot to say to each other. I think this corner is the least draughty and the floor's dry. We can sit on my coat and spread the rest of it round both of us, like this. All right? Going to be fairly warm?'

Under the enfolding coat, his arm about her, holding her strongly. She could feel the warmth of him gradually reaching her chilled body. Too tired and worn to make her mind think of anything but his nearness and the comfort of his protecting arm, she leaned her head against his shoulder and was silent.

'Who's going to start?' he asked her. 'You or I?'

She had never heard him speak like that, not even in the far-off days of their engagement, nor felt before that the barriers between them were down. Glancing fleetingly at his face she had never seen it wear just that expression, indefinable, comforting.

'What is there to say?' she asked in a tired whisper.

'First—this, Diana,' he said, and bent his head to hers and kissed her mouth and held it with his own until she responded with a swift uprush of emotion, her lips moving beneath that firm, demanding pressure.

When he let her go she lay back and the waves of that undreamed-of emotion swept over her. It was Andrew who had kissed her like that – Andrew ...

He was smiling into her eyes.

Hers wore a strange look, fascinated yet deeply sad. Even in that tremendous upsurge of feeling, she was remembering her baby, the price she was paying for what Andrew was offering her.

'Have you been home yet?' she asked him, the words coming with difficulty.

He nodded.

'That was how I knew where to find you. Mrs. Barrett told me you had said you were going to walk on the downs.'

'And—Brouette and Poucet?'

She could not speak of the baby. The pain was too great.

'They've gone, darling.'

She closed her eyes on the slow, hot tears. She felt his lips and the close holding of his arms, wondered if this new love for him would in time make her forget her anguish.

His voice came to her as if from a long way off.

'I know, my darling,' he said. 'Everything. The thing you were willing to do for me.'

'You know? Andrew, what do you know?' she asked, startled.

'That you would have done this idiotic, this magnificent and— unforgettable thing for me. Oh, my love, how far away we went from each other that you could ever think I wanted you to do that, that it could possibly make me happy! What a monster you made of me, my little love, my foolish, wonderful little love.'

'Andrew, my baby?' she asked him quiveringly, imploringly.

'Is where she should be. In her own home. Oh, Diana, to have thought of such a thing!'

'I thought you hated to have her there,' she quavered. 'You never go to her or look at her or even speak of her, and I thought—thought you would feel better about it if she were not there to remind—and she's so like Paul—'

'We've both been prize idiots, my sweet. Why, I love the little thing! If I've appeared not to notice her it was because of you, because I've wanted to show you that—how shall I put it?'

'Oh, Andrew, my darling, put it any way you like!' she told him, smiling through the tears that were now of happiness. 'You can't hurt me now. Not any more, whatever you say—now.'

'I have known how you always wanted something of your own,' he said, trying to pick his words, trying not to seem to criticize or blame her. 'When I first knew you I realized that. You had your dogs, but you could not keep them when you had to leave Mayne Downe so that they seemed no longer yours. I belonged to you, even then, but you didn't love me, so I could not let you know how completely I was yours. It wouldn't have been fair to you to lay on you the obligation of such a—possession,' with his quiet, kind smile. 'Then you went to Paul and when I found you again you had lost him, though I think perhaps you never felt he was entirely yours.'

'No, I never did feel that,' she told him in a low voice. 'I don't think he'd ever belong to anybody but himself.'

'I felt that. You were so lost, my darling, so forlorn and afraid. Then when you told me about the baby, and that nothing would induce you to get rid of it even if you could, I realized that at last you were to have something really your own, all your own. When she was born there was in your eyes the look I had feared would be there. It seemed to shut me out so that I couldn't find the way to you, and I thought that in your heart you had returned to Paul because she was so obviously his—'

'I never returned to Paul,' said Diana. 'Oh, Andrew, I think that all the time I have been yours, that you've kept some part of me even when I was with him, and now—all of me, Andrew, all of me,' and she turned in his arms and for the first time lifted her lips to him of her own accord, asking for his kiss.

'I do love you,' she said. 'I do love you, Andrew.'

'And do you believe now that I love you? That there are no sacrifices to be made? That I want you as you are, and with all you have, or ever shall have, or ever will be?'

'I know. Oh, Andrew, at last I know!'

They were silent and still, content to cling together and to be so absorbingly aware of each other.

A noise outside drew their attention at last, and Diana sat up.

'What on earth's that?' she asked.

'I think Simon's decided to dig up the hut,' he said, and as he spoke a board of the crazy little shelter gave way and admitted a soft golden muzzle, covered with earth and blowing ecstatically at the discovery of their nearness. Diana took the soft nose in her hand and shook it in playful tenderness.

'Perhaps we'd better go,' said Diana almost regretfully, when they had extricated him and dusted some of the earth off him.

Her tiredness had gone, though she still felt stiff. But there was warmth and life in her heart again, a light in her eyes and a new tenderness in the mouth which Andrew had kissed.

He held her for another long moment before they went down.

'No more secret thoughts and no more distrust, my darling, ever,' he said, and she shook her head but could not speak.

'Sometimes I think I know you better than you know yourself,' he went on, looking deep into her eyes. 'I love you. You know that now, don't you? And you, thank God, love me, and I say that with reverence and humility because it is the thing which, in my quite unorthodox way, I have prayed for. There have been other loves for both of us. I loved someone before you came, and I lost her. You know that. You also have loved, Diana. Don't let us belittle those other loves or even try too hard to forget them. They've had their place and their value because through them we have become what we are today; the Diana, the Andrew, who have found each other. You believe that, my sweet?'

'Yes, I believe it. If I had not—run away from you and known Paul. I could not think you so wonderful and so utterly lovable as I know now that you are,' and she laughed a little at her own earnestness, but tenderly and with a most touching simplicity.

'Let's go home then, Diana,' and hand in hand they went down the hillside to where their small house, lamp-lit, sent out its welcome to them.

Mrs. Barrett stood in the open doorway. It was she who, alarmed and puzzled by the orders she had received, and by the look of death in Diana's face, had taken matters into her own hands and telephoned to Andrew so that he could come posthaste and by a providentially convenient train, to get everything under control. Brouette and Poucet had been as relieved as Mrs. Barrett by his prompt appearance.

'Oh, madam, thank heaven you've got back!' cried Mrs. Barrett when they reached her. 'You must be frozen and famished. I've lit a fire in your bedroom and I'll bring your supper there to you.'

'For me too, Mrs. Barrett, please,' said Andrew. 'Get your wet things off whilst I draw you a hot bath.'

Wrapped in their loving care, Diana had truly come home.

She lay in the hot, scented water, into which Andrew had tipped a whole jar of her favourite 'Ebe' bath salts, and then, wrapped in her warm dressing-gown, went back to her room and to the blazing log fire and the small table set ready for them in front of it.

Andrew rose from one of the deep chairs and came to her.

'Shall we go first and say good night to the small one?' he asked, and she nodded her head, the foolish tears of weariness and happiness springing to her eyes again, though she blinked them away furiously and smiled at him.

Their arms entwined, they went down the passage and into the nursery where little Brouette lay asleep. In the normal way Diana would not have risked wakening her, but tonight the joy of seeing her there again, safe and still hers, overruled every other consideration, and she stooped and lifted the sleeping baby and held her close to her breast.

Andrew watched them, saw her eyes raised to his with a new and lovely light in them, a look of confidence and contentment.

'Will you give her to me?' he asked softly.

'Oh, Andrew, yes! Yes!' she said, and put the child into his arms.

# Give Back Yesterday

Helena Clurey has it all – a devoted husband, money and family. She is happy and secure, but her apparent contentment is about to be shattered by a voice from the past. Mistress she may have been, but that is not the way it is put to her: 'you were not my mistress - you were, and are, my wife.'

# The Weir House

Philip wants to marry Eve. It is her way out - he is rich, not too old, and has been in love for years – but not a man she can accept. He has even secretly funded her lifestyle, such that it is. Eve feels trapped. Unlike her friend Marcia, who cheerfully accepts an 'ordinary' life without complaint, Eve has known better and wants better. A chance encounter then changesthings – Lewis Belamie pays her to act as his fiancée for a week. Adventure, ambition, and disappointment all follow after she journeys to Cornwall with him, where she eventually nearly dies after what appears to be a suicide attempt because of a marriage that has seemingly failed. However, the mysterious and mocking Felix really does love her. Just who is he; how does Eve end up with him; and what part does 'The Weir House' play in her life? Has Eve's restlessness and relentless search for stability ended?

# Through Many Waters

Jeff has got himself into a mess. It is, on the face of it, a classic scenario. He has a settled relationship with one woman, but loves another. What is he to do? It is now necessary to face reality, rather than continually making excuses to himself, but can he face the unpalatable truth? Then something beyond his influence intervenes and once again decisions have to be made. But in the end it is not Jeff that decides.

# Misadventure

Olive Heriot and Hugh Manning had been in love for years, but marriage had been out of the question because of the intervention of Olive's mother. Now, at last, she was of age and due to gain her inheritance and be free to choose. A dinner party had been arranged at the Heriot's home, 'The Hermitage' and Hugh expects to be able to announce their engagement. Things start to change after a gruesomely realistic game entitled 'murder', which relies on someone drawing the Knave of Spades after cards are dealt. Tragedy strikes and other relationships are tested and consummated – but is this all real, or imagined?

Printed in Great Britain
by Amazon